Some dream

He put his hand... [weight of that da...] back so that he could plunder her mouth, so that he could taste her.

Hell, in that moment, he wanted to consume her.

His body ached for her. Need pulsed through his veins, and if they weren't in some pit of hell, if the bad guys weren't just down the hallway...

Drew lifted his head. "Then you'd be mine," he rasped.

Tina blinked and shook her head. "What?"

He kissed her once more, just because he had to do it. *There's no way we're dying.* The woman was full of secrets, and he'd be sure he had the chance to discover every single one.

UNDERCOVER CAPTOR

BY
CYNTHIA EDEN

Published in Great Britain 2014
by Mills & Boon, an imprint of Harlequin (UK) Limited,
Eton House, 18-24 Paradise Road, Richmond, Surrey, TW9 1SR

© 2014 Cindy Roussos

ISBN: 978 0 263 91348 4

46-0214

Harlequin (UK) Limited's policy is to use papers that are natural, renewable and recyclable products and made from wood grown in sustainable forests. The logging and manufacturing processes conform to the legal environmental regulations of the country of origin.

Printed and bound in Spain
by Blackprint CPI, Barcelona

New York Times and *USA TODAY* bestselling author **Cynthia Eden** writes tales of romantic suspense and paranormal romance. Her books have received starred reviews from *Publishers Weekly,* and she has received a RITA® Award nomination for best romantic suspense novel. Cynthia lives in the Deep South, loves horror movies and has an addiction to chocolate. More information about Cynthia may be found on her website, www.cynthiaeden.com, or you can follow her on Twitter (www.twitter.com/cynthiaeden).

This book is for all of the fantastic
Harlequin Intrigue readers out there
—thanks for loving mystery and romance!

Chapter One

"You're making a mistake!" Dr. Tina Jamison shouted as she was hauled out of the nondescript brown van and pushed into the dimly lit parking garage.

But the four men—all wearing black ski masks—didn't seem to care that they'd grabbed the wrong woman.

And they *had* gotten the wrong person. They must have made some kind of mistake. There was no way these armed gunmen could actually want *her*.

The man on the right jabbed his gun into her back. "Move!"

When someone shoved a gun at her, Tina knew exactly what to do. *Move.* Just as the man had ordered. But Tina was scared and she stumbled, nearly slamming face-first into the cement as she hurried to follow the guy's order.

This can't be happening. This can't be happening.

She'd been safe in her hotel room less than an hour ago. Sleeping. Minding her business.

She'd woken to find a man leaning over her. His hand had flattened over her mouth before she could scream. Then he'd put a gun to her head and told her that if she wanted to live, she'd follow his orders.

Tina wanted to keep living.

One of the men pushed open the stairwell door. Then the gun was poking into her back once more. Tina got the

message loud and clear, and she started double-timing it
up those concrete stairs.

Why? Why have they taken me? "Look, you've got the
wrong girl." She tried telling them this fact for what had to
be the fiftieth time. They needed to see reason and listen
to her. "I'm a doctor, okay? Just a doctor who—"

"We know exactly who you are," the man with the gun
replied in a hard, lethal voice. "And we know just what
Mercer will pay to get you back."

Her blood iced as Tina grabbed for the stair railing. Mercer. Oh, no. With the mention of Bruce Mercer's name, the
situation went from bad to unbelievably, terribly worse.
Because Bruce Mercer was the director of a covert group
of agents who conducted secret missions for the United
States' government. Bruce Mercer operated the EOD, the
Elite Operations Division.

Bruce Mercer was also her boss.

*But I'm not an agent! I'm a doctor! The one who patches
up the wounded after a battle.*

Because Tina had learned long ago that she didn't mix
so well with danger.

Her heart was about to gallop out of her chest right
then and, taking a breath— Oh, yes, it was hard. Painful.
She was very afraid that she might be about to hyperven-
tilate. Her breath sure seemed to be wheezing out with
each frantic exhale.

"Can you…" Tina huffed. "Move the gun?" If the guy
stumbled, that gun could accidentally discharge. She knew
firsthand the kind of severe damage a shot to the spine
would do to a victim.

"No, I can't." The gun jabbed harder into her.

"Look, I—I…" She tried to suck in air. *Don't panic.
Don't.* "I'm not who you think I am!" She wasn't an EOD
agent. If these men were taking her because they mistak-

enly thought that she had some kind of classified information she could give to them, they were dead wrong. She didn't have the clearance level needed to access that sort of intel.

"We know you're not an agent," the man snapped. "Now keep climbing. *Faster.*"

She climbed until her legs burned. Flight after flight. Finally a door opened above her. The scent of fresh air and the mighty Mississippi River teased her nose as Tina was led outside.

Stars glittered overhead. Glancing around, she realized they were on a rooftop. And…and she could hear the *whoop-whoop-whoop* of an approaching helicopter.

This is so not good. As if masked men with guns could be good. But any group that came equipped with their own helicopter sure equaled a whole world of trouble in her book.

Fear had Tina shaking, but she made herself turn to face the gunman. "I-if you know I'm not an agent…" She had to raise her voice, nearly shouting, to be heard over the helicopter's approach. The wind from its blades blew against her, and she trembled. "If you know that, then let me go! I'm of no use to you."

The masked man—the fellow had to be the leader because no one else had done any talking—shook his head. "Mercer's daughter is going to be plenty of use to us."

Mercer's daughter? Tina's eyes widened. Definitely the wrong person. "I'm not his daughter!"

A rough, twisted bark of laughter escaped from the gunman. "Sure you aren't, sweetheart." A Texas accent. She could just hear it slip around his words. "That's why Mercer pays for your apartment in D.C. and why he sprung for the fancy hotel here in New Orleans. Why he's been paying your bills for years." More laughter. "At first, I thought you might be his lover, and that connection would have been just as useful to me."

The helicopter circled around to land. Her abductors had given her time to dress—a humiliating task since they'd watched her every move. The wind from the landing helicopter made her T-shirt cling tightly to her chest and it tossed her hair wildly around her face.

"Then I got intel that revealed your true identity." He let the gun trail over her cheek. If she *had* been an agent, Tina would have done something incredibly cool right then. Such as wrestle the gun from him or give him a sharp right hook.

Then take *all* of these jerks out.

But she wasn't an agent. She knew how to heal, not how to hurt.

"You've been the one constant in Mercer's life since you got out of med school. You're that constant because you're Bruce Mercer's daughter. The daughter he tried to hide after your mother was killed in that attack in France."

She swallowed. The fact that she'd been born in France was really going to work against her here.

"Of course, if you're not his daughter, you can just prove that to me."

The gun was still at her cheek.

The helicopter's blades had stopped.

"Prove who you really are," the man in the mask murmured. There were slits over his eyes so that he could see out, but the rest of his face was concealed. All she knew was that the guy was big, with narrow shoulders and hips, and that his words carried a slight Texas accent. She couldn't physically identify *any* of the men who had taken her.

"Are we ready?" another voice called out as heavy footsteps approached from behind her. This voice didn't hold a Texas accent. This one just sounded bored.

It also sounded familiar.

Tina felt her cheeks turn ice-cold, then they burned red hot.

Those footsteps kept approaching. "Yeah, we got our package," the gunman said with a quick nod. "Though she's been whining the whole time about us having the wrong woman."

The weapon finally left her cheek. Moving slowly, carefully, because she sure didn't want to set anyone off, Tina turned to face the man. The helicopter waited behind him, perched perfectly in place.

There was a ski mask over this man's face, too. Slits for his eyes, a hole for his mouth. As the others, he was also dressed in black from head to toe.

But she *knew* him; knew those broad shoulders, the tall, tough build. He towered over the other men by several inches and he walked with a slow, stalking grace.

Relief swept through her and Tina felt dizzy. *Drew Lancaster.*

"If she's been talking so much…" his familiar voice rolled over her, edged with a Mississippi drawl, "then maybe you should have just gagged her."

Wait. W*hat?* Tina's eyes widened in horror. That wasn't what Drew was supposed to say. Drew wasn't a criminal. He was a good guy. He was a federal agent with the EOD.

He moved behind her, and put his hand over her mouth. "See?" Drew murmured. "Easy enough to stop her from talking."

She nearly bit him.

But Drew bent and put his mouth right next to her ear. "Stay calm." A bare whisper. One Tina wasn't even sure she hadn't imagined. But she'd felt the warm rush of his breath against her ear and a shiver slid through her body.

Drew kept his hand over her mouth as his head lifted a

few inches. His eyes glittered down at her. She knew those eyes were golden, the color of a jungle cat that she'd seen once in the D.C. zoo.

Drew had always reminded her of that great cat. Because he was wild and dangerous, and he'd scared her, on an instinctive level, from the first moment they'd met.

"I didn't realize our cargo tonight was a woman," Drew charged as he glanced over at the lead gunman. "Maybe next time, you should clue me in on that."

The guy grunted. "Need-to-know basis, Stone. Need to know." Then he jerked his thumb toward the chopper. "Now are you ready to get us out of here?"

Stone. Her lips pressed against Drew's palm. She hadn't seen him in two months. Not since he'd left for his last mission.

Drew shifted his body and glanced down at her. This time, Tina could see past her fear and she easily read the hard warning in his eyes.

Drew was undercover. These men—they knew him as someone named Stone.

And something else that Tina realized… Drew wasn't about to blow his cover.

Not for her.

Her shoulders slumped. Things were going to get even worse before they got better.

"I'm ready," Drew said. He dropped his hand and backed away from her.

The gun was jabbed into her back once more. She didn't tense this time.

But Drew did. "Is that necessary?" The words seemed gritted.

"Yeah, it is. Now get that bird off the ground!"

Drew's gaze dropped to the gun then his stare slid back to Tina. She knew that she had to look terrified.

Because she was.

"Do you seriously think she's going to get away?" Drew glanced around the rooftop. "No one's up here but us."

The gun didn't move.

"Her hands are tied. She's not going any place." Drew exhaled. "And I don't see—"

"She's Bruce Mercer's daughter!" the gunman snarled. "You think he didn't train her? Until we're clear, I'm keeping my weapon on her."

Drew blinked. "Bruce Mercer's daughter," he repeated softly, considering the information it appeared.

No, I'm not!

But did Drew know that?

"I guess that changes things," Drew said. Then he turned away and hurried back to the chopper without even a second glance. In seconds, all of the men had climbed in behind him and Tina found herself secured in the backseat.

The blades were spinning again, matching the frantic beat of her heart, and the helicopter rose high into the air.

HIS COVER WAS about to be blown to hell and back.

Drew Lancaster slowly lowered the chopper onto the landing pad. His jaw was locked tight, his hands held the controls securely and rage beat at his insides.

Tina Jamison.

When he'd landed the bird on that roof, the pretty little doctor had sure been the last person he'd expected to see. But she'd spun toward him, her eyes wide and desperate behind the lenses of her glasses, and he'd realized that he was in some serious trouble.

She'd known who he was. Without even seeing his face, Tina had known. Maybe his voice had given him away. He hadn't bothered to change accents with this particular group. He'd just wanted them to think he was a slow-talking, ex-soldier from Mississippi. A man with a grudge against the government. A man willing to do just about anything for cash.

Tina's face had lit with hope when she'd seen him. Such a beautiful face it was, too. He'd found himself admiring it more and more during his visits to the doc at the main EOD office. She'd been all business, of course, checking his vitals, talking to him about stress in the field.

He'd been imagining her naked.

Before the blades had stopped spinning, Lee Slater was already out of the chopper and dragging Tina with him. The jerk still had that gun far too close to her for Drew's peace of mind.

How am I supposed to get her out of here?

With narrowed eyes, Drew watched Tina and Lee vanish into the main house. More armed men followed them inside.

They were in the middle of Texas, at a dot on the map that most folks would never find. It wasn't as if the cops were just going to rush in and rescue the kidnapped woman.

He was deep undercover. Working under the alias of Stone Creed. The men here—they were looking to cause as much chaos on U.S. soil as they possibly could. They were into drugs, into weapons and into wrecking the political powers that be.

And, in particular, it seemed that the men were looking to take out the EOD. Or, more specifically, they wanted to destroy Bruce Mercer.

Drew climbed from the chopper and checked his own gun.

"Can you believe it?" the excited voice asked from behind him.

Drew looked back just as Carl Monroe yanked off his ski mask. Yeah, that mask wasn't exactly necessary anymore. Not since they were back on their own turf. They didn't have to worry about unwanted eyes seeing them here.

Carl grinned. "We got the EOD director's daughter!"

No, they hadn't. Drew swallowed. Bruce Mercer did have a daughter, all right, but that daughter wasn't Tina Jamison.

What would happen when the men realized that they'd taken the wrong woman?

She will become a dead woman.

He couldn't let that happen. He'd been sent in to gather intel on this group, to determine just how much of a threat the individuals known as HAVOC posed—and, once his assessment had been made, his team was supposed to eliminate that threat.

It sure looked as if his timetable had just been accelerated.

"She sure is pretty," Carl said. Like Lee, Carl was a Texas boy, born and bred. He was also very, very dangerous. Carl liked to use his knife—often. And, according to his file, Carl enjoyed watching his victims slowly die from their knife wounds. Torture and pain were all part of Carl's twisted package.

"You should have seen her," Carl continued, voice thickening, "when we found her in that hotel room. She was all tousled and—"

Drew whirled on him. "Are you going to help me secure the chopper?" His words rapped out. Fury had coiled in his gut. No way, no damn way, should Tina have been put at risk like this. At his first opportunity, he had to contact the other EOD agents assigned to the HAVOC mission. They needed to work an immediate extraction on her.

And if they didn't, then he would.

Carl's smile stretched. "You thought she was pretty, too, didn't you? It's those glasses... Sexy."

He wanted to drive his fist into Carl's face.

But Carl turned away and went to work on the chopper.

Drew exhaled slowly as he tried to bring his control back in check. He was still the new guy in this crew. Useful because he could fly anything—and kill anyone instantly. Sure, his dossier had been faked, but his skills were plenty real enough.

During his time in Delta Force, Drew had been turned into a lethal fighting machine. He didn't need a weapon to take out a dozen men. He could do that just with—

A scream cut the night. *Her* scream.

Drew was running toward the main house before he could even think about his response.

The door was shut, so he just kicked his way right through it. The wood banged against the wall.

"*Don't!*" Tina yelled. "Please, I—"

Her cry was abruptly cut off.

Drew felt the familiar ice encase his fury. That was the way it had always been for him. When it came time for a battle, he went ice-cold. No emotion. No room for mistake.

He'd been called a robot by some of his teammates before.

He'd been called a hell of a lot worse by his enemies.

Why had Tina stopped screaming?

Another door was in front of him. A tall, blond guy with a gun at his hip tried to block Drew's path. "Stone, man, I don't think they want you right now."

Drew shoved the guy out of his way. He went *in* that room.

The first thing he saw was the blood. Fat drops that were sliding down Tina's arm. Lee Slater stood next to her, a knife in his hand. "I think that's what we need."

In his mind, Drew saw himself rushing across the room and breaking the guy's wrist. The knife would clatter to the floor, falling from Lee's slack fingers. With him out of commission, Drew would turn on the other two men there. He could have them all on the floor in less than a minute.

But he didn't attack. Not yet. Because he'd been given very specific orders from Bruce Mercer.

The job was top priority. The fear was that these men— men from the U.S., from Mexico and from parts of South America—had access to classified government intel. There had been a leak at the EOD just months before, and they were still tracking to determine just how much information had been taken from headquarters.

They'd followed the trail to HAVOC. Drew was supposed to be days away from meeting the group's leader.

Days.

Getting an up-close audience with the man named Anton Devast wasn't an easy task. Those who got close usually wound up getting killed.

Drew locked his jaw. "Why'd you cut her?"

They'd cut Tina *and* gagged her. The gag would explain why she'd stopped screaming. Damn it, the gag had been his suggestion, but he'd only said it to clue her in to the fact that she needed to stay quiet about him.

Her eyes—so green and bright—found his. There was a desperate plea in her gaze.

A plea that he couldn't answer right then. Not if they wanted to both keep living.

"I was just showing her," Lee said softly, "what would happen if she tried to escape. We can treat her well…" He lifted the knife. Blood coated the blade. "Or we can make this little stay turn into her worst nightmare."

A tear leaked down Tina's cheek. She had high cheekbones, a slightly pointed chin and the cutest damned nose with its spray of freckles.

Normally her face was full of soft color and life.

Right then, fear had etched its way across her face. He didn't like for Tina to be afraid. Not one bit.

"You showed her," Drew growled. "She got the message. Now put the knife up."

Lee's dark eyes narrowed. "I don't take orders from you."

Fine. Drew stalked toward him. He grabbed the guy's wrist. *Don't break it, not yet.* But the threat was there, and Lee would know it. "You think the boss would like it if you killed Mercer's daughter? Seems to me she's a tool that he can use. Not something to be damaged."

Lee swallowed. The guy liked giving pain, but he couldn't handle being on the receiving end of it. He was also afraid of Drew, mostly because Drew had gotten into HAVOC by fighting his way in. He'd taken down five men, left them bloody and broken. The initiation had been hell.

But so was life.

"It's just a cut," Lee said dismissively. "No big deal."

"Don't cut her again. If the boss wanted her, then the boss will get her." Maybe he could use that. Surely, Devast would want to come in for a personal look at Mercer's daughter.

That visit would give Drew his chance to eliminate the man.

After all, eliminating Anton Devast was his job. At his core, Drew was a killer.

Still holding Lee, Drew let his gaze return to Tina. He didn't like seeing tears in her eyes.

And—her glasses were cracked. He let his hold on Lee tighten a little more. "I'll take first watch on her," Drew said.

Lee was trying to yank his hand free. Failing. "What?"

He hadn't stuttered. "I'll take first watch." Because he didn't trust anyone else with her. Definitely not Lee or Carl.

Lee's eyes were angry slits, but he gave a grim nod. "Fine, you do that." His short, red hair looked as if he'd raked his fingers through it. "You can stay with her while I get some sleep."

He made his words sound like an order. Whatever. As long as the guy got out of there...

Drew released the man.

It only took an instant for Lee's smirk to come back. "I'll see you again soon, sweetheart," he promised Tina. His gaze flickered to Drew. "And I'll see you later, too, Stone." A threat hung in the words.

He'd have to stay extra alert. The way Lee was eyeing him, Drew knew he might find a knife shoved into his own ribs during an unguarded moment.

Not like that would be the first time.

Drew lifted his hand and his fingers traced over the thick scar on his right cheek. "You sure will." He made certain that his words held just as much of a threat as Lee's had.

Actually they held *more* of a threat. Showing a weakness with these guys was a mistake, because they'd most definitely attack that weakness.

Drew didn't move until Lee and his two cronies were out of the room. When the door shut behind them, he exhaled slowly.

Tina was still staring at him with her wide, desperate eyes.

He wanted to tell her that everything was going to be okay, but he couldn't be sure listening devices weren't in the room. When he'd first reached the compound, he'd found two bugs in his bunk room.

It only figured that there would be some in there, too.

He glanced toward the door. Even though Drew had said that he'd take first watch, Lee might have stationed a guard outside.

"Mumph."

His attention slid back to Tina.

"Mumm-mph…" She jerked in the chair. Someone had tied her to the chair. Probably Lee.

He crossed to her side and knelt on the floor so that they'd be at eye level. "The ropes were tied too tight," he muttered, feeling anger try to push past his control once more.

Can't have that. Must maintain cool.

The other agents had him all wrong. They thought he was made of ice. That he didn't feel when he went out on his missions.

The problem was that he felt too much. And if he didn't control his fury… *Then I'm too dangerous.*

He loosened her binds. He glanced up at her, his gaze colliding with hers.

A crack ran across the right lens of her glasses, looking like a spider's web. He reached up.

She flinched.

"Easy," Drew murmured. "I'm just checking you out."

He lifted the glasses away from her face.

She blinked at him.

Hell. She was just as sexy without the glasses as she was with them. He'd thought maybe it was just a hot-librarian-type thing working for him, but no. The woman was simply temptation.

He didn't need temptation. He had a job to do.

She's the job right now. The words whispered from within him.

He put her glasses on the nearby table.

"Mumph!" Ah, now Tina was sounding angry behind the gag. He wasn't sure what would be better for her. Fear or anger. Unless they were careful, both might just get her killed.

He leaned toward her. Brought his mouth right to her ear just as he'd done before. Her scent, light, sweet strawberries, wrapped around him.

Because of Tina, he'd developed one serious addiction to strawberries over the past year. Not that she knew it. Not that she knew *anything* about him. To her, he was just another agent.

Another adrenaline junkie that she had to patch up and keep alive.

Only now it was his turn to keep her alive.

"Be very careful what you say," he barely breathed the words against the delicate shell of her ear.

Tina shivered.

Was that shiver from fear? Had to be. In these circumstances, he was foolish to think it could be from anything else.

But, just in case, he filed that reaction away for future notice. Because he'd sure like to know every sensitive spot on Tina's gorgeous body.

"They could be listening." His mouth brushed across her ear.

She gave the faintest of nods.

Her smell was incredible.

Focus.

He lifted his hands and undid the gag. The cloth dropped from her mouth.

Tina licked her lips and sucked in a deep gulp of air. "Thank you."

His own mouth tightened. She shouldn't be thanking him. He hadn't saved her. "I'm going to patch up your arm."

She blinked once more, and her gaze found his. She was still breathing deeply, gulping in air as if she'd been starved for it.

Her skin was porcelain pale and he wanted color staining her cheeks once more. He wanted the fear gone from her eyes.

Trust me. He mouthed the words to her.

After the faintest of hesitations, Tina nodded.

The ice melted a little around him. He turned away from her. Fumbled through the drawers in the room until he found some first-aid supplies. The men—and women—at the compound were always ready for battle, so that meant they had to be ready for the cleanup after that battle. He'd quickly learned that there were first-aid supplies scattered all around the place.

Tina didn't wince when he began to clean her wound with an antiseptic cloth. "It's not deep enough for stitches," he said as he put the bandage on her arm. "You're lucky."

Both her brows shot up.

Fine. So "lucky" hadn't been the best word to describe her current situation.

He grabbed a chair and pulled it toward her. She was still tied up, and he had to keep her that way or the others would wonder what the hell was happening. "You're going to be all right."

Tina's gaze just stared back at him.

He realized that she didn't believe him. Maybe that was good—because Drew hated making promises he couldn't keep.

"Mr. Mercer?"

Bruce Mercer looked up from the files that were spread across his desk. His assistant, Judith Rogers, stood in the doorway. Judith hated buzzing him. She'd said once that buzzing was too impersonal for her, and she usually came in to tell him when he had a visitor.

So her standing there…walking in unannounced…that wasn't unusual.

The fear in Judith's eyes *was* unusual.

"Tina Jamison is missing," Judith told him as she twisted her hands into fists. "I just got the call from an agent at her hotel. The lock on her door was broken, and Tina—she's gone."

Mercer didn't let the expression on his face alter.

This situation had been one that he feared. He was playing a deadly game, and Tina could have just become a pawn in that game.

If he wasn't careful, he might lose his pawn.

He might lose the whole damn game.

"Get me Dylan Foxx," Mercer demanded. "Right *now.*" Because he was going to need agents in the field to work this case and to make sure that Tina survived the battle that was coming.

He'd foolishly positioned Tina right in the middle of that battle.

I'm sorry, Tina.

He didn't make mistakes often, but when he did…they were deadly.

Chapter Two

"It's time for me to take over." The gruff voice had Tina's head jerking up.

She'd actually fallen asleep. How was that even possible? Tina blinked bleary eyes and found herself staring at Drew.

He was right in front of her. His gaze held hers an instant, then he turned his head and looked at the guy who'd just come into the room.

Tina had no idea who this blond man was. As he watched her, his hard brown eyes glittered. There was a holster at his hip—she could see the butt of his gun. And he had a knife strapped to his left side.

After her last encounter with a knife, Tina wasn't exactly eager to go another round with a blade.

"Lee said for me to relieve you," the man said in that same gruff voice. He shrugged. "So here I am."

Tina wanted to reach out and hold tight to Drew, but that wasn't possible.

Mostly because she was still tied up, but at least the gag was gone. That horrible, terrible gag. If she hadn't gotten her medicine just a few hours before the men had taken her, she wouldn't have been able to handle the gag. Tina wouldn't have been able to breathe.

"Keep that knife in its sheath, Carl," Drew told him flatly.

Oh, no. Oh, that wasn't *good.*

Drew's face—handsome, hard, fierce—seemed to tighten even more as he studied the other man.

Drew Lancaster was a warrior. She knew it. Had known it from the first moment she'd seen him. He'd been dripping blood at the time, courtesy of a fresh bullet wound. He hadn't even flinched when she'd dug that bullet out of him.

He was big; about six foot three, with wide shoulders, narrow hips and what she thought of as a go-to-hell golden gaze. His skin was tanned from hours under the Mississippi sun, and that slow drawl that crept out every now and then…

That drawl was temptation in a dangerous package.

She knew how lethal Drew was. She'd gotten a glimpse into his file once, thanks to her friend Sydney Ortez. Sydney controlled all the intel at the EOD, and when she'd noticed that Tina was spending a bit too much time gazing after Drew, Syd had wanted Tina to know exactly who she was day dreaming about.

Not a white knight.

More like a killing machine.

Drew's gaze slid to her once more. His face was all tough angles and planes. The scar that cut across his right cheekbone just made him appear all the more dangerous.

Her breath felt too hot in her lungs.

After a tense moment Drew gave a curt nod and rose to his feet. There was a tiny window in the room and sunlight spilled inside that window. The light fell on Drew as he passed it.

"Told you she was pretty," the one he'd called Carl mumbled.

Drew leaped at the other man. In an instant Drew's lower arm was under the guy's chin and Drew had him pinned against the wall. "And I'm telling you...*keep your hands off her.*"

The other man blinked. Then Carl smiled. "Like that, huh? Calling her yours already?"

I am in a nightmare. And Drew wasn't calling her anything.

But he was leaning in even closer to the blond male. "If you hurt her, if you so much as bruise her, I'll make you pay." A deadly promise.

The blond man gulped. "No worries, man. I'm just watchin' her."

Drew stepped back. "See that you do." He fired one more glance at Tina.

She had to press her lips together so she wouldn't cry out and basically beg him to stay.

He was undercover. He had a job to do. But she knew that he'd get her out of there.

She just had to hold on long enough for the rescue to work.

Drew turned and left the room without another word.

Carl eased toward her. "Guess you two got cozy, huh? Figured old Stone was a secret ladies' man."

He dropped into the chair near her. His hand went to the hilt of his knife.

Tina tensed, but he made no move to pull out the weapon.

His gaze swept over her face. "Such a pity," he murmured. "I hate it when pretty girls have to die."

HE WAS TAKING a risk. A huge one, Drew knew it, but he had to make the call. He slipped away from the others at the compound and headed toward the old fence on the right side of the property. He'd scouted before, and this was the weak spot in security. No cameras could see this location, but, thank goodness, there was actually cell service here.

Sydney Ortez had been the one to tell him about this sweet spot. Before Drew had gone in undercover, Sydney had used her satellites and her computer magic to try to find him a safe contact zone.

Safe, but not one hundred percent secure. Because in a situation such as this one, you never knew when the enemy might decide to take a stroll and blow your plans to hell.

Drew fired a quick glance over his shoulder. The phone was clutched tightly to his ear. One ring…

"I know about your problem," the voice on the other end of the line said. No identification was necessary. Drew instantly recognized the voice of his team leader, Dylan Foxx. The former SEAL had been the one to convince Drew to join the EOD in the first place. The two men had become old friends on the battlefield, on missions that they'd never discuss. So many years—so many missions. Through them all, Dylan always had Drew's back.

"Yeah?" Drew surveyed the area around him, trying to make sure no one was close enough to hear him. "So what the hell are we going to do?"

"Keep her alive," Dylan responded instantly. "Mercer knows what's happening. He says that Dr. Jamison's survival is priority."

Mercer knew. Right. The guy had eyes and ears everywhere.

I'm a set of eyes and ears for him now. "Does he realize I'm the one undercover here?"

"He does, and he said that you should make certain you stick to the doctor."

"They think she's his daughter," Drew stressed. How long would they keep working under that wrong assumption? How long until someone figured out they'd screwed up?

There was silence from Dylan, then he asked, "Is she?"

No. But Drew didn't give that immediate response. He trusted Dylan, of course he did, but there were some secrets he couldn't share.

Drew was one of the few people in the world who knew that, yes, Bruce Mercer actually did have a daughter. But that daughter wasn't Tina. "Hell if I know," he said.

It was a good thing Dylan wasn't there to see him. The guy had always said that he could read any lie on Drew's face. Lucky for Drew, the bad guys didn't have such an easy time of seeing past his deception.

"Tina Jamison wasn't supposed to be involved in this case," Drew growled. "No way. Who messed up? How did this happen?" Tina wasn't the bait for the trap they needed.

"I don't know." He could hear the frustration in Dylan's voice. "That's why I asked if she actually *is* his daughter, because that's the only thing making sense on my end. We gave Devast's men the false trail. They were supposed to follow it to *our* operative, not to Dr. Jamison."

Something had gone wrong. Very wrong. Now Drew had to stop the train wreck before Tina was killed.

There was a murmur in the background then Dylan said, "Get back to her. Word just came down that someone is about to send proof of life to the EOD."

Drew ended the call and started back toward the main house. Proof of life could be anything. Providing proof was the standard deal in an abduction case. That proof could be a video of the prisoner. A phone call from the captive.

It could be a severed finger. An ear that had been sliced off. That kind of physical evidence was actually often needed. High-profile prisoners were valuable and, before they were ransomed, their DNA had to be confirmed.

He couldn't let anyone cut into Tina.

He checked his weapon. Fully loaded.

Then he kicked up his speed and raced frantically back to Tina.

THE REDHEAD WAS BACK. Tina stared up at him—no, she stared into the guy's phone. He'd turned the phone sideways; he was video-taping her.

"This is what we call proof of life," he murmured. "We need you to prove to your dear old dad that you're still alive."

They weren't proving anything to her father. Her father *was* dead. So was her mother. They'd both died shortly after Tina's eighteenth birthday.

Their blood had soaked her fingers. She hadn't known how to save them.

I do now.

"Look into the camera," he ordered her. "Say your name."

The door opened behind him. Drew. Drew was back.

It got easier for her to breathe then.

She stared toward the redhead and his phone. "My name is Tina Jamison."

"Good girl," the redhead murmured. *Lee.* That was his name. She'd heard one of the other men call him that earlier. "Now tell us the date."

She did. Her voice didn't tremble. Tina was proud of that fact.

"Bruce Mercer, we have your daughter," the redhead said. His voice was cold and flat. "She's alive right now, but, if you don't follow our orders *exactly,* she won't be alive for long."

Tina kept staring at him.

"We want an exchange," Lee continued. "Her life for yours."

That wasn't going to happen. Not ever. Mercer was too important. He had ties to too many governments, too many agents, too many secrets.

She was just the doctor who patched up the team members.

I'm expendable.

Bruce Mercer wasn't.

"For every day that you delay, we will hurt her."

Oh, wait. *What?*

"We gave you proof of life," he continued. Her eyes narrowed. Was he recording these images of her? Or streaming them live to Mercer? If the fool was streaming them, the EOD would be on top of this group in hours. Sydney would trace the signal back to this location.

His hold tightened on the phone. "Now it's time for proof of pain."

He'd barely even got the words out before the other guy—the blond who'd kept her terrified for the past hour—came at her with his knife.

Tina tensed, but the knife just went to the ropes that bound her. Carl cut through the ropes that circled her right hand.

"What the hell…" Drew began.

"Slice off her finger," was the order that followed.

Carl smiled.

Tina tried to jerk her hand back.

She couldn't. He was too strong.

"Stop!" Drew bellowed.

He wasn't stopping. The knife pressed toward her hand.

Tina looked away.

But the blade didn't slice her skin. Instead she heard

the brutal thud of two bodies colliding. Her head whipped back toward that sound. Drew had just slammed into Carl. He'd tackled him, and both men had hit the floor. The knife clattered away.

"What are you doin', Stone?" Finally, Lee had dropped his phone. The video show seemed over.

Drew pounded Carl's head into the floor. Then he leaped to his feet. "You aren't cutting her, Lee."

"I'll do anything I want!" His chin jutted out, and Lee motioned to the other two men who stood against the back wall. "Take that fool down."

They ran toward Drew.

But they were the ones that hit the floor.

As he fought, Tina began to yank at the ropes still around her. Now that her right hand was free, she could escape. Her fingers were shaking as she undid the knots on her left hand. Then she started jerking at the ropes that tied her feet to the legs of the chair.

Grunts filled the room. The crunch of bones. The fight was brutal and—

More men were rushing inside.

Drew put his body in front of hers.

She untied the last knot and jumped to her feet.

"You aren't hurting her!" Drew shouted.

Then she heard a new sound. A very, very loud boom. A gunshot.

Drew's body jerked at the impact, but he didn't stop fighting the men who came at him. Of course, he didn't stop.

A killing machine.

He took down another man. Broke the nose of the fourth guy who rushed at him.

Hard hands grabbed Tina. A gun was shoved against her temple. Then Lee ordered, "Stop!"

Drew whirled. His gaze dipped to Tina's face, then back to the face of the gunman—Lee. "You aren't killing her," Drew said. His lips twisted into a humorless grin, one that was ice-cold. "She's no good to you dead."

"True." The gun lifted away from her. "Though it seems that *you* are no good to me alive."

He was going to shoot Drew again. Kill him while she watched. *"No!"* Tina yanked free of Lee's arms with a wild burst of strength. She put her body in front of Drew's. "Don't!"

Lee hesitated. His gaze went from her face back to Drew. "Interesting."

"I'll cooperate," she said, desperate because more men had run into the room. Alerted by the sounds of battle, they'd rushed inside. Now she and Drew were surrounded by guns and by men who looked as though they were ready to fire those guns at any moment. "I'll do whatever you want. I'll get my...father to meet your demands." Such a lie. "But, please, don't hurt him."

Carl had dragged himself off the ground. Blood dripped from his busted lower lip. "T-told you," he stuttered to Lee. "Stone here got sweet on the girl during his night duty."

"I think it's more than that," Lee said. A shrewd understanding filled his eyes. "Get some cuffs. Snap 'em on him." His head cocked to the right. "Cuffs will hold him better than rope." Then his lips lifted into a cold grin. "Even better, cuff him to *her*."

So much for keeping his cover in place. He'd sure blown that fast enough.

As soon as that knife had come close to her fingers, he'd attacked.

Where was the ice? When the knife had hovered over

her delicate hand, rage had ignited within him, driving right past his control.

The cuffs bit into his wrists. He wasn't surprised they'd used cuffs on him instead of rope. But when it came to thinking that the cuffs would be more secure than the rope, Lee was dead wrong.

They'd taken him and Tina into another room, a smaller room, with no window and sealed with a heavy, metal door. They'd cuffed one of his hands to hers, and his other hand—they'd cuffed it to a metal pole that came straight out of the floor.

Carl smirked at him. "That will hold you until it's time for us to play."

Play. Right. Wonderful.

Lee stood in the doorway behind Carl. "You know, Stone, there was something about you that I never liked."

Carl drove his fist into Drew's gut. He grunted. The jerk sure knew how to deliver some pain with a hard punch.

Lee sauntered into the room. He pushed Carl back and glared at Drew. They'd taken Drew's weapons. They'd also given him plenty of punches in the other room, despite Tina's pleas for them to stop.

They weren't exactly the type to show mercy. He didn't expect any.

"You've got secrets, don't you, Stone?" Lee said. His left brow rose. "If that's even your name."

Drew smiled. "You know you're a dead man."

Lee's lashes flickered. The flash of fear was obvious as the guy stepped back.

"I'm sending the video to Mercer. The video of his daughter…and the video of you, getting your butt beat."

Drew shrugged. "I don't think Mercer will care that some jerk he doesn't know was attacked."

"Maybe. Or maybe…just maybe…he does know you." Lee's gaze cut to Tina. "You made a mistake."

Saving her? No, it hadn't been a mistake. Saving her had been worth every second of pain.

"You looked at her with a lover's eyes, and you've never looked at anyone like that before."

Every muscle in Drew's body stiffened. Lee wasn't as dumb as he looked. *He's too observant.*

"I've seen you with plenty of women. You play around, you drink, and you don't care what they do when you're done." Half of Lee's mouth hitched up in a taunting smile. "But when you looked at her, when you burst into that room and saw me cutting her, your eyes were different. *I saw you.*"

This was bad.

"And you went crazy when I let old Carl loose on her."

He forced his back teeth to unclench. "Carl shouldn't be turned loose on any woman."

"She's not just any woman, is she? You know her."

Tina wasn't speaking beside him. But he could hear the sounds of her breaths, coming far too fast.

Then Lee advanced toward her. He grabbed Tina's chin. "And you know him, don't you?"

"No!" Tina cried.

Drew could almost believe her denial.

Almost.

"Well, I'll find out. I'll send this message to Mercer, and then I'll be back to see just what secrets you have… you and Stone here. When I let Carl begin to cut him, I'm betting either he'll talk—" Lee's fingers tightened on her chin "—or you will."

"Leave her alone," Drew ordered.

Lee shook his head. "See, that's what I'm sayin'. You get too protective for a man who doesn't know her, and that makes me wonder… Just *how* do you know her? How would a man like you know Bruce Mercer's daughter?" Menace layered his voice. "Want to know what I'm suspecting?"

"Not really. I don't give a damn," Drew retorted. He just needed Lee and Carl to get out of there so he could escape and get Tina to safety.

"I think one of Mercer's agents would know her. I think you're a man with a certain set of skills, skills a guy like Bruce Mercer would appreciate."

"You're thinking way too hard," Drew told him. "Don't hurt yourself."

Lee's eyelids flickered. "Getting an agent in here, monitoring us…that would be a Mercer move," Lee continued as he stepped away from Tina. With a nod, he said, "Maybe you are the killer I thought you were—only you're killing for the U.S. government. Not for HAVOC."

Drew made himself smile. The bullet was still in his shoulder, and it hurt, throbbing and burning constantly. But he was used to ignoring pain, so he shoved that burn deep into the back of his mind. "If I am EOD, then you need to be watching your back. 'Cause *maybe*—" he deliberately tossed the word back at Lee "—I got a team here, backing me up. *Maybe* this little place of yours is about to explode around you."

No, it wasn't. Drew's team wasn't close enough for that fast of an attack. They wouldn't even realize he'd been compromised at this point.

But Lee didn't know he was bluffing. And all of a sudden the guy started to sweat as worry sank in deep. "We need to sweep the perimeter!" Lee said as he spun toward Carl. "I have to make sure the place is secure."

With the big boss coming in, the guy wouldn't want any screw-ups.

Lee grabbed Carl's shirt. "You get outside that door. You make sure that no one enters and no one leaves until I get back." His hold tightened on Carl. "I trust you. You came up with me through the ranks."

How wonderful for them. Drew's eyes narrowed as he filed that little piece of information away for later.

"In case this jerk has any other teammates here undercover, I want *you* securing him. No one but me comes in here, got it?" Lee demanded.

Carl nodded. "Got it."

After firing one last fuming glare at Drew, the two men marched from the room. The door slammed and Drew heard the distinct sound of the lock setting into place.

"I'm sorry." Tina's voice was hoarse.

He grunted and yanked against the pole. He didn't have anything with him that he could use to pick the lock on the cuffs, so he had to find another means of escape. Yanking down the pole seemed like a fairly good option number two.

"The bullet is still in you, isn't it?"

"That's the least of our trouble." As soon as Lee realized that EOD agents weren't about to swarm the place, the guy would be back. He'd torture Drew then kill him, and Tina would get an up-close seat for that bloody show.

The pipe began to groan.

"What are you doing?"

Drew figured there was no point in sugarcoating things with her. "You know this is a torture room, right?"

Her breath rushed out.

"See the drain over there? It's so they can hose the place down when they're done and just wash the blood right away. Fast and easy cleanup." Lee had transferred them into that room so that he could fully take advantage of the facilities.

Lee had plans.

Drew was ready to destroy those plans.

"He should've checked the equipment," Drew said softly. "Sloppy mistake." Lee had probably cuffed other prisoners to this pole before to hold them in place.

But one thing Lee seemed to have missed...desperate prisoners struggled. The men and women that Lee had hurt in the past would have struggled desperately to escape from the pole—and the pain.

And their struggles had loosened the pole. It wasn't fully embedded in the hard floor any longer.

Perfect.

"Drop with me," Drew ordered in a low whisper. He didn't want Carl hearing them.

Without a word, Tina dropped with him. The floor was cold and hard, and it smelled of blood. Hell, he wanted her out of that place. No way did Tina belong in a room like this. He yanked again against the pole and then... then Tina was there, adding her strength to his. She'd positioned her body closer to his, and she was jerking on the pole with him.

It groaned again, and Drew stilled. "Wait." Because he didn't want to alert Carl, not yet.

But Carl didn't come rushing into the room.

"Again," Drew whispered.

They yanked again, and the pole lifted off the floor, just a few centimeters, but that was all Drew needed. He slid his cuff under the pole and his left wrist was free.

Hell, yes.

He jumped to his feet and Tina rushed up with him. "What about this one?" she said, tugging on the cuff that connected their wrists.

"That one's going to have to stay." Until he could find something to pick the lock or find a saw to cut the cuffs off. And if she was going to stay cuffed to him, then Tina needed to realize… "We're going to be targets."

Her eyes were wide. Stark.

No glasses.

He swore. "Just how much can you see?"

"I'm fine. I'm near-sighted, so I can see up close pretty much perfectly."

Which should work, since she had to stay up-close with him.

"I'll be your eyes for distance," he said.

She licked her lips and, of course, that just made his gaze drop to her mouth.

Focus.

He exhaled slowly and let the ice sweep over him. "You follow my every order, understand? No hesitations, no questions. Because a hesitation will get you—or both of us—killed."

She nodded. Her dark hair brushed over her shoulders.

"These are bad men, Tina." Bad was an understatement. "You know what they want to do to you." Cutting off her finger would just be the start of their fun.

Her gaze held his.

"So just be prepared for what I have to do…to them." Their escape wasn't going to be some walk in the park. It might even turn into a blood bath.

"What can I do?" She shook her head. "I want to help you, not just be some burden that you have to carry out of this place."

"Help by staying alive."

Her lips tightened. "That's not what I meant."

He knew, and Drew also knew that he didn't want to risk her. *But she will be risked.* There was no escaping the danger surrounding her. "How the hell did you even get in this mess?"

"I don't know."

His left hand lifted. The loose cuff dangled from his wrist. He touched her cheek.

Tina flinched.

"Easy." He wouldn't hurt her, ever. Didn't she realize that? "Before I open that door…" *And I run the chance of losing my life before I get the one thing I've wanted for so long…* "There's something I need to do."

A faint line appeared between her brows. "What?"

He was a bloody, bruised mess. When he'd imagined this moment—and he had, many times—it had been different.

Oh, well. So much for his best-laid plans.

"What?" Tina asked again.

"This." He put his mouth on hers. Drew had to do it. He had to find out if the woman would be as good in reality as she was in his dreams.

At first Tina didn't move at all. She'd frozen on him—maybe his ice had transferred to her.

Some dreams were better than reality. He began to pull away.

Then Tina leaned toward him. Her lips parted beneath his and she kissed him back with a wild, reckless passion he hadn't expected.

Some dreams couldn't touch reality.

He put his hand under her chin, aware of the weight of that dangling cuff. He tilted her head back so that he could plunder her mouth, so that he could taste her.

Hell, in that moment, he wanted to consume her.

His body ached for her. Need pulsed through his veins, and if they weren't in some pit of hell…if the bad guys weren't just down the hallway…

Drew lifted his head. "Then you'd be mine," he rasped.

Tina blinked and shook her head. "What?"

He kissed her once more, just because he had to do it. *There's no way we're dying.* The woman was full of secrets, and he'd be sure he had the chance to discover every single one. "I've wanted to do that since the first time I walked into your office and you told me to take off my shirt."

Her gorgeous eyes widened. "Your shirt was covered in blood."

As if a little matter of a bullet wound could have stopped him from wanting her. "It is now, too." *A bullet wound won't stop the need.* He rocked back on his heels. "Remember, no hesitation."

Her lips were swollen from his mouth. She was so sexy right then. Sexy, but still scared. Talk about terrible timing.

That was the story of his life.

He backed her up against the wall on the right side of the room. Drew calculated that this would be his best attack spot.

He rolled his shoulders, pushed down his fury. He had to take out his prey one at a time. First, Carl would go down. Carl who'd wanted to slice away one of Tina's fingers.

Rage... Drew swallowed and pushed the rage down again.

Carl would be taken out first. Then Drew and Tina would rush down the hallway. Another guard would be at the door that led outside. Maybe two guards would be there. Drew would have to take them out, too.

He and Tina would stay low, keeping to cover. There was a motorcycle waiting in the garage. One the others thought was out of commission, but that Drew had taken the time to ensure was actually fully operational.

He liked having backup plans available.

His muscles were tight, battle ready. Tina watched him with wide eyes.

Protect her. Get her out.

Once Tina was safe, he'd come back to finish this mission. *I have to eliminate Anton Devast.*

He gave a little nod. "Okay, Doc, it's show time." He waited a beat, then said, "Scream for me."

She didn't scream.

Hadn't they talked about not hesitating? Drew was sure that he'd gone over that part with her. "Scream!"

She screamed.

An instant later Carl rushed through the door.

Chapter Three

Tina screamed. She screamed as loudly as she possibly could. She'd always had a rather good scream—horror-movie good—and her scream had Carl racing back into the room.

But her scream was cut off when Drew's fingers locked around her throat. "You're dead," he growled.

"What's goin' on here?" Carl demanded.

Drew's grip was strong, but not painful. The look in his eyes—that was terrifying. He should have given her a head's up about this little bad cop—uh, agent—routine.

"You ruined everything for me," Drew told her. "Everything."

"You can't hurt her!" Carl snapped. "That's what I'm doing—"

He grabbed for Drew's shoulder.

His mistake.

Drew swung toward him. The loose cuff on Drew's left wrist flew out and hit Carl in the face. Then Drew punched Carl in the face. A fast, brutal hit. Carl stumbled back. The weapon in his hand started to rise.

But Drew wasn't done. He chopped down with his hand, hitting Carl's arm, and the weapon fell from Carl's fingers.

A few more hits from Drew—Tina jerked forward

because when he moved, so did she—and Carl was on the floor.

His eyes were closed, and he was *out*.

Drew leaned over Carl and scooped up the gun. "Nice scream you got there, Doc."

And nice, brutal fighting skills he had there. Tina cleared her throat. "Ah, thank you."

He looked back over at her. "Ready?"

She nodded.

Drew led the way out of that prison. He eased open the room's door and peered down the hallway. She wondered if anyone else had heard her scream. No one else appeared to be racing toward them.

"Lee has most of the guys stationed outside. They're probably searching for my team." His voice was so quiet she had to strain to hear it.

His team. "When will they get here?" Hopefully, any moment. Then—

His gaze slid to hers. "They won't."

Her heart sank at that news.

"Don't worry, I've got you."

She would be more reassured when they were safely away from all of the bad guys with guns. Tina wanted to know who these guys were, why Drew was undercover there—what was happening!

But now wasn't the time for her questions. Now was the time to focus on survival—escape.

He searched the immediate area once more. "Clear." They rushed down the hall. Drew held the gun in his left hand. She'd known that he was ambidextrous; the man could wield a weapon just as easily with either hand. She'd watched him do just that on the shooting range once. That ambidextrous talent was a real good thing, since his right hand was still locked to her.

They approached another door—a heavy, wooden door.

"This will take us outside," he said, pausing briefly. "I don't want to use the bullets unless I have to because they'll just bring more company running toward us."

She wasn't in the mood for company, either.

He gave her the gun.

Wait. What?

"Use it, but only if you have to."

Then he opened the door. They slipped outside.

And a man with a gun immediately appeared in their path.

"Stone!" He glared at Drew. "You traitor! Lee warned me about you!" He brought up his gun.

Drew kicked out at the guy; his boot connecting with a snap. The gun went flying, and so did the man. His head slammed into the cement behind him.

"Got you!" a voice snarled from Tina's right, a bare moment before hard hands wrapped around her. Those hands tried to rip her away from Drew's side, but with the cuffs, that wasn't happening.

But the vicious pull did make Drew attack. He spun and struck out with his fist.

The attacker let her go, but only for an instant. Only so he could lunge at Drew.

No.

She hit the guy with the butt of her gun.

He went down with a groan.

Drew curled his cuffed fingers around hers. "Nice job, Doc. Now let's *go.*"

Because no one else had seen them, not yet. Darkness

had fallen once more, and the glittering stars were above them as they raced toward what looked like an old barn.

They stayed to the shadows. Drew stopped her several times, lifting his hand and freezing when a rustle of movement sounded.

Then they were in the barn. Only, Tina quickly realized, it was more of a garage than a barn. Broken-down cars waited inside. Rusty tools lined the wooden walls. And, from what she could see, there was no means of escape. This plan wasn't working. "We need the helicopter," she said, grabbing his arm. The helicopter was their best bet. They could fly right out of that place.

"The chopper's too secure," Drew softly replied as he pulled her toward a thick, dark tarp. "We wouldn't be able to fuel it and get out of here before every man in the area swarmed us."

A swarming sounded bad.

"This is what we need." He tossed the tarp aside.

She saw the curving body of a motorcycle. One that looked as if it had seen better days a very long time ago. "Uh, I'm not sure…"

He'd already climbed on the motorcycle, the movement, of course, propelling her forward.

Tina dug in her heels. "There are tools here. Maybe we can cut the cuffs." So what if most of the tools looked to be about ten years old? There could be a sharp saw in there, somewhere.

"Our priority is getting to freedom right now, before a patrol comes through here." His eyes glittered at her. "We don't have any more time to waste. Get on the bike."

"I don't see a helmet."

She heard voices then, rising from outside.

He heard them, too. His body tensed. "Get on the bike!"

She'd just broken the no-hesitation rule of his again. Tina jumped on the motorcycle just as someone threw open the door to the garage.

"What the hell?" the guy in the doorway demanded. "Stone?"

Drew revved the motorcycle's engine. Because of their linked hands, Tina had to stretch her arm out next to his and had to press her body intimately close.

"Hold on," Drew told her.

She already was. For dear life.

The bike leaped forward, heading straight for the man in the doorway. Tina clamped her lips together so that she wouldn't scream.

After all, there was no need for her to scream. The man in the doorway was doing plenty of screaming.

Then that man was diving out of the way. Drew drove the motorcycle right through the door and out into the night.

Wind whipped against Tina's body, her hair flying behind her and— Oh, *no,* she realized that she'd dropped the gun.

Not exactly the pro move of an agent.

But then, she wasn't an agent, and she needed both hands to hold tight to Drew because he wasn't heading for some nice, paved road.

He was heading straight for a fence. One that had barbed wire at the top.

"Uh, Drew…"

"Don't worry, Doc. I got this."

At least, that was what she thought he said. It was hard to tell for certain over the roar of the bike. They were going faster and faster and— Was that a ramp? No, no, that was just boards, propped up against the fence. He couldn't possibly ride up on those—

He could.

He did.

They hurtled over the fence, clearing the barbed wire with inches to spare, even as voices shouted behind them.

When the bike touched down, Tina nearly flew right off the cracked seat. Luckily, the handcuff—and her death grip on Drew—had her jerking right back down.

The motorcycle's wheels spun. Dirt flew in the air. But Drew righted the bike before they could crash.

They hurtled forward once more.

Bullets thudded into the ground behind them.

Drew didn't stop. He gunned the engine and they raced off into the night.

Tina clung tightly to him. *Breathe. Just breathe.* The nightmare had to end—sooner or later.

"WE HAVE A PROBLEM."

Dylan Foxx glanced up at those quiet words. Rachel Mancini stood just inside the doorway of the small office. Her dark hair fell in a perfect, straight line to her chin. Her eyes—a bright blue that always seemed to look through him—reflected worry.

Rachel didn't worry often. There wasn't much that *could* make the ex-Marine worry.

"Another one?" Dylan muttered as he yanked a hand through his hair. He'd just finished a second phone call with Bruce Mercer. The big boss was furious and demanding action.

It was time for the team to move. They couldn't give Drew any longer on his own.

"Drew didn't check in."

He sucked in a sharp breath at the news. Yeah, that counted as a problem. Dylan surged out of his chair. As he walked toward her, Rachel's shoulders seemed to stiffen.

She did that around him. Always tensing up. Always closing him out.

He locked his own jaw. "Maybe he was delayed. Maybe—"

"Drew's never missed a check-in. I waited ten minutes, and he didn't make contact." She shook her head. "And I picked up some radio noise—something is happening out there. All of the men were called to action."

Hell. Rachel had been monitoring the radio waves and transmission signals from the HAVOC compound, extra ears in case Drew got into trouble.

She wet her lips. "There's…something else."

Her tone told him this was even worse.

"Drew's tracker went off-line."

Every EOD agent in the field had a tracking device implanted just beneath the skin. In case the agent was taken by the enemy, Mercer wanted to be able to get a lock on the missing man or woman. The EOD didn't like to lose agents.

Dylan had no intention of losing a teammate, and a friend.

"Maybe it's a system error," he said, even though his gut told him otherwise.

"I checked in with the techs at the EOD. They said his signal was transmitting fine until an hour ago, then it went dead."

Hell. "And there's no tracker implanted on Dr. Jamison."

"No, she's not an agent. Mercer never saw a need for her to be monitored. She wasn't supposed to be at risk."

Now she'd been taken and Drew had gone off the grid.

They had to get into the field. ASAP. Dylan hated being away from the action, especially when his team needed him. Especially when—

His phone rang. He glanced down and swore when he saw the number. He knew they were about to have more problems coming their way. With his eyes on Rachel, he answered the call. "Foxx."

"I just sent you a file that you need to view immediately." The voice on the other end of the line was feminine, husky, and one that was used to giving orders. *Sydney Ortez.* When it came to EOD Intel, Sydney was the go-to girl. She was also Mercer's right-hand woman. If something was happening within the organization, Sydney knew about it.

The fact that Sydney was *supposed* to be out on maternity leave as she prepared for the birth of her twins—well, the fact that she was calling him meant that something serious had gone down.

He put Sydney on speaker and pulled up the file on his phone.

Tina Jamison's face filled the screen. Her eyes were wide with terror.

"Look into the camera," a hard voice ordered. Dylan couldn't see the speaker. He figured the voice probably belonged to the man recording the video. "Say your name."

"My name is Tina Jamison."

"Good girl," the guy murmured.

Her voice held fear. The same fear that filled her eyes. Tina wasn't supposed to be in the field. Her place was in the office.

And Dylan knew why. Mercer had briefed him during that second phone call. Told Dylan all of Tina's secrets.

"Tina Jamison is my *friend*," Sydney said softly. "I want her back. The EOD wants her back."

"Bruce Mercer, we have your daughter," the rumbling voice said on the video then.

"Tina isn't his daughter," Sydney said at the same instant. "The kidnappers are mistaken about her identity.

When they realize that mistake, Tina will become expendable to them."

Rachel raised her dark brows. "They took the wrong bait," she said sadly.

Yes, they had. The EOD's careful plans had gone horribly wrong.

Before Dylan could reply to Rachel, the voice from the video was talking again. "We want an exchange," the man continued. "Her life for yours."

Dylan whistled. Mercer had suspected this would happen.

"For every day that you delay, we will hurt her."

Tina stared out of that video, her eyes wide. But, wait, did her gaze just flicker to the left? It looked as if some of the tension had eased from her shoulders.

"We gave you proof of life," the male voice said. "Now it's time for proof of pain."

Another man approached Tina. All Dylan could see was the guy's back, his blond hair and the knife in his hand.

"Oh, dear God," Rachel whispered.

"Slice off her finger," the grating voice ordered.

The knife lowered toward Tina's hand.

"Stop!" A familiar bellow. Drew's bellow.

But the knife didn't stop.

Tina looked away.

After that, all hell broke loose. Or, rather, Drew Lancaster broke loose. He leaped forward and attacked the blond. The video image twisted, flew sideways, and Drew pummeled the guy on the floor.

Then another image filled the screen. A man wearing a black ski mask stared straight ahead and said, "We have your daughter, Mercer, and we have one of your precious EOD agents. If you don't come for them, if you don't trade yourself, they'll both die. I can promise you, their deaths will be long and very, very painful."

The video ended.

Rachel slowly exhaled. "That would explain why Drew isn't making contact."

Because he'd had to blow his cover to protect Tina.

"There is no exchange," Sydney told them. No emotion had entered her voice. For a moment she almost reminded him of Drew. "You have to extract Tina and Drew, immediately. Backup agents will be sent down to assist your team."

"And the original mission?" He wasn't just going to let a domestic terrorist group walk away unscathed. If those SOBs escaped, thousands could die.

Not on my watch.

"Contain Devast's group. Local law enforcement has already been alerted, and they'll move on your command."

This was a mess. A terrible, dangerous mess. "What about the group's boss? If we just get the underlings, we don't stop Anton Devast." That was why Drew had gone in. To take down the real threat. Not just the lackeys.

"We'll work to make his men turn on him. If he isn't there, if we can't get Devast in this raid, then we'll use any prisoners that are taken against him."

But they might not turn on their boss. If they were afraid enough—or stupidly loyal enough—they wouldn't.

He ended the call with Sydney. He understood exactly what had been said and what hadn't.

The EOD wasn't like other government agencies. They didn't follow official protocols, and they didn't always tie up their cases with nice, neat little bows.

More often, their cases ended in bloodshed and death.

Their cases were the darkest. The most dangerous.

An extraction wouldn't be easy, and attacking that compound—that attack could turn into a full-on war.

"Are you ready?" Dylan asked Rachel. Because sometimes, it didn't take an army to fight a war.

It just took a few well-trained soldiers.

She nodded.

"Then let's do this." Before any more innocents were pulled into the fray.

HE'D LOST THEM, for the moment. That moment wouldn't last long, though.

And, unfortunately, neither would he.

Drew blinked, trying to keep his eyes open. He'd driven for at least two hours, stopping when he thought he saw lights in the distance, making sure that he didn't turn on his own lights because he hadn't wanted to alert the enemy to his location.

He'd gotten Tina away from those men. He'd done his best by her.

But now he was about to collapse. Too much blood loss. Not enough sleep. He couldn't even remember the last time that he'd slept and, normally, that wouldn't be a problem but—

The bullet's still in me. The wound was making him too weak. He had to find a place to hide. A place to rest so that he could get that damn bullet out of him.

Or so Tina could remove it. He had a doc. He was going to use her.

He saw the small ranch, a dot in the distance. Cautiously he drove toward it. The fence was broken, the grass overgrown. No signs of cattle or horses. No sign of anyone.

The windows were boarded up. The roof slumping.

"Are we going there?" Tina asked, her voice barely rising over the rumble of the motorcycle's engine.

He shook his head. Not there. If their pursuers came this way, they'd search the ranch first. But…

Drew drove past the ranch. He kept heading across that overgrown field.

Then he saw the shack. Maybe it had been used as a storage building once or even as a small house for a ranch hand, but time hadn't been kind to the place.

The front window was broken. Two boards had been crisscrossed over the window and nailed in place.

The little structure was nestled behind some trees, so it wouldn't be immediately visible to anyone who came by. And, besides, if their pursuers *did* come this way, they'd check the ranch first.

And I'll hear them.

"We're stopping here." He killed the engine.

Tina climbed off the bike, wincing a little, and he followed right after her. They walked the motorcycle to the shack where he hid it in the back and then Drew reached into the saddlebag.

"What's that?" Tina asked as she leaned in close.

"Emergency supplies." Because he believed in being prepared. Would the burner phone work? Only if they could get a signal in the middle of nowhere. It had been hard enough to get a signal at the compound.

Out here…doubtful.

He'd gotten the pack ready cautiously, always knowing that he could need to flee at any moment. Some food, medical supplies—and that burner phone. Everything that a guy on the run could possibly need.

He tucked the bag under his arm and hissed out a breath when his wound throbbed.

"Drew?"

"I'll need your help, Doc." Sure, he'd taken out bullets on his own before, but when he'd stitched them up, he'd done hack jobs on his body. Besides, with the way he was feeling, Drew was afraid he might pass out halfway through the bullet extraction.

He went back to the front of the shack. The door was locked, so he just pulled up his strength and kicked it in.

Inside, dust coated the place. The shack smelled closed-in—but, lucky for them, there weren't any critters.

And the place *had* been a house. Once. He pulled a flashlight from the pack and shone the small ray of light around the interior. An old bed. A table. Some chairs.

He hauled the chairs back against the door and braced them under the now-broken doorknob.

Drew dumped his pack on the wobbly table. He reached inside and pulled out another flashlight. Drew handed it to Tina. "We can't keep the light on for too long. If the folks looking for us come this way, it will alert them."

She nodded.

He lifted the phone.

He realized that Tina was holding her breath.

He hated to break it to her but… "There's no signal here." He'd try to go outside. Walk the perimeter. Maybe he'd find—

His knees buckled. He almost hit the floor. And he almost took Tina down with him.

"Drew!" She braced him against her.

"Sorry, Doc, stood as long…as I could…" He licked his too-dry lips. "Do me a favor?"

"Of course! Anything, I—"

"Dig out the bullet."

She grabbed for the first-aid supplies and helped him to the bed. He fell back and she came tumbling down with him. When he hit the mattress, she fell in close to him. Her mouth was just inches from his. "Want you," he managed to rasp, and maybe he was starting to get a little delirious from the pain and blood loss because he hadn't meant to tell her that. Talk about bad timing. "Got to…stop bleedin' first… Can't die on you…"

"No, *you can't.*" Her voice was sharp. She pushed up to stare down at him. But he'd dropped his flashlight when his knees buckled, and he couldn't see her face clearly. Just the darkness.

He wanted her mouth again.

He also wanted to just sleep.

Then he heard fabric ripping. He realized his eyes had sagged closed. He opened them and saw the flash of light. Tina still had her flashlight, and she was shining it on him.

She'd ripped away his shirt.

"How were you even moving?" Tina whispered. "You drove for so long."

Soldiers didn't stop moving. Not until the mission was done. He'd needed to get Tina to safety.

He had.

"Drew!"

He realized that she'd been calling his name. Again and again. He frowned at her.

"I'm going to remove the bullet, and I'll sew you up, but I don't have anything to numb the area. The kit had some alcohol and some antibiotics, but—"

"Do…it," he growled. They'd have to run again, soon. He needed the wound closed by then.

She climbed over him. With them bound, he knew that Tina had to be creative with her movements.

If he hadn't been hurting so much, he would have truly enjoyed having her straddle him.

Next time.

She put the flashlight at the top of the old headboard so that it shone down on him. "One hand," she muttered. "I can't believe I have to do this with one hand."

He jiggled their connected wrists. "Use me."

"You're about to pass out on me." She nibbled her lower lip. She'd taken the gloves from the first-aid pack. Put them on. "Don't get an infection. Don't get an infection…"

He didn't think she was talking to him anymore. She seemed to be repeating that mantra to herself.

When she started applying pressure and digging that bullet out, he pulled in a deep breath. He locked his gaze on her face. Focused only on her.

He'd been shot on another mission, just a few months back. He'd been lured into a trap. Hit before he'd had a chance to call for backup. When he'd woken in the hospital, Tina had been there. "You were…worried about me," he said, remembering.

She glanced at him. "Are you staying with me, Drew?"

"Always," he whispered.

"Good. Because I'm not planning to let you go." Her lips curved. She was so gorgeous when she smiled. Did she realize that?

She even had a dimple in her left cheek. A little slash that would peek out every now and then.

The dimple wasn't showing at that moment. Tina had to really smile, had to really laugh, for it to come out. He'd caught her laughing with her friend Sydney once. That was when he'd first seen the dimple.

He'd been lost, staring at her.

"Stitching you up," she said. "Just a little bit longer."

He'd watched her that day, and he'd wanted. But there had been another mission waiting for him. There always was. And, even if there hadn't been, he didn't know how to approach a woman like her.

Wining and dining. Those were tricks that other guys used. He didn't know anything about romance.

He just knew too much about death.

"All done."

Drew glanced down. She'd put a bandage over his wound.

"Thanks, Doc." He owed her. He'd find a way to repay that debt.

"Thanks for getting me out of that place," she whispered back to him. A soft, wet cloth pushed over his skin and smoothed down his chest.

He tensed.

Her hand lightly stroked him. "Easy. It's a bacterial wipe from the kit. I'm just going to clean the blood away."

"Tina…"

Her hand stilled. She looked up at him.

Focus. "Don't…leave the house."

She nodded then smiled. One of those real smiles that flashed her dimple.

Gorgeous.

"I can't," she told him. Then she was the one to wiggle their cuff. "I can't go any place without you."

The darkness pressed in on him. "Damn straight," Drew heard himself mumble. "That's the way it's going be… here on out…"

And, with Tina's hands on him, with her smile the last sight he'd seen, Drew let the pain finally take him away.

"WHERE ARE THEY?"

Lee Slater froze at the demand. Oh, hell, he hadn't thought the boss would be showing up so soon.

"Did you think I wouldn't hear about this screw-up?" Anton Devast demanded as he stepped forward. Lee could easily hear his footsteps and the *thud, thud, thud* of his cane. "The men here are loyal to me, not you, Lee."

Lee squared his shoulders and spun to face the boss.

The guy in front of him didn't look intimidating. Older, with gray hair at his temples, a slight slump to his shoulders, and the fingers of his right hand curling so tightly around that cane—the guy didn't look like a threat at all.

He was. He was the deadliest man that Lee had ever met. "I've got men tracking them now—"

"You let Bruce Mercer's daughter escape."

Cold. But when he looked into the boss's eyes, that dark blue gaze seemed to burn.

"Sh-she had help." He was stuttering. Because he'd seen the boss in action. The guy was faster than men half his age. "We think... We think an EOD agent was undercover."

"I know. Carl told me."

Carl. Damn it. The guy should have waited for Lee to break the news to the boss.

"Don't be angry at Carl. I *convinced* him to tell me everything as soon as I arrived."

Lee realized that there was blood at the bottom of that cane.

It wasn't just a cane, he knew. A deadly blade could extend from that tip. *Sorry, Carl.*

"An EOD agent, in *my* operation." The boss began to pace around the room. *Thud, thud, thud.* "I should've eliminated Mercer years ago. The same way he tried to eliminate *me.*"

The boss had to use the cane because Bruce Mercer had nearly killed him twenty years before. The boss had almost lost his leg in that explosion.

He had lost his son.

Devast stopped pacing. He lifted the cane and pointed it at Lee. "You have six hours to find them."

Lee nodded quickly. "My men—"

The cane pushed against his throat. The blade extended

just a bit. "No, not your men. *You*. Get out there. Kill the EOD agent and bring that woman back to me."

Lee nodded.

The blade withdrew. The cane dropped.

Lee rushed for the door.

"If you can't bring her back to me, then you'll be the next one to die."

It wasn't an idle threat. Lee grabbed for his backup weapon. He hurried out of the compound and headed toward the helicopter. They hadn't been able to see much at night, but now that day had broken, he was sure he'd be able to track the agent and the woman.

He wasn't dying.

They were.

Chapter Four

The knife was coming toward her hand. The man with the cold eyes smiled as he prepared to slice off her finger. Tina tried to jerk her hand back, but it was caught on something.

"Easy."

Her eyelids flew open.

Drew stared down at her. "You're safe," he said, the words a low, deep rumble. "You're with me."

Her breath eased out as the nightmare—memory—faded.

They were on the old bed. Still cuffed. And Drew was leaning over her.

A much more aware, focused Drew than she'd seen a few hours ago. Right before he'd passed out on her.

Tina swallowed. Her throat was parched. It must have been at least eight hours since she'd had something to drink, but she figured the dry throat was the least of her worries. Her voice was husky when she asked him, "How are you feeling?"

"More human."

Good. A fast glance showed that there had been no additional bleeding since she'd last checked him. "I don't even know how you stood on your feet for that long. Much less controlled that bike." Anyone else would have been down the instant the bullet hit.

Not Drew. The guy seemed to have a will made of iron.

And now that he wasn't down for the count, she became aware of the fact that they were in a highly intimate situation.

In bed.

His body over hers, his arm curving around her.

Her heart slid into a double-time beat, and that faster pounding wasn't just from fear.

His eyes were on hers. Golden eyes. She'd never seen a man with eyes like his before. They always looked a little wild.

His eyes were so startling because other than his wild stare, he'd always been so controlled in every encounter they'd had back at the EOD offices.

"I—I'm not Mercer's daughter." She wasn't sure why she blurted that out right then. Especially since she'd been staring at him and thinking that his lashes were incredibly long... That his lips were sexy...

That she wanted him to kiss her.

"I know."

He was— Wait. "You do? How?"

He just stared back at her.

He knows who Mercer's real daughter is.

But then, so did Tina. But she only knew because Mercer had been so determined to protect one particular agency "asset" a few months ago. On a case that had caused Drew to wind up with more bullet wounds and an emergency trip to the hospital.

The asset had been in that hospital, too, and guarded by other EOD agents. Mercer had wanted to transfer the woman out of that hospital, to move her ASAP. He'd even gone so far as to order the woman drugged.

But, fortunately for the woman in question, EOD Agent Cale Lane had been there. Cale had fallen fast and hard for the asset and he hadn't been about to let anyone threaten her.

Not even the woman's own father.

"You...you worked on her protection detail," Tina said slowly as she put the puzzle pieces together. That was how he knew her identity.

Drew shook his head. "Bruce Mercer doesn't have a daughter." Flat. Hard.

Her brows lifted.

"Bruce Mercer doesn't have a daughter," he said again. "Because if he did, the woman would be a constant target. She'd never be safe."

She understood. Oh, heck, yes, after the past twenty-four hours, Tina definitely understood. "He doesn't have a daughter," Tina repeated. Did Drew think that she wouldn't protect the other woman? She could have sold her out at any time, if that was what she wanted. "I'm not like that," Tina said, suddenly angry because, after everything that had happened, Drew actually thought she'd trade someone else's life for her own. She shoved against him.

But Drew didn't back away. "What's wrong?"

"You think..." Now she was the one gritting out words. "That I would throw someone else at those animals? Knowing that they'd just torture her? Kill her?" She wouldn't stand by and watch an innocent suffer. That wasn't who she was. "I *wouldn't.*" She'd had to watch her parents suffer.

Their deaths had almost broken her.

He pinned her hands to the bed. "Calm down."

"You calm down!" Tina snapped at him. "I've been kidnapped, cut, locked up, handcuffed—and I've held it together!" She'd even saved his hide. Where was her thanks?

"I'm not going to betray the EOD, and you should know me better than that."

His hold didn't loosen. "Torture can break anyone, Doc. I've seen seasoned warriors crumble with the right pressure."

"Maybe you should have more faith in me," she told him, the anger snapping in her words. "Now let me go before I damage those stitches!" Because she was fighting mad.

Drew shook his head. "You won't. You won't hurt me. You're a healer. That's what you do." He brought his head close to hers.

Before she could snarl at him, Tina heard a new sound rising in the distance. The unmistakable whir of a helicopter's blades.

She stilled.

"It's okay," Drew told her, but his voice had dropped to a whisper. "They're just doing a sweep. They're not going to see the bike, and they're not going to see us."

She didn't have that confidence. "Maybe they're searching for houses. Places that we could have used for hiding. They could land here—"

He laughed softly at that. "They'll be lucky to land anywhere. A guy named Grayson was the only other pilot there, and when I went up with him once, he could barely hold the bird steady. That's why they were so quick to bring me on board. They needed me."

She still wasn't exactly feeling reassured. Especially because the whir of the helicopter's blades was getting closer and closer—louder and louder.

"Don't think about it," Drew told her. "Think about this."

Then he kissed her. She was still angry at him and scared about the helicopter.

But she had a weakness. One very distinct weakness. She liked kissing him because the man sure knew how to use his mouth.

His tongue licked lightly over her lower lip then it thrust into her mouth. He kissed her slowly, deeply, as if he were savoring her.

She was sure savoring him.

She wanted to wrap her arms around him, wanted to feel the broad expanse of his shoulders, but he still held her hands pinned to the bed.

Other parts of her body could sure feel, though. His arousal pressed against the juncture of her thighs. He'd moved, shifted his weight, so that he was positioned between her legs.

His mouth slipped from hers. He began to kiss his way down her neck. Her breath was coming in fast gasps, and—

"The helicopter is gone," she whispered as she realized an intense quiet had swept over the area.

He kept kissing her neck.

Right. Gone chopper. But focused man. "Drew?"

His head lifted. Those golden eyes seemed to blaze. "I want you."

Her breasts were tight, aching, and when had she started arching her lower body against his? She wasn't normally one to have desire ignite with just a kiss.

But Drew wasn't a normal kind of guy, and the way he made her feel was definitely not normal, too.

Maybe that wasn't bad. It sure didn't feel bad.

It felt incredibly good.

"But our first time together isn't going to be in some shack." That Mississippi drawl slipped in and around his words. "And we won't be covered in blood and grime." He sucked in a deep breath. "I know you deserve better than that." He backed away from her. "But, Doc, to be safe, you better keep that sexy-as-sin mouth away from me, 'cause when I get your lips beneath mine, I lose control."

He'd moved to the edge of the bed. She sat up next to him. Their linked hands were so close. *We might as well be holding hands.* Tina swallowed and tried to steady her breathing. "I didn't think control was a problem for you." Wasn't he supposed to be the cold-blooded agent?

His fingers caught her chin, tilted her head back so that he stared into her eyes. "Don't believe everything you hear." A warning.

"I don't." Tina forced a smile. The tension was thick, and she ached. "If I did, I'd think I was Bruce Mercer's daughter."

His lips twitched again. His fingers fell away from her chin and he glanced toward the cuff on their wrists. His tentative smile faded. "Hell, you're bruising."

She looked down. The skin around the cuff was starting to turn dark. "It's okay." She'd always bruised easily.

He slid from the bed, pulling her with him. "The hell it is. Now that I'm not delirious from pain, I bet I can find something here to get that thing off you."

Tina followed him. Actually bumped into him when he spun back around to face her.

"Don't think it's over," he said, eyes sharp.

What?

His gaze searched hers. "A promise is a promise," he murmured. Then he was heading toward the small table. She followed right beside him, wondering just what he was talking about.

"Making love, Doc. I'm talking about me and you, being naked on clean sheets and enjoying pleasure that lasts all night long."

Oh, man, had she asked her question out loud?

Tina realized that her mouth was hanging open.

"Got it," he said with a satisfied nod.

He had what looked like an old, thin, twisted piece of metal in his hand. It wasn't any bigger than a bobby pin, and when he shoved it into the handcuff lock, Tina knew he hadn't "got" anything.

"That's not going to work," she told him, clearing her throat because she was still thinking about…*being naked on clean sheets and enjoying pleasure that lasts all night long.*

So that was the promise he intended to keep.

"Sure it will work. Trust me. I learned to pick locks early on."

"You did?" *Stop focusing on being naked.* She glanced up at his face. Drew wasn't looking at her. He was concentrating on the lock. "Back before your Delta Force days?"

"Back in my screwed-up-kid days." Said without any emotion. "My dad cut out on my mom and me. She had to work two jobs to cover me and my sisters."

Sisters? Any family information was kept strictly confidential at the EOD.

"Guess you could say that I had a lot of anger about what was going on around me. Growing up dirt poor in Mississippi isn't exactly an easy path. I was a mad kid, in the wrong part of town."

The lock *snicked*. The cuff opened, freeing her wrist. He took care of the cuffs still on him then he lightly stroked the skin of her wrist. "I ran wild back then. Picked up some habits that I shouldn't have."

His touch felt so good on her skin. "I thought you were the one who always played by the rules."

"These days, I try." His gaze dropped to her mouth once more. "But sometimes there are some rules that I have to break."

He was going to kiss her again. She wanted him to—

Drew's head jerked to the left. Toward the broken window. "Hell. Company."

She yanked her hand away from him. "The helicopter left."

"And when Lee spotted the ranch, he might have given orders for his men to search the place." He reached for his pack. "I thought he might do that."

Her body had tensed. "You should have mentioned that 'thought' to me sooner."

He pulled a knife from the pack. "I didn't want you to worry."

Uh, she was worrying plenty right then.

Drew hurried to the window. "I heard their vehicle. The sound of one engine, but I can't see them. Not yet."

She looked around for her own weapon. "Do we make a break for it?" Jump on that motorcycle and ride fast and hard?

He shook his head but didn't glance back at her. "They're searching to push us into a panic. With that chopper in the air, Lee would see us on the bike. No, we don't leave." She saw his grip tighten on the knife. "We hunt."

A HELICOPTER SWOOPED overhead.

Dylan paused beside his truck. He was on the side of the old road, standing next to the apparently broken-down vehicle. The hood was up and his hands were dirty with grease.

"That's the second time that chopper has flown over us," Rachel murmured as she strolled to his side. "Something is definitely going on in this area."

Dylan tilted back his head. "They're searching for—"

He broke off because he'd just spotted another vehicle coming down that long, lonely stretch of Texas road.

There was only one place at the end of that road—the enemy compound.

And the gray pickup that was heading toward him? Those guys were coming from the compound.

The weight of his gun pressed into his lower back. The weapon was hidden beneath his jacket.

They'd planned to get in close to the compound, and this was their first step.

It was also a step that might be ending a little too soon.

The gray truck braked next to him, sending a pile of dust up into the air. Two men were in the vehicle. They were young, both in their early twenties, with dark hair and suspicious eyes.

"You got trouble?" one of the men demanded.

Uh, yeah, didn't it look as though he did?

"The engine overheated," Rachel said easily as she walked toward the truck. "My boyfriend here...he's not so good with cars."

The men's attention fixed a little too quickly on her.

Dylan slammed the hood shut. "She'll be working fine now, *honey*."

"It's not them," one of the men muttered. "Leroy, we need to keep lookin'."

Not them. That was exactly the intel Dylan had needed. He headed toward the men, toward Rachel. Dylan made sure his steps were slow and easy. As nonthreatening as possible. He wrapped his arm around her waist and kept his gun concealed. "I think I'm a little lost," he said, giving them a sheepish smile.

One of the men, a fellow with ruddy cheeks and a small gap between his front teeth, eyed Dylan with suspicion. "Where are you headed?" *Leroy.* His buddy had called him Leroy. Dylan filed that name away for later.

"Toward Baker's Ranch," he replied easily. "A dude ranch in—"

"There's no dude ranch this way," he was flatly told. "So get your pretty girl, get in your truck and get the hell out of here."

Rachel stiffened. Her eyes widened as she gave a little gasp. "Is that— Are you threatening us?" Fear slid into her voice. Rachel was a damn fine actress.

"No, 'honey,'" Leroy told her as his gaze slid back toward her. "I'm giving you a warning. There are some dangerous people out in this area. We're hunting them right now."

"Are you a cop?" she whispered. The fear was gone. Now she was sounding all impressed.

Dylan squeezed her hip. *Not too much, Mancini.*

The fellow's chest puffed up. "Something like that," he said.

Wrong. Nothing like that.

"And the guy we're looking for? He's a killer. A cold-blooded, shoot-you-in-the-face killer."

Rachel trembled.

Dylan pulled her closer. "Then we need to get out of here." He gave a quick nod. "Thank you, gentlemen. We appreciate you stopping to try to help us."

As if the guys had even offered help. They'd just ogled Rachel and given their get-out-of-here warning.

But the men had been helpful. *They're looking for Drew.*

There was no point in trying to get inside the compound for an extraction. Not when Drew had to be long gone.

Dylan and Rachel climbed back into their vehicle. Dylan thought he heard one of the guys give a wolf whistle when Rachel's shorts hiked up as she eased into the high seat. Jaw clenching, he cranked the truck and turned it around, heading away from the compound.

"They're watching us," Rachel said as her fingers tapped lightly against her thigh.

He glanced into his rearview mirror. The men were standing in the middle of the road. Just staring after them.

"Now we know why Drew didn't make contact," she added.

He nodded. "Because he's on the run."

"No," Rachel corrected softly, "*they* are. The guy said 'hunting them.' Drew's in the wind, and he took the doctor with him."

That had been Drew's new mission assignment. Protect the woman. And when the blond in that proof-of-life video had gone toward her with that knife, Drew had run out of options.

Dylan's gaze scanned the empty terrain around him. He heard the whir of the helicopter approaching once more. "We have to find Drew before they do."

Because if they didn't, he'd be dead.

"We need to call Sydney," he said, "see if she was able to remotely activate his tracker."

Only…this part of Texas was hell when it came to satellite transmissions and tracking. Cell phones barely worked, and locating Drew's GPS signal could be near impossible.

It was a good thing Dylan liked a challenge.

THREE MEN CLIMBED from the vehicle. A quick check revealed that they were all armed. The HAVOC group always was. "They're coming toward us," Drew said. The men had already checked the ranch and now were splitting apart as they searched the surrounding land.

Tina stood just behind him. She'd grabbed a broken leg from an old wooden chair and was clutching it like a baseball bat. He had no doubt that, if necessary, she'd be ready to swing.

The men had made short work of searching the house. After they'd cleared that place, they should have just gotten in their Ranger and rode the hell out of there.

They hadn't.

Lee must have given orders to thoroughly search the area. So that was exactly what those three bozos were doing.

One suddenly called out, voice excited.

You don't call out. That alerts your prey. Amateurs.

But Drew realized they'd seen the shack. He backed away from the window as he planned his attack.

"I want you to stay inside," he told Tina. He didn't want her in the line of fire but he didn't have a whole lot of options. *I'll keep her safe.*

"I can help you," Tina said as her grip on her makeshift bat tightened.

"You will help me." He hated to do this but... "You're going to be my bait."

Her eyes narrowed. "Say that again. I'm going to be your what?"

"When those men get close enough, I want you to call out and beg for help. You're the prize they want. They aren't going to fire on you."

He wouldn't give them the chance to fire.

But he did need them distracted.

"Stay against the wall when you call out. Do *not* let them see your body at all, understand?"

"I understand that I don't like this plan." Her jaw had firmed.

Damn but she was cute. "Think positive. Maybe I'll take 'em out before they even get close enough to hear you." He'd do his best. Drew turned away from her.

Tina's hand wrapped around his arm. "Be careful."

She was worried about him? "Don't worry, Doc, we have unfinished business, right?"

Her fingers jerked back as if he'd burned her.

Ice shouldn't burn.

He left her quickly, ready to eliminate this threat and move on as fast as he could. He exited from the back of the small house. He kept his body positioned close to the old walls. He'd need to circle around for his attack. The problem? There wasn't a lot of cover. So those men had to stay totally focused on what was happening *inside* the house.

Not what was going on outside.

He could hear their footsteps rushing toward them, coming closer and closer with every tense second that passed.

Now, Doc. I need you now.

As if on cue… "Help!" Tina shouted. "Please, help me!"

The footsteps moved even faster. Drew crept around the house. He peered around the corner and saw the men at the front door. They weren't even looking his way.

Mistake.

He tossed his knife and it sank into one man's side. The guy cried out, and down, down he went.

The other men spun at his cry, but it was too late. Drew grabbed the second guy, applied the right amount of pressure, and he was unconscious seconds later. A fast, hard kick slammed the third man into the side of the wall. His head connected with a thud and he fell with a groan.

"You…*bastard!*"

Technically, he wasn't. Drew spun toward the new threat. The attacker had yanked the knife out of his side and blood dripped down his body as he advanced toward Drew. "I get to kill you," he said, eyes bright. "Lee said you didn't have to come in alive. Not you, just her."

Drew backed up, trying to lead the man away from the house.

"I will *kill*—"

Tina rushed from the house. She swung her chair leg at the man's hand. The knife hit the ground while he howled.

Drew drove his fist into the guy's face.

No more howling.

The guy crumpled on the ground just as nicely as the other two men had.

Tina's breath was coming fast and hard; panting.

Her cheeks were too pale.

Drew frowned at her. "You okay?"

She lifted her hand. "Just give me…" She sucked in more deep breaths. "A minute."

He didn't like the pallor of her cheeks. He reached for her and wrapped his hands around her arms.

Her breathing seemed to slow.

In. Out. In. Out.

"You were great," he whispered to her. "I knew you'd be a slugger with that chair leg."

Faint color rose in her cheeks. Her breathing was definitely easier now. After a moment Tina eased away from him and stared down at the unconscious men. "You know I'm going to have to stitch that one up, right?"

"I know we're cuffing them and tying them up." The old bed cover inside would work perfectly once he cut it into strips. He glanced over at the ranch. "Then we're leaving them here and we're taking their ride." Because if Lee saw the Ranger high-tailing it down the road he'd just think his men were continuing their search. The vehicle would be their perfect cover.

Tina smiled. "We're going to make it, aren't we?" Hope lit her face.

He nodded, but Drew didn't actually speak. He'd learned long ago that some lies could taste too bitter on the tongue.

LEE'S HANDS WERE sweating. There was no sign of Mercer's daughter, and if he didn't turn that woman back in to the boss... *I'm dead.*

Anton Devast wasn't exactly big on giving second chances. You messed up once with him and you were dead.

He motioned to Grayson, and the pilot circled the chopper around. The bird jerked in the air, then steadied. Lee hissed out a sharp breath and stared below with grainy eyes. He saw the familiar Ranger heading down the narrow, broken road. Reynolds, Morris and Sanchez. They'd been sent out to the abandoned ranch that he'd spotted. He'd given them orders to radio in if they saw anything suspicious out there.

He squinted as he stared down at them. Their vehicle was moving in the wrong direction. They weren't heading back to the compound. They were going east.

He glanced over at Grayson. "Get Reynolds on the radio." Where the hell was that man going? No one stopped searching, not until Stone was dead and Mercer's daughter was contained.

Lee's life was on the damn line.

No one stopped.

TINA STARED AT the small radio cradled in Drew's hand. It had crackled to life a moment before.

"Report!" a man's voice demanded.

Drew glanced over at her. One hand was on the wheel. The other was tightening around the radio. "Clear," he barked. Only that wasn't his normal voice. He'd responded in a voice that was harder, sharper.

"Any—" more crackling "—sign?"

"Not there. Checking to the east. Interference—" Then he slammed the radio into the dashboard.

It splintered into several big chunks.

"Like I said," he muttered, "interference."

She couldn't pull in a deep enough breath. She was trying hard to stay calm, but the panic wanted to rise. Did Drew know? He'd heard her deep, heaving breaths back at the abandoned ranch. Did he realize just how much of a risk she posed to him?

Breathe. Relax. Picture the air sliding deep into your lungs.

"You think…they bought that?"

"If the chopper lands in front of us, then they didn't."

The chopper was about fifty yards away and it was—

Leaving.

Tina finally got that deep breath.

"Any signal on the cell?"

She glanced down. "Not yet."

"When we get to Lightning, we'll call in my backup. They can pick up the men we left back at the ranch, and they can get you out of here."

"Lightning?"

"A speck on the map. One of the tiniest towns you've never seen." His lips hitched as he glanced toward her. "As far as rest stops go, it's the only option we have."

"But…but won't those men be looking for us there?"

"Yeah, they will be, and that's why we have to make sure they don't find us." He gave a grim nod. "It's also my backup plan."

"Good to know you have a plan," she said as her fingers curved around the cell phone.

"My team has eyes in that town. They'll be able to back us up. Doc, you may even be on your way to your D.C. apartment by dawn."

That sounded like heaven to her. Going to New Orleans had been such a horrible mistake. And to think, she'd originally believed it would be the perfect, easy assignment. A way to get out of D.C. for a while.

If only she'd known about the danger that awaited in the Big Easy.

But Drew was right. Soon she would be going home once more.

She just had to get through a few more hours of hell first.

DREW HAD BEEN RIGHT. The town of Lightning was so small that if she'd blinked, Tina was sure she would have missed the place. When they drove in, a rumble of thunder followed them.

They passed boarded-up buildings. Two empty gas stations. She saw a diner to the right that looked as though it hadn't been open in years.

"Storms come in here like clockwork," Drew told her as he fired a quick check into the rearview mirror. So far, there had been no sign of company. "Lightning messes up all the electrical equipment in town. Most folks don't like the storms, so they don't stay here long."

Well, that would sure explain the town's name.

He eased off the main road. Well, what passed for the main road anyway. He parked the vehicle behind the diner. "No sense leaving it too close," he said as he took her hand. He'd taken the cowboy hat and a shirt from one of the thugs back at the old ranch. The shirt was a little too small and it stretched over his wide shoulders.

His fingers curled around hers. "Come on. Another storm will be hitting soon."

The sky was pitch-black. More thunder rumbled. She'd

just taken a few steps with Drew when the first raindrops hit her.

Then the dark clouds really opened up. The rain pelted them, hard and fast, as they ran down narrow streets toward an old motel.

The orange Vacancy sign glowed brightly.

It sure was a beautiful sight.

Drew pushed open the motel's office door. A little bell jingled overhead.

No one was inside. No one waited behind the narrow counter. Tina shoved back her wet hair. Her shirt clung to her like a second skin and—

"Good thing you two are here." A woman's voice came from the back corner of the office, making Tina jump. "No one should be out in weather like this."

Tina realized that she'd put her hand over her heart. She was ready to stop having so many scares.

"Hi, ma'am." Drew flashed the woman a smile and tipped back his wet hat. "My wife and I need a room." He pushed some cash across the counter. More than enough cash to cover a room.

And enough to stop any questions?

But the woman—her white hair and the deep lines near her eyes put her in her seventies—was staring at Tina's hand. No. At the dark circle on Tina's wrist.

Frowning, the lady asked, "You okay, miss?"

Tina dropped her hand and forced a big smile. "I'm fine. Just had a little…accident." With a pair of handcuffs.

The woman's gaze slid toward Drew. Now she was looking suspicious. A small name tag on her left breast-pocket indicated the woman's name was Sarah.

"Maverick," he said softly.

And, just like that, the woman's face cleared of all emotion. She handed Drew a room key. "Room six. Last one on the end." She turned around and headed into the back room.

Tina blinked. What was that about?

Drew reached for Tina's hand. His fingers stroked her wrist. "We'll get some ice for that."

A bruised wrist wasn't especially high on her list of worries right then.

They had to run back into the rain to get to their room. But, less than three blessed minutes later, they were inside room number six. The place was small but clean, so wonderfully clean, and dry.

Lightning flashed outside the window. Thunder rumbled and the window glass trembled.

Drew locked the door behind her.

Tina wrapped her hands around her stomach. "There's a phone on the nightstand." A landline. She'd never been so happy to see one of those before. "Are you going to call Mercer now?"

"I don't need to." He tossed away his hat and wiped his hand over his hair. The hat hadn't exactly kept his dark hair dry. Droplets of water fell around him. "Sarah knows the score. She's already made contact with the base group."

"Sarah?" Her eyes widened. "That sweet old lady at the desk—"

"She's ex-EOD. She recognized my code word. She'll make sure that word spreads fast that we're here. My team will come for us."

That was good. That put her one step closer to ending this nightmare. It also meant that she was one step closer to leaving Drew.

Not so good.

He turned toward the window. "Why don't you go shower off? You'll feel more human after—"

"After I wash the blood and dirt away?" Tina finished.

Yes, she would. But she felt as though there was more she should say to him. If the cavalry was coming in to swoop her away at any minute, there *had* to be more she told him. So she started with the basics. "Thank you."

He turned toward her.

Another bolt of lightning flashed, illuminating the area just beyond the window.

The thunder rumbled a moment later.

"You blew your cover to save me." No, more than that. Tina's gaze held his. "You risked your life." He'd taken a bullet for her. How was she supposed to repay that kind of sacrifice?

He took a step toward her.

"I didn't ask who those men were." Because she knew the way the system worked. Need-to-know info.

She wasn't an agent. That meant, according to Mercer, the less she knew, the better. Even if her life had been put on the line.

"You're better off not knowing," Drew said, sounding way too much like Mercer for her peace of mind right then. His jaw tightened. "They're some of the most dangerous SOBs that I've crossed."

"You could have died saving me."

He took another slow, gliding step toward her. Then one more. She tilted her head back. Trembled as the rain water began to dry on her skin.

"Doc, I wasn't leaving you behind." His eyes raked her. "And I wasn't going to let them hurt you anymore. Carl wasn't using that knife on you."

She was so out of her league. Not just in the middle of this blood fest, but with Drew.

The guys she dated were nice, safe. They didn't know how to take down enemies in hand-to-hand combat. They didn't know how to pick the locks on handcuffs.

And those men didn't make her feel the way Drew did.

When the cavalry did come through that door, she'd leave the motel. Drew would go back to his missions, and she'd see him when he came in for his checkups at the EOD.

They'd go back to business as usual.

She didn't want that.

What she wanted—was him.

Unfortunately she was a sopping-wet mess at that moment. No doubt, she appeared like a drowned rat.

A seduction routine wasn't going to work right then.

Tina nodded and tried to pull herself together again. "I'm glad you were the agent who was there, Drew." Then she swept around him before she did something crazy—such as throw her arms around the guy and hold on tight.

Or point out the fact that the bed behind them appeared very, very clean.

She opened the bathroom door and rushed gratefully inside. Before she shut the door, she heard him mutter, "I'm glad, too, Doc."

They'd escaped. Not just escaped, but seemingly *vanished*. Lee stormed away from the helicopter. He had to tell the boss that the search hadn't turned up the missing woman. This wasn't the way he wanted things to go down.

He hurried by the base's parking area. More of the search teams had come back in, but they'd turned up nothing.

"You didn't find them." *Thud. Thud. Thud.*

Lee froze. The boss wasn't inside the compound. He was right there waiting to attack. "I'm going back out. They must have gotten to a town. Got shelter. We'll get them—"

Thud. Thud. "No, if they made it to a town, then the

agent will be calling for backup. He'll be bringing in men to take the woman away."

"Boss, look—"

His words were interrupted by the loud banging of a horn. "What the hell?" Lee said as he turned toward the sound.

He recognized the pickup heading toward him. Leroy and Guan were coming in hell-fast, but three men were hanging on to the back of their pickup.

Reynolds? What the hell was he doing with Leroy? Reynolds had radioed that he was heading east to search.

Lee ran toward the truck. Reynolds was trying to jump off the side of the vehicle's bed. He was missing his shirt and dried blood coated his skin.

"Ambushed us…" Reynolds yanked up his hand—a hand that was connected by a handcuff to Adam Morris. "SOB took our ride and headed out!"

Lee's heart raced faster. "East." He snarled that one word.

"We found 'em," Guan was saying, "when we went over to do a backup sweep at that abandoned ranch. They were tied up in some shack."

"Head east!" Lee bellowed. Because that was where the Ranger had been going. East. There was only one safe spot within a two-hundred-mile radius that way. "Lightning."

They'd gone to that old town.

Now he knew exactly where his prey was hiding.

Thud. Thud.

He whirled around. "Don't worry," Lee said quickly to Devast. "I've got them." *My six hours aren't up.*

He'd blow up that whole town if he had to, but he'd get that agent.

Or I'll die trying. Because the look in his boss's eyes

clearly said that if he came back empty-handed, death would be waiting on him.

ANTON DEVAST WATCHED Lee Slater rush away. Slater was proving to be a disappointment to him.

When he was disappointed, it meant it was time for people to die.

If Slater couldn't catch the EOD agent and the missing woman, Anton would just have to find someone else to get the job done.

He smiled. Mercer had infiltrated Devast's group. *Thought you were clever, didn't you, old friend?*

It was Anton's turn now. And he'd use one of Mercer's men against him.

In their business, loyalties were bought and traded every single day. You just had to know the right price to offer.

With the right price, you could buy anything.

You could even buy your way into the EOD.

Chapter Five

The storm wasn't letting up. In fact, the rain pelted down even harder as Drew gazed out the window. His team was coming. He hadn't used the landline to call them. Even in a place that was supposed to be secure… Well, he knew better than to take risks.

Risks would get a man killed.

Sarah had instantly recognized his code word. She would have gone into the back and made contact through a secure system. As a backup—because Drew always believed in backups—he had used his burner phone to check in with Dylan. Now that they were in the town, he'd managed to get a signal strong enough to make the call. His friend and team leader had given him an ETA of less than thirty minutes.

Thirty minutes, and then Tina would be gone.

That's not enough time with her.

The bathroom door opened with a soft creak. He turned to look at her. Steam drifted lightly from the small bathroom.

A loud crack of lightning seemed to explode outside the motel room.

The room—the whole motel from the look of things—was immediately plunged into darkness.

"Drew?"

Even in the dark, he saw her form easily. Drew had always been gifted with excellent night vision. He stalked toward her. "Told you," he said softly, "the storms come in and cause chaos in the town." The lights might come back on in a few minutes or it could be a few hours before the electricity was restored. *She'll be long gone by then.*

His fingers lifted and curled around her shoulder. Her *bare* shoulder. Her skin was like hot silk beneath his callused fingers.

In that one moment, before the lights had flashed off, he'd seen her standing in that doorway. She'd just been wearing a towel.

Desire, need for her, pulsed beneath his skin. He'd be sent back into the field. If not on this case, then out on another one. How long would it be before he saw her again?

Now that she was compromised, now that the crazies with HAVOC mistakenly thought that she was Mercer's daughter, what would happen to her? She wouldn't be able to go back to her old life.

Not with that threat hanging over her.

I'll eliminate that threat.

"My clothes had blood on them," she whispered. "I just... I hated to put them right back on, but I didn't have anything else to wear."

He motioned toward the bed. It was just a big, dark shadow. She probably didn't even see his hand moving. "Sarah brought you some jeans and a fresh shirt."

She didn't move to get those clothes.

"I have a confession," Tina told him softly. "I've... watched you." Her voice was husky in the dark. "At the EOD offices."

He'd watched her plenty, too.

Intrigued now, he waited.

"I know I'm not your usual type of...of date—"

"Oh?" He was even more curious now. "You think I don't go for the smart and sexy women?" Because Tina was most definitely his type. His sleepless nights could attest to that.

"You live on the edge. You love danger and action. And I hide in the background."

No, she *tried* to hide in the background. She failed at that job. A woman like her could never just disappear.

"I don't want to hide from you," Tina told him. Her hands rose and her fingers settled around his shoulders. She was so small, seemingly fragile in front of him. "I want to be with you."

He stiffened as desire sharpened within him. "You should be very careful what you say." Especially to a man like him. A man who'd lived for too long wanting things that he couldn't have.

One of those things was right in front of him.

"It's just us," she said, and her voice was pure temptation. "No gunshots. Not even any lights. Just us. Alone in the dark." She rose onto her tiptoes.

His fingers locked around her waist. "I warned you before about what would happen if I kissed you again." *Naked. Pleasure...*

"I don't want a warning. I told you, I just want you." Then she kissed him.

The need, the raw lust that he felt for her, shot through him and electrified his whole body. Her kiss was tentative, and he needed more than that. So much more. He lifted her into his arms, holding her easily despite his wound.

Tina was right. They were alone. He'd been imaging her spread out in that big bed and, with the lights off, with the dark around them...

I'll make her mine.

And when she was taken away from him, Tina would remember what they'd shared.

Drew knew he'd never forget.

Her lips were open and soft beneath his. His tongue slipped into her mouth, and she arched against him. Two steps and he was at the foot of the bed. His knees bumped into the mattress. He lowered her onto the covers, but he couldn't make his hands let her go.

There was too much silken skin to touch and explore. The towel had come loose, and it barely covered her breasts. His fingers eased up her arms. Trailed over her shoulders then moved down her sensual curves.

He got that towel out of the way, yanked it aside.

His mouth followed the path of his hands. Drew kissed her shoulders. He inhaled her sweet scent—still strawberries. Even after everything she'd been through.

Her breasts thrust toward him.

Thunder rumbled once more.

He bent his head over her breast. Put his mouth on one tight nipple. She arched toward him and her fingers sank into his hair.

He liked the sounds she made when he touched her. But even more, he liked the way she was becoming wild for him.

His arousal strained against the fly of his jeans. He wanted to be flesh to flesh with her, to be as close as he could possibly get.

His hand slid down over the curve of her stomach. Her hips were still lifting toward him. His fingers eased between her legs.

"Drew?"

She was warm and responsive and so amazing to touch. He had to explore her. Every single inch.

The fantasy between them would end soon. But he'd take these moments. He'd hold them tight.

And she won't forget me.

He stroked her, caressed her and made sure that her desire wound tighter and tighter with every press of his fingers. Her body trembled against his. Her breath came faster.

He found the center of her need. Right there. Right—

A cry of pleasure spilled from her lips. She held him tighter as she shuddered against him.

Hell, yes. And that was just the beginning.

He reached for the snap of his jeans.

And heard footsteps outside the motel room.

Drew tensed.

"Drew—"

He put his mouth on hers and kissed her deeply once more. He could taste her pleasure.

His own body ached. He wanted to drive into her more than he wanted his next breath.

But the footsteps were coming ever closer.

"Outside," he whispered against her lips.

When she stiffened, he knew she understood. Their visitors could be his backup, or it could be the men from HAVOC.

Though it hurt him—*so close*—Drew slid off the bed. He handed Tina the clothes that Sarah had brought for her.

She dressed quickly.

He grabbed the gun Sarah had brought to him.

Drew eased toward the door. Tina's heady scent still filled his nose. He could still taste her.

But their moment of reprieve was at an end. *Too soon.*

He pulled back the curtains, just a tiny space, and gazed outside. Darkness.

That was all right.

The darkness wouldn't last forever.

Lightning flashed.

He saw the outline of two bodies.

A man and a woman. No weapons in their hands, but he could see the holsters for their guns.

He studied the two figures in that instant of light.

And the tension eased from his shoulders.

Drew opened the door. "As always," he said to Dylan Foxx and Rachel Mancini, "your timing is hell."

Dylan grinned at him. "Good to see you, too—"

Thunder blasted.

The hell that was thunder!

Wood splintered from the top of the door as Dylan and Rachel leaped inside the motel room.

Drew knew they'd also recognized that sound for exactly what it was—gunfire.

Drew shoved the door closed even as more bullets came flying through the air. "Anyone hit?" he demanded.

"Just a graze," Rachel panted. "What a...*jerk.*"

The glass in the window shattered. The shots were coming so quickly that Dylan knew they were looking at more than one shooter.

"You were followed," Drew said as he immediately took up a fighting stance. His gaze swept the room. Tina had ducked behind the bed. Good. She was safe.

Now to eliminate this threat.

"Bull," Dylan snapped. "We know how to cover our trail."

"Looks like you didn't cover it well enough this time." Drew hated being pinned in that motel room. The only way out would be through some back windows, and there might be men out there, waiting to take a shot at them.

"Let's just hope all of HAVOC isn't out there," Rachel

said as she checked her gun. "'Cause this could be one very long fight."

A bullet ripped through the wood on the motel room door. "Tina!" Drew cried out as worry snaked through him. Innocents got hurt too easily in firefights. "Make sure you stay down." Because when he rushed outside, the bullets would start coming twice as hard and twice as fast.

But there wasn't a choice for Drew.

They weren't going to stay trapped.

Dylan slanted a glance at him. They'd worked together for so long, the guy would know exactly what Drew was planning. "You sure about this?"

He rolled the tension from his shoulders. He'd gone from touching heaven to facing hell in five short minutes. "Just give me cover."

Rachel eased closer to the window. She took aim.

Dylan took a position right next to her. They opened fire.

And Drew rushed out the front door.

DREW LANCASTER was *insane*.

The man had just run out into a hail of bullets. He *had* to be insane.

The thunder was pretty much continuous around Tina then. She could hear the bullets thudding into the walls. Hear the shattering of glass and—wow—the bedside lamp had just blasted into about a hundred small pieces.

You'd better be alive, Drew. Do not get yourself shot.

Tina stayed low. She didn't have a weapon to use in this battle. She also couldn't let herself become any kind of handicap to the agents. Her heart was racing, her hands shaking, but she breathed in and out, in and—

Silence.

Tina started to lift her head.

"I count two men down." That was Dylan Foxx's voice. Deep, rumbling, no accent at all. She'd seen Dylan plenty of times at the EOD office.

"There were at least four shooters," Rachel Mancini said. Her voice was softer, and Tina had to strain to hear it. Usually, if Rachel was around, Dylan wasn't far away. They always worked missions together.

Rachel and Dylan were still safe but...

Where is Drew?

"I'm going out," Dylan said.

Great. Now two of them were rushing into enemy fire.

I can help. She crawled forward. Keeping her head down was a definite priority, but so was making certain that Drew was safe. She grabbed Dylan's leg. He jerked toward her. "Give me a gun," she said, gazing up at him and hoping that he didn't notice her body was shaking. "And I'll help cover you."

He hesitated.

Fine. She yanked up his jeans, revealing his ankle holster. The guy always carried his backup. "I'll just take this one," she told him.

He blinked.

There was still no more gunfire. The silence out there was scaring her as much as the bullets. "Go find Drew."

Dylan nodded. His gaze darted toward Rachel.

The dark-haired agent gave an almost imperceptible nod.

Then Dylan was easing open the motel-room door. He slid into the night.

Tina's knees brushed across the broken shards of glass from the window. The rain still poured from the sky, and the darkness seemed so complete outside. The brief flashes of lightning lit up the scene, and every time it flashed, she strained to see—

"He's got a gun!" The figure lurched up from the darkness and aimed right at the motel room.

Rachel fired.

Tina did, too. The bullets hit the would-be shooter, and the man stumbled back.

Her heart slammed into her ribs. The frantic beating was so powerful that she ached.

"Clear!" That sharp voice calling out—it was Drew's.

She didn't release her death grip on the gun.

"Four men down," Drew shouted. "I need the doc out here!"

He was hurt. In an instant Tina was on her feet. She grabbed for the doorknob.

"Wait—" Rachel began.

No, Drew needed her. There was no waiting.

She ran from the room. Another flash of lightning illuminated Drew. He was on the ground. She could smell blood. "Drew?" Tina reached for him.

He turned toward her. Rain water dripped down his face. "I'm okay, Doc." He pointed to the man on the ground. "He isn't."

Another flash of lightning showed her the face of the man who'd held her hostage. Drew had called him Lee. *Lee.* The man who'd used his phone to record her video proof of life.

The guy who'd callously ordered that her finger be cut off.

"The others are dead," Drew said as the rain hit them. "Lee is the only one left alive out here."

Lee was choking on his own blood. Bullet wounds lined his chest. His eyes were wide and stark, terrified.

This was the man who'd wanted to use her. To hurt her.

Tina sank to her knees. *I need tools.* "I have to get the

bullets out." *Have to stop the blood. Have to try to stabilize him. His blood pressure will be dropping. And—*

She heard the wheeze coming from his lungs. When she leaned forward and looked at his mouth, she could see the small mist of blood shoving past his lips.

"He's got a bullet in his lung." She grabbed Lee's shirt and ripped it apart. The rain kept pelting down on her. She needed to get him inside and—

There were two holes in his chest. One bullet had hit his lung. One had driven in close to his heart. Too close.

A hard hand closed around her wrist, jerking on the bruised skin.

"Don't even think about it, Lee," Drew snarled in the same instant.

Lee had a tight hold on her. He was trying to sit up.

The man should have realized that he didn't have strength to waste fighting her. He should also have realized—

Drew had his gun locked on the man.

"You don't need that," Tina said softly, sadly. Because unless she could get serious help to the injured man within the next few moments…

He'll be gone. He won't be able to hurt anyone.

"M-Mercer's…daughter…" The words were forced from Lee's throat. Blood dripped from his lips.

"You need to take it easy," she told him. No one's last moments should be filled with agony.

But Lee smiled at her. "Y-you're gonna die…"

No, you are. In just a few moments. Had she done this? Had her shot hit him?

She'd seen brutal death just like this before. Her father had been hit in the chest with a bullet. Her mother had been hit in the heart.

The wrong place. The wrong time.

They'd gone into the local bank, so happy. They'd planned to close out Tina's savings account right before she went to college.

They'd walked into death.

The bank robbers hadn't cared about her family. The robbers had just panicked when Tina began having one of her attacks.

They'd killed her mother instantly.

Her father—it had taken him longer to die. His lungs had slowly filled with blood.

It wasn't going to take Lee as long to die. Not with that shot so close to his heart. Had it nicked the heart? A valve? She glanced over at Drew. "His heart—"

"I can…feel it…" Lee muttered. "Know…what's comin'…"

Her gaze slid to him once more. Under the flash of lightning, Lee didn't look scared. He looked furious.

"Think you're…winnin'…agent…" Lee's lips twisted into a gruesome smile. "But he's not…done…"

Drew pulled Tina away from the dying man. "Who's not done?"

Footsteps rushed toward them. Dylan and Rachel.

"We checked the rest of the perimeter," Dylan said as he closed in. "We're clear."

The rain eased up, dripping lightly over them instead of pelting down.

The thunder had stopped.

No more thunder. No more gunshots.

"Devast…wants…her…" Lee's voice was a harsh rasp. "Won't…stop…until he gets…*her*…"

"Devast won't touch her," Drew swore. "He's out at the compound now, isn't he? Your boss? I'm going after him. I'm going to—"

"Devast…won't stop—"

A sharp breath slipped from Lee.

"Anton Devast?" Drew demanded as he bent over Lee. "I know how many lives he's taken. He won't—"

Tina put her hand on his shoulder. "He's gone." She'd heard that last, hard wheeze that had stilled in Lee's throat.

"Damn it!" Drew surged back to his feet.

Tina leaned over the body. She felt for his pulse, just to be certain, but with the massive trauma to his chest...

Gone.

She shivered as the raindrops trailed down her body. The past and the present both slid through her mind.

You can't save them. The cops on scene had told her that over and over again as she'd clung desperately to her parents.

Tina glanced at her hands. Even in the dark, she could see the blood.

"Get her inside," Drew said to Rachel as his fingers closed around Tina's shoulders. "Dylan and I will handle the cleanup."

Cleanup. Because there were other bodies out there. Wait, maybe... "Are you sure they're all dead? Maybe some of them are still alive."

Drew shook his head.

She turned toward the motel room. The place looked totally trashed from the outside. Sarah was there, and Tina saw her edging toward them cautiously.

The chill of death seemed to permeate the air. Tina squared her shoulders. "I'm ready to go home now." It was time to leave Drew's bloody world behind.

Time to leave...him.

THUD. THUD. THUD.

Anton Devast slowly walked toward the waiting helicopter. The compound was being evacuated. The few men left were scattering.

This base wouldn't be operational—not when the EOD agents swarmed. And they would swarm.

One of those bastards was here.

Mercer was smart, and his agents were smart. It had only been a matter of time until they'd infiltrated his network.

But it didn't matter. He'd found Mercer's weakness. *Tina Jamison.* He had pictures of the woman. Videos.

She wasn't escaping from him.

Lee hadn't checked in. That meant the man was either dead or running. If he had tried to flee, well, Lee would be dead in hours.

Anton stared into the waning night. He'd waited years for his vengeance. He'd bided his time, made powerful connections and planned so carefully.

He didn't have many days left on this earth. The cancer that had ravaged him before was coming back. Before he died, he had to finish his job.

It wasn't about destroying the U.S. government. Wasn't even about taking down the EOD and the agents who thought it was their job to stick their noses into private affairs.

It was about Bruce Mercer.

About making the man suffer.

Bruce hadn't agreed to trade his life for his daughter's. That had been his mistake. He'd had an option. A chance.

There would be no more chances.

It wasn't about a trade anymore.

It was about a life.

One life for another.

Vengeance.

Mercer would understand his pain now. He'd feel the

same agony that Anton had experienced. But there would be no relief from that pain. There was *never* any relief.

"Burn the place to the ground," he ordered as he left the ranch.

Thud. Thud.

The base had already been set to ignite. The first explosion detonated and the flames burst into the air. The scent of fire drifted on the wind. He didn't look back at the flames.

He was too busy looking ahead—and planning for Tina Jamison's death.

Chapter Six

Tina wasn't looking at him. She hadn't looked Drew directly in the eyes since Lee Slater's death.

They were at the airport; a small strip that was used just for government operations. A plane waited behind Tina.

This was the moment he was supposed to let her go. *Why won't she look me in the eyes?*

"Thank you," Tina said. Her voice didn't sound right. Too stilted. Too polite. "I can't ever repay what you did for me."

He didn't care that they had an audience. Drew took her hand in his. Her skin was incredibly soft—he'd never get used to that silken feel beneath his rough fingers. "I want you to watch your back."

Her eyelashes flickered. "Rachel is going to D.C. with me. I'll be perfectly—"

"You won't be safe, not until we have Anton Devast in custody." She'd heard the name already, when he'd been trying to force a last-ditch confession from Lee, so he wasn't breaking any clearance by telling her. Hell, after all she'd been through, the woman *deserved* to know who was after her.

He didn't care about Mercer's rules right then. Not with her life on the line.

Tina glanced at him. Wet her lips. "Do I want to know... the things that he's done?"

No. Drew didn't even want to know. The tortures. The murders. Anton's network stretched halfway across the world. Getting to the man, eliminating him, had been a goal of the EOD for years.

But Anton Devast was a hard man to kill. Getting close to him was practically impossible.

I was almost there. One more day. I would have been up close and personal with the man.

But Tina had come first. His hold tightened on her. "He's not just going to walk away from you. He's convinced that you're Mercer's daughter. Stay alert."

"And you stay alive." She gave him a sad smile. One that made his chest ache. "I've grown rather fond of you, Agent Lancaster. I know there's more than just ice running through your veins."

For her, there was fire.

She looked back at the plane that waited. The pilot stood outside, his hands on his hips.

"We need to go, miss!"

Drew just didn't want to let her go.

It's not about what I want.

If he had his way, he'd be the one sticking to her like glue. But Mercer's orders had come down. This flight was Tina's safe passage back to D.C.

Drew's job wasn't finished. He was to head back to the Devast base. He was supposed to start picking up the pieces of this mission and track the HAVOC ringleader once more.

What he wanted... He wanted to kiss Tina. To taste her again.

Not here.

Drew cleared his throat. "Remember what I promised you we'd have?"

Naked, tangled together.

Her pupils widened. Her lips parted.

"I keep my promises."

He let her hand go.

Tina stared up at him. Finally, *finally,* she was looking deeply into his eyes. "You'd better."

She turned away. She and Rachel began heading toward the plane.

Watching someone walk away had never been harder.

BRUCE MERCER DRUMMED his fingers on his desk. Tina Jamison was safe. She was on her way back to him.

Dragging her into this mess had been a mistake. A miscalculation. He didn't make those often, but when he did…

The phone vibrated on his desk. Not the confidential office phone.

His personal phone.

Only a handful of people knew his number. He picked it up instantly, thinking it was his daughter, Cassidy.

Unknown number.

Tension tightened his body as he read the message on the phone's screen. He answered the call with a curt, "Hello?" He didn't identify himself. Never would.

"Hello, old friend." That voice—that familiar voice—stopped time for him.

Twenty years… It had been twenty years since he'd last heard from Anton Devast.

How had the SOB gotten his private number?

"You always underestimated me," Anton murmured. "That was such a shame."

Mercer didn't speak. He wouldn't. There was no sense giving the man any more information than Devast already possessed. And for Devast to get his private line…

He has far more intel and connections than I realized.

"I know where your daughter is…"

No, the guy didn't. He didn't even know who Mercer's real daughter was.

My Cassidy is on her honeymoon now. With one of my best agents at her side. A man who'd die for her in an instant. She's safe, and you can't touch her.

"Your girl is flying through the sky. Safe?" Anton laughed. "No. She's not safe. You know what I do best."

Destroy. Terrorize.

"There won't be anything left of her." More laughter. "You should have agreed to the trade. Then you would be the one dying and she'd still have a shot at life."

Click.

Sweat slickened Mercer's temple. That call could have been a hoax. A trick to mess with his head. To cause panic and force him to make a mistake.

Except…

Anton Devast doesn't make threats.

The bastard delivered promises.

In the next second Mercer was dialing fast and frantically on his phone, calling the one agent who should be able to help him.

Don't be too late. Don't be…

THE PHONE IN Drew's pocket vibrated. Frowning, he yanked it up to his ear. Dylan had just given him the replacement phone an hour ago. There weren't many folks who should be trying to reach him then.

He began, "Hel—"

"*Get to Tina Jamison.*" Bruce Mercer's voice barked the order.

Drew's head snapped up. Tina was heading onto the plane.

Drew started running.

"Get to her, Lancaster. Secure her. You saved her before and you damn well better save her now—"

"Tina!" Drew bellowed.

Tina turned toward him. Her head tilted, the sunlight glinting off her dark hair and the replacement glasses that she'd been given.

Rachel was just steps behind her. Rachel frowned at him. "What's happening?"

Rachel had a phone. Rachel was the one who'd been assigned guard duty to Tina. Why hadn't Mercer called her?

"Drew? What's wrong?" Tina took a few steps away from the plane.

The pilot had vanished. Was he inside? Getting ready for takeoff?

Tina shook her head. "I don't understand—"

Mercer was shouting something in his ear.

He needed to get to Tina.

He needed to—

The plane exploded.

BRUCE MERCER STARED at the phone in his hand. He'd heard an explosion, then...nothing.

"I can't get anyone to check in at the scene."

He looked up at his assistant's voice. Judith Rogers stood in the doorway, her eyes wide and worried.

"Keep trying. Someone is there." *Someone has to be.* He'd called Drew because he trusted the man to protect Tina. Bruce was good at observing people, and he'd watched Lancaster and the doctor.

Drew will keep her safe.

Judith didn't look reassured. "Tina...?"

"She's fine." This was *his* fault. But he'd fix it. "Drew Lancaster was on scene. I gave him orders to protect her."

Drew had always followed mission orders. The guy did his job and he didn't hesitate. "Drew has her."

But his palms were sweating.

"I hope you're right." Judith turned away. Judith knew most of his secrets. "Because if you're not, I'm not sure how you'll sleep tonight."

Yes, she knew his secrets and his sins.

"Tina!"

Drew was yelling her name again.

He seemed to do that a lot lately.

Her eyes cracked open. Drew was hunched over her. His face was haggard. And— "Do I smell smoke?"

He yanked her into his arms and nearly squeezed the breath from her.

With that crushing embrace, memories flooded back through her mind. She'd been about to board the plane. She hated small airplanes like that one, but she'd been determined to suck up her fear. Then Drew had called out to her.

And the world had exploded.

Smoke thickened the air around her. Tina pulled away from Drew and glanced over her shoulder. The plane was still burning out on the tarmac. "Rachel?" Fear cracked the word.

"She's okay. Dylan has her." Drew rose, pulling Tina to her feet, too. He kept a steady hand on her. "I thought I was going to be too late."

She couldn't take her eyes off the plane. Had the pilot gotten out in time? The flames were wild, burning so high and bright.

Sirens wailed behind her.

"A bomb, Devast's weapon of choice." Drew's words

vibrated with fury. "But how did he get close enough to plant it with so many agents here?"

"The pilot…" She licked her lips, tasted fire and ash. "He's dead?"

"Pierce didn't come out of the plane," Drew said grimly.

Her heart squeezed in her chest.

Another minute and she would have been on that plane, too. She wouldn't have come out.

Dark smoke swirled in the air around her. She tried to suck in air.

Breathe in. Breathe out.

But her normal routine for calming an attack wasn't working.

A fist had her heart. Her lungs were burning. Clogged. Her eyes watered as she tried to pull in air. The muscles of her neck and chest were tightening. Clenching.

"Tina? Tina, what's wrong?"

Her streaming eyes found his. "At-tack…" She needed her medicine. The inhaler that would help her.

But there was no inhaler there. Not in the middle of that burning tarmac. No medicine. No help. And she remembered another time. Another place.

At the bank…she'd struggled to breathe. Her lungs burned. Her chest ached. The men with guns were shouting and fear clawed through her. Her father and mother had rushed to her because they'd known what was happening. Her father had reached into his jacket, grabbing for the inhaler he always carried, ever since her first attack had put her in the hospital at three years old. When he'd reached for that inhaler, one of the masked robbers yelled—then shot her father.

Her breath wheezed out. The smoke was so thick and dark. The smoke surrounded her. She couldn't get air in—

"I need help!" Drew yelled. He was rubbing her back. "Baby, breathe for me. Nice and slow, okay?"

Didn't it appear as if she was trying?

"Look at me."

Her gaze flew to his once more.

"Breathe with me," he said. "In and out."

It wasn't that easy. It wasn't some mind-over-matter thing right then. She was wheezing, and soon—soon she wouldn't even be able to do that. She could barely pull in any air at all.

Tina knew the power of a severe attack when it struck her.

The pilot is dead. I was nearly on that plane. People are dying—because of me.

Blood. Death. Everywhere.

"Tina. Tina, focus on me."

She wanted to, but dark spots were dancing in front of her eyes. Her body trembled.

He caught her before she could fall. He scooped her into his arms and started running toward the sounds of those sirens. "I need a medic, now!"

The smoke was too heavy in the air. Even when she did manage to pull in a breath, it was coated in smoke.

"Her lips are blue, damn it. Help me!"

She saw the swirl of flashing lights. Finally something other than the darkness of the smoke. The EMTs reached for her and pulled her away from Drew.

She didn't want to leave him. Her hand flew out, caught his.

"Don't worry, Doc." His voice was steady and strong. "I'm not going anywhere."

The EMTs loaded her in an ambulance; a breathing mask was slid over her face.

Drew was right beside her.

The ambulance roared away as the team got to work on her.

SHE FELT AS if she'd been hit by a truck. Tina sat on the edge of the narrow hospital bed, clad in a thin, paper gown, and she let her breath whisper slowly past her lips.

At least I'm still alive.

They'd given her medication to stabilize her breathing. The medication had stopped what might have just been the worst attack of her life.

She'd been helpless. A prisoner, beaten by her own body.

And he'd seen her. Drew had been there every moment. Now he knew just how weak she truly was.

The door opened. She didn't glance up. She'd been told by Dylan that guards had been posted outside her room. It seemed that she couldn't go anywhere without a guard now.

Because she was targeted for death.

"Why didn't you tell me?"

She'd known that it was him, of course. Whenever Drew was in the room, her body responded with an awareness that was almost frightening.

Tina wasn't sure that she liked being that tuned to another person.

His fingers brushed over her arm. "Doc?"

She forced her shoulders to straighten. "There wasn't anything you could do while we were on the run. It wasn't like you were going to have asthma medication in your back pocket—or even in your handy motorcycle saddlebag."

She'd been managing to keep the asthma in check. She'd handled the motorcycle ride just fine. Tina had thought she could keep controlling the asthma. Until the plane had exploded. Until the smoke had choked her. Until— "Has Pierce been recovered?"

Drew shook his head. "There's…not going to be much left to recover."

Right. Her eyes closed for an instant. That last little bit of hope left her.

"Tina?"

Her eyes opened. "How did Devast know I was getting on that plane?" The EOD had made arrangements for her flight out of Texas. She should have been safe.

"I slipped into his network," Drew said quietly, his gaze watchful on her face. "And it looks like he managed to slip someone into ours."

Her heart seemed to ache with each beat. From past experience, she knew the soreness would last for a while. "You're saying we have some kind of double agent in the EOD?"

He nodded. "It looks that way."

"Who?"

"That's what we have to find out. And we *will* find out."

"Before," she demanded because it was too much, "or after I'm dead?"

His hands rose and curled around her shoulders. "I'm not letting you die."

Didn't he get it? "You saw me." She pressed her lips together so they wouldn't tremble. Shame burned in her, but she pushed past it. "When an attack hits me, there is nothing I can do. I'm too vulnerable. If there's a double agent in the EOD, he can find out my secret." *If he doesn't already know.* "I'm easy to kill." The paper gown scraped across her knees as she shifted uncomfortably. "Too easy."

"I'm not letting you die," he said again, voice rougher.

"You can't save everyone, you know." That was a lesson she'd been taught long ago. Sometimes you couldn't even save the ones who mattered to you the most.

"You aren't everyone." A muscle jerked in his jaw. "You *aren't* dying." His head bent toward her. "You scared me."

She didn't think anything scared him.

His lips brushed against hers. "You were dying in my arms. There was nothing I could do."

Tears stung her eyes. Her father had died in her arms.

"Come back to me."

Those harsh, rumbling words had her blinking.

And getting lost in the gold of his gaze.

"You think I don't know," Drew began as he eased ever closer to her, "when you leave me? I can tell when you slip into your mind, into the past that has left those scars inside you." His lips thinned. "I don't like it. Don't focus on whatever the hell happened to you. Focus on now. On me."

He kissed her again. Harder. This wasn't a kiss of comfort. This was a kiss of pure, wild need.

His mouth didn't hesitate—it took. He was demanding a response from her and, raw and vulnerable from all that had happened, Tina had no barriers to protect herself from him.

So she just…let go.

Her mouth met his. Hungry. Desperate.

Her hands came up and locked around his shoulders. She pulled him against her. She needed him as close as she could get him.

Her heart pounded. Ached.

When he kissed her, she didn't feel weak. She felt sensual, powerful, *alive.*

Nothing else mattered in that instant. Desire twisted through her; a want that couldn't be denied. Her breasts ached, her legs shifted restlessly. She needed to be closer to him.

Needed…*him.* Her short nails dug into his arms.

His mouth pulled from hers. Just a whisper of a space

separated their lips as he growled, "Stay with me." He began to kiss her neck.

Her breath was fast, it was—

He stilled. "Are you okay? What am I doing?"

And, just like that, he'd done the one thing she'd feared. He'd discovered that she was weak.

So now he was treating her as if she'd shatter too easily.

He stepped back, a hurried, almost clumsy move for a man who usually moved with such grace.

"Tina? Tina, answer me. Are you all right?"

She'd been more than all right a few seconds ago. Unfortunately reality was back. "Kissing me doesn't kill me." She'd had other men who treated her as though she was some kind of broken china doll once they'd seen her attack.

His eyes narrowed. "I didn't..." His hands fisted and he backed up another step. "I don't mean to be so rough with you."

She didn't want him to back away. "I don't need you to treat me like I'm...I'm going to shatter."

He stared back at her. Drew seemed to absorb what she said as his eyes narrowed and swept over her face. "I won't make the mistake again."

She jumped off the bed. She could taste him on her lips. Desire still pulsed through her blood. A desire that seemed to burn too hot and fast whenever they touched. Was it from the adrenaline? The danger? Something else? "What is happening between us?" Then Tina forced herself to say the painful truth. "You didn't even notice me before that group took me prisoner—"

He caught her hand. His head moved in a hard, negative shake. "That's bull. I noticed you every moment."

He sure hadn't seemed to see her. Only when he'd been in the lab with her for his checkups, and then he'd been gruff. All business. Never lingering to chat or—

One dark brow rose. "Calling me a liar?" His head tilted to the right as he studied her. "Doc, I've wanted you in my bed from the first moment I saw you. I came into your office, expecting some kind of quick clearance check from a stuffy M.D., and the next thing I knew...you were in every dream I had."

She sure hadn't expected that. He'd treated her with the same icy indifference that he seemed to show everyone at the EOD.

"Yeah, I noticed you," he continued, his voice seeming to deepen with memories. "But I knew that you were afraid of me, so I stood back."

She didn't deny her fear. What would have been the point? He was a dangerous man. A man who could kill as easily as most men could kiss. There were shadows that clung to him—and always would.

"You're still afraid," he charged, "but I'm done with stepping back. You're not going to get away from me now."

She hadn't been the one stepping back a few moments ago. She'd been the one digging her nails into him. Drew had put the brakes on things. Before she could speak, someone was rapping at the door.

Tina's gaze jumped to the door. It swung open and Dylan, looking at little singed and blistered, came striding inside.

"That perfect timing again," Drew muttered. "Work on it, man. Work. On. It."

Tina frowned at him.

Dylan lifted a plastic bag and seemed to focus just on Tina. "I've got new clothes for you. The doctors here said they'd give you medicine to take with us. They wanted you to stay but—"

"It's too dangerous," Tina finished. She understood. The longer she stayed, the easier it would be for her location to be compromised. It was too hard to keep secrets in a place as public as a hospital. "Does that man—Anton Devast—think I'm dead?"

If he thought she'd died in the explosion, then she'd be free. Wouldn't she? His men wouldn't look for her any longer, and she wouldn't have to be worried about waking up in the night to discover a gun pressed to her head.

But Dylan's tense expression shot down those hopes. "He's not going to believe that, not if he had a man on the scene. And a guy like Devast…he doesn't take chances. He would have wanted to *see* you die."

Great. She snatched the bag from him. So much for being safe again. Safety wasn't going to come easily.

"Mercer received a call." This detail came from a watchful Drew. "Right before the explosion, Devast called his private line and told Mercer that you were about to die."

Her cheeks felt a little numb. Even she didn't know Mercer's private line, and she'd worked for the guy ever since she'd finished her residency. "That's how you knew what was happening. Why you ran to me—"

Drew nodded. "Devast's man must have told him that you were on the plane. He knew we were at that airport and that you were getting ready to take off."

"In order to place the bomb," Dylan said with a roll of his shoulders, "they had to know *before* our team got on scene. They tapped into the EOD system, and they figured out your most likely departure spot."

Then they'd placed the bomb and waited for her to board the plane.

She would have been on board when the bomb detonated, if she hadn't stopped to talk to Drew once more. If she hadn't tried to tell him thank-you before she left.

And if he hadn't promised her—

Naked bodies.

So much for delivering on that promise. She was still waiting.

Tina cleared her throat. She was feeling a draft in the back of her gown, and she needed to get dressed ASAP. First, though, she demanded, "What happens now? Am I still headed back for D.C.?" This was her life, and she needed to pick up the pieces and keep going.

Dylan slanted a fast glance toward Drew.

She didn't like that secretive glance. "What happens now?" Tina repeated, the words a little sharper.

"Devast got his start by making bombs, dirty devices that he'd place for the highest bidder." Dylan spoke slowly. "He loves to use his fire to destroy anyone or anything in his path."

So she'd figured out with that up-close brush with death. She'd felt the scorch of fire all along her skin as she was propelled through the air.

"He burned down the ranch his group was using out in Texas."

"HAVOC," Drew said.

Dylan's head jerked in a nod.

Tina frowned as she tried to understand. "So he creates havoc, that's his big thing?"

"No." Drew exhaled slowly. "He *is* HAVOC. It's a terrorist group. They're global, and their main goal is destruction. Devast started the group. He used his bombs to create it from fire and destruction and fear. He's a threat that needs to be eliminated."

"You're giving me this intel because he keeps coming after me…" Mercer must have finally given them the all-clear to reveal this information. All it had taken was—what?—a few attempts on her life. One attempt that had nearly been too successful. In return for nearly dying, she got HAVOC clearance. *Thanks, Mercer.* Her boss could be a real jerk.

"That's not why we're telling you." The intensity in Drew's voice worried her.

Her bare feet curved over the cold floor. She waited.

"We're telling you because we need your help," Dylan said. "The EOD needs you."

"What?" Sure, if they needed her to patch up the wounded, then Tina was their girl. But if they were talking about a mission in the field… "No, no, you've got the wrong woman—"

"That was the problem," Dylan continued roughly. "You weren't the woman who was supposed to be picked up as bait. Another EOD agent was. Rachel was the bait who should have been taken, but Devast followed the wrong trail of breadcrumbs."

Drew's lips were a thin, grim line. "You weren't ever supposed to be brought into this mess. Hell, you didn't even have a tracker on you! There was no way we thought that HAVOC would ever come after you."

A tracker. She stiffened. Tina had placed trackers in plenty of agents. The small devices were inserted right under the skin, a precaution in case of capture. The EOD could follow the signal sent from the tracker and locate the agent almost any place.

"Once we realized Drew had left the ranch, we activated his tracker. That's how we got to you both so fast in Lightning. Before Drew and Sarah checked in, we were already en route." Dylan's face tightened. "I'm sorry you were brought into this mess. It wasn't supposed to be you."

"But now it is." She was tangled up in HAVOC without any chance of escape.

Dylan nodded. "And now we need your help."

"Dylan…" A warning edge entered Drew's voice.

Dylan's gaze flashed. "The orders came from Mercer. As long as Devast is out there, she's not going to be safe." He jaw hardened as he stared at Drew. "Do you want that? Do you truly want her to be constantly at risk, always looking over her shoulder, always wondering when another attack might come?"

Drew's hands fisted.

Tina clutched the bag of clothes a bit tighter. "What is it that you want me to do?"

Dylan focused back on Tina. "We don't want you to run. We don't want to hide you."

Drew swore. "I told you already. I *don't* like this plan. We have other options that can work."

"Nothing that we can do now. Nothing that will be as effective as—"

"As what?" Tina demanded.

Dylan hesitated a moment, then said, "We want you to help us catch Devast."

"SHE'S STILL ALIVE."

Anton didn't let his expression alter when he heard this news. "That is disappointing. You'd…assured me that she was on the plane."

"That agent—he stopped her. I thought she'd already gotten on board, but the guy stopped her for some damn sweet talk." Disgust thickened the words as they drifted over the phone line. "Those two must be involved. I don't know how the hell I missed that."

"Apparently, Agent Lancaster is a man who is very good at keeping secrets." Drew Lancaster…not Stone Creed. That had just been an alias the agent used when he got close to HAVOC. Now Devast understood who the fellow truly was. And it was time to unearth every secret Drew Lancaster possessed.

Know your enemy. When you knew your enemy, it was easy to attack his weak spots.

"They took Tina Jamison to a local hospital then they cleared out of the place. But don't worry, I'll find them. Just give me a little time."

Anton sighed. Why did everyone always think that he would tolerate failure? "Time isn't on your side. You'd better find them, fast." But he was already talking to a dead man. Whether this man delivered Tina Jamison or not, he was dead.

Anton had no use for traitors. Men like the agent on the phone…they'd sell out anyone.

He stared down at the photo on the desk in front of him. Drew Lancaster.

He'd already managed to pull up some records on the man. Born in a small Mississippi town, abandoned by his father. The guy had been trouble as a kid, thrown in and out of juvenile halls. He was always running from the law.

Lancaster's mother had worked herself to death.

And Drew Lancaster…he'd fought his way out of that life and joined the army.

Became very, very good at killing.

Anton hung up the phone and kept staring at Drew Lancaster's image. A man who'd come from nothing. Who existed only to kill.

Right now, Drew Lancaster was one of Mercer's attack dogs, but, as Anton had already discovered, some of Mercer's men could be bought…if the price was right.

Anton was good at making the price right.

He smiled as he stared down at Lancaster. Another dead man, one who just didn't know it yet.

But, before Drew Lancaster died, Anton planned to use him.

Use him, then dispose of him.

Chapter Seven

The Dallas skyline stretched in front of Drew. He stared at the buildings, noting the sweep of architecture as it bled into the red evening sky.

He and Tina were in a plush hotel room. Five star all the way. No dusty sheets or wobbly chairs would be found in this place. For security, Drew had requested two adjoining rooms. Dylan and Rachel were stationed right down the hall in another set of adjoining rooms.

Dylan was determined to go through with Mercer's ridiculous plan. They wanted Tina to continue with the deception of being Mercer's daughter. Wanted her to play that part—and to keep Anton's focus on her—until their team could bring down HAVOC and its leader.

He hated that plan. Tina wasn't trained for a situation such as this one. Putting her into the middle of this fight could very well get her killed.

I won't have her death on my hands.

The door squeaked open behind him.

Soft footsteps came toward him.

He kept staring out at the setting sun. Its light reflected off the high-rise towers.

The scent of strawberries drifted in the air.

His fingers curled into fists. "Why did you say yes?"

Because she had, and with that one word, Tina had changed everything.

She'd agreed to Dylan's too-dangerous plan, and she'd made saving her even harder.

"I agreed because Devast is determined to kill me, and no matter what you do or say, he isn't going to believe I'm not Mercer's daughter."

My fault. That burned like acid in his gut. He and his team had thought they were being so smart.

Mercer's real daughter, Cassidy Sherridan, had needed to vanish. Intel had leaked out about her—not her specific name, but the fact that Mercer had a daughter he'd hidden for years—and the sharks had started to circle. They'd needed to get the sharks off their blood scent.

We needed bait.

But the bait was supposed to be Rachel. Not Tina.

They'd left a trail of evidence including phone calls and a log of private meetings connecting Rachel and Mercer. They'd wanted all those circling sharks to think that Rachel was the one connected so intimately to Mercer.

When the sharks came in to attack, Rachel and the team would have been ready.

But the main shark had gone after the wrong prey in New Orleans. Tina had been down there—why?—and Devast had connected her to Mercer.

"I'm sorry," he told Tina, and he meant the words. Drew was sorry that he'd screwed up her life, and that his team had brought her into this twisted mess. He turned toward her.

She stood just a few feet away, her eyes wide, her cheeks a soft pink.

She's so beautiful. Does she even realize what she does to me?

He cleared his throat. "Why were you in New Orleans? You weren't supposed to be there."

"The call came down that an EOD doctor might be needed on scene." Her smile was wry. "Considering some of the locations the agents travel to, visiting New Orleans sounded like a really good option for me. I can't... I can't always go into the field. It was—"

"Safe," he finished as he edged toward her.

She nodded. Her hair brushed across her cheeks with that slight movement. "I thought that would be the perfect trip for me. I needed a break from D.C." A rough laugh eased from her. "I guess I got my break."

"A break is one thing." He tried to keep his anger and fear leashed. "Signing on to *finish* this mission? That's something altogether different. You're risking your life." The anger spiked, sharp and hard, within him. "You don't belong in the field, Doc. You need to get back in an office. Go back to—"

"I know his daughter."

Hell. He'd wondered if Tina had put the puzzle pieces together. The woman was sharp. She'd been working in the EOD office when Cassidy Sherridan had gone in a few months back. Cassidy hadn't headed to the office willingly. She'd been hunted, nearly shot right outside on the street in front of the EOD office.

"She's trying to escape, isn't she?" Tina asked.

Yes, Cassidy wanted out of the prison that had held her in check for her entire life. "Not at the cost of someone else's life." Cassidy would never go for a plan like that.

"It's not just about her." Her gaze seemed shadowed. Since when did Tina keep secrets from him? "I want to stop Devast, too. I want to help."

He had to touch her. He shouldn't. She was still recovering but...

His fingers trailed down her cheek. Like warm silk. "Help by staying alive."

"I can do *more*." Now she had anger of her own pushing through the words. "So I'm not an agent. I've been working with the EOD for years. I can keep a level head. I won't panic. I have my medicine now, so I can control my attacks. I can *do* this."

The problem was that he didn't want her to "do this." What he wanted was for her to be far away from danger. He forced his hand away from her and took a step back so the scent of strawberries wouldn't be so tempting. "Go to your room. You should get some rest." He turned away.

"*Stop it.*"

That wasn't anger coming from Tina. It was full-on fury. He glanced over his shoulder.

Her cheeks weren't just a soft pink any longer. They were flushed a dark red. "Uh, Tina…"

"I don't take orders from you, Lancaster. Whether I'm completing this mission or not—that isn't your call. It's mine. It's my life."

"A life that you could lose!"

"Pierce Hodges already lost his life."

Pierce. His body tensed. Pierce Hodges had been the pilot on that plane. A good guy. Drew had worked with him before and—

"Pierce died because Devast was coming after me. Devast is going to keep coming. If we don't stop him, innocent people are going to die."

This was what she didn't seem to get. "You're innocent."

Tina shook his head. "Not in his eyes. You really think you're going to be able to convince him that he made a mistake? My life has been bound with Mercer's since I was eighteen. You were trying to link him to Rachel, but you overlooked the fact that he's been linked with *me* for too long."

Eighteen?

"I won't have more deaths on me. Not when I can do something to stop this."

"You don't know what you'll be facing—"

Her chin lifted. "Maybe you don't remember, but when we were in that hellish room and that jerk with the knife was getting ready to cut me—when he was getting ready to take a finger from me—I didn't make a sound."

He shook his head. He didn't want to remember that moment. It twisted his guts.

"I'm not going to crumble. I don't have your training, I get that. But I can do my part."

He stared back at her.

Her eyelashes flickered. "I know what this is about."

He doubted it. He was good at keeping his secrets.

She stalked toward him, stabbed her index finger into his chest. "It's because of the attack I had. You can't get past it."

Drew shook his head. "That's not—"

"I am not some little piece of fluff. Do you understand me? Yes, I had an asthma attack. My asthma gets severe—especially if smoke is billowing around me! But I've got it under control. I'm fine now."

But he'd never forget how terrified he'd been. "I'm not going to risk—"

Her finger stopped its stabbing, but her eyes were bright with fury. "I'm not yours to risk, Agent."

I feel like you are.

"I told you already. This is *my* life."

But he felt like she was his.

"You think I'm some green girl who doesn't know

what she's doing? That I'm just a healer. That's what you said, right?"

There wasn't any "just" about it. She saved lives. She'd saved plenty of agents. That was damn important.

"I killed a man when I was eighteen."

There was that magic number again, only now he realized it was attached to a dark story that had changed her life.

"I can do it again, if I have to."

She'd killed a man? His doc? Drew shook his head.

Her smile was sad. "Anyone can kill, under the right circumstances. Those circumstances…" The smile vanished as she swallowed. "They didn't give me a choice."

His heart was pounding in his chest, racing fast, but when Drew spoke, his voice came out flat. "What happened?" He had to know. It was getting to the point where he felt as though he had to know everything about her.

She backed up a step.

He caught her wrist, held her there. "What happened?" She didn't get to drop a bombshell like this one and just walk away from him.

She straightened her spine. Her whole body seemed to tense as if she were bracing herself for the memory. "It's one of those 'wrong place, wrong time' stories. They always end badly, you know."

Pain echoed in her voice and seemed to strike right at his heart.

"My parents and I got caught in the middle of a bank robbery. When we walked into that bank, we didn't realize what was happening until we heard the teller scream."

She eased out a slow breath and continued. "My dad, he was a cop. He had his dress blues on that day. He always looked so good in them. My mom would call him her 'handsome cop.' And he did look handsome that day. I was proud of him. Always so proud."

She pushed her left hand through her hair. Her eyes were on his, but Drew didn't think Tina was actually seeing him. Her gaze seemed to be focused only on the pain of the past. "We went inside, thinking that we'd be in and out. We had dinner reservations at six that night." She pushed out a hard breath. "We didn't make dinner."

"Tina…"

"As soon as they saw my dad, the robbers panicked. They screamed for him to get on the ground and to lift his hands up."

He wanted her in his arms. But Drew didn't move.

His thumb rubbed lightly against her wrist. The beating of her pulse seemed to steady him.

"I had an attack. They were worse back then. I used to get them more frequently." Her breath eased out slowly. "My dad always carried medicine for me. He was reaching for it, but the robbers thought he was reaching for his gun."

Hell.

"They shot him. My mother ran at them and they shot her, too." Tears glimmered in her eyes. "My mother died instantly, but my father didn't. His blood was all over me, and there wasn't anything I could do. I was trying to pull in air, begging them to help my dad, and when I looked up—" She blinked and finally seemed to see Drew once more. "The shooter had his gun pointed right at my head."

Drew didn't speak. He found that, for once, he couldn't.

"Sirens were screaming. Help was coming, but it wasn't going to get there fast enough. I knew I'd die. Just like my mom. I didn't want to die."

Every muscle in his body had locked.

"I had been trying to stop the blood from flowing out of my dad. My hand was just inches from his holster—from the gun that he had never grabbed." A tear slipped from her eye. He carefully wiped it away. "I lifted it and I fired, right before the shooter did. I killed him."

"You saved yourself." Eighteen. He'd never imagined that her life had been so dark. No, he hadn't wanted it to be dark. He'd always liked to think that only good things happened to the doc. *She's my good thing.*

But it seemed danger had stalked her for far longer than he'd realized.

"What happened to your dad?" he forced himself to ask.

"He died right after the police stormed inside."

Hell.

"Mercer was there."

So this was how Mercer fit into the puzzle of her life.

"He and my dad…they were friends. He was at the funeral. He stayed with me, made sure that I was set for college. Med school."

Med school. He understood. "You wanted to be able to save lives."

"I did but…I still couldn't save that man at Lightning. No matter what, you can't save everyone."

She pulled away from him; headed for the connecting door. The room immediately seemed colder without her near.

Tina paused and glanced back at him. "I didn't tell you that story so that you'd feel sorry for me."

"Sorry isn't what I feel." She was even stronger than he'd thought.

And I always thought she was damn tough.

"You can't save everyone," she said again as she gazed back at him. "You should have realized that by now."

He had. He wasn't interested in saving everyone.

Just her.

"You don't know what's going to happen next. You don't

know if you can save me. Whether I agree to the plan or not, Devast is hunting me."

You don't know if you can save me.

She was right. He didn't know. He had no idea how this case would end.

Tina slipped into her room then quietly shut the door.

He stood there, far too aware of the silence around him.

After a few moments Drew found himself staring down at his own hands. Tina had killed one man. He didn't want to remember all of the lives he'd taken.

She's my one good thing.

His head lifted. He looked toward that connecting door. Then Drew took a breath and a step. He kept walking until he was in front of that door.

He didn't knock. Didn't hesitate. He just swung that door right open.

If it hadn't been unlocked, he probably would have broken the damn thing down.

Tina stood near the bed. When the door bounced against the wall, she spun toward Drew and her eyes flared wide with surprise.

"I know that I have to try to save you." He felt as if a force was pulling him toward her. A moth to the burning flame. She was the fire he craved. "Because I need you." Then he kissed her.

With the press of his mouth to hers, Drew got that fire.

The desire seemed to ignite in his blood. Her mouth was soft and warm, and she kissed him back eagerly.

This wasn't a time for fear. Not a time for death.

This was their time.

"I made you a promise," he growled against her mouth. "There's something you should know. I always keep my promises."

"So do I," she whispered back. Her hands were between

them, seeming to singe him right through the thin fabric of his T-shirt. Then she was shoving up that T-shirt.

He tossed the thing across the room. "No going back," Drew told her, voice rough. He was rough.

She was silk.

"I don't want to go back."

With those words, Tina sealed both their fates.

He lifted her and put her in the middle of that big bed with its clean, white sheets. Her hair spread out behind her.

She reached up for him.

She was the most perfect thing he'd ever seen. And this time, for her, because it was *her,* he was going to show her that he could be more than the wild lover who consumed.

Though he sure as hell wanted to consume her.

He stripped the hotel robe off her. Let it drop to the floor. Her breasts were round and perfect, with light pink nipples. He put his mouth on her and tasted. "Strawberries..." he whispered. His arousal shoved hard against his jeans.

She arched her hips toward him. "That's my...ah... lotion. I found some in the gift...ah—shop!"

He made a mental note to buy her a case of strawberry lotion. "Love that scent on you." He loved touching her, kissing her. His lips feathered over her flesh. He licked her nipple, caressed her and held tight to the reins of his control.

He was trying to be gentle and easy.

Tina wasn't.

Her nails raked over his back. Her fingers pushed between them and fumbled with the zipper of his jeans.

"I don't want to wait," she told him. "All I want is *you.*"

Her voice was the best sin he'd ever heard. She was every thought he had right then.

He ditched his jeans, but made sure to keep the protection he'd shoved into his back pocket. Yeah, he'd visited that gift shop, too. *Because I knew I wouldn't be able to keep my hands off her.*

And protecting her, always, was his priority.

His hands pushed her thighs farther apart. Drew nearly lost his mind when he touched her and found her so ready for him. He took care of the small foil packet in a flash.

He heaved in a deep breath—*hold on to your control, hold on to it!*—and positioned himself at the entrance to her body.

He started to thrust into her, but then Drew stilled and she glanced at him. Tina's eyes were wide and eager, her lips parted. Desire was on her face. Desire wasn't enough.

He wanted to see her pleasure.

"No going back," he said again. This moment would change everything for them. She needed to realize that. This wasn't just some adrenaline-infused hook-up sex.

Tina's hands caught his. Their fingers threaded together.

He thrust.

Too good. Drew growled out her name. He withdrew, thrust again. Her legs wrapped around his hips. The pleasure built, rushing fast and hard toward him. This wasn't just sex. He'd had sex with plenty of other women.

This was more. So much more.

He thrust faster. Harder. His control ripped. No, shredded.

He'd wanted to show her that he could be a considerate lover.

But he was starving for her.

Her sex squeezed around him. He was staring straight into her eyes, and he saw her gaze go bright and blind with pleasure.

His climax hit him. The pleasure slammed through him, took his breath, and he held on to her as tightly as he could.

Drew kept thrusting. The pleasure wasn't ending. His back tightened. His muscles strained. Tina whispered his name. She was so beautiful. So perfect to him.

The release crested. The surge was the most powerful climax he'd ever had.

When it ended, when the shudders stopped racking their bodies, Drew could only think—

No going back.

He always kept his promises.

IT WAS THE ringing of the phone that woke Drew hours later. The steady peal came from his phone, a weak and low sound since he had fallen asleep in Tina's room.

In her bed.

He glanced over at her. His arm was curled around her stomach. Her lashes swept over her cheeks. She breathed easily. Slowly.

The phone kept ringing.

Drew slipped from the bed. He yanked on his jeans and padded quietly to his room. He grabbed for the phone.

He didn't recognize the number, but in the EOD, that didn't mean anything. Burner phones and untraceable cells were used every day. "Hello?"

"Agent...*Lancaster?*"

He turned away from Tina's door and headed toward the skyline view. Darkness had fallen over the city now, but the lights from the skyscrapers still gleamed. "Who is this?"

"I believe you've been looking for me," the voice said. It was a male's voice. No accent. No inflection. "And I've been looking for you."

He glanced toward the connecting door. He could still see Tina in there. Safe in bed. "I think you've got the wrong number." His gut clenched and his body went on high alert.

Laughter. The cold kind. "No, I've got the right number, and I've got the right man."

Drew strained to hear any background noise that might give the guy's location away, but, unfortunately, he heard nothing.

"How valuable is she?" the voice asked him, still as calm and easy-as-you-please.

"Sorry, man, I don't know what you're talking about." His voice came out the same way. He could play this game all night long.

Devast. The big boss had actually called him. Called him on what should have been a secure line. Who was giving the guy this intel? They'd thought that the EOD had outed its traitor months back. A guy in the tech department who was now in a cold grave.

Someone else was on Devast's side. The bombing on that plane and Devast's access to his personal number proved it.

A sigh drifted to his ear. "Don't waste my time, Agent Lancaster. I know exactly who you are. You know who I am. And you know what I want."

Tina.

Fine. His cover was blown with the guy, so he could cut through the bull. "You're not getting her."

The laughter came again. "Why? Because it's your *job* to keep her safe?" A taunt.

"Something like that." He made sure to step away from the glass and yank the curtains closed. He was up so high that Devast shouldn't be able to take a shot at him, but Drew had never been the type to take chances.

"I've learned a lot about you recently. After you killed my men, I had no choice but to learn."

The guy spoke of death far too easily. But then, Devast

had been an instrument of death for most of his life. "You sure don't seem upset about losing them."

"And you don't seem upset about killing them."

Once more, his gaze returned to Tina's still form in that bed. She thought that she was safe right then.

She wasn't.

Drew couldn't track the call—he didn't have the equipment handy—but was Devast tracking *him?* Right then? The HAVOC network was massive. And inside the EOD. "This call is over," he said. He wasn't going to risk revealing Tina's location to—

"I want to make you an offer," Devast said quickly. "Consider it a business deal. You give me what I want, and I'll give you a million dollars."

What? One million dollars was one hell of an offer.

"Like I said," Devast continued, and now the guy sounded way too confident. "I learned a lot about you. I know that you're a man who would once do anything for money. Lie. Cheat. Steal. And now…for Mercer…for *his* money, you kill."

His back teeth had locked. "You don't know as much about me as you seem to think." He didn't auction off his services to the highest bidder.

"Give me what I want," Devast said, "and I'll give you enough money to finally kick all of that poor Mississippi mud off your shoes."

The bedcovers rustled softly from the other room. He turned away from the room and hunched his shoulders. "Who says there is anything wrong with that mud?"

Silence. Then… "Think about my offer. Think long hard about it. I'm giving you one chance. The money—and your life."

For Tina's life.

"I don't give second chances, Agent Lancaster. This is your one opportunity. Be smart. Take it."

The floor squeaked behind him. The scent of strawberries drifted in the air.

"Bring her to me. Forty-eight nineteen Demopolis Way. The old factory on the east end."

Devast sure thought he'd found Drew's price. "When?"

"Sunset. That will give you plenty of time to get her away from the other agents."

And it would give Devast plenty of time to lay his trap. Drew was no fool.

I won't betray her.

The floor gave another low squeak. Tina would be close enough to hear every word that Drew said. "I'm surprised you don't just want me to kill her right now."

He heard the sharp, indrawn breath behind him.

"I won't have another mistake on my hands. I want to *see* Mercer's daughter die."

Drew turned his head. He could look straight into Tina's eyes then.

"Make the trade, Agent Lancaster."

The line went dead in his ear.

Fear flashed in her eyes. "Drew, what's happening?"

He glanced down at his phone. Had Devast traced them? And if the EOD traitor had hacked into the system already... There could be no safe place for her.

No safe place, but with him. Drew rushed toward her and locked his fingers with hers. "We need to leave *now*."

ANTON DEVAST SMILED as he put down the phone. The seed had been planted. Now, it was just about letting it take root.

Drew Lancaster could trade the woman. Or he could die.

A simple enough offer.

Anton looked to the right. Dallas waited. So did his prize.

When I'm done, I'll send you a piece of her, Mercer.

Then his old friend would know that they'd finally come full circle.

A child for a child.

Payback.

MERCER STARED DOWN at the faded headstone. Weeds were trying to grow over it, so he bent and jerked them back.

The stone was cold to the touch.

No flowers. No mementos marked the grave.

The man buried there had been gone for nearly twenty years. No one but Mercer ever came to visit the grave. He knew—he'd had eyes on this cemetery for years.

"Who is he?"

He didn't glance back at the agent's curious voice. He was bringing Cooper Marshall on to the case because he needed backup. The mission was going to get tough, Anton wouldn't hesitate to kill—and Cooper Marshall, well, he was an agent who never hesitated.

He was also a guy who didn't seem to understand fear. Sometimes that lack of fear was a weakness.

Sometimes it was an advantage.

"He was a man who got caught in the cross fire." A cross fire that had come from Mercer. "And his death started a war that I need to end."

He backed away from the grave. His gaze slid around the area. The spot hadn't changed much in twenty years. The trees were still heavy, lush. A pretty spot.

Jon might have liked it.

Grief pulled at him, but Mercer pushed the memories away. "You've been briefed on the situation with Dr. Jamison?"

He couldn't bring in a full force of agents on this case. The more people who knew, the more potential for word to spread about his "daughter"—and that couldn't happen.

He'd already sent a message to Cale Lane, his real daughter's husband. The agent was on high alert, and he had strict orders to keep Cassidy out of the U.S. until this nightmare was over. Cale also had orders *not* to tell Cassidy what was happening. If she thought that someone else was being risked in her place…

Cassidy would be back here in an instant.

He didn't want her in that kind of danger. He'd begun the whole ruse with Rachel Mancini to protect Cassidy.

The plan had been for Rachel to draw out his enemies—in particular, Devast. The agents would have taken Devast down, and Mercer's "daughter" would have died in the cross fire. They'd arranged to stage Rachel's death so perfectly.

With that fake death, the hunt for his daughter would have ended. Cassidy would have been safe to live a normal life. A life she'd never had before.

But now that perfect plan was in ashes.

"I have been briefed, sir," Cooper replied.

Mercer's gaze slid to him. "Dr. Jamison has volunteered to assist in the rest of the investigation. She wants to help us catch the man behind her abduction."

"Anton Devast," Cooper said. His blue stare drifted to the grave—and to the name on the headstone.

Jonathan Devast.

"Devast is a very dangerous, unpredictable man." Mercer cocked his head as he studied Cooper. "You're rather unpredictable, too." A point that had almost kept the man out of the EOD.

Cooper Marshall was an ex-U.S. Air Force Pararescueman. He jumped into danger any chance he could get. Literally.

A faint smile lifted Cooper's lips. "Yes, sir, I've been told that I am."

They were alone in the graveyard. No eyes. No ears. "You've been on a mission in Afghanistan for the past seven months." Mercer exhaled a slow breath. "And I have someone who has been in my agency, someone who has been selling secrets, straight to Devast. Since I personally sent the plane to pick you up on your mission—"

"You think I'm not the traitor."

"I *know* you're not." He knew every single secret that Cooper Marshall possessed. He should. The man was family.

Some secrets, Cooper didn't even know.

"So you want me to go in and join the others who are already on point," Cooper began.

Mercer shook his head. "No, I don't want you making any contact with the other agents."

Cooper's blond brows rose. The sunlight glinted off his hair. *Not as golden as my Cassidy's. Much darker.*

Cooper cleared his throat. "Sorry. I'm a little confused. If I'm not to join the team, then just what is my assignment?"

"To make sure you're not seen. To follow Tina Jamison. To keep your eyes on her and to report to me anything or anyone that threatens her."

"And the agents with her— What, you don't trust them? You think one of them could be the traitor?"

He wanted to trust them. On paper, Drew Lancaster, Rachel Mancini and Dylan Foxx were all good agents.

But somewhere in the EOD, there was an agent who was selling him out.

So, yes, he wanted to trust them, but he'd learned long

ago that he didn't always get what he wanted. And he wouldn't put Tina's life in jeopardy. "Money can tempt a man to do just about anything in this world." The right offer, to the right man... "This isn't the first time that one of the EOD's own has turned." Not the first time and, unfortunately, not the last. When you moved in the circles that he did, betrayal was a fact of life.

It was a fact that had killed his wife.

It had taken time, but Mercer had traced that brutal attack back to the man who'd been his friend.

His gaze returned to the grave.

"I want extra protection on Tina Jamison. She's not an agent, and I'm not going to have her sacrifice her life because she's trying—" He stopped because Cooper had no reason to know the rest. *Tina is trying to repay a debt to me.*

He knew exactly what Tina was doing. Because he knew her. Tina was smart, incredibly so. She always had been. Her father had kept smiling pictures of a young Tina— holding her slew of academic awards—all over his desk.

Mercer had never been able to show pictures of his own daughter. But he had one of Cassidy, one that he carefully hid from others.

Cassidy and her mother, Marguerite.

Tina was grateful to him. He knew that. She'd told him time and again. But he hadn't done anything for her. She would have graduated college on her own. Gone to med school—*on her own.*

Sometimes, he felt as though all he'd done was put her in a cage. He'd offered her the position at the EOD because she was a damn good doctor.

But... *Did I also offer her the job so that I could keep an eye on her? To protect her, the way her father would have done?*

Only, Mercer's protection had turned into a trap.

The same way I trapped Cassidy.

And if he'd known about Cooper Marshall sooner...

He shoved out a hard breath. "You're on Dr. Jamison's security detail. You watch her. You protect her. If you think she's compromised, you move immediately to retrieve her." He leveled his stare at Cooper to make sure the man got the point. "Your priority isn't bringing down Devast. It's keeping Dr. Jamison alive." Because if a choice had to be made...

Cooper nodded.

Then Mercer wanted his agent to make the right choice.

Chapter Eight

"He wants a trade," Drew said as he paced the small confines of the house.

A safe house, or so he'd said. The guy had hustled her out of that big hotel fast. Told her that their location had been compromised.

Then he and the other two agents had burned some serious rubber getting to this new spot.

A spot that was a lot less glamorous than their five-star hotel. The little neighborhood had looked abandoned at first glance. Houses in disrepair, roofs slumping, windows boarded up.

The streets were dark, and Tina sure hadn't seen anyone walking in the area.

Tina glanced around the small, single-story house. There were burglar bars on the windows. Instead of making her feel safe, they just made her feel like a prisoner.

"Tina, did you hear me?" Drew paced toward her. A frown pulled his dark brows low. "The SOB called me. I don't even know how the hell he got my number—"

"Sydney's working on that," Rachel murmured. There was a dark bruise on her temple. A cut on her cheek. Little mementos from the explosion that had nearly killed her and Tina. "She thinks someone hacked into the system because he called Mercer's private line, too. She'll find the link back to the hacker, just give her some time."

"We don't have time." Dylan looked as grim as Drew. "What we have is a terrorist who's locked on us. He's killed to get to Tina already, and he'll do it again. He won't hesitate to take out anyone in his way."

Was that why they were on that forgotten street? To minimize any collateral damage? The hotel had been full, right in the middle of the bustling city, but the houses on the street were pitch-black and empty.

"We have to be prepared for his attack," Dylan said. "It could come at any moment."

Tina found her gaze sliding back to Drew. He'd been quiet, too reserved, since they'd left the hotel. "What aren't you telling me?" There was something else, she knew it.

"A killer is after you!" It was Rachel who answered a little too quickly. "Isn't that enough, Tina?"

No, right then, it wasn't. "What kind of trade did he offer?"

"One million dollars." Drew's gaze was guarded. "For you."

One million— "Didn't realize I was worth so much." She had to ask because morbid curiosity compelled her. "Is that alive...or dead?"

His pupils widened, the dark spreading into the gold as he stared at her. "Alive." The word seemed to drip ice. "I guess, after what happened before, he wants to kill you personally. To make sure the job gets done."

The man who stood in front of her— *I feel like I don't know him.* With his careful words, his dark gaze and his expressionless face...this wasn't the man who'd made love to her so passionately. As if he couldn't get enough of her.

This was the tough agent. The one with ice in his veins. She hadn't...expected to see this agent return. Not after what had happened between them. She hadn't wanted to see him again.

Tina squared her shoulders. So much for not going back. He seemed to have flipped their relationship right back to the starting point on her. All thanks to one phone call. "Then I guess this is our chance."

"Are you sure?" Dylan asked. "Before we go too far, we can—"

"We've already gone too far." Every time she shut her eyes, she saw the plane exploding around her. *I'm so sorry, Pierce.* She kept thinking about the pilot. Was his family waiting for him to come home? Had they already learned of his death?

Her eyes stung, but Tina blinked quickly, refusing to let any tears fall. She could be strong now. She *had* to be. Tina lifted her hand and adjusted her glasses. Rachel had brought them to her. She'd even given Tina a backup pair in case these got smashed.

The backup glasses were in her bag. Right next to Tina's inhaler. *I won't be going anywhere without it.*

When the HAVOC group had taken her from the hotel, they sure hadn't stopped long enough for her to get her medicine. But she would *not* be that vulnerable with them again.

Can't be vulnerable. Won't. "I need a gun."

The breath expelled from Drew in a hard rush. "You need to think about this. We can get to Devast another way."

"What way?" She rose from the chair and paced around the room. The familiar weight of her glasses strangely re-assured her. "How long has the EOD been trying to get Devast?"

"Years," was the mutter from Dylan. "We got lucky when Drew was able to infiltrate the group. Their main pilot was caught in an explosion a few months back—one of their own bombs—and they were desperate for another pilot."

And in stepped Drew.

"You're not going to get so 'lucky' again," Tina said. "Devast will be even more suspicious of new faces now." She wasn't saying anything they didn't already know. "If we want to take him down, I'm the ticket that you can use. I'm the one who will get up-close access to the man." She forced a smile even as she wiped her damp palms on her jeans. "So how does this work? He calls Drew again—"

"He already told me when and where to make the exchange."

She blinked. "Well, then, you just have to tell Mercer. His men will be there, and the trap will be sprung." A relieved smile spread over her lips. This agent business wasn't as hard as she'd thought. "He's caught himself."

Drew shook his head. Then he walked slowly toward her. He stopped less than a foot away. She could feel the warmth of his body surrounding her. "It's not that simple, Doc."

When he said "Doc," the word dripped and rolled. It sent a shiver over her.

He called her doc the way some men might call their girlfriends sweetheart or baby.

Emotion was breaking through his mask once more, and she sure was glad to see the real Drew. "Then tell me how it's harder."

"If he picks the location, if we go by what he says, then we could walk right into a place that Devast has already got wired. He'll blow it up and kill every agent there."

"All while he stays back, nice and protected," Rachel added. She'd taken a seat on the old couch.

Dylan stood close to her. He always seemed to be close

to Rachel. "We don't go by Devast's rules. We make him come to us."

"So...what? You're saying that if we go by his orders, the guy probably wouldn't even be at the exchange?" She'd just have a bomb waiting for her?

Drew shook his head. "I'm saying we aren't ready for the meeting yet. I have to guarantee that Devast will be there. To do that, I have to *make* the trade personal."

She glanced toward the burglar bars. "Did he know we were in the hotel?" Was that why they'd rushed out so desperately?

"He had my phone number. Devast called me and deliberately kept me on the line long enough for a trace." Drew shrugged. "It was a safe bet. Only a fool would have stayed put then. I wasn't just going to wait for the hotel to explode beneath my feet."

She swallowed. No, Drew wasn't a fool. And she wasn't exactly game for anything exploding beneath her feet.

Make this personal. "What are Devast's weaknesses?" Tina asked as she tried to figure out a plan. "He has to have them, right? Everyone has a weakness."

"If he has one," Rachel sighed, "then we haven't found it."

Drew's phone rang.

Tina glanced down at it. He'd placed it on the table when they'd entered the safe house.

"Sydney's monitoring his calls. If that's Devast, she'll get a lock on him," Rachel said, eagerness pushing in her voice.

Drew picked up the phone. His face didn't so much as change expressions.

"Syd will get her trace," Tina said, "but Devast will get one on us, too." That was how it worked. But...was that what the agents wanted? "Is this some game of see who hits the fastest?"

"I told you, I have to make this more personal for him." Drew pushed the button to activate the speaker on his phone. "Calling me again already?" She was surprised by the mocking tone of his voice.

Laughter filled the room. Chill bumps rose on Tina's arms.

"You left the hotel so fast, Agent Lancaster. Did you truly think that you could run from me?"

Drew's gaze focused on Tina.

"I'm a step ahead of you," that hard voice said. "Your bars won't keep her safe. And if you won't give her to me, then I'll just take her."

Your bars.

He knew where they were.

Rachel had leaped to her feet. Her gun was out and she was at the window on the right, carefully searching the area outside.

"Doctors, police officers, even agents…they can all be bought."

Drew hadn't taken his eyes off Tina. "You haven't named the right price for me," Drew said. "You haven't bought me."

Silence.

"Why pay, when I can get her for free now? Thank you for showing me exactly where she was."

"Come on and try to take her." There was no fear in Drew's voice at all. Just a dark challenge. "Let's see how fast your men die. I took 'em out before, and I'll do it again."

"We'll see…"

"Yeah, we will. You want her—then you're going to have to *track* me yourself." A deliberate taunt.

Then the call was over, just like that. Dylan had gone to the back of the house, and Drew closed in on Tina.

"Does he know? He said 'bars' as if he could see where we were." She fisted her shaking fingers. "And when am I going to get a weapon? *When?*" If Devast was about to come storming into their not-so-safe house, she needed a weapon.

His hand closed around her shoulders. "You stay by my side, okay? No one is taking you. I've got this worked out."

Oh, great, wonderful to know but before he'd even finished speaking, she heard the eruption of gunfire. The fast blasts came from the back of the house.

Tina flinched.

"Two men!" Dylan called out.

"Three up front!" Rachel said at the same moment.

Devast hadn't been lying. He had found them. Trailed them? But they'd been so careful when they'd left the hotel. They'd switched vehicles, left false trails... "How did he do it? How did he track us?" Even if he'd had a trace on the phone call, he shouldn't have been there so quickly. It took time to triangulate signals and then to actually get an attack force to the right location.

But his team was already here. He didn't have to wait for a lock on the phone.

Devast shouldn't have been able to find them.

Unless...

Tina's eyes widened. The GPS trackers. The trackers implanted in the agents. If he'd accessed the EOD system, then Devast could have found Drew—and through him, Tina—by following those tracking signals.

Rachel was returning fire to their attackers. So was Dylan. Instead of joining the firefight, Drew was trying to pull Tina down the narrow hallway. She dug in her heels, then she ducked when a bullet whipped by her. She fell to the floor and her hands slapped against the hard wood.

Tina looked up. Drew had dropped with her. She met his stare even as a cold knot twisted in her belly. "You said that Devast had hacked into Syd's system?" Just months before, the EOD computer system had come under attack. Agent intel had been compromised.

They'd thought the leak had been controlled but...

Maybe Syd wasn't looking in all the right areas.

"If Devast knows you're with me, he could be tracking you," she said. Literally, damn it. He could have a direct feed into the small tracking device that she'd implanted in Drew's back. "If the EOD is compromised," she said as more bullets flew, "then you're compromised." Because Devast had definitely outed his identity. "We have to deactivate the tracker."

The only way to deactivate it was to cut the tracker out of Drew.

"Not yet. I want him tracking me." He grabbed her hand and pulled her down the hallway. "First order of business— *staying alive.*"

Wait! He *knew* Devast was following his GPS signal? His mocking challenge for Devast to "track" him made chilling sense to her.

Drew led Tina into a back room. The windows were boarded up. As far as exit strategies went, this sure wasn't looking like a good one to her.

He tossed aside the faded rug that had been spread over the floor.

With the rug gone, Tina easily saw the trapdoor in the floor. "Is that a basement?"

He hauled up the trapdoor. The hinges groaned. "It's our escape plan. You didn't think we'd actually bring you to this place without being sure we could get you out alive?"

The sound of gunfire still thundered from the other rooms. "But what about Rachel and Dylan?"

"They're coming. They're just leaving a little something for Devast." His eyes glittered at her. "We needed to buy some time, so we had to lay the trap."

What?

"After what he said on the phone back at the hotel, I figured he was tracking me, and I wanted that SOB to follow me here." His fingers tightened around the door. "Because here, the guy will realize that he can't just stand back and let his flunkies chase after us."

Rachel and Dylan burst into the room. "They're set. Let's go."

What was set?

"We're going to use some of HAVOC's own techniques against them." Drew took her hand. "There's a tunnel under this house. Stick with me. Stay low."

A tunnel? With dust and mold and— *Breathe. In. Out.* She had her medicine. This was fine. She could handle a tunnel. She had to. Tina nodded quickly and hurried down with him.

There wasn't any dust. No mold, either. Just a small, narrow tunnel, maybe three feet tall and three feet wide. She had to crawl, and she did it, double-timing her movements so that she could get out of there as fast as possible.

The sound of their breathing seemed loud in that small space. Rachel was leading the group. Tina was right behind her, with Drew following close. Dylan closed in the back.

"We're clear," Rachel said. She'd stopped. She shoved open another trapdoor, one that led them into the darkened interior of yet another house.

Tina scrambled from the tunnel. Drew grabbed her hand. "Easy. We're about a quarter of a mile away, and we don't want to do anything that would give away our position."

So they stayed in the dark. She quickly realized that they'd already stocked this house. Food. Water. First-aid equipment. Binoculars. Night-vision equipped, of course. These agents were definitely prepared.

Rachel took the binoculars and peered through the thin blinds that lined a narrow window. "They're surrounding the house. Do it."

"Do what?" Tina asked, almost afraid to find out. Her eyes had adjusted to the darkness enough for Tina to see Dylan pull a small box from his pocket.

"Time for Devast to experience some HAVOC of his own," Drew said. His arm brushed against hers.

Dylan pressed a button. An explosion seemed to rock the street. Through the blinds, Tina saw the flare of fire flash high up into the night.

The house they'd been in had just exploded.

"They're falling back," Rachel whispered.

Yeah, because the fire was driving them back.

Drew's fingers slid down her arm. "He tried to kill you with a bomb before, so we just gave him what he wanted."

She turned toward him, frowning. "Are you sure Devast is going to believe this? You think he'll buy that I'm dead?"

He pulled a knife from the sheath strapped to his ankle. "No, I think the explosion will just make him even angrier. And when he sees my GPS signal moving fast soon, he's going to track it. He'll come after me with everything he's got."

Instead of letting Tina be the bait in this deadly game, Drew was using himself. "Why?" she whispered.

"Because I don't want you in his sights."

And she realized why he hadn't told her about this plan sooner. Because he didn't intend to use her to finish this investigation. She'd agreed to cooperate, but he was the one calling the shots. He wanted her out of Devast's path, and he'd just blown up a house to make sure Devast couldn't get to her.

Drew offered her the knife, handle-first. "I need you to cut the tracker out of me. You know it emits a signal that covers a one-mile radius, not an exact location, so, for the moment he'll think I *could* be in that blaze."

Her fingers closed around the knife. "What are you going to do with the tracker?"

A muscle jerked in his jaw. "Rachel and Dylan are going to take it. They'll lure Devast into Mercer's web, and I'll take you out of here. No signal will link back to you and me. You'll be safe." His eyes glittered at her. "My job is to protect you. That's what I'm doing." He stripped off his shirt and turned his back to her.

Rachel and Dylan hurried into the other room, saying they had to check in with Mercer.

The knife's handle was cold. Her fingers were slippery with sweat. She rose onto her toes. She knew exactly where Drew's tracker was located because she'd been the one to implant it. The blade sliced over his skin.

The guy didn't flinch.

Carefully, she pulled out the tiny device.

"Here." Rachel was back with bandages. Tina gave her the tracker and began to patch up Drew.

"We'll rendezvous just like we planned?" Rachel asked him as she pocketed the tracker.

"Dawn," Drew agreed with a curt nod.

Rachel glanced toward Tina. "This is the best way. Mercer agreed. The big boss wants to make sure Devast can't ever threaten you or anyone else in the EOD ever again." Rachel nodded once more and then she was gone.

Tina smoothed the bandage over Drew's back. The knife was still in her left hand. His blood was on the blade.

Drew turned toward her. "We don't have a lot of time

here. We need to clear out, just in case those guys out there wise up and start searching the houses." He took the knife. Stepped away and dug in a chest of drawers. A moment later he was clad in a fresh shirt and tossing her—a leather jacket?

"I know you like motorcycles," he said with a wry grin.

Uh, no, not so much.

"Time to ride."

Her head was spinning.

"All of the other houses on this street are abandoned. That fire is going to blaze until the EOD tips off the fire department. And Devast's men? They're not leaving until he gives them an order to clear out." He took her hand. "So we leave *them*. The motorcycle is stashed a few blocks away. Ten minutes, and we'll be clear."

She slid on the leather jacket.

Then he gave her a very blond wig.

"Just in case you're spotted." He pulled a baseball cap low over his brow. He'd retrieved the cap from the same drawer that held the jacket. "We can't be the ones they are looking for. That would wreck the plan."

She balled her hair up, secured it, and became a blonde in moments. She also ditched her glasses. Or rather, Drew took them and carefully stored them in his pocket.

A few minutes later they slipped out the back door. She could hear voices yelling, could hear the faint crackle of flames in the distance.

"Stay close to the buildings. Stay close to me," Drew whispered into her ear.

Right. She had this.

Her fingers shoved into the pocket of the leather jacket and they curled around—medicine?

She felt the familiar shape. An inhaler. Drew had made sure that she had an inhaler close by.

Their footsteps were silent as they snaked through alleys and around old houses. The area looked so abandoned but she knew they couldn't take any chances.

Drew caught her in his arms. He spun her around and pressed her back into a brick wall.

"What's happening—" Tina began.

Drew put his lips on hers. He kissed her hard and deep, and his body seemed to completely surround hers.

Then she heard the thud of footsteps advancing toward them.

Drew's hand moved between their bodies. His fingers brushed over her stomach. What was he doing? There? This didn't seem like the place to—

His lips pulled from hers. He kissed her jaw, brought his mouth to her ear.

"I've got my gun," he said.

Oh. *That* was what he'd been reaching for.

The footsteps were coming closer. They hadn't gotten away clean, after all. So much for the grand plan.

"Get a room!" an angry voice called out.

Then the thudding of those footsteps continued as they rushed past Tina and Drew.

Tina glanced up. She saw the back of a man's head. He had a baseball cap on, too. He was rounding the corner, not seeming to care about her and Drew at all.

Her shoulders slumped in relief.

"We're almost there." Drew's body still brushed against hers. "You ready?"

Tina swallowed and nodded. She glanced once more toward the left, but the other guy in the baseball cap was long gone.

Her fingers curled around Drew's. They hurried into the darkness.

It seemed to take forever, but in reality, Tina knew only

about five minutes had passed before they were on the promised motorcycle. The bike vibrated between her legs when Drew kicked the engine to life. The motorcycle shot into the night. She held on tight to Drew.

And they got the hell out of there.

COOPER MARSHALL WATCHED the lights of the motorcycle vanish as he pulled his baseball cap lower over his forehead.

He had his own ride waiting, but he didn't want to follow Drew Lancaster too closely.

He hadn't realized that Drew and Tina would be coming down that alley. He'd seen the flames and thought that he'd been too late to help the doctor.

Nice job getting her out of there. He had to hand it to Lancaster—the agent had a certain style.

And Cooper knew that he'd been lucky, too—if there had been more light in that alley, Drew would have recognized him.

Recognition wasn't on Mercer's agenda. Not then.

He wondered if Mercer knew just how involved Drew had gotten with the good doctor. Because Cooper had seen the way the guy touched her.

The touch of a lover, not an agent.

He'd have to brief Mercer. Drew might not be up to his usual standards of ice and detachment on this particular case.

When cases got personal, they all too often got messy.

As far as Cooper was concerned, personal involvement always led to danger.

Tina Jamison was already in enough danger as it was.

"I DIDN'T GIVE any order for a bomb!" Anton snarled. "What the hell happened?" He wanted to shatter the phone.

"B-boss, the house just exploded. They were inside—all of 'em! They've got to be dead."

His back teeth ground together. He spun around and tapped on his keyboard. The feed on Drew Lancaster's tracker immediately came up. According to the signal, Drew Lancaster was moving fast down Bridge Avenue.

His eyes narrowed. *I've got you.* Drew thought that he could throw up a distraction and escape with Anton's prey?

Not happening.

The agent should have taken the money. Now he'd just die.

And so will the woman.

TINA'S ARMS WERE locked around Drew's waist.

He eased the motorcycle to a stop, pulling it up near the wall of a bar. It was hitting close to 3:00 a.m., and the bar was about to shut down.

Perfect timing for him.

Drew shoved down the motorcycle's kickstand.

"Why are we stopping here?" Tina asked quietly.

He knew the place didn't look like much of a safe house, but that was why they were there. Appearances could be plenty deceiving.

He tucked his helmet under his arm. "You need a place to crash." They both did. "By morning, this case will be all over." Because Devast would have followed their breadcrumbs straight to Mercer.

Drew had told Tina that he had to make the situation *personal* for Devast. And he had. The bomb at the house on Moyers would have infuriated Devast. As soon as Devast had pulled up Drew's tracking signal and realized that he'd escaped the flames…

The SOB would have decided that he had to go after Drew himself.

After all, Devast had told him that he didn't give second chances. Devast's men weren't catching Drew and Tina.

So you have to get involved in the job yourself, don't you, Devast?

Devast would follow their planted trail. Mercer and the EOD agents could capture him.

And Tina would be able to head back to her old life.

He pushed open the bar's door. His gaze swept the area, checking for any threats and, when he was satisfied, Drew gave a nod to the bartender. The redhead raised her brows when she saw him. Like Sarah, this woman had ties to the EOD. The bartender's brown gaze flickered toward the Staff door.

A band was playing. A somebody-did-me-wrong slow tune. Three couples were still on the dusty dance floor.

Drew eased past them. Tina glanced over at the couples, hesitating.

"Come on, Doc," he said. "We need to go."

A sad little smile tilted her lips, but she followed him. Just past the Staff door, a narrow flight of stairs waited for them. Drew had actually been to this bar a time or two before. He'd crashed here between missions, so he knew exactly how to find the hidden key to the upstairs apartment. They headed inside, and he secured the door.

"The bar will close by four," he told her, putting the motorcycle helmets down. "Then it will be dead quiet, and you can have plenty of time to rest."

That same smile—one that looked a little sad and a little lost—curved her lips as Tina ditched her blond wig. "And when I wake up again, I'll go back to my old life?"

He nodded. "That's the plan." A fast and frantic plan that he'd had to make as soon as he realized exactly how Devast must be tracking them.

The music drifted lightly in the room, muted, so that he

couldn't clearly hear the singer's words, but he could easily hear the guitar's strains. The low melody was sad and soft.

Tina brushed her hand through her hair. "I never thought so much could change for me in just a few days."

"You'll be back to safety soon."

"Safety." She seemed to be tasting the word. "Yes, I guess I will be safe again." She glanced toward the bed. Narrow, only built for one.

Drew cleared his throat. "You take the bed." He could crash in the chair. *If* he could crash. Ever since he'd gotten that call from Devast, his body had been tight with tension and too much adrenaline.

He's not the first person who thinks he can buy my allegiance.

But this wasn't about allegiance. Not really.

It was about Tina.

There were some things in this world that money would never be able to buy.

Tina didn't advance toward the bed. Instead she turned and walked closer to Drew.

The tension in his body got even worse. Hell, if the woman was about to try her hand at seducing him, she wasn't going to need to try too hard.

Any time she got close to him, desire pushed through him and he *wanted*. Not an easy need. Frantic and fast. Consuming. Not safe, when safety was what she seemed to need so badly.

"Drew..."

The way she said his name had him clenching his hands into fists. Husky, sexy. She'd been running for her life that night. He needed to back off, but if she was saying—

"Will you dance with me?"

That was not what he'd expected the doc to say. Drew just stared at her.

Then he saw the color flood her cheeks. The embarrassment because she thought he was rejecting her.

"Never mind." She spun away from him. "That was stupid. I—"

He caught her shoulders in his hands and slowly pulled her around to face him. "I'm not much of a dancer."

Her lashes lifted. She gazed up into his eyes. "Neither am I."

No, she didn't understand. "My life is about missions and violence. Following orders and getting the job done." His left hand slid down to the curve of her waist. His right caught her hand and cradled her fingers in his.

Her breasts brushed against his chest as she stepped closer to him. Her scent filled his head. Strawberries shouldn't make a man feel drunk, but her scent worked better than wine on him.

"There wasn't a lot of dancing when I was young," he confessed to her. The music was still playing from downstairs. "There wasn't a whole lot of anything." Except a kid on the path of destruction. A mother with a heart that was breaking because she couldn't seem to stop her son.

His feet moved. Slowly. Carefully. "I won't ever be the polished guy." Not the one who could blend in at any party or ball.

Her movements matched his. But she wasn't awkward. She was graceful and perfect.

His doc.

He took his time, trying to give her what she wanted because making her happy mattered to him.

"There's more to you," Tina said softly as she glanced up at him with eyes that seemed to gaze right into his soul, "than just bullets and combat."

She didn't understand. It was the combat that had saved him. "When I was eighteen…" His fingers tightened around hers. At eighteen, Tina had watched her parents die. And at eighteen, Drew had been trying to find his life. "I had a choice. Get my life in order, join the army, or find myself in jail."

"Jail?"

"I told you before I wasn't the good guy back then." He'd been the guy always looking for trouble, and finding it. "I was on a crash course with destruction. I knew what waited in my future, and it wasn't pretty."

"Why?" No judgment. No censure. Just curiosity. "What was happening to you?"

The music kept playing. So he kept dancing with her, bringing her even closer to his body as they moved so slowly around that little room.

"My old man didn't want to be a father, and my town... Hell, 'poor' didn't even describe it. There was no way out for us. My mom was trying, but she couldn't make enough to take care of me and my three sisters."

For an instant she stilled.

"Crime was the way to make money for them. So I did whatever I could. Whatever I had to do. The only law I followed was my own."

He waited for her to stop looking at him with such trust in her eyes.

Only, she didn't.

They kept dancing.

"I stole," he confessed. "I cheated. I found myself in the back of a patrol car a dozen times."

"What made you change?"

The money had been good. He'd finally been able to buy nice clothes for his sisters. For his mother. *My mom...* "My mother cried over me. When the cops came—when they were taking me back to juvie—she begged me to stop."

He could still see her tears. "I wanted to help her, but all I was doing was hurting her worse."

"I'm sorry," Tina whispered.

Drew shook his head. He wasn't telling her the tale because he wanted her pity. Pity was the last thing he wanted from her. "I wanted her to be proud, not to be holding her head down in shame because of what I was doing."

Then Drew realized why he was telling Tina about his past, when he'd tried to bury those Mississippi memories as deeply as he could.

He wanted Tina to know that he couldn't be bought, not anymore. That he wasn't going to trade her for money.

That he was better than that.

He pulled in a deep breath. "I joined the army. I sent her my checks. She used them for the girls." Kim, Heather and Paige. "Things started to change for my family. Things changed for *me.*"

Did she understand?

"I'm not the same boy I was back then."

Tina shook her head. "I never thought you were."

And it was still there. That blind trust in her eyes. When she'd been on that godforsaken rooftop and Lee had put his gun to her head, Tina had looked over and seen Drew. She'd recognized him, even when he'd had on that damn ski mask.

Trust had been in her stare then, too.

"Why do you have so much faith in me?" She shouldn't. It was dangerous. *He* was dangerous. "You know about my missions." She'd dug the bullets out of him, seen the scars from the knife attacks. "You know everything I've done."

"Yes, I do." She pushed up onto her tiptoes then. Her mouth brushed against his.

She knew, and Tina wasn't afraid. She wanted him—good, bad and everything in between.

And he just *wanted her*.

His mouth pressed harder on hers. Need and desire twisted within him. He licked her lower lip, and loved the little moan that she gave in response.

They weren't dancing any longer. They were at the edge of that too-small bed.

Tina's hand slid down his chest, rested over his heart.

"Before I get my safe life back," she whispered against his lips, "I want to be with you again."

Nothing could have stopped him from being with her.

The bed groaned beneath them, the old mattress and springs buckled. He didn't care. He stripped her, kissed her, caressed every silken inch of her body.

She put her mouth on his neck. Sucked. Licked. Made him shudder and ache.

He'd used all of his control before.

This time, in this moment, knowing that she was going to slip away from him soon...

There was no control.

There were frantic hands. Deep kisses. Clothes that were tossed to the floor.

He stroked her everywhere. Couldn't stop touching her. He had to see all of her.

He tasted Tina. Every single inch of her. Her fingers sank into his hair and she arched against him.

When the first release hit her, he tasted her pleasure.

When the second hit, he was *in* her, driving as fast and as hard as he could. He'd pulled away from her only long enough to grab protection from his wallet, and even leaving her for that long had made sweat break out on his forehead.

Again and again he thrust into her.

The bed slammed into the wall. Her hips arched toward him.

His fingers were locked with hers. Their bodies moved in perfect rhythm.

Tina stiffened beneath him. Then her legs curled around his hips and she held him even tighter as pleasure flew across her face.

The release crested, thundered over him, and left Drew growling her name.

His heart thudded, racing too fast in his chest, and his breaths shuddered out.

Tina smiled up at him.

Such damn trust.

He was afraid he'd destroy it. The way he'd destroyed too many other things in his life.

I don't want to destroy her.

Because she was coming to be the one thing in his life that mattered the most.

THE TRACKING SIGNAL had stopped. Devast had followed Drew Lancaster's tracker all the way to the outskirts of the city. An old factory, one that sat, abandoned, boarded-up, with the faint light of dawn just touching its weathered roof.

No cars were outside. No vehicles of any sort.

Devast stared up at the factory. So this was to be the endgame location. Interesting choice.

Mercer must truly think that he was a fool.

You shouldn't underestimate me, Mercer. That mistake would be fatal.

Anton would show his old friend.

He parked his car. He'd come alone. There was no sense losing any more men on this mission. Not when he knew exactly what he was doing.

Delivering a message.

Some messages were best delivered in person.

Anton headed toward the main entrance. This moment had been such a long time coming. Anton made sure that his steps were slow. Made sure to lean heavily on his cane. After all, he was frail. He was weak.

Very helpfully, someone had undone the chain that sealed that main entrance.

He heaved the chain out of his way. Deliberately, he wrestled with the chain as if it were a struggle to lift its weight. The chain fell to the ground. He pushed against the door. Once. Twice.

Then the door was sliding open. Anton waved the dust aside and entered the factory.

Silence.

Darkness.

"I know you're here!" Anton called out. His voice seemed to echo back to him. "Why must we play these games?"

Footsteps padded behind him. In front of him. To the left— The right—

And they attacked.

A gun was shoved into his back. A knife put to his throat.

"Got you," a man's hard voice snarled.

Anton shrugged. "So it would appear." But he wasn't interested in talking with a flunky. He wanted to see one man. *Needed* to see him. "Where's Mercer?"

Because he knew that Mercer would have been pulled out of his office. For a case this personal, there would be no sitting on the sidelines for him.

Lights flickered on in the factory. One after another, flashing on in rows.

Anton didn't even blink at the onset of all that too-bright illumination in a factory that should have been without power for years.

I know how appearances can deceive. Hadn't he been the one to first teach Mercer that lesson?

Anton's gaze cut to the left. The man with the knife had short, dark hair and a gaze that said he'd seen plenty of death.

Good. Then there would be no surprises when he saw it again.

Anton pounded his cane against the floor. "I asked for Mercer." He let his shoulders hunch inward. A frail old man was what he appeared to be. "I know…he's here…" He huffed out a ragged breath. "Where…is…he?"

"Right here, Anton." Mercer's strong voice rang out.

Then he was there. The devil himself was striding from behind the old machinery and walking so confidently toward Anton.

You think you've won.

It was time for the man to see exactly what he'd lost.

Anton hunched forward even more. The knife was cutting into his throat, but he didn't care. He'd never minded a bit of blood.

He wasn't the squeamish sort.

But then, neither was Bruce Mercer.

He clutched his cane then jerked it up in a flash. Before the knife could slash his jugular, he drove the handle of his cane into the man's side. The man stumbled back, but Anton was already attacking a second time.

He whirled around. Pushed the handle of his cane to deploy his own blade—

And he drove that blade into the stomach of the fool who'd pulled a gun on him.

The gun discharged. The bullet drove into Anton's chest.

Good thing he'd been wearing a bulletproof vest.

He laughed when the second agent fell. He was still laughing when he turned to face Mercer—

And the gun that Mercer had aimed right between Anton's eyes.

"Rachel?"

Ah, yes, that would be the agent with the knife—now he seemed to be desperately trying to save his partner.

Pity. Anton had sliced her nice and deep. Saving her might prove difficult.

"It's over, Anton," Mercer said, voice flat and hard. "You're done."

Hardly. "Actually, I'm just getting started." But he dropped his cane and raised his arms as if surrendering. "Can't just kill me now, can you?" Mercer and his code of honor. He wouldn't shoot an unarmed man in the head.

Mercer's gaze glittered. "Yes, I can."

Anton lost his smile. "That would be a pity. Because then you'd be killing *three* innocent women."

Mercer hesitated.

Right. The code of honor. It would be the death of Mercer. Just not at that moment.

Others had to die first. What good was revenge if your victim didn't suffer?

"Where is Agent Lancaster?" Anton glanced around the factory. He expected more agents to swarm him.

They didn't. Others were there, but they were hanging back. No doubt, by Mercer's order.

"Shouldn't he be here for this little party?" Anton asked. Lancaster had lured him there. The agent must have stashed Mercer's daughter first, then headed to this factory.

Clever, but not clever enough. Anton would get to her, soon.

Mercer reached into his pocket and tossed something at Anton's feet.

"We need an ambulance!" The other agent. Still so

frantic. He must really care for the woman—hadn't he called her Rachel?—dying in his arms.

Mercer tapped the transmitter on his ear and barked a command for help.

Ah, maybe Lancaster would come in with that aid.

Anton's gaze slid back to the object Mercer had tossed toward him. He squinted, then realized—

"Agent Lancaster isn't here. He never was," Mercer told him.

Anton laughed. "Well played." *Not well enough.*

Footsteps rushed inside toward him. More agents came in the door and a few EMTs appeared with them.

He slanted a glance toward the injured agent. A pretty woman, but one currently bleeding out on the dirty floor. "Better get her to a hospital," he advised, rather helpfully, he thought. "Or that will just be another death, on *you,* Mercer."

Mercer's fingers tightened on the gun. "You're done, Anton. No more bombs. No more threats. No more deaths."

Someone snapped handcuffs on his wrists. The metal bit into his skin.

Anton shook his head. "It's a pity that Lancaster wasn't here, but how about you deliver a message to him?"

Mercer marched toward him. When they were good and close, Mercer lowered his voice and said, "It was an accident. You know it was. Why the hell did you start on this path?"

Not an accident. A life lost. Payback. "Tell Lancaster that I know his price now."

"Agent Lancaster doesn't have a price." Disgust thickened Mercer's tone. "Get him out of here," he ordered as he stepped back and motioned to his men. "Maximum security. We're going to—"

"Three lives," Anton said as hard hands grabbed on to

him. "The first woman will die in three hours. The second in six, and the third in nine. One life, every three hours."

Mercer jerked his hand in the air and the motion froze the agents who were trying to drag Anton toward the door. "What the hell are you talking about?" Mercer demanded.

Pleasure filled Anton. Oh, but he'd finally found a way to break his old friend. And he'd use the man's own agent to do it. "Agent Lancaster's price. I told him that I wanted your daughter. Instead of delivering her, he hid her from me."

"I don't have a daughter," Mercer snapped.

"Of course, you do. Marguerite's daughter. Beautiful Marguerite." He could see her so clearly in his mind. "She died for you."

"You *killed* her." A muscle flexed in Mercer's jaw. His eyes blazed. Ah, but the mask was falling away. The real man—the real monster—glared at Anton.

"You're missing the point," Anton said as the memories flared in his mind. Painful, dark memories. "And you're costing Lancaster time that he doesn't have. One woman, every three hours…"

"What women? Who are they?"

This was the fun part. The part that would set his plan into real motion. "Lancaster's sisters. I have them. And my men will kill them, unless I get exactly what I want."

Chapter Nine

"The music has stopped," Tina said softly. She wasn't even sure when it had stopped. She'd been too caught up in Drew.

In the pleasure that he gave to her.

They were in bed. Tangled together. His heart beat beneath her hand, and the steady rhythm made her feel safe.

But that was the way Drew always made her feel.

He says I'm going back to my safe life. But I am safe, right here. Right now. With him.

She pressed a kiss to his shoulder. Then a kiss to the scar that cut across his cheek. He'd gotten that scar on his first mission with the EOD. The first but not even close to the only battle wound he'd received.

He'd suffered. He'd survived.

His fingers brushed over her jaw. "Tell me this… Why the hell does a girl like you want someone like me?"

She frowned at that. *Someone like me.* "Because you're a good man." Strong. Brave. Sexy.

"You should be running as far and fast from me as you can," he said, shaking his head. His hair looked so dark against the white pillow. "Not letting me touch you. Because, Doc, every time I touch you, I want more."

Her throat seemed to go dry at that. "Good, because you make me want more, too." Maybe—maybe they could have more. There had to be some way for them to work things out. Dawn had come. She could see the faint light trickling through the windows. Devast would be in custody by now. She'd be clear. Drew's current mission would be over.

Maybe they could take some time together. She'd like that. Being with him… *Yes.* She'd definitely be game for more time with Drew.

A hard knock shook the door.

Tension slipped into Tina's body. Their last few surprise visits hadn't exactly gone well.

"It's okay," Drew said as he eased from the bed. "I didn't bring a phone because I wanted to make sure I wasn't traced. That's Kelly from downstairs. She was going to tell us when we were clear."

Right. Clear. The nightmare was over.

Drew pulled on his clothes. Tina didn't want to be found naked in that room, so she fumbled to quickly dress, too.

The pounding came again. Harder. More desperate.

"Open up!" a woman's voice shouted. "I've got orders— They need you, Drew.*"*

The Drew that had been in Tina's arms moments before seemed to vanish. At the woman's tense words, all emotion left his face as he hurried toward the door.

Tina yanked her shirt into place and hauled up her jeans.

Drew pulled open the door.

Tina caught sight of the pretty redhead who stood on the threshold. "There's a problem," the woman said. "A big problem."

"Devast got away." Drew yanked a hand through his hair. "I knew that SOB was tricky. He's not getting his hands on Tina, though. I'm not going to let him—"

"They have Devast." The redhead's brown stare darted to Tina then slid back to Drew. "But Devast… He says that he has your sisters."

Drew shook his head. He took a step back.

Tina reached for him. "Drew—"

He flinched away from her. "That's not possible. The bastard is just bluffing. Playing another of his games."

The redhead paled a bit more. "Mercer doesn't think so. He wants you to come and meet him. The women..." Now her gaze held sympathy. "He says they are going to start dying soon, unless Devast gets what he wants."

Tina glanced down. Drew's fingers were clenched so tightly that the knuckles were white. "What does he want?" Tina whispered.

She glanced up at the silence that followed her question. The redhead was staring right at her.

"You," the woman said. "If Drew trades you, then Anton said that his sisters will be let go."

THE ELEVATOR DINGED, the doors opened and Drew stormed through the third floor of the Dallas FBI office. Tina was at his side, as if he would have left her with anyone else. His mind was a mess of chaos and fury, but one thought remained constant—*must protect her.*

Rage was building inside him, cracking through his surface. His sisters? He hadn't seen them in more than a year. He tried not to bring his darkness to their doors because he knew that he had enemies.

He sent them money. Had been sending those checks to his family ever since his enlistment. Every month, just like clockwork. His mother had passed away a few years ago, but he hadn't stopped his checks. He just wanted to help his family.

But now they might be in danger...because of me.

His fingers squeezed Tina's even tighter. She seemed to be his only link to sanity right then.

Maybe he's lying. That had been Tina's response to

Kelly's dark announcement. *You don't know yet, Drew. Let's find out what's going on.*

He'd find out all right.

Kelly had told them to meet Mercer at the FBI office. Mercer had pulled his strings—as usual—and taken over the third floor of the building.

Agents rose at his approach, their gazes suspicious. Yeah, he knew he probably looked like hell right then, and he wasn't in the mood for any bull.

One FBI agent made the mistake of stepping into his path.

Drew tensed, ready to swing.

"Easy." Mercer's voice boomed out. "Agent Lancaster isn't someone you want to tangle with."

The FBI suit backed up.

Drew marched toward his boss. "Where's Devast?"

Mercer pointed down the hallway. "We've got him in secure holding. Two agents in the room with him. Two at the door. He's not going any place."

"Does he have Drew's sisters?" Tina asked, her voice soft and worried.

Mercer focused on her. "I'm sorry you were brought into this mess, Dr. Jamison." He pulled her away from Drew. "Rest assured that you are safe now. Devast will not be threatening you again."

But Tina shook her head. "Don't 'Dr. Jamison' me," she replied crisply, notching her chin up into the air. "We usually play that game, but not now. I'm not going to pretend—" She sucked in a deep breath and squared her shoulders. *"Does he have Drew's sisters?"*

Mercer's stare slid back to Drew. After a tense beat he quietly said, "We've confirmed that your sisters are missing."

Drew fell back a step. *Kim. Heather. Paige.*

"We haven't confirmed that Devast has them yet. He came to the factory, with no backup, no men in sight, and he said—"

"I want to talk to him." Because Drew would find out in five seconds if Devast was telling the truth or if he was just spinning another web of lies.

Mercer nodded. He pointed down the hall. "The second room. There's a two-way mirror in there so that—"

"Watch what happens, I don't care." Drew had to force the words past a tight throat. The darkness of his life should never have touched his sisters. Never.

Kim was planning a wedding.

Heather... Heather had just started a new teaching job.

And the baby of the family... Paige had entered college two months ago. He'd sent her some extra money, just in case she needed—

"Don't kill him." Mercer's hard voice had Drew's head snapping up. "Do you hear me, Agent? Do. Not. Kill. Devast. That's an order."

Mercer thinks Devast is telling the truth.

"Drew..." Tina stepped in front of him. "What can I do?"

"Nothing." *The rage was cracking the ice.* "If he has them, I'll find out where they are." He'd get them back.

He walked around Tina. She didn't follow him. The two agents at the holding room door tensed when they saw him approach.

"Let him in," Mercer ordered from behind Drew.

They stepped to the side.

Drew shoved open the door. Anton Devast was seated at a small table. Both of his wrists were cuffed to the table's legs. He lifted his head at Drew's approach and smiled.

"Ready to make a deal with me now, Agent Lancaster?" Anton asked quietly. "I know your price."

TINA STARED THROUGH the observation glass. Her whole body was so stiff with tension that she ached. Mercer was by her side, quiet, intense, his gaze on the scene unfolding.

"You don't know anything about me," Drew said to Devast. His voice was cold and empty, totally lacking feeling.

This is the agent they whispered about. The one with ice in his veins.

Anton Devast, old, frail, but with evil seeming to ooze from his pores, shook his head. "I know plenty. You're a man who thinks that he needs to atone for the past. You try to wash the blood from your hands but you just can't."

As Tina watched, Drew placed his hands on the table and leaned toward Anton. "The EOD caught you. You aren't going to blow up any more buildings. You're not going to destroy any more lives. You walked into our trap. Followed every breadcrumb that we left for you, and now you're trying to throw out some desperate, last-minute—"

"Mercer can't locate your sisters, can he?" Anton's voice was mild, but the smile on his face was satisfied. "I'm sure he said that it's just a temporary situation. That he has agents on the ground in Mississippi, and that he *will* find them." Anton shook his head. "I gave him a timeline. I told him, one woman, every three hours. There's not a lot of time left before the first woman dies."

Tina turned stunned eyes on Mercer. "Why didn't you tell—?"

"We can't negotiate with terrorists," Mercer said flatly, but she saw the emotion in his eyes. The storm of anger. "Anton Devast is a terrorist wanted in over a dozen countries. We won't agree to any of his demands." He shook his head. "Especially when that demand involves killing an EOD employee."

Me.

"I want proof of life."

Her attention jerked back toward the glass when Drew said those five cold words.

Anton's smile widened. "I thought you would say that. Proof is coming. Mercer will be getting a call any moment."

Drew kept staring at the killer. "If you have them, if you hurt my sisters in any way, I will see you dead in the ground."

One dark brow lifted as Anton stared back at him. "It was your mistake. Any pain they feel is on you. I offered you fair money. You should have taken it and walked away." Anton gave a little shrug, as much of a shrug as his handcuffs would allow. "You could have even sent the money to the women, the way you send all the other checks to them."

"Hell," Mercer snapped, "that's it." He ran a shaking hand over his face. "That's how he found them. He followed the money trail Lancaster left behind."

Tina wanted to rush into that room with Drew. She wanted to *help* him. She'd thought the nightmare was over, but now Drew was facing the hardest fight of his life. "His sisters are all he has." He'd tried to control the emotion when he talked about them, but his voice had broken when he referred to the "girls." Without them, Drew would be lost.

Drew straightened to his full, imposing height as he glared down at the cuffed man. "I'm going to destroy you," he said.

"Promises, promises," Anton taunted. He wasn't even sweating. Surrounded by guards. Captured by the EOD. But still smug.

"He's calling the shots," Tina whispered. Because he held all the power.

"I can't negotiate," Mercer said again.

Her gaze slid to him. Cool under fire, Mercer was

sweating. As she watched him, Mercer hurriedly pulled out his phone.

"Sydney is already monitoring my phone from D.C. Any call that comes in, she'll be able to trace it back to the source. If that bastard really does try to send proof of life, we'll find them."

The door opened. Drew stood there, shoulders tense. "Have you gotten a call?"

Mercer shook his head. "He's playing with us. He knows that we have him, and he's just trying for one last mind game."

Tina wanted to believe that—

Mercer's phone rang.

Drew surged forward.

Mercer stared down at his phone. Tina was close enough to see the Unknown Number message flash across the screen. Mercer put the phone to his ear.

Tina could clearly hear the scream that broke across the line.

Drew yanked the phone away from the EOD boss. He hit the speaker button and the scream seemed to echo in the room. "Who the hell is this?"

"Drew!" The scream changed into his name. "Drew, please, say that's you! I-it's Paige. They told me that you're going to come and get me. Please come for me! *Please!*"

Drew's gaze didn't stray from the phone. His voice was ice-cold when he said, "When you were seven years old, what did I give you for Christmas?"

"You carved me a jewelry box. It had a…a P on it. We didn't have any money, but you said you'd buy me jewelry for it one day—" She broke off, screaming again.

"Don't hurt her!" Drew roared. The ice and control were gone. Only fury and fear remained in his voice.

The line went dead.

Mercer grabbed the phone from him. "Sydney was tracing. She'll get them—"

"Not if the call wasn't long enough." He turned away and stared through the glass at Anton. Anton stared back, as if he could see right through the mirror.

Tina reached for Drew's arm but he jerked away from her touch.

Her hand fisted. "We'll get them back. Whatever we have to do—"

"The EOD doesn't negotiate with terrorists," Drew said. The words were growled. And they were almost word for word exactly what Mercer had said. Drew spoke those words as if repeating some long-memorized rule. Then, whispering, he said again, "The EOD doesn't negotiate with terrorists." His breath sawed out as he glanced toward Mercer. "Consider me out of the damn EOD."

Drew stormed from the room.

"Sydney?" Mercer had the phone to his ear. "Tell me you got them. They gave us proof of life, and we only have an hour left before the first woman dies."

Tina's heart was racing. She pulled in as many deep breaths as she could. Drew was back in the interrogation room.

Anton had his smug smile in place once more. "Talked to your sister, did you?"

"*Where* in Louisiana?" Mercer demanded. "I need specifics, and I need them now."

One man knew specifics. One man knew everything.

The man smiling as he taunted Drew.

Tina rushed for the door. She wasn't going to let this happen. Not to Drew. Not to his sisters.

The agents guarding the room tensed when they saw her. But they knew she'd just been in the observation room with Mercer, and she had treated these EOD agents before.

They understood she wasn't the enemy, so she just said, "Mercer wants me in there as backup."

They weren't used to her lying, so they let her in.

She hurried into the interrogation room just as Anton said, "If you want them alive, then you'll give me what I want."

Tina squared her shoulders. "Here I am."

Drew whirled toward her. *"Tina."*

She didn't look at his face. Right then, she couldn't. Tina focused completely on Anton. "You wanted me, and I'm here."

His smiled faded as his gaze raked her face. "What I want is you dead."

Drew stepped in front of Tina, blocking her from Anton's sight. "You aren't getting what you want."

"Then you don't get to see your sisters alive again." His voice had gone low and rough and mean. "Because if you did want them back alive, you'd be bending down, taking that knife from the sheath you keep strapped to your ankle, and you'd shove it into her heart, right now."

Tina locked her knees.

"I kill her," Drew rasped the words. "Then how do I know you won't still let my sisters die? I'm not a fool. I know how you operate. You turn on everyone that you can. Your only loyalty is to yourself."

The door was shoved open again and it banged against the wall. Tina glanced over her shoulder. Mercer was there, chest heaving. His eyes blazed at her. *"Out!"*

Anton laughed. "Brave is she? Coming in here, getting away from you. Maybe she's more like Marguerite than I first thought."

Marguerite. Tina had heard that name before. Not from Mercer, but from her real father. He'd been talking to Tina's mother once and he'd said, "Bruce won't ever be the same. Losing Marguerite broke him."

Mercer grabbed Tina's wrist. "Come on. I told you—"

We don't negotiate with terrorists. "I have a deal," Tina said flatly. "A deal that I want to make."

The room got real quiet. The tension was so thick she could feel it pushing at her.

Tina tugged free of Mercer. She stepped around Drew. And she faced the nightmare in that chair. How many lives had he destroyed?

You won't destroy any more.

"You can't be trusted," Tina said simply as she stared at Anton.

"Neither can he," Anton immediately replied as his head jerked toward Mercer. "You think he's so good? That he's on the side of the law?" His lips thinned. "You're losing your life, dear girl, because of him. Because of what he took from me. Your father says that he works for justice— but how was killing my Jonathan justice?"

Mercer shoved past Drew and slammed his fists into the table, sending spider-web-like cracks across the top. "That attack was meant for you! How the hell was I sup- posed to know you'd brought your boy into that life? *You* were behind the attack on Marguerite. You killed her—"

"She wasn't meant to die!" Anton tried to surge to his feet, but the handcuffs jerked him right back down. "I was taking her. Taking your daughter. It was leverage because you were too close to finding out—"

"That you were a traitorous bastard who'd sold out not one but two countries? Yes, Anton, I figured that out!"

They were fighting over lives long lost. What about the lives still hanging in the balance? "Neither of you can be trusted," Tina said. Her breath rushed in and out. In and out. "And we're running out of time."

Anton and Mercer both swung their attention back to her. She focused just on the man who was pulling the puppet strings, even while in EOD custody. "We already know the women are in Louisiana."

His eyes narrowed.

"We'll run the rest of the trace down soon enough." She tried to keep all emotion from her face and eyes, just as the others had done. Maybe she was learning how to be an agent. "Tell us where they are."

Anton glanced toward Drew. "Still haven't gone for the knife yet… I guess you don't care that much for your sisters after all."

"You planned better than this." Tina shook her head as she tried to puzzle through the nightmare. "You wouldn't just count on Drew killing me."

"Drew?" Anton murmured. "How intimate. I thought for sure he'd just be Agent Lancaster."

She'd slipped up.

"Drew and Tina," Anton continued, as if tasting their names. "Perhaps I see now why the sisters don't matter as much. They can't matter as much as a lover."

"Get out," Drew snapped. His eyes pinned Tina and then Mercer. "Both of you." His steps were slow and certain as he advanced around the table and got close to Anton. "Turn off any video feeds. Secure the room. Leave him to me. I won't *negotiate*." He spat out the word. "I'll make him tell me."

"Anton has been tortured before," Mercer said, voice grim.

"You should know," Anton told him with a sly glance Mercer's way. "I won't break."

This had to stop. "Take me. Take Drew. Take us both to the place where you have his sisters. As soon as Drew gets them…y-you can kill me." *Or, a much, much better option—we'll find another way out of this mess by then.*

Mercer grabbed Tina's wrist once more. "You're done here."

No, she wasn't. She kept talking and focusing on Anton. "You have men close by, you have to. A guy like you wouldn't leave anything to chance." She ignored the burn in her chest and spoke even faster as she said, "You knew Agent Lancaster wouldn't just kill me without making sure his sisters were safe. You wanted an exchange—so here's one. Get your men to come in. Take us to the women. Then, I'll—"

"Die?" Anton finished.

"No," Mercer snarled.

"I'll trade my life for theirs," Tina said.

Anton smiled. "I was wondering when someone would finally see reason."

She didn't think this man had seen reason in a very, very long time.

Anton's lips pursed as he seemed to think about her offer. The silence and the tension stretched in the little room until—

"Mercer stays with me," Anton finally said as he inclined his head. "Every minute. I want to see his face when he learns of your death."

He was going to take her offer.

"You and your agent there… I'll tell you exactly where to go. My men don't need to take you there. They'll just be *waiting* for you to arrive."

No, more like waiting for them to walk into a trap, but Tina stayed quiet. He was talking, and that was what she'd wanted him to do.

"They're hidden in a Mardi Gras float graveyard in New Orleans." He rattled off the address easily, almost as if it didn't matter. "You'll find it near the river. Get down there, and only *you two* go in. The place is wired, and if more agents show, my men have orders to detonate. They'll kill the women in an instant."

Tina forced herself to speak through numb lips. "We can't get down there fast enough. The time you gave us—"

He laughed. "Bring me a phone. Mercer's phone will do nicely. I'll tell the men to keep them alive, until you get there."

We can't believe anything he says.

"Remember, dear, only you and your agent Lancaster are to go in. Try to send in any cops or other agents first and you'll watch the world explode."

DREW DRAGGED TINA out of the interrogation room. His hold was too hard, too rough, but he couldn't let her go.

He pushed her into the first empty office that he found. His glare made sure no one followed them inside. He slammed the door. Rounded on her. "What the hell are you doing?"

Her cheeks were flushed. Her eyes glittered up at him. "Saving your family."

"By sacrificing yourself?" He wanted to shake her. He wanted to *kill* Anton Devast.

"I'm not going to die." She said the words with total confidence. "We just bought time, and we'll be able to figure this out."

Oh, damn it, that trust again. She had to stop seeing him through rose-colored glasses. *See me for what I am.* "We go in that building, we find them—and we are going to face off against at least a dozen of Anton's men. They aren't just going to let me grab my sisters and walk away. They're going to try to take *you*."

"That's why we will have backup. Anton said that other

agents couldn't go in first. They can be there, though, waiting for the perfect moment to attack—"

She didn't understand. Tina hadn't lived her life, day in and day out, with evil. She wasn't getting the way that men like Anton Devast operated. "The minute we walk in that door, he could order the explosion. End us all in one instant. Backup won't do any good then. There will only be pieces left of us."

Tina flinched.

I'm hurting her. He immediately dropped his hold. Stepped back.

"It's not much of a plan," Tina said, voice soft. "But it's the only one I had. Now we know where your sisters are. We have their location. We can get them out."

And all I have to do is trade your life for theirs.

"You're not even his daughter." He'd go back in there. Tell Devast the truth—

"That doesn't matter anymore." Then she laughed, and it was a bitter sound, so unlike anything he'd ever heard from Tina. "Actually, maybe the lie is the only thing that *does* matter at this point. Because if Anton thought I wasn't Mercer's real daughter, then your sisters *would* be dead. He wants us in New Orleans. He wants us in that building, and as long as we are still alive—we have a chance."

He hated this. "I don't want you at risk."

She walked toward him and closed the space he'd created. Tina touched his cheek. Her fingers were light against that rough scar. She'd never minded his scars.

I can't let her die.

But he couldn't stand aside and let his sisters suffer.

"We won't go in unarmed. We'll get hooked up to EOD surveillance. Mercer and his men can watch our every step. Sharpshooters can be placed around the building." She was speaking so quickly now, her words tumbled together.

"They can learn the locations of Anton's men from us. They can give us backup. We *can* do this."

He pulled her against his body. Put his mouth on hers. Kissed her—hard and deep and desperately.

She was trying to be so confident, but she was wrong. He'd been on so many missions that had gone to hell without warning. You couldn't predict every moment. Could never plan for every contingency.

They were taking the bait Anton offered, but were both of them coming out alive?

It was a long shot.

"I trust you," Tina whispered against his mouth. "We can do this."

She shouldn't trust him. Drew put his forehead against hers. "I don't want to lose you."

"You won't."

No, he wouldn't let her die.

But I still might lose her.

The door opened behind her. Mercer stood there, filling the doorway. "This is a suicide mission." His voice was grim. The lines on his face were deeper than Drew had ever seen them.

Tina turned in Drew's arms so that she could face the director. "It's only suicide if we don't come back." Her shoulders brushed against Drew's chest. "We will."

Mercer swallowed. His Adam's apple bobbed. "I never wanted this for you. If your father were here, he'd—"

"My father was a brave man. He wouldn't leave three innocent women to die."

Mercer advanced into the room. "You're innocent."

"They're Drew's sisters." Her voice broke.

Drew's own heart squeezed. She was risking everything—*for him.*

"You're a lot like your father," Mercer whispered. "He

was always so damned proud of you." Mercer straightened his shoulders. His gaze turned to Drew. "I know you'd prefer for your own team to have your back on this one, Lancaster, but Mancini is recovering in the hospital right now. She's out, but Dylan is on his way to the airport. Two other EOD agents—Gunner Ortez and Logan Quinn—will meet you in New Orleans. Gunner is the best damn sharpshooter I have. I want his eyes on that building at all times. On *you*."

Gunner Ortez was Sydney's husband. Drew knew first-hand just how deadly a duo Gunner and Logan Quinn could be. He'd admired their work before—and seen them in ruthless action.

"More personnel will be on the ground," Mercer added. "I'll wire you both. At the first sign that this plan is compromised, you use the code word to call in the troops. Understand? Don't hesitate to call us in."

Drew nodded, but as far as he was concerned the plan had already gone to hell.

"What's the code word?" Tina whispered. Her body trembled against Drew's.

"Escape."

MERCER STARED THROUGH the observation glass. Devast thought he had them dancing on his string.

He was wrong.

Mercer glanced over at Cooper Marshall. "You have your orders."

Only Drew and Tina going into that warehouse? *Hell, no.*

He wasn't about to lose them.

Mercer stared at Anton as he spoke. "Disable the bombs. Take out the suspects. You'll have your own team in place. Use any means necessary." He pulled in a deep breath. "Get the civilians out and make sure that Dr. Jamison comes back alive."

"Yes, sir."

Anton continued to sit there, cuffed but smug.

He wants to look into my eyes when my daughter dies.

The same way that the bastard had been looking into Mercer's eyes when he'd found out that Marguerite was dead. Anton had pretended sympathy then.

There was no pretense any longer.

Mercer checked his weapon. The end was coming— for Anton.

Chapter Ten

They'd gone back to New Orleans. It was strange to return to the city, especially since she'd been taken from this place days before.

"Full circle," Tina said softly as the plane landed.

Drew glanced over at her, his jaw set, his eyes grim.

She wanted to comfort him, but she didn't know how. She was doing the only thing that she could do.

Offer herself up in the deadly game.

When she left the plane, two agents were waiting to meet her. Tina instantly recognized Gunner Ortez and Logan Quinn. Gunner was married to Tina's close friend, Sydney. Normally, Gunner hung back from Tina—from most people, actually. He was the tall, dark and deadly quiet kind of guy. But when he saw Tina leave that tarmac, he pulled her into his arms.

"Nothing will happen to you," he promised against her ear. "If you come out of this mission with so much as a bruise, Syd will have my hide."

A choked laugh escaped her. Tears stung her eyes. "Thank you, Gunner."

His words had been so low that only she could hear them.

"I'll have a lock on you," he told her, pulling back a bit

so he could study her with his steady and determined gaze, "every step of the way."

That was good. She blinked away the tears. Then Tina quickly followed the agents into the hanger. She was wired, hooked up and given a bulletproof vest in mere moments.

She'd worn a bulletproof vest before, during the few times she'd gone into the field. The weight should have reassured her. It didn't.

A knife was slipped into the sheath that had been attached to her ankle. Now she matched Drew. The agents even gave her a gun. Finally.

"They'll probably take the weapons from you as soon as you go inside," Logan Quinn told her. *So much for the gun.* "But they won't be aware of *everything* that you and Drew have."

Because Drew had being loaded down with weapons. Multiple guns. Knives.

She was given backup weapons, too. Now if only she'd had the training to go with them, then she'd be a serious threat.

"Just point and shoot," Logan told her, staring her dead in the eyes. Logan Quinn—Alpha One. He was the team leader of a group of EOD operatives known as the Shadow Agents. In combat, he was lethal. "If they're coming at you, they're coming to kill. You don't hesitate."

Tina nodded. She wished she could have a few minutes alone with Drew.

Time to tell him goodbye.

His shoulders were straight. His spine up. Fear had to be twisting through him, but he showed no emotion on his face or in his voice.

He was barking orders. Checking equipment.

How could he be so calm?

"If you don't compartmentalize," Gunner said from her

side, "then you're no good in the field. You have to be able to turn the emotions off."

That was exactly what Drew was doing.

She couldn't do the same. She looked at Drew and she hurt.

She didn't want this for him.

She wanted his family whole. Wanted him happy.

Because I love him.

Too fast? Too sudden? She'd known him for several years. Fantasized about him for nearly that whole time. Then when they'd been thrown into close quarters, the reality of the man had far exceeded any of her expectations.

She'd never forget dancing with him in that little room above the Texas bar. He'd let her slide past his guard in those precious moments; she knew that he had.

Logan's phone rang. He stepped aside.

Gunner turned away.

Tina reached for Drew. "I— Can we talk?"

His gaze collided with hers. "I flew you out of this city just nights ago."

She nodded. "I was terrified then."

In that emotionless voice he said, "I was furious. I wanted to destroy those men because they'd hurt you." He paused. "I *did* destroy them."

There was such a dark, dangerous intensity clinging to him. Drew was dressed all in black, and he seemed to be a part of the shadows.

"When I saw you on the rooftop," Tina told him, "I knew that I'd be okay."

His lips thinned. "Stop having so much faith in me."

"I can't." This was the part he needed to understand. "And I need you to have the same faith in me. I won't let you down, Drew. I can do this."

His eyelids flickered. "What if you have another attack?

What if they grab you and put a gun to your head? Are you going to be able to 'do this' when they're ready to shoot a bullet into your brain?"

Tina swallowed. Not such a nice visual. "I'll do anything necessary."

"Now you sound like Mercer." But his hand had lifted. Curled around her shoulder. "I don't want you doing anything necessary. I want you saving lives. I want you *safe.*" He shook his head. "I should have known, though. It seems like everything I touch gets destroyed."

"You don't destroy me." He made her stronger. He made her—

"We've confirmed the location," Logan said as he strode toward them.

Drew's hand tightened.

"We'll make sure there are no civilians nearby," Gunner assured them. "We'll clear the area, damn quietly."

Because if the building exploded, they didn't want civilians getting hurt.

"Time to roll," Logan said.

Tina nodded.

Logan added, "Dylan Foxx is going to meet us on scene. We'll surround the building and make sure we're ready to advance on your command, Drew."

Drew stepped back. He wasn't looking at Logan. His focus seemed to be just for Tina. "You're getting out of this alive, Doc."

Tina grabbed his hands. "So are you."

But he didn't answer her, and a chill encased Tina's heart.

THE TWO-STORY BRICK building waited at the end of the street. A tall, chain-link fence, topped with barbed wire, circled the property.

Four cars were parked outside the building. Two SUVs. Two vans.

One man stood at the main door. Even from a distance, Drew had no trouble seeing the bulge of his weapon.

"Got a man at the back door," Gunner said into Drew's earpiece. "And one canvassing the east side."

"And the west," came Logan's voice. They were all linked, but the transmitter in Drew's ear was so small the enemy shouldn't be able see it, not until it was too late.

Drew climbed from the rental car. He walked around the vehicle and opened Tina's door. When she stepped out, the sunlight glinted off her glasses. Her dark hair brushed over her cheek. She was pale, but her eyes were determined.

She was risking everything for his family.

"Doc, you are the most incredible woman I've ever met."

She blinked and looked a little lost as a furrow appeared between her eyes.

He leaned in close. Put his mouth to her ear. "And I will damn well die before I let them hurt you."

They needed to be clear on that.

His life, not hers.

Never her.

Their hands locked. Together, they approached the building.

The man at the door tensed. He lifted his weapon and aimed it right at Drew.

"I'm Agent Lancaster, and I think you were waiting on me." He paused. "On us. For a trade."

Gunner would have his sites locked on that guy right then. If the fellow moved to fire, all bets were off. Gunner would take him out, and the agents lying in wait around the property would swarm.

But the man didn't fire. Instead, he approached the gate. He fumbled and undid the padlock and let Drew and Tina inside. Then they headed for the door. The wood groaned as it opened. The building was dark and quiet inside.

And Drew could smell blood.

Paige.

He didn't rush forward, though. Because his gaze had slid to the left. He saw the bomb that was planted there, just a few feet from the entrance.

"Well, well, well…" a familiar voice called out. "If it isn't….*Stone*…coming back into the family once more."

Hell. Drew focused to the right. The man walking from the shadows had bright blond hair. Angry brown eyes. And a knife in his hand.

Carl Monroe.

He'd been hiding just behind one of the bigger parade floats that filled the large warehouse.

"Figured I'd be seeing you again," Carl said. His gaze slid eagerly toward Tina. "I was sure hopin' that I'd be seeing you both again."

"THEY'RE IN THE building," Mercer said as he glared at Anton. He shoved his phone across the table. He'd uncuffed Anton's right wrist. "Now make the call. Get your men on the line. Tell them to release Agent Lancaster's sisters. If those women aren't out in the next sixty seconds…"

Anton laughed and reached for the phone. "I don't care about his sisters. I never did. They were just the means to an end." His eyes narrowed on Mercer. "Your end."

Mercer held his gaze. "Make. The. Call."

Anton punched in numbers. He smirked. The phone was answered on the second ring. "Carl?" Anton said. "Are Lancaster and the girl standing right in front of you?"

Mercer leaned toward Anton.

"Good. Good. Now listen carefully. Let the agent's sisters go…."

TWO MEN HAD come up behind Drew and Tina and taken their weapons. Most of them. Drew figured he still had about three blades left on him. They should have done a better job of searching them.

Carl's phone rang. The man answered it, then called out, "Bring the women."

Drew stopped breathing. From the back of the building, he heard the sound of footsteps. Shuffling. Slow. He craned to see, but the floats were in his way. One was a massive green dragon with flames coming from its mouth. Another was a mermaid, her tail crashing into faded blue waves.

But then…then they appeared.

He saw Paige first. Blood trickled down her cheek. So did tears. Helpless to stop himself, he took a step toward her.

And Drew found his own gun shoved at his temple. "That's not the way this works," Carl snapped. One of Carl's hands still held the phone. The other held the gun.

"Tell your sisters that you love them, *Stone,* and then they can walk away."

Kim and Heather were behind Paige. They looked scared, but unharmed.

"Drew?" Paige whispered as more tears slid down her cheeks. "What's happening?" Pretty little Paige. She looked just like their mother. That long, blond hair. The big, blue eyes.

Drew looked like their father. A constant reminder of the man who'd left them. Who'd let them all down.

"You're going to be safe." His voice was cold and flat. The rage was buried as deep inside as it could go. "Just walk out through the front door, go past that fence and you'll be fine."

But Paige shook her head. "You're coming, too?"

No. He wasn't leaving. Not yet.

"The agent doesn't go, honey," Carl cut in. "Not yet."

"I'm not leaving you—" Paige began.

"Then you can die." Carl motioned toward one of his men. The man lifted his gun.

"No!" Tina screamed. "That wasn't the deal. You can't kill them!" She'd rushed toward Drew's sisters. And she put herself right in front of the gun. "Let them go. Let them walk out of here."

Her chest was heaving. Her voice trembling. Fear brightened her eyes and flushed her cheeks.

She was the most beautiful thing Drew had ever seen.

Carl smiled. "Right. You're the one we want…" He waved toward the door. "Go," he said to Paige and the others. "Before you're dead on the floor."

Kim and Heather dragged Paige toward the door. When they crossed the threshold, when they were clear outside, Drew exhaled slowly.

Alive.

He knew that Dylan, Gunner and Logan would make sure they stayed that way.

The door closed behind them.

"Now it's your turn," Carl said. He took a step back from Drew. What? The better to aim?

Drew kept his muscles loose. His legs were braced apart, his hands at his sides. He'd attack as soon as the moment was right.

Carl backed up. One step. Another. Then he had his gun at Tina's head.

"All right, boss," Carl said into the phone. "Are you ready for me to pull the trigger?"

ANTON STARED INTO Mercer's eyes. How long had he waited for this moment? And it was everything that he'd hoped it would be.

"Tell your man to stand down," Mercer ordered him.

As if Mercer had the power to give him orders.

"Is the agent still there?" Anton asked softly. "Can he see Tina Jamison very clearly?" Because the agent would need a good, up-close view of what was coming.

"Yes," Carl replied.

Carl. Such a useful man. They both shared a love of pain. This would be a wonderful moment. "Don't pull the trigger, Carl."

He saw Mercer's shoulders relax. Some of the tension slipped from Mercer's face. "I knew you could do the right thing," Mercer said. "I knew—"

You knew nothing. "Use your knife on her instead," Anton told him quickly. "Make her hurt, make it last, make her suf—"

"No!" The door to the interrogation room flew open. Mercer whirled around.

A beautiful blonde stood in the doorway. Her eyes were bright, angry; they were—*Marguerite's eyes.*

"Get out!" Mercer barked at her. A tall, dark-haired man stood just behind the woman. His face was granite-hard. "Agent, I'm giving you an order." Mercer tried to push her away.

The man—the agent—pushed Mercer right back. "She wants to be here. I wasn't going to keep the truth from her."

"Damn it," Mercer swore, his voice a growl. "I told you—"

"I had the wrong woman." Anton barely breathed the words. He couldn't take his gaze off the blonde. He could *see* Marguerite in her.

The sight was almost painful.

Mercer stormed toward Anton. "You're dying. You think

I don't know about the cancer eating you up again? How much time do you have left? Weeks? Days?" He shoved the phone at Anton. "You tell your man to stand down. Tell him not to hurt a hair on Tina Jamison's head."

"She wasn't your daughter." He had to give Mercer credit. He'd outsmarted him damn well. Led him down the wrong trail all along.

The blonde came fully into the interrogation room. Her guard—the agent had to be her bodyguard—shut the door behind her.

"I'm Mercer's daughter. The woman you're trying to kill just got caught in the cross fire." Her gaze was steady, direct. "She's not of any use to you now. Let her go."

"Boss? *Boss?*" Carl demanded, his voice cracking from the phone.

"I won't be able to kill you," Anton said as he realized the truth. There just wasn't enough time left. "But it's okay. I wanted him to suffer, as I suffered…" He forced his gaze off Marguerite.

No, she's not Marguerite.

He didn't know her name. Right then, he didn't want to know.

"You will suffer, Mercer, because that woman down in New Orleans might not be your blood, but I heard the emotion in your voice when you talked to her. Sometimes, it's not just blood that makes a family, is it?" He didn't even feel the pain in his chest anymore. The pain that had eaten at him for so long. This was his moment. "Go ahead, Carl," he ordered as he raised his voice so the man would hear him. "Kill her."

"No!" the blonde screamed.

She was too late.

There was no going back now.

CARL SMILED. He tossed aside his phone. "I've got my orders. She's gonna die. I'll cut her, again and again, and she's gonna scream for me."

Tina wasn't making a sound right then.

"The hell she is," Drew snarled at the bastard.

Footsteps shuffled behind him. He tensed. Two men, armed. Were they coming to kill him? *Let's see you try.*

"They can take you outside," Carl said, surprising him, "or you can die right here with her."

Why were they trying to make him leave? That didn't make sense. Anton Devast was a sadistic freak. He would want to take out everyone in his path.

So why free my sisters? Why try to let me go?

This scene wasn't adding up to Drew.

Rough hands grabbed his arms and hauled him back.

Tina still wasn't speaking. She was just watching him with those wide, resolute eyes of hers.

That knife was so close to her throat. If he fought the two men right then, in front of Carl, the SOB could slit her throat while he watched.

No, he couldn't risk it. He had to pick a better moment to attack. *Hold on, Tina. I'll get you out of here.*

That was what he tried to tell her with his stare, but what he said was, "Goodbye, Doc."

She blinked back tears.

They pulled him away. Shoved him toward the door.

When he tried to turn back, the taller man put a gun to Drew's head. "Now walk away, hero. Don't look back. Just go."

Was Carl already using his blade on Tina? He didn't hear a sound coming from her.

"There's going to be no escape for you two," Drew said, deliberately using the code word because he wanted the

EOD agents to swarm. "You won't be able to just walk out of here. You have to know that's not going to happen."

But the men just smirked at him. "Who said anything about walking?"

Drew was directly in front of the main entrance. A few more steps and he'd be out of the building.

Only, he didn't plan to leave.

"Why just follow orders?" he demanded even as he palmed the small blade he'd tucked beneath his belt. *You missed that one on your weapons search.* "Why let Devast use you? He's going to make sure you all die, too. Don't you realize that?"

But the men started laughing. Drew's hold on his weapon tightened.

"You don't really think we're letting you all go, do you?" the taller guy demanded.

"Ten, nine, eight…" his sidekick began.

Drew tensed. "What the—?"

"Your sisters were wired, *Agent* Lancaster. Hell, I don't think they even knew those collars we snapped around their necks were set to blow—"

Drew spun for the door. He rushed outside.

"The EOD agents got them, right? Those guys who are surrounding us? Guess they'll all go boom soon enough."

"Three…two…"

An explosion erupted, shaking the ground and sending Drew flying.

TINA SCREAMED WHEN she heard the explosion.

The knife sliced the side of her neck.

"That will keep those agents busy." Carl smiled at her. "I'm supposed to take my time with you, so let's go, honey. Let's go enjoy ourselves."

More men rushed inside. They all headed to the back of the building. Carl was trying to haul her that way, too.

More explosions erupted, only this time they were *in* the building. The detonations seemed to come one right after the other. Devast's men were destroying everything—and making it impossible for anyone to follow them as they fled through the float graveyard.

Chunks of the old floats flew into the air. A dragon's papier-mâché head ignited a few feet from her.

"You think Devast didn't plan this end?" Carl jerked her head back with a painful grip on her hair. "He made sure we could escape—and that we'd take you with us. Mercer will be getting pieces of you sent to him for weeks."

They were sick. "I'm not…going…" The smoke was rising. Filling her lungs.

Breathe.

They'd taken her inhaler. When they'd searched her at the door, they'd taken her weapons and her medicine.

The smoke made her eyes burn. The flames heated her skin.

The men kicked open the back door. Fresh air blew inside and she tried to take deep, greedy gulps.

But then gunfire erupted. The *rat-a-tat* sent the men scrambling back inside the building. Tina tried to duck for cover, but Carl wasn't letting her go.

The back door swung open. A man raced inside. His blond hair gleamed in the faint light. He wore black, and she could see the bulky outline of his bulletproof vest. He had a gun in each hand, and his bullets hit with deadly accuracy, slamming into the men who'd thought they'd had an easy escape.

With the EOD, nothing was ever easy. Devast had underestimated his opponents.

"Stop!" Carl yelled. Tina was in front of him. His human shield. "Throw down your weapons and get back or she *dies!*"

But the man shook his head. He lifted his guns. Seemed to be aiming—

At me? Yes, he was.

"You aren't getting away. The EOD doesn't negotiate with terrorists." She didn't recognize the agent's unaccented voice, but she sure recognized Mercer's familiar line.

He's going to shoot me. To take out Carl, she realized the agent would need to get rid of Carl's protection. Tina braced for the pain.

Before another gunshot erupted, someone slammed into them. She and Carl both hit the ground with an impact hard enough to crack bones. Tina was pretty sure she *did* hear one of Carl's bones break, and that savage sound made her heart race faster. The knife had sliced over her collarbone when she fell, and more blood soaked her shirt as Tina rolled away from her attacker.

She pushed up to her knees and saw—

Drew.

He'd come back. She'd known that he would. Happiness and hope fought inside her.

But…his expression was brutal. Wild. He was driving his fist into Carl's face again and again.

Carl's head slammed into the concrete, and he stopped moving.

"Come on!" It was the EOD agent. The one she didn't know. He was grabbing her arms and pulling her up to her feet. "My orders are to get you out of here!"

The flames were spreading. Would more bombs be detonating soon?

"The whole place is going to blow—it's their distraction. They thought they'd get away while the whole block burned."

His hold on her wrist was unbreakable.

Drew rose to his feet.

Tina tried to reach for him. "Drew! Come on!"

He looked up at her.

Her heart stopped.

Something was…wrong. Drew's eyes looked dead. His face was a mask of fury and rage—but his eyes were *dead*.

"Drew?"

Another detonation shook the building. Cracks ran across the remaining walls and chunks of the ceiling fell, narrowly missing them.

"They were timed to start right after Lancaster went out the door," the agent shouted. "Come on, we have to *move*."

Wait, Drew had gone out and then come back through that hell? He'd walked back into the flames?

Her breath heaved out as she fought to break the mysterious agent's hold and get back to Drew.

But the agent wasn't letting her go.

"Drew!" He seemed frozen. He needed to move.

Because Carl was moving again. Carl had just grabbed the knife from the floor. He wasn't unconscious; he'd just been waiting for his moment to attack. He lunged up and went straight for Drew's back.

"Behind you!" Tina screamed. The fire was crackling so loudly she wasn't sure he even heard her. "Drew!"

At the last moment he spun around. He grabbed Carl's hand, stopping that knife before it could shove into his body.

Drew twisted Carl's hand. Carl howled—she could hear the stark cry of pain rising over the flames—then Drew plunged the knife into Carl's chest.

This time, when he hit the ground, Carl wasn't pretending to be unconscious. He was dead.

"Have to do this…" the agent muttered as Tina kept struggling against him. She needed to get to Drew. "Orders…"

Forget orders.

Drew looked up then, staring at her with the eyes that weren't his.

He shook his head, as if waking up, then he ran toward her. Tina stopped fighting the other agent. She ran with him—and Drew.

The smoke was choking her, her lungs were burning, but she wasn't about to let the attack stop her. Not now, not when they were home free.

The fresh air was just steps away.

Steps—

"Bomb!" Drew yelled. "Above the back door. The timer's counting down—"

She could see it. The seconds were showing in a digital red flash. They only had four seconds. *Four.*

They raced outside. She couldn't pull in any breath. Her legs just kept going. *Escape.* That had been their code word. She just needed to—

When the last bomb detonated, the force tossed Tina as if she were a rag doll.

Chapter Eleven

Anton Devast inclined his head. "And then there was nothing left." He'd been watching the clock on the stark, white interrogation room wall. If Carl had followed his orders, if he'd stayed on the schedule Devast had made for the detonations, then the float graveyard had just blown up in New Orleans.

The whole block would be a wreck.

His chaos. His havoc.

Mercer had his phone out. He was pulling the pretty blonde from the room. Demanding to know the status—

The door shut behind Mercer.

Anton exhaled slowly. It wasn't the revenge he'd wanted.

But it would have to do.

"TINA!"

Drew wiped the blood from his eye as he leaped to his feet. His clothes were singed, blisters covered his arms and— *Where was Tina?*

She'd been in front of him before the last detonation. He'd tried to reach for her, but the blast had torn her away from him.

His gaze searched to the left. The right. Smoke billowed all around him. Tina couldn't stay in this smoke. It would hurt her.

Maybe that's why she wasn't calling back to him. Maybe she was having another attack. The smoke had set it off before, on that runway, and maybe—

"D-Drew…" Just a whisper; a strangled gasp that he heard above the flames.

That gasp was the sweetest sound to his ears. It meant that she was alive.

He ran to her, following that gasp. She was on the ground, struggling to sit up. He shoved his hand into the hidden pocket on his vest and pulled out her inhaler. "Easy, Doc, I've got you."

Always.

She took the inhaler. Her lashes lifted so that her eyes met his.

The fire was still spreading, surging higher and higher. Sirens wailed in the distance.

"I have to get you out of here." He scooped her up into his arms. It wasn't about a mission or priorities. He didn't think it ever had been. It was only about her.

Now, she truly was the only good thing left in his life.

He looked up. The other agent was there—the man who'd come up behind the building and taken out most of Devast's men. Cooper Marshall. Drew knew the guy by reputation, but had never worked with him. Cooper's blond hair stuck to his temples, slick with sweat. He had a gun in his left hand. "Get her out," Cooper barked. "I'll make sure we're clear."

And that no more of Devast's men had survived to attack again.

Drew held tight to Tina as he raced away from the scene. He'd gotten her out of that inferno. She was in his arms. *Safe.*

When he'd learned about his sisters—

No.

Drew immediately slammed the door on that thought. *Not now. Can't think of them now.* He was barely holding together as it was.

He had to protect Tina first.

Tina, then—

Paige had wanted to stay with me.

His back teeth ground together. His eyes burned.

His arms clung even harder to Tina. He kept running with her cradled against him. The smoke was so thick that he could barely see as he rushed forward.

She had her medicine. She was safe. Alive.

His sisters…

I'm so sorry. He'd failed them. Let them all down. They'd died, because of him.

The sirens were wailing. He could see the lights of an ambulance approaching.

Grief threatened to choke him, but Drew kept running toward that ambulance.

Police were on the scene now. Drew caught sight of Gunner and Logan. They were keeping the local authorities back.

They'd all have to stay back until they made sure there weren't any more bombs. The rescue teams would be held in a safe zone until the bomb squad completed their sweeps.

He had to make it to that zone.

Just a few more steps…

Made it.

The EMTs reached for Tina. They put her on a stretcher. She shoved their hands back. "Drew—"

"You're safe." Ash stained the hand that he slid over her cheek. "It's over."

His heart was leaden in his chest. His whole body seemed numb. He'd used his control in the field more times than he could count; locking his emotions away. But this was different—

My family is gone.

Tina grabbed his hand when he would have stepped back. "Wh-what…h-happened?"

The EMTs were trying to work on her, but she kept pushing them away and clinging to Drew.

"Your eyes…" Tina whispered. "They're wrong…some-thing…happened."

He didn't know what she meant about his eyes. Other than the fact that they kept burning as if they were on fire. Drew shook his head.

"T-tell me…"

His shoulders bowed. "They killed my sisters…" He should have known the exchange was too easy. His dark-ness, his job—it had cost Kim, Heather and Paige their lives.

"Drew!"

His head whipped up at that frantic call. That had—had just sounded like Paige.

"I can…see them," Tina said, voice husky. Her gaze slid over Drew's shoulder. "Not…dead."

He spun around.

Walking through the smoke, he saw Dylan—and his friend was right beside Paige, Kim and Heather.

Alive. All of them were *alive!*

Drew shook his head. No, no, the explosion—

Paige ran to him. She hit his chest so hard that he took a step back. She was crying and laughing and holding on to him as tightly as she could.

Drew's stunned gaze rose and met Dylan's.

"Devast used devices like those collars two years ago, back in Brazil." Dylan's lashes flickered. "Those vics didn't get free in time. I wasn't going to let the same thing happen again."

Then Kim and Heather were there. All holding him. All laughing and crying as the smoke drifted in the air.

The ambulance's siren wailed once more. He looked back. The ambulance's door had just slammed.

The EMTs were taking Tina away.

He tried to head toward the ambulance, but his sisters tightened their hold on him.

Drew needed to make them understand. "I have to—"

"I thought we were all going to die," Paige whispered as the tears slid silently down her cheeks. "Is this…is this what you do?"

"You risk your life like this, all the time?" Heather's face was stark, white. Fear lit her eyes.

He couldn't answer her. Families weren't supposed to know about the missions he faced.

Families also weren't supposed to be pulled into his battles.

"I'm sorry," he said, the words rough and rumbling from deep in his throat.

Dylan pressed his hand to Kim's shoulder. "We need to get you ladies to the hospital. We want you all checked out."

And the scene wasn't safe.

Tina's ambulance had left.

Another ambulance was waiting, its back doors open. The EMTs came forward to help his sisters.

Drew caught Dylan's arm. "Thank you."

Dylan inclined his head. "Man, you should know I always have your back."

He did.

The flames were burning, raging so brightly behind them. More havoc.

The group's name had come from the destruction they left behind.

Destruction and death.

Only this time there had been survivors, too. Innocent lives had been saved.

Devast wouldn't hurt anyone else.

No, you bastard, you didn't know my price.

And Devast never would.

SWEET OXYGEN FLOWED into Tina's lungs. The ambulance rolled and bounced as it raced from the scene.

Drew's sisters had been hugging him.

She swallowed.

They'd made it out alive. The mission was finally over.

Now it was time for her to go back to the life that waited for her.

Time for him to return to his life. His missions.

They'd see each other at the EOD.

She'd remember. How could she ever forget what they'd shared?

"Miss? Miss…are you hurting?"

A tear had dropped down her cheek. Tina shook her head. There wasn't anything the medics could do for the pain that she felt.

"WHERE THE HELL IS SHE?" Drew demanded as he slammed his hands down on the nurses' station desk.

"Sir, you need to calm down."

"What I need is to find the patient who was brought in! Dr. Tina Jamison! She came in by ambulance two hours ago."

Two of the longest hours of his life. He'd stayed on scene, needing to make sure the last arm of HAVOC was truly destroyed. He'd gone in on the bomb sweeps, checked all the nearby buildings to make sure they also weren't set to blow.

They'd used the bomb-sniffing dogs. Gone in and out—searching every possible area. They'd found two more bombs.

The bomb squad had disarmed them with seconds to spare.

Sweat coated Drew's body as he glared at the nurse in front of him. He'd been through hell, and he needed to see his damn angel. "Where is she?"

"We have no record of a Tina Jamison, sir. She didn't come in here. You must have the wrong hospital."

No, he didn't, and Drew was perilously close to tearing the place apart with his bare hands.

"They took her back to Dallas."

He stiffened at Gunner's voice. Drew glanced over his shoulder.

Gunner inclined his head to the right. "Come with me."

If Gunner was giving him information on Tina, then he'd go anyplace with the guy. His steps hurried, Drew followed Gunner to a quiet corner and, once he was sure no one could overhear him, he squared off against the sharpshooter. "Why wasn't I told about her transfer?"

"Because you were still on scene, defusing bombs." Gunner lifted a dark brow. "Your lady is all right. You can rest easy on that. Tina was stable when she boarded the flight."

Your lady... Gunner had always been observant. Drew nodded and tried to calm his racing heart. "You saw her then?"

"I did. Cooper was with her. Hell..." He ran a weary hand over his face as he muttered, "That guy is a ghost. I didn't even know he was working the Devast case until I saw him jump in the ambulance with her on scene."

Cooper had been in the ambulance?

"Seems Mercer gave him orders. Protect Dr. Jamison at all costs."

Drew stiffened. "Mercer didn't think I could do the job?"

Gunner's gaze was steady. "Mercer knows that when emotions get involved, even good agents can get compromised."

"I wouldn't have traded her safety for *anything*. I was going back in after her—"

"You dying for her wouldn't have saved her life. And we both know that was exactly what you planned to do." Flat, cold words.

True words. He would have traded his life for Tina in an instant. Drew didn't look away from Gunner's direct stare.

"Does she know?" Gunner asked quietly.

He had to get on a flight to Dallas. "Know what?"

Gunner laughed. The sound caught Drew off guard. As far as he knew, the guy never laughed.

But then, as far as the rest of the agents seemed to be concerned, Drew didn't feel, either.

Ice in my veins.

No, he had fire in his veins right then.

"Why don't you take some friendly advice from someone who's been where you are…?" Gunner's lips twisted in a wry smile. "Don't just stand back and let the thing you want the most slip away from you."

The fire burned ever hotter inside him. "But what if I'm not right for her? She needs someone—"

"Let her decide what she needs. Who she needs. Go for what *you* want." Then Gunner turned away from him. "I'm going home. My wife is waiting for me."

His wife. His very pregnant wife. Gunner had a wife who loved him—and twins on the way.

"How did you—?" Drew stopped.

Gunner glanced back at him.

"Weren't you afraid? That what we do… Weren't you scared that it would spill over on them?"

But, no, Gunner's wife, Sydney, she was part of the EOD. She'd worked for years in the field. She knew all about danger. "Never mind," Drew said, shaking his head. "I shouldn't have—"

"I was more afraid," Gunner admitted, voice low, "of trying to live my life without her."

Drew thought of his life. The missions. One after the other. Coming home.

Being alone.

He'd looked forward to his visits to the EOD office— *because I knew I would see Tina.*

Is that what he wanted to happen? Would he return to only seeing Tina every few months? He'd keep his emotions sealed off and try to go on with his life without her?

He'd watch life from the outside? Day in and day out, he'd long for what he couldn't have.

I told her there would be no going back. Because he didn't want to go back to a life that didn't involve Tina. He needed her far too much.

He walked down the corridor. His sisters were in a private room. Police guards made sure they weren't disturbed.

Paige had gotten stitches. Kim and Heather had been bruised, but otherwise unharmed. They'd been very, very lucky.

He stepped into the room with them. Shut the door behind him.

No one spoke at first. Drew realized that he didn't know what to say.

He hadn't been in a room with the three of them since—

"I miss you," Paige told him. A bandage was on her neck. On her arm. White bandages against her skin.

"We all miss you," Kim added in a soft tone.

Drew swallowed. *No ice.*

"Why don't you ever come home?" Heather asked him.

He didn't have a home. Not anymore.

Paige walked toward him. The baby. The kid sister. Did she know that he'd kept every letter she'd ever sent him?

"My life…" He stopped, cleared his throat and tried again. "I never wanted it to hurt you."

But it had. Their worlds had collided. "It was my fault that you were hurt. A very…dangerous man tracked the money I'd been sending to you."

Paige stood in front of him. "Is he going to come after us again?"

Drew shook his head.

Her pale lips curved. "We don't want your money, Drew. We just want you."

And he wanted them. He wanted his family back.

He wanted a *life*.

Not ice.

Maybe it was time to take the risk—and to take what he wanted most.

TINA WALKED SLOWLY down the hallway of the FBI's office in Dallas. Cooper Marshall was at her side. The guy seemed to be her constant shadow.

She was his mission—at least, for about five more feet, she was.

Tina stopped in front of Mercer's temporary headquarters. He'd commandeered the biggest office in the place. Figured. That was Mercer. Always making friends left and right.

"Thanks, Agent Marshall," Tina said. "I'm here, safe and sound."

Cooper inclined his head toward her. He didn't talk much. The agent sure seemed to be the quiet and intense type.

Once, Tina would have described Drew the exact same way. Except—

He seemed to talk plenty when they were together.

We aren't together any longer. The mission is over. So are we.

The door opened. Mercer stood there. "Dr. Jamison, come in…"

She stepped across the threshold.

Cooper started to follow.

"Sorry, son," Mercer said, sounding not the least bit actually sorry as he held up his hand to block Cooper, "but you don't have clearance for this."

Then he shut the door in Cooper's surprised face.

Tina took a few tentative steps inside the office. She glanced around the room and she instantly realized just why Cooper didn't have clearance.

Two other people were waiting in that office.

She knew the EOD Agent, Cale Lane. She'd patched him up a few times. And the other woman—the woman with the blond hair and the perfect face—that was Cassidy Sherridan.

Well…technically she was Cassidy Sherridan *Lane* now.

The blonde was Mercer's real daughter.

She was also rushing across the room and *hugging* Tina. "I'm so sorry," Cassidy told her, squeezing her tightly. "As soon as I found out, I came right away. I told Anton who I was."

"And I damn well told *you* to keep her away," Mercer growled to Cale.

"I'm not lying to my wife." Cale was resolute. Determined. Protective.

Cassidy pulled back a bit to study Tina. "I can't ever make this up to you."

Tina frowned at her and shook her head. "There's nothing to make up. You didn't do anything to me. It was all Anton." She glanced toward Mercer. His arms were crossed over his chest, but his gaze was on her—and it was worried. "Is his network contained? Is it over?"

"Yes."

Her shoulders slumped. "Then we saved lives. The risk was worth it."

"But you shouldn't have been risked," Cassidy whispered as she stepped back. "You should never have been in harm's way."

Tina had to smile at that. "And you should have been? We can't help who we are…or who we're not." She felt… different standing in that room with Mercer and Cassidy. Before the nightmare of her abduction, Tina had always been a bit in awe of Mercer and all the EOD agents.

And she'd been…afraid. Of so much. Of letting her weakness hurt others. Of being caught in the cross fire once more.

"I'm not weak," Tina said.

Mercer's eyes narrowed.

Cale stood beside Cassidy.

"Who the hell said you were?" Now anger lit Mercer's eyes. "If Lancaster—"

Tina shook her head. "I'm the one who thought it. Drew never said anything." She pushed her glasses—another replacement pair because she'd lost the others in the blast down in New Orleans—up a bit on her nose. "I've been hiding for a long time, and I don't want to do that anymore." She *wouldn't* stay in her labs. Wouldn't live through the actions of others.

It was time for her to seize her own adventures.

Only, maybe these new adventures wouldn't involve death and destruction.

"You let me hide," she said to Mercer because she'd seen through his mask.

His jaw hardened. "I wanted you safe."

Cassidy laughed softly. Sympathy flashed across her face. "Oh, Mercer…when you keep us safe, sometimes you keep us caged."

Tina didn't want to be caged anymore. Not by Mercer and not by her own fear.

The past couldn't haunt her, and she wouldn't spend her days afraid of what might come.

Mercer stared into Tina's eyes. "What about Lancaster?"

He always saw so much. "He did his job. It's over now."

There had never been any talk of a future from him. Never any talk of emotions.

Tina knew what she felt, but as for Drew…

Maybe I couldn't ever get past the ice.

It sure had felt as if she had, though. His torch had seemed to scorch right to her very soul.

Frantic pounding sounded on the door.

Mercer jerked his head. Cale immediately reached for Cassidy, and they slipped out a side door.

No wonder Mercer picked this office.

When they were clear, Mercer yanked open the main door. "I'm in a private meeting, what do you want?"

Cooper stood to the side. Two FBI agents—decked out in pressed suits—stared at Mercer with wide eyes.

"The prisoner is seizing, sir. We've called medical personnel but—"

"It could be a trick," Mercer snarled as he rushed past them.

Tina was right on his heels. There was only one "prisoner" who would have sparked this kind of reaction from Mercer.

They zigged and zagged through the halls. Then they were entering a small room that she hadn't seen before. No windows. Only one narrow door to gain entry into that place.

Anton Devast lay slumped on a narrow cot in the room. Two agents were with him, trying to turn his head so that he could breathe.

Anton's eyes widened when he caught sight of her. "Dead…"

No, she wasn't.

Tina fell to her knees next to him. His breath was jerking out, his heart—beating too slowly.

She stared at his skin, noting the blue tinges and the sunken lines around his eyes and mouth.

He tried to lift his hand to reach for her.

But he didn't have the strength.

His eyes flared. His lips trembled as he tried to speak. Only, he couldn't talk anymore. It was too late.

Anton Devast was still staring at Tina when he died.

IT WAS BACK to business as usual at the EOD.

Tina stepped into her lab, the white lab coat she wore a familiar comfort to her. After Devast's death, she'd been caught up in a whirlwind. A whirlwind controlled by Mercer. Before she'd barely blinked, she'd found herself back in D.C.

With, of course, Agent Cooper Marshall at her side.

She hadn't seen Drew again. Hadn't heard from him.

His sisters were safe, alive— She carried the image of them embracing him in her mind.

But Drew…he just seemed to be gone.

Had he already taken another mission? Gone out on another undercover assignment? Was he in the U.S.? Already halfway around the world?

She didn't know.

But Tina would find out.

Her hair was twisted into a small bun and her steps were sure as she searched around her lab. *Less than a week.* How could one life change so quickly?

Hers had, irrevocably, and there was no going back now.

She realized the full meaning of Drew's warning to her. When he'd said there would be no going back, she should have paid more attention. Her old life had vanished, destroyed in the heat of their passion.

Her new life seemed too cold. Too sterile and stark, without him.

I miss him.

The door squeaked open behind her.

"Be with you in a second," she said, throwing the words over her shoulder as she bent to peer into the low cabinet.

"Take your time," a slow, drawling voice told her, the smallest hint of Mississippi deepening those words. "I'm not going anywhere."

Drew.

She straightened slowly, then turned toward him. He stood just inside the doorway, his shoulder propped against the door frame. His eyes were on her.

And he was staring at her as if he could eat her alive.

Only fair, she was probably ogling him the same way.

"I missed you in New Orleans." He stepped away from the door. Locked it. "And in Dallas." He stalked toward her.

"Mercer wanted me to come back—"

"I'm not real interested in what Mercer wants."

Neither was she. Her gaze slid over him. Tall. Dark. Deadly. That was Drew. But his eyes—they were bright. They seemed to shine with emotion.

But Tina didn't know if she could trust what she was seeing in his gaze.

"Don't." He stopped in front of her.

"Don't what?" Why was her voice so husky?

"That's not the way you usually look at me."

She swallowed, not sure what he was talking about.

"Usually, you stare at me with trust. I look into your eyes, and I want to be the man you think I am."

He was.

She made herself ask, "How am I looking at you now?"

"Like you've lost faith in me." The faint lines near his mouth deepened. "Doc, *don't.* I've been tracking you. I've been steps behind you all the way home."

"I—I thought you might be on another mission."

He nodded. "I am. The most important mission of my life."

Oh, right. Now she understood. Another mission meant he had to be medically cleared for the field. She cleared her throat. "In light of what's…happened…another doctor here can—"

"I don't want another doctor." His hands wrapped around her waist and he lifted her up. He sat her on the exam table. Put them eye-to-eye and leaned in real close to her. "You're the one I want. The *only* one I want."

"Drew—"

He kissed her.

Kissed her with passion, with need, with raw lust.

Kissed her as if he were desperate.

Kissed her as if she were his life.

She kissed him back just as fiercely. Her arms curled around his neck and she pulled him tightly to her.

She didn't care where they were. She had him in her arms again, and she'd take this moment while she could.

It was her new philosophy. Grab life. Hold on tight.

She was sure holding tight to him.

When he licked her bottom lip, a delicious shudder slid over her.

"I love you."

It took a minute for his growled words to sink in. When they did, Tina shook her head.

He pulled back, just a few inches, and his golden stare held hers. "I. Love. You."

"You don't have to say—"

"The truth? Yeah, Doc, I do." He brushed back a lock of hair that had escaped from her bun. "I wanted to tell you in New Orleans. I wanted to tell you in Dallas. Hell, I even wanted to tell you in Lightning."

What? No, he could not have just said that.

"I haven't loved another woman, haven't gotten close to anyone, the way I have with you." His fingers curled under her jaw. "You slipped right past my walls. Made me want things…things I never thought I *could* have."

If this was a dream, she had better not ever wake up. "You can have anything."

He smiled at her. "You're what I want."

Her tall, dark and deadly agent was staring straight at her—and looking at Tina as if she was his world.

"I know you don't love me," he said, and he spoke those words with a determined pride that made her heart ache, "but give me a chance. That's all I'm asking for. A chance to show you that we can be good together. No bombs. No danger. No threats. Just you and me. Give me the time to—"

"No." That one word sent silence through the room.

His hand slid away from her. He swallowed. The soft sound was almost painful to hear. "Then I won't push you anymore. I'm sorry. I—I guess I should have let you go."

Never.

She grabbed his arm when he tried to ease away. The new stitches that she had on her neck—courtesy of that jerk Carl—pulled a bit. Tina ignored the little flash of pain. Some things were more important than pain. "I don't need to take any kind of chance on you. I *know* that I love you."

He blinked at her.

Ah, so she'd finally caught her agent by surprise. Only fair. He'd sure broken into her world and turned everything upside down.

"I loved you in New Orleans," she told him softly. His pupils widened. The darkness fought the gold of his eyes. "I loved you in Dallas." She smiled at him and hoped that he could see the emotion in her eyes. "And I loved you in Lightning." She'd tried to tell him, to show him, in a million small ways.

Tina leaned forward and brushed her lips over his. She reached around him, her hands sliding over his coat.

She frowned when she felt the small bulge in his pocket.

Her brows lifted as her fingers slid inside that pocket. She touched the familiar form of an inhaler.

"I want you to always be safe," he whispered. "I want you close to me, and I want to make sure I can help you."

"You've been carrying this—"

"Since I found out what you needed. I want to be the man you need. The man who makes you smile in the morning." A wicked glint lit his eyes. "The man who makes you moan at night."

"You are." Her heart was beating faster—because she was happy. The happiest she'd been in years.

It wasn't about taking a chance on him. Wasn't about the unknown risk of falling for a dangerous agent.

It was about what the heart wanted.

About trust.

About love.

"My sisters want to meet you," he said as his lips lowered toward hers. "They want to meet the woman who saved them."

"But I didn't—"

"Yes, you did. Doc, you're the bravest, strongest woman I've ever met. And I don't know how I got so lucky as to find you, but I don't ever want to let you go."

She tilted her head back. "You don't have to let me go." Fair warning time. "Because I'm not going to let you go."

"Forever?" Hope was there, in his eyes. Hope and love and happiness.

In his eyes. In his voice. On his face.

"Forever," Tina promised. She kissed him and knew that she'd found the right man. The only man for her.

Epilogue

Bruce Mercer gazed down at the busy Washington, D.C., streets below his office. The sidewalks were full of people, and cars bustled on the pavement.

Those people lived their whole lives without realizing the danger that truly stalked the world. The danger his agents faced every single day.

"The last case was too close," he said quietly. He'd almost lost Tina, *and* Cassidy's true identity had nearly come to light.

Good thing only a dead man had heard Cassidy's confession.

Devast had gotten intel that the man *never* should have possessed. The EOD tracking devices had been designed to protect the agents.

Not put them at increased risk.

Devast was dead, but the case wasn't over. Not completely. There was a traitor in the EOD. Someone in his organization was selling out agents who were already risking their lives.

That traitor would have to be stopped.

Mercer turned away from the busy street and gazed at the agent who sat, silent and still, in the leather chair. "It was close, but you did a good job on this mission, Agent Marshall."

Cooper Marshall inclined his head.

"Now I've got another case for you." Bruce stalked slowly toward him. "I want you to find my traitor, and I want you to stop him."

Cooper gazed up at him for a moment. "You're sure it's one of our own?"

"Yes." And that just made the betrayal even harder to take. "Trust no one on this case, Marshall. A man—or woman—who will sell out his own teammates—that person will be the most dangerous enemy you've ever faced."

And that enemy was *in* the EOD. He or she could be walking through the offices right then.

Mercer had thought he'd already cleaned house at the EOD. Every employee there *should* have been carefully screened.

But he'd messed up. He'd trusted the wrong person, and now his agents were paying for his mistake.

They can't pay with their lives.

"Stop the traitor," Mercer ordered him again. "By any means necessary."

* * * * *

Read on for a special sneak peek of
THE GIRL NEXT DOOR,
the next installment of the
SHADOW AGENTS: GUTS & GLORY *miniseries,*
coming from Intrigue March 2014!

Chapter One

Cooper Marshall burst into the apartment, his gun ready even as his gaze swept the dim interior of the room that waited for him. "Lockwood!"

There was no response to his call, but the stench in the air—that unmistakable odor of death and blood—told Cooper he'd arrived too late.

Again.

Damn it.

He'd gotten his orders from the top. He'd been assigned to track down Keith Lockwood, an ex-Elite Operations Division agent. Cooper was supposed to confirm that the other man was alive and well. He'd fallen off the EOD's radar, and that had sure raised a red flag in the mind of Cooper's boss.

Especially since other EOD agents had recently turned up dead.

Cooper rounded a corner in the narrow hallway. The scent of blood was stronger. He headed toward what he suspected was the bedroom. His eyes had already adjusted to the darkness, so it was easy for him to see the body slumped on the floor just a few feet from him.

He knelt, and his gloved fingers turned the body just slightly. Cooper pulled out his penlight and shone it on the dead man's face.

Keith Lockwood. Cooper had never worked with the man on a mission, but he'd seen Lockwood's photos.

Lockwood's throat had been slit. An up-close kill.

Considering that Lockwood was a former navy SEAL, the man shouldn't have been caught off guard.

But he had been.

Because the killer isn't your average thug off the streets.

The killer was also an agent with the EOD, and the killer was trained just as well as Lockwood had been.

No, trained *better*.

Because the killer had been able to get the drop on the SEAL.

Cooper's breath eased out in a rough sigh just as a knock sounded on the front door.

The front door that Cooper had just smashed open moments before.

He leaped to his feet.

"Mr. Lockwood?" a feminine voice called out. "Mr. Lockwood...i-is everything all right?"

No, things were far from *all right*. The broken door *should* have been a dead giveaway on that point.

"It's Gabrielle Harper!" the voice continued. "We were supposed to meet..."

His back teeth clenched. Talk about extremely bad timing. He knew Gabrielle Harper, and the trouble the woman was about to bring his way just was going to make the situation even more of a tangled mess.

Cooper holstered his weapon. He had to get out of that apartment. *Before* Gabrielle saw him and asked questions he couldn't answer for her.

He rose and stalked toward the bedroom window. His footsteps were silent. After all of his training, they should be.

Gabrielle's steps—and her high heels—tapped across the hardwood floor as she came inside the apartment.

Of course, Gabrielle wasn't just going to wait outside. She was a reporter, no doubt on the scent of a story.

And she must have scented the blood.

She was following that scent, and if he didn't move, fast, she'd follow it straight to him.

Cooper opened the window, then glanced down below. Three floors up. But there were bricks on the side of the building, with crevices in between them. If he held on just right, he could spider crawl his way down.

The floor in the hallway creaked as Gabrielle paused.

She should have called for help by now. At the first sign of that smashed door, Gabrielle should have dialed 9-1-1. But, with Gabrielle, what she *should* do and what she actually *did*—well, those could be very different things.

If she wasn't careful, the woman was going to walk into real danger one day. The kind she wouldn't be able to walk away from.

He slid through the window. Since it was after midnight, Cooper knew he'd be able to blend pretty easily with the darkness when he climbed down the backside of the building.

He'd make it out of there, undetected, provided he didn't fall and break his neck.

He eased to the side, his feet resting against the window's narrow ledge. He pulled the window back down and took a deep breath.

"Mr. Lockwood!" Gabrielle's horror-filled scream broke loud and clearly through the night.

She'd found the body.

Jaw locking, Cooper made his way down the building.

Gabrielle had just stumbled into an extremely dangerous situation. Now he'd have to do some serious recon to keep her out of the cross fire.

"I'm going to stay with you tonight."

She straightened. "You will not."

"Yes, I will. At least until we find out who was asking about you yesterday."

"Jake, you cannot stay at my house. What will people think?"

"Since when do you care what people think?" The woman he'd known before had made a point of flouting public opinion.

"Since I moved to a small town where everyone knows me. I'm a schoolteacher, for God's sake. I have a reputation to protect."

"So you're telling me nobody here sleeps with anybody else unless they're lawfully married?"

"I'm sure they do, but they're discreet about it."

"So we'll be discreet. Besides, I never said I was going to sleep with you—unless that's what you want..."

She straightened. "No, you're not."

ROCKY MOUNTAIN REVENGE

BY
CINDI MYERS

The text is word for word the same as the original and intended for general reading and reference purposes only. It does not replace or serve as the equivalent to the original version of this text, or under any circumstances to, any adverse or litigious events or incidents. This requirement is strictly unregulated.

This book is sold subject to the condition that it shall not, by way of trade or otherwise, be lent, resold, hired out or otherwise circulated without the prior consent of the publisher in any form of binding or cover other than that in which it is published and without a similar condition including this condition being imposed on the subsequent purchaser.

® and ™ are trademarks owned and used by the trademark owner and/or its licensee. Trademarks marked with ® are registered with the United Kingdom Patent Office and/or the Office for Harmonisation in the Internal Market and in other countries.

First published in Great Britain 2013
By Mills & Boon, an imprint of Harlequin (UK) Limited,
Eton House, 18-24 Paradise Road, Richmond, Surrey, TW9 1SR

© 2012 Cynthia Myers

ISBN: 978 0 263 91348 1

46-1213

Harlequin (UK) Limited's policy is to use papers that are natural, renewable and recyclable products and made from wood grown in sustainable forests. The logging and manufacturing processes conform to the legal environmental regulations of the country of origin.

Printed and bound in Spain
by Blackprint CPI, Barcelona

MILLS & BOON

Published in Great Britain 2014
by Mills & Boon, an imprint of Harlequin (UK) Limited,
Eton House, 18-24 Paradise Road, Richmond, Surrey, TW9 1SR

© 2014 Cynthia Myers

ISBN: 978 0 263 91348 4

46-0214

Harlequin (UK) Limited's policy is to use papers that are natural, renewable and recyclable products and made from wood grown in sustainable forests. The logging and manufacturing processes conform to the legal environmental regulations of the country of origin.

Printed and bound in Spain
by Blackprint CPI, Barcelona

Cindi Myers is the author of more than fifty novels. When she's not crafting new romance plots, she enjoys skiing, gardening, cooking, crafting and daydreaming. A lover of small-town life, she lives with her husband and two spoiled dogs in the Colorado mountains.

Chapter One

Elizabeth Giardino had died on February 14. For three hundred and sixty-four days, Anne Gardener had avoided thinking about that terrible day, but on the anniversary of Elizabeth's death, she allowed herself a few minutes of mourning. She stood in her classroom at the end of the day, surrounded by the hearts-and-lace decorations her students had made, and let the memories wash over her: Elizabeth, never Betsy or Beth, her hair streaked with brilliant purple, leaning dangerously far over the balcony of her father's penthouse in Manhattan, waving to the paparazzi who clicked off shot after shot from the apartment below. Elizabeth, in a ten-thousand-dollar designer gown and impossibly high heels, sipping five-hundred-dollar champagne and dancing into the wee hours at a St. Tropez nightclub while a trio of morose men in black suits looked on. Elizabeth, blood staining the breast of her white dress, screaming as those same men dragged her away.

Anne closed her eyes, shutting out the last image. She'd gain nothing by remembering those moments. The past was the past and couldn't be undone.

Yet she couldn't shake a feeling of uneasiness. She looked out the window, at the picture-postcard view of snow-capped mountains against a turquoise sky. Rogers, Colorado, might have been on another planet, for all it resembled New York City. Those lofty peaks did have a mesmerizing effect, anchoring you to the earth in a way. Part of her would like to stay here forever, too, but she doubted she would. In a year, or two at most, she'd have to move on. She couldn't afford to put down roots.

She drew a deep breath, collecting herself, then gathered up her purse and tote bag, and shrugged into her coat. She locked the door of her classroom and walked to the parking lot, her low-heeled boots clicking on the scuffed linoleum, echoing in the empty hallway.

Her parking space was close to the side entrance, directly under a security light that glowed most mornings when she arrived. But there was no need for the light today, though the shadows were beginning to lengthen as the February sun slid down toward its nightly hiding place behind the mountains.

The sudden descent to darkness had made her uneasy when she'd first arrived here. Now she accepted it as part of the environment, along with stunning bright sun that shone despite bitter cold, or the sudden snowstorms that buried the town in two feet of whiteness as soft and dry as powdered sugar.

She drove carefully through town, checking her rearview mirror often. People waved and she returned their greetings. That, too, had unsettled her at first, how people she'd never met greeted her as an old friend within a few days of her arrival. She'd never lived in a small town before, and had to get used to the idea that of course everyone knew the new elementary schoolteacher.

Dealing with the men had been the biggest challenge

at first. More men than women lived in these mountains, she'd been told, and the arrival of an attractive young woman who was clearly unattached drew them like elk to a salt lick. Elizabeth would have been in heaven— the men were ski instructors, mountain climbers, cowboys, miners—all young and fit, rugged and handsome, straight out of a beer commercial or a romance novel. But Anne rebuffed them all, as politely as she could. She wasn't interested in dating anyone. Period.

A rumor had started that her heart had been broken in New York and this was why she'd come west. The sympathetic looks directed her way after this story circulated were almost worse than the men's relentless pursuit.

Things had calmed down after a few months. People had accepted that the new teacher was "standoffish," but that didn't stop them from being friendly and kind and concerned, though she suspected some of this was merely a front for their nosiness. People wanted to know her story and she had none to tell them.

She stopped at the only grocery in town to buy a frozen dinner and the makings of a salad, then drove the back way home. She tried to vary her route every few days, which wasn't easy. There were only so many ways to reach the small house in a quiet subdivision three miles from town.

The house, painted pale green with buff trim, sat in the middle of the block. It had a one-car garage and a sharply peaked roof, and a covered front porch barely large enough for a single Adirondack chair, which still wore a dusting of snow from the last storm.

She unlocked the door and stood for a moment surveying the room. A sofa and chair, covered with a faded floral print, filled most of the small living room, the television balanced on an old-fashioned mahogany table with barley-twist legs. An oval wooden coffee table and a brass lamp completed the room's furnishings, aside from a landscape print on the side wall. The place had come furnished. None of the items were things she would have picked out, but she'd grown accustomed to them. No sense changing things around when she couldn't stay.

She stooped and picked up her mail from the floor, where it had fallen when the carrier had shoved it through the slot. Utility bills, the local paper, junk—the usual. Nothing was amiss about the mail or the house, yet she couldn't shake her uneasiness. She eased out of the boots and padded into the kitchen in stocking feet and put away the groceries. She wished she had a drink. She had no liquor in the house—she hadn't had a drink since she'd left New York. It seemed safer that way, to always be alert. But today she'd welcome the dulling of her senses, the softening of the sharp edges of feeling.

She put water on for tea instead, then went into the bedroom to change into jeans and a comfy sweater. Maybe she'd start a fire in the small woodstove in the living room, and try to lose herself in a novel.

The bedroom held the only piece of furniture in the house she really liked—an antique cherry sleigh bed, the wood burnished by years of use to a soft patina. She trailed one hand across the satin finish on her way to the closet. She stopped beside the only other piece of furniture in the room, a sagging armchair, and slipped out of the corduroy skirt and cotton turtleneck. Sensible clothes for racing after six-year-olds. Elizabeth would have laughed to see her in them.

She opened the closet and reached for a pair of jeans. She scarcely had time to register the presence of another person in the room when strong arms wrapped around her in a grip like iron. A hand clamped over her mouth, stifling her scream. Panic swept over her, blinding her. She fought with everything she had against this unknown assailant, but he held her fast.

"Shhh, shhh. It's all right. I won't hurt you." The man's voice was soft in her ear, its gentleness at odds with the strength that bound her. "Look at me."

He loosened his hold enough that she could turn her head to look at him. She screamed again as recognition shook her and choked on the sound as she stared into the eyes of a dead man.

Jake Westmoreland watched the woman in his arms closely, trying to judge if it was safe to uncover her mouth. He wasn't ready to release his hold on her yet. Not because he feared she'd strike out at him, but because he'd waited so many months to hold her again.

She was thinner than he remembered, fragile as a bird in his hands, where he'd never thought of her as fragile before. Her hair was darker too, cut differently, and the bright streaks of color were gone. He'd seen her picture, so he should have been prepared for that. But nothing could have really prepared him for meeting her again, not after the trauma of their last parting. For months, he hadn't even been sure she was still alive.

"I thought you were dead," she said when he did remove his hand from her mouth. Tears brimmed in her eyes, glittering on her lashes.

"I was sure Giardino's goons would go after you next."

"Your friends got to me first. But they never told me

you were still alive. How? The last time I saw you…"
She shook her head. "So much blood…"

They told him later he had died, there on the floor of
the suite at the Waldorf Astoria. But the trauma team
had shocked his heart back to life and poured liters of
blood into him to keep his organs from shutting down.
He'd spent weeks in the hospital and months after that
in rehab—months lying in bed with nothing to do but
think about her.

He brushed her hair back from her temples, as if to
reassure himself she was real, and not a dream. "Elizabeth, I—"

The pain in her eyes pierced him. "It's Anne. Elizabeth doesn't exist anymore. She died that day at the
hotel."

He'd known this, too, but in the moment his emotions
had gotten the better of him. He stepped back, releas-
ing her at last. "Why Anne?"

"It was my middle name." Her bottom lip curved
slightly in the beginnings of the teasing smile he'd come
to know so well. The old smile he'd missed so much.
"You didn't know?"

"No." There was so much he hadn't known about her.
"Can we sit down and talk?" He nodded toward the bed,
the only place where two people could sit in the room.

A piercing whistle rent the air. He had his gun out of
his shoulder holster before he even had time to think.

She stared at the weapon with an expression of disgust. "Are you going to shoot my tea kettle?"

He put the gun away.

"Let's go into the living room," she said. She pulled
a robe from a hook on the closet door and wrapped it
around herself, but not before he took in the full breasts

rounded at the top of her black lace bra, the narrow waist fanning out to slim hips—and the scar on her lower back.

"Your tattoo's gone," he said. She'd had the words *Nil opus captivis* at the base of her spine, in delicate script. *Take no prisoners*. The motto of a woman who'd been determined to wring everything she could from life.

"I had it removed. They told me I shouldn't leave any identifying marks."

She led the way into the living room, going first to the kitchen to turn off the burner beneath the kettle, then to the front window to pull the blinds closed. He sat on the sofa, expecting she would sit beside him, but she retreated to the chair, her arms wrapped protectively around her middle.

"How did you find me?" she asked.

"I still have friends at the Bureau. People who owe me favors."

"No one is supposed to know where I am. They promised—" She broke off, her lips pressed together in a thin line. He could read the rest of her thoughts in her eyes. This wasn't the first time the government had broken promises to her. What about all the promises *he'd* made?

"I never meant to lie to you," he said. "I was trying to protect you."

"You didn't do a very good job of that, did you?"

He clenched his hands into fists. "No. Tell me what happened after I left. I heard you turned state's evidence."

"If you're still with the FBI you should know all this."

"I'm not with the Bureau anymore."

She raised her brows. "Oh? Why not?"

"Officially, I was retired on disability."

"And unofficially?"

"Unofficially, they thought I was too much of a risk."

"Because of what happened with my father?"

"That, and...other things." He'd committed the cardinal sin of developing an intimate relationship with a person he was supposed to be investigating. Not that Elizabeth Giardino had been the target of his investigations, but she was close enough to her father to raise questions about Jake's integrity and his ability to perform his job. "Tell me what happened after I was shot," he said.

"My father's goons did try to drag me away, but they didn't know you had the place surrounded. When the cops broke in, everyone was too focused on keeping my father safe to worry about me. Someone hustled me into a car and took me downtown."

He tried to imagine the scene. She'd been covered in his blood, wild with fear. They'd have put her in an interrogation room and turned up the pressure, grilling her for hours, trying to break her. At one time he would have said she wasn't a woman who could be broken, but now he wasn't so sure. "They wanted you to provide evidence against your father."

"They didn't have to persuade me. After I saw what he did to you...I wanted to make him pay."

Was it because of him, really? Or because her father had destroyed her trust? In one blast of gunfire she'd gone from pampered daddy's girl to enemy number one. It must have made her question everything.

"I laid all the family's dirty secrets out in public and he swore he'd kill me," she continued. "He stood there in court and cursed me and said I was dead to him already." She swallowed, and he sensed the effort it took for her to rein in her emotions.

"After that it was too dangerous for you to remain in New York," he said.

She nodded. "It was too dangerous for me to be me. Within a month my father had escaped prison and disappeared, but we all know he's still out there somewhere, and he hasn't forgotten anything. The feds gave me a new identity. Elizabeth Giardino died in a tragic boating accident in the Caribbean and Anne Gardener came to Rogers, Colorado, to teach school."

"I never imagined you as a schoolteacher."

"I had a degree in English from Barnard. The Marshals Service pulled a few strings to get me my teaching certificate. They found this job for me, and this house." She looked around the room. The plain, old-fashioned furniture was as unlike her hip Manhattan apartment as he could have imagined. "I suppose they thought this place was as anonymous as a town could be." Her gaze shifted back to him. "Yet you found me."

"I had inside information."

"Other people can pay for information."

Other people being her father and his goons. "I knew about this place. That it was on a list of possible hideouts. I persuaded a former colleague to let me take a look at the accounting records for the period after you disappeared and I found payment to a Colorado bank. I was able to trace that to this house."

"But you still didn't know I was here."

"I looked online, through the archives of the local paper. I saw the announcement last summer about the new teacher. The timing was right, and I thought it might be you."

"You make it sound easy."

"Not so easy. There are a lot of layers between you and the feds. Layers I helped design."

"I forgot you started out as an accountant." She gave a rueful laugh. "Not the picture most people have of the rough-and-tough federal agent."

He'd been hired straight out of university to work as a forensic accountant for the Bureau. Following the money put away more criminals than shootouts. But then they'd needed someone to go undercover in the Giardino family and he'd volunteered, wanting a change from sitting behind a desk. He hadn't counted on getting in so deep. He hadn't counted on Elizabeth.

"How are you doing?" he asked. "Do you like it here?"

"I don't dislike it. The people are friendly. I love the children."

He tried to imagine her surrounded by first graders. He'd never thought of her as the mothering type, yet the image seemed to suit this new, quieter side of her. "It's very different from the life you lived before," he said.

"I'm very different."

"Yeah." A person didn't go through the kinds of things they'd been through without some change. "How are you doing, really?" he asked.

"How do you think?" Her voice was hard, the accusation in her eyes like acid poured on his wounds. "It's hard. And exhausting, being afraid all the time."

"You don't feel safe?"

"You of all people should know the answer to that. You know my father—he'll do anything to get his way.

And he meant it when he said he would see that I was dead. If you found me, he can too. Why did you come here?"

"I wanted to see you."

"Well, you've seen me. Now you can leave." She stood, and cinched the robe tighter around her waist.

He rose also. "Eli—Anne. Listen to me. I need your help."

"For what?"

"I need you to help me find your father."

"Why? You said you're no longer with the Bureau."

"No. But if we find him he'll go back to prison—and they won't let him escape this time."

"I can't help you. All I want is to stay as far away from him as possible."

"Don't you want to put an end to this? Don't you want to be safe again?"

"What are you talking about?"

"I'm talking about finding your father and making sure he's punished the way he deserves."

"Revenge?" She spat the word, like a curse. "You want revenge?"

"Call it that if you want. Or call it justice. He's killed too many people. Someone has to stop him."

"Well, that someone won't be me."

"I'm not asking you to risk anything. I just want you to talk to me. To tell me where he might be hiding."

"I already gave you everything I could. Why do you want more?"

She had given him everything—her body and her beauty and a willingness to risk that had made his own bravery seem a sham in comparison. "I need your help," he said again.

"You're as bad as he is—you only want to use people to get what you want." Without another glance at him she left the room, the door to the bedroom clicking softly shut behind her.

He stared after her, feeling sick. Maybe her words hurt so much because they were too close to the truth. He did want to use her. She was the only link he had to Sam Giardino. The only way he could do what he had to do.

Chapter Two

Anne leaned against the closed bedroom door, her ear pressed to the wood, listening. The silence in the house was so absolute she imagined she could hear Jake's heart beating—though of course it was only the frantic pounding in her own chest. Footsteps crossed the room, moving away from her, the heavy, deliberate echo of each step moving through her like the aftershock of an earthquake. She bit her lip to keep from shouting at him not to leave. Of course she wanted him to leave. She didn't want any part of the kind of danger he represented.

The front door closed with a solid click. She held her breath, and heard the muffled roar of a car engine coming to life. The sound faded and she was alone. She moved away from the door and sagged onto the bed, waiting for the tears that wouldn't come. She'd cried them all out that night at the hotel, believing he was dead, knowing her life had ended.

Jake. One of the other agents at the Bureau had laughed when she'd called him that. "You mean Jacob? No one ever calls him Jake."

No one but her. And everyone in her family. It was the way he'd first introduced himself to them. His name—but not his name. Like everything else about him, he'd built a lie around a kernel of truth. He wasn't really a low-level official with the Port Authority, wanting to get in on the Giardino family business. He was an undercover operative for the FBI. Not even a real cop, but an accountant.

By the time she'd learned all this it had been too late. She had already been in love with him.

So what was he doing back in her life now? Hadn't he done enough to ruin her? Before he came along she'd been happy. She'd had everything—looks, money, friends, family. She wasn't an idiot—she'd known her father didn't always operate on the right side of the law. He'd probably done some very bad things. But those things didn't concern her. They didn't touch the perfect life she'd built for herself.

Jake had made her take off the blinders and see the painful truth about who her father was.

About who she really was.

She pushed herself off the bed, pushing away the old fear and despair with the movement. Not letting herself stop to think, she dressed, grabbed her keys and headed out the door. She couldn't sit in this house one more minute or she'd go crazy.

She drove back into town, to the little gym one block off Main. A few people looked up from the free weights and treadmills as she passed. She nodded in greeting but didn't stop to talk. She changed into her workout gear, found her gloves and headed for the heavy bag and began throwing jabs and uppercuts, bouncing on her toes the way the gym's owner, a former boxer named McGarrity, had shown her.

She'd taken up boxing when, shortly after her arrival

in Rogers, she'd come to the gym for what was billed as a ladies' self-defense class. Turned out McGarrity's idea of self-defense was teaching women to box. Anne had fallen in love with the sport the first time she landed a solid punch. She'd never been in a position where she had to fight back before. Now, at least, she was prepared to do so.

She'd worked up a sweat and was breathing hard when a woman's voice called her name across the room.

Maggie O'Neal taught second grade in the classroom across the hall from Anne. A curvy woman with brown, curly hair, dressed now in pink yoga pants and a matching hoodie, she was the closest thing Anne had to a best friend. "Maybe I should take up boxing," Maggie said. "You look so healthy and...dewy."

Anne laughed. "I'm sweating like a pig, you mean."

"It looks good on you."

"What are you doing here?"

"I just got out of a yoga class. Marcie Evanston teaches one every afternoon at this time. You should join us sometime."

Anne had tried yoga once. While everyone else lay still in *savasana,* her mind had raced, unable to grow quiet. She needed physical activity—punching the heavy bag or an opponent in the ring—to shut off the voices in her head and drown out the fear.

"Can I talk you into a break for a smoothie or some juice?" Maggie asked.

"Sure."

Anne stashed her gloves in the cubby marked with her name and the two women made their way to the juice bar next door to the gym—McGarrity's latest effort to squeeze more profit out of the facility. The idea seemed to be working—the juice bar was usually busy, favored by tourists and local office people as well as gym members.

They sat at the counter and ordered banana-berry smoothies.

"Look what Ty gave me for Valentine's." Maggie extended her pinky, showing a gold ring with a row of tiny diamonds.

"It's beautiful," Anne said. "Was it a surprise?"

Maggie nodded. "We saw it in the window of a store over in Grand Junction last month and I remarked how I've always wanted a pinkie ring. When I saw the ring box on my plate this morning, I squealed loud enough to wake the next door neighbors." She smiled at the ring. "Did I get lucky or what?"

"You got very lucky." Anne ignored the pinching pain at her heart. In her party-girl days she'd dismissed love as some fanciful notion from novels and movies. She'd liked being with men, but she hadn't needed one to make her happy. And the thought of wanting to spend the rest of her life with one had seemed ludicrous.

And then Jacob Westmoreland—she'd known him as Jake West—had walked up to her at one of her father's clubs and asked her to dance. She'd thought he was handsome and a decent dancer, but then she'd looked into his eyes and her world had shifted. A flood of lust and longing and locked-in connection had rocked her like a tidal wave. Nothing had ever been the same after that.

And now he was back. She didn't have the strength to go through that heartache again.

"Did you see your picture in the paper? Great promo for the carnival."

Anne realized Maggie had been talking for several minutes about something. "My picture?"

"In the Telluride paper today. You made the front page."

She fought back the nervous flutter in her stomach. "I don't remember anyone taking my picture."

"You remember that reporter who came around Saturday, when we were working on our carnival booth? He must have taken some candid shots after he talked to us. He got a perfect picture of you framed by the heart cutout in the side of the booth. I think you leaned out to say something to Ty."

"He should have asked me before publishing it."

"Oh, come on! I know you don't like having your picture taken, but it was a great shot, I promise. I'll save my copy for you. And maybe it will pull in a few more people to our booth at the carnival."

"That's great." Anne managed a weak smile. The first and second grades were teaming up to sell hot chocolate and cider at the Winter Carnival in the town park next weekend, an annual fundraiser for local charities. She wanted to do her part to help, but the thought of her picture circulating in the public made her uneasy. What if someone from her old life saw?

She shrugged off the thought. After all, it was just a small-town paper, a very long way from New York.

"Hey, ladies, how you doing?" A stocky man with broad shoulders and a shaved head came to stand beside their bar stools. Evan McGarrity was rumored to be in his sixties, but he looked two decades younger, and had the energy of a man half his age. "Annie, did your friend find you?" he asked.

Anne went cold. "What friend?"

"There was a guy in here earlier, asking about you. Said he was a friend of yours from New York."

Aware of Maggie's eyes on her, Anne kept her expression noncommittal. McGarrity must mean Jake. "What did he look like?"

"Not too tall. About my height, maybe. Good set of shoulders on him. Looked like he might have played football. Dark hair. Expensive suit."

Jake was tall, with sandy hair and a slim build. This wasn't Jake. She stood, knocking the half-empty smoothie glass onto its side as she groped blindly for her purse.

"Anne, are you all right?" Maggie asked. "You've gone all gray."

"I'm sorry about the mess." She stared numbly at the purple liquid spreading across the countertop. "I really have to go."

She ran to her car, still dressed in her workout clothes, not feeling the icy evening breeze against her bare legs, ignoring the shouts of her friends behind her.

Someone had found her—someone who wasn't Jake. Someone who might mean her harm.

ANNE'S FIRST INSTINCT was to go to Jake for help. But she had no idea where he was staying. And maybe he'd led them here. She could call Patrick Thompson, the marshal who'd been assigned to her, but he was hours away in Denver. By the time he got here, it might be too late.

She drove home and raced into the house, locking the door behind her. In the bedroom, she dragged her suitcase from the top shelf of the closet and began throwing things in it. She'd wait until after dark, then she'd leave. She'd drive as far as she could toward Denver. It was easier to get lost in the city. She'd ditch the car there, maybe buy a new one or take a bus. She couldn't travel out of the country. The feds wouldn't let her get a passport—letting her leave would be too risky, they said.

But she had to leave. The last time she'd seen him, her father had vowed to erase her. That was the word he'd used—*erase*. As if she were a mistake he needed to blot out. She'd never seen such coldness in his eyes before. His daughter was dead to him already—disposing of her body was of no consequence.

Never mind that she still had plenty of use for that body.

A knock on the door made her freeze. She tried to think. Would the man who was looking for her knock and announce himself?

Yes, she decided, he would. He'd want her to open the door. To let him inside where he could dispose of her quietly, without the neighbors seeing. He'd slip away without anyone noticing and tomorrow, when she didn't show up at class, someone would find her. Someone else would discover her true identity, and the newspapers and gossip magazines would print the news in bold headlines. *Mob King Takes Revenge on Daughter Who Betrayed Him* or *Mafia Princess Gets Hers*.

She waited, but no second knock came. No friendly voice called out in concern. She forced herself to breathe, ragged, metallic-tinged breaths that tasted of terror.

When she could stand the tension no more, she tip-toed into the front room and peered out a gap in the blinds. The street in front of her house was empty. Dark. After another half hour of stillness, she decided no one was there. But maybe they were waiting across the street, waiting for her to open the door.

She pulled on her coat and gloves, then took the loaded pistol from her bedside table and slipped it into the pocket of her coat. When she'd asked for the gun the Marshals had dismissed her, saying she had no need to be armed. She was merely an innocent schoolteacher. Patrick Thompson had assured her the U.S. Marshals Service would provide all the protection she needed. She'd argued with him to no avail.

But three days after her arrival here she'd received a package in the mail. The handgun, ammunition and an unsigned note. *I hope you never need this*, the note read. *But just in case...*

One hand on the pistol, she slipped out the back door. The temperature had dropped twenty degrees with the setting sun. The air was brittle with cold, the ground crisp beneath her feet. Staying close to the side of the house, she moved toward the street. She took a step, then waited, listening. She repeated this process all the way down the side of the house, so that twenty minutes passed before she reached the corner. She craned her head around to look toward her front door.

The small porch was empty, the light shining down on the doormat and a rectangle of white that lay on the mat.

Chapter Three

Anne studied the rectangle of white that gleamed on the doormat. It looked like an envelope, and a simple envelope shouldn't be so ominous. But this one was out of place. The mail carrier delivered letters through the slot in the door. Other people who had messages for her telephoned, or contacted her at school. Did this envelope contain an explosive to injure her, or a poison?

Neither of those things were her father's style. He believed in personal retribution—not necessarily from him, but from his goons. His representatives, he called them. She remembered overhearing him on the phone with a contractor he suspected of double-crossing him. His words had been so calm, in sharp contrast to the menace in his voice. "I'm sending a couple of my representatives over to discuss this with you."

When the police found the man, he was floating in the sound, his face gone. Cut off, she'd heard later, while he was still alive.

Shivering with cold and fear, she turned and raced back around the side of the house and through the back door. She ran to the front, opened the door just wide enough to snatch the envelope from the mat, then sat on the sofa, shaking.

She turned the envelope over and read the childish printing. *Miss Gardener* was rendered in uneven printing. Below that, a more adult hand had penned *Happy Valentine's Day.*

Inside the envelope was a crooked heart cut from construction paper, decorated generously with silver glitter and stickers bearing images of cupids and more hearts. The crayoned signature was from one of her students, a wide-eyed little boy who clearly had a bit of a crush on his teacher.

She stared at the words through a blur of tears, hating how the sordidness of her old life had reached out to taint this sweet, innocent gesture. If she ran away, all of that ugliness would follow her, to whatever new town she settled in.

She had friends here in Rogers. A place in the community. She wasn't ready to give that up, not until she absolutely had to.

"ARE YOU STAYING in town long, Mr. Westmoreland?"

The desk clerk at Rogers's only hotel smiled at Jake, all but batting her eyelashes at him. He returned the smile. It never hurt to be friendly with the locals, especially in a place this small. You never knew who might give you the information you needed, or put you in touch with the one contact who could help you break a case. "A few days. I'm not sure, really." He plucked a brochure advertising Telluride ski area from a rack on the counter. "This is such a beautiful place, I might stay longer than I planned."

"We've got plenty of scenery, that's for sure," she said. "Not much excitement, though."

"I don't need excitement." He'd had enough to last

a lifetime. As soon as he was done with this last job, he'd stick to crunching numbers for the rest of his life.

"You might stick around for the Winter Carnival next weekend," the clerk said. "That's kind of fun."

"What's the Winter Carnival?"

"It's this little festival in City Park. Ice skating, ice sculpture, a broomball tournament. A bonfire. Different groups have booths selling food and hot chocolate and stuff. Real small-town, but a lot of tourists like it."

"I might have to check it out. Thanks." The phone rang, and when she turned away to answer it, he took the opportunity to set the brochure aside and leave before she questioned him further.

Outside, the sun was so bright he squinted even behind his sunglasses. The windshield of the car he'd rented in Grand Junction was thick with frost. He turned the heat on full blast and sat in the driver's seat, debating his next move.

He'd driven by Anne's house last night, after midnight. Her car had been parked in the driveway, a single light in the back of the house glowing yellow behind the shades. Her bedroom. He'd thought of stopping, but she'd made it clear she wanted nothing to do with him.

Not that he intended to take no for an answer. He understood she was angry with him—upset and hurt by the lies he'd told her. Sooner or later she'd see he'd had to lie to protect them both. The fact that he'd failed so miserably made him more determined than ever to make it up to her.

She was afraid; that was clear. Who wouldn't be, in her position? Helping him would force her to admit that fear—that weakness. For all the changes in her life and her appearance, she was still a woman who never liked to admit any weakness. *Take no prisoners*. She could erase the words from her skin, but Jake was certain they were still inscribed on her heart.

Approaching her at her house had been a tactical error. He could see that now. They needed neutral territory. With other people around she wouldn't be so guarded.

He spent the morning at the library, reading through back issues of the *Rogers Reporter,* learning what Anne's life had been like these past nine months. Other than the announcement of her hiring, the new first-grade teacher had stayed out of the spotlight. She was playing by the rules of the Witness Security Program, keeping quiet and fitting in.

At three o'clock he drove to the school, a low-slung group of buildings set one behind the other at the foot of a mesa. The elementary classrooms were in the last building, next to a fenced playground where children in parkas and snowsuits climbed a jungle gym and kicked a soccer ball in the snow.

Jake spotted Anne standing with a shorter woman with curly hair. He waved and strode toward them. Anne stiffened, and the other woman eyed him warily, but he kept a pleasant expression on his face. *I come in peace.*

Up close, she looked tired, gray smudges under her eyes, her skin pale beneath the makeup, as if she hadn't slept well. Had thoughts of him kept her awake? Memories of what had happened between them? "Hello, Anne," he said, stopping in front of her.

"What are you doing here?" She didn't look angry— more resigned, he decided.

"I was hoping I could take you for a cup of coffee."

He was aware of the other woman staring at him, suspicion in her eyes.

"Is this the man McGarrity was talking about?" the woman asked.

"What man?" Jake asked. "Who's McGarrity?"

Anne shook her head. "This isn't him."

Jake turned to the other woman and offered his hand. "I'm Jake Westmoreland. A friend of Anne's from New York."

"Margaret O'Neal." Her hand brushed his lightly before retreating. "Anne doesn't look like she wants to see you."

"It's been a long time. I wanted to apologize for what happened the last time we met."

"What happened?" Margaret and Jake were the only ones talking, but at least Anne was listening. She hadn't walked away.

"Anne left before I could say goodbye." He spoke to Margaret, but his gaze remained fixed on Anne. She stood with her arms folded, her body angled away from him, her shoulders stiff with tension. "I've always regretted that."

"We don't have anything to say to each other," Anne said.

"We have a lot to say to each other. I came two thousand miles to talk to you. Please don't turn me away now."

"You can't say no to a man who says please." Margaret touched her friend's shoulder. "A cup of coffee can't hurt."

Anne's eyes telegraphed the word "traitor" to her friend, but she kept silent. She glanced at Jake. "One cup of coffee, then you leave me alone."

"One cup of coffee." He wouldn't leave her, though. He couldn't.

"Call me," Margaret said, and left them, smiling to herself.

Anne moved closer to Jake. "Now you've done it," she whispered.

"Done what?"

"Everyone will think you're the long-lost boyfriend who broke my heart."

The words were so melodramatic they were almost comical, but he felt the pain behind them. "Is that what happened, Anne?" he asked, his voice as gentle as he could make it.

"No!" Her eyes sparked with anger, the energy in them a jolt to his system, a glimpse of the woman she'd been. "But it's what people want to think. They think I don't know about the stories they've made up to explain me, but in a town this small, gossip always eventually gets around to everyone. They say I came here all the way from New York to recover from a broken heart. It's the reason I don't date anyone now. The reason I won't talk about my past."

"It's a good story," he said. Maybe part of it was even true, but he didn't say this. He didn't want to risk making her angrier.

"That's the only reason I let them think that. It's a good story."

"Have coffee with me and tell me your real story."

"You already know my real story."

"Then maybe it's time I told you mine."

Her gaze met his, sharp and questioning. "Come with me," he said. "Listen to what I have to say and then decide how you feel."

She hesitated, then nodded. "All right."

She insisted on taking her own car, and led the way to a coffee shop tucked between the library and a church. At this time of day the place was practically deserted, and they settled into a pair of upholstered wing chairs, facing each other across a low table. She cradled her coffee cup in both hands, legs crossed, back straight, elegant even in her schoolteacher's denim skirt and turtleneck sweater. "Tell me your story, Jake," she said. "Or should I call you Jacob?"

"I always liked the way Jake sounded when you said it."

"But Jake West wasn't your real name."

"No. But Jake West was close enough to Jacob Westmoreland my handlers thought I wouldn't get confused in a tense situation." He shifted, balancing his coffee cup on the arm of the chair. "I wasn't even supposed to be there at all. I was auditing the accounts at one of your father's companies, looking for some proof of mob connections. I needed some more information so I made a personal visit. Completely unauthorized, but when I hit it off with the manager there, my bosses saw a way in. They gave me a crash course in undercover work and sent me off to find out what I could. They never expected I'd blow the whole organization open."

She traced one finger down the side of her cup. Her nails were short and unvarnished, different from the perfect manicure she'd always sported before. "Was seducing me part of the plan?"

"You were never part of the plan," he said. "I didn't even know you existed until I saw you at the club that night."

"You were investigating my father and you didn't know about me?" She looked scornful.

"I was investigating his business. I didn't care about his personal life. And I don't read the society pages."

"Why did you dance with me that first night?"

"Because I couldn't not dance with you. The moment I saw you, we might as well have been the only two people in the room." He leaned toward her. "Don't tell me you didn't feel it, too."

She looked down at her lap, avoiding his gaze, but the blush in her cheeks warmed. "Yes," she breathed, scarcely louder than a whisper.

Attraction pulled at him now, as strongly as that first night. He'd arrived at the club late—almost midnight. Andy, the manager he'd befriended, who was one of Sam Giardino's lieutenants, had invited him for drinks. A social call, though Jake suspected this was the night he was going to meet Sam himself.

He and Andy had been standing at the railing overlooking the dance floor of the club in the East Village. A D.J. played techno-pop too loudly and dozens of young people crowded the dance floor. How he'd even spotted her in the confusion was a mystery, but his gaze had zeroed in on her like a laser. She had been dancing with a group of girlfriends, hands in the air, twirling. Laughing with such joy. He'd stared, knowing for the first time what the word "gobsmacked" really meant. He'd never seen someone so full of life and energy. So beautiful and vibrant.

And he'd never wanted anyone so much. Forgetting why he was there and all he might be risking, he'd pushed his way through the crowd until he'd stood in front of her. She'd immediately lowered her arms, and her smile had faded. "Dance with me," he'd said.

"Why should I?" she'd asked, her voice cool.

"Because I asked nicely." He'd smiled, coaxing her. "Please."

He'd expected a few moments' dancing facing each other, not touching even, but she'd surprised him by moving into his arms. As if the deejay played only for her, the music had switched to a slow number. She'd cuddled up to him like a kitten, and laid her head on his shoulder. "If you want to dance with me, you have to do it properly," she'd cooed.

And that was how he'd met Sam Giardino, with the don's daughter wrapped around him, closer than any father likes to see his daughter next to another man. Of course, he hadn't known she was Giardino's daughter, but the horrified look on Andy's face clued him in that something was very wrong. When Elizabeth had stepped back and murmured, "This is my father," he figured he'd just made the biggest mistake of his career.

But Sam had surprised him. "Elizabeth is a very good judge of character," he'd declared. "If she likes you, I like you."

And that was it. With one dance he'd gone from suspicious stranger to practically a member of the family. Weeks went by when he scarcely returned to his own apartment, living at the Giardino penthouse in Manhattan. He ate dinner with the family four nights out of five. He saw Elizabeth every day. And he collected reams of evidence he hoped to use to one day put her father away. His work never felt like a betrayal of her; she was too good for her father. Jake was going to rescue her from that life.

He'd never asked if she wanted rescuing. He could see now that had been a mistake. "I'm sorry things worked out the way they did," he said.

"It could have been worse. At least we're both still alive." She sipped her coffee. "Elizabeth's gone, but I'm still here."

"Are you okay with that?"

"Would I rather be living the life of the carefree, wealthy socialite in the most exciting city in the world?" She shook her head. "Even if it was possible, I couldn't go back to that life—not after you showed me what was really going on, where the money that paid for my designer clothes and nights on the town really came from."

"I always knew there was more to you than most people gave you credit for."

"Right. They didn't give me much credit after my father was arrested. If I wasn't the poor little rich girl who was biting the hand that fed her, I was the gold-plated harpy who was no better than a criminal herself."

"I guess I missed all that."

"How long were you in the hospital?"

"Five weeks. Then I was in a rehab facility for four months after that."

"Why aren't you in the witness protection program?" she asked. "If my father knows you're alive he'll do everything he can to change that."

"You thought I was dead—he probably does, too. And even if he doesn't, I fought too hard to keep my life to turn around and leave it behind. Not that I blame you for making that choice."

"Maybe it was easier for me because I didn't want to be who I was anymore. But I still don't feel safe. Aren't you afraid?"

"If I let myself think about the danger, I'd be afraid. But I've learned to put it out of my mind."

"To compartmentalize."

"Is that what it's called?"

"The marshal who's assigned to me—a guy named Patrick Thompson—used to talk about it. He told me that's what I had to learn to do—to lock the fear away in a separate part of my mind and not let it out, like a file I'd sealed."

"Good advice. Did you take it?"

"I tried. It works sometimes. And then something happens to remind me...." She looked away, her lower lip caught between her teeth.

"Has something happened lately?" he asked. "Something that's made you afraid again?"

She didn't answer, and kept her face turned away from him. He leaned forward and took her chin in his hand, gently turning her head until her eyes met his. "Tell me."

Chapter Four

Jake noticed Anne's hesitation, as if she was debating whether to trust him. "I'm the only one who knows your story," he said softly. "The only one who can understand what you're going through."

She took a long sip of coffee, then set the cup down and looked him in the eye. "Yesterday, after we talked, I went to my gym. The owner told me a man had been in there asking about me. Was that you?"

He shook his head. "I haven't been to any gym. And I didn't ask anyone in Rogers about you. I came straight to your house as soon as I got here."

The lines around her eyes deepened. "McGarrity—that's the gym owner—said this guy was dark, and built like a football player."

"Could be one of your father's goons."

"Yes. It could be." Her shoulders sagged. "I started to leave last night—to throw what I could in the car and just…run away."

"Why didn't you?"

"What would that solve? I'd still be afraid, and alone. More alone even than I am now. I like it here. I've made friends. And there are people here who depend on me. Kids. I don't want to let them down."

"You've always been a fighter. That's one of the things that drew me in. Even that first night on the dance floor, you made your own rules. Everyone else had to follow them or get out of your way."

"You make me sound like a pushy witch."

"You could be that, too. But it's kept you alive."

She shook her head. "I'm not like that anymore. I've learned the wisdom of staying in the background and letting others take the lead. I just want to do my job and live a quiet life."

"Wouldn't it be better if you didn't have to be afraid?"

"You mean if my father weren't around to threaten me?"

"Yes."

"I'm not going to help you, Jake. I did what I could to punish my father and I wasted my breath."

"You won't be wasting your breath this time."

"What are you going to do? You're not with the Bureau anymore. You don't have any authority. If the government can't find Sam Giardino, with all their resources, what makes you think you'll have better luck?"

"You know your father better than anyone. You know his habits and the people he associates with. The places he likes to vacation and where he stays when he goes out of town."

"You can learn all those things without me. Your friends in the Bureau have files filled with that kind of information."

"They know facts. They don't know emotions, or the reasons your father does what he does. You can tell me those things. You can help me predict what he's going to do next."

"And then what? You confront him and end up dead yourself? Or you lead him to me and I'm dead?"

"I won't let anything happen to you. I promise."

"You can't make that promise. Not when so much is out of your control."

"I'm going to stay with you tonight."

She straightened. "You will not."

"Yes, I will. At least until we find out who was asking about you at your gym yesterday."

"Jake, you cannot stay at my house. What will people think?"

"Since when do you care what people think?" The woman he'd known before had made a point of flaunting public opinion.

"Since I moved to a small town where everyone knows me. I'm a schoolteacher, for God's sake. I have a reputation to protect."

"And me spending the night with you is going to ruin that reputation? You're a grown woman."

"This isn't New York. Some people here still care about morality."

"So you're telling me nobody here sleeps with anybody else unless they're lawfully married?"

"I'm sure they do, but they're discreet about it."

"So we'll be discreet. Besides, I never said I was going to sleep with you—unless that's what you want."

The color rose in her cheeks. "It doesn't matter what we're actually doing. It's what they think we're doing."

"But I'm the long-lost boyfriend come back to beg forgiveness," he said. "Doesn't everyone love a lover?"

"No. You can't stay with me."

"Fine. Then you come stay with me. At the hotel."

"That's even worse. Sneaking off to a hotel together."

He laughed. "We're just a sordid pair. Honestly, I think you're making something out of nothing."

"You don't live here. I do. And I don't want to do anything to call attention to myself."

"Too late for that. I'm here. And this other mysterious stranger is here, asking about you. What are people going to say about that? The new teacher's gotten very popular all of a sudden."

"Just go away, Jake. Please? I'll handle this on my own."

"No."

"You don't think I can handle this?"

"I'm not going to leave you. Not until I know you're safe."

"I'll call the Marshals office in Denver. They'll send someone to babysit me for a while."

"Another strange man come to town to hang out with the teacher. Won't that set people talking?"

She made a face. "Maybe they'll send a woman. I'll tell people she's my sister."

"Then tell them I'm your brother."

"As if anyone would believe that."

"Why not? Siblings don't have to look alike."

"You don't act like any brother."

"Maybe not like your brother. What's Sam Junior up to these days?"

"I have no idea. As far as I know, he thinks I'm dead."

"Sammy was what, twenty-four when I saw him last? He'd just had a baby with that woman—what was her name?"

"Stacy. She was the daughter of some guy who owed my father a favor. It was practically an arranged marriage. I don't think she was very happy."

He didn't remember much about the girl, or her husband, for that matter. "Sammy Junior was in law school, wasn't he?"

"Yes. I imagine he has his license by now."

"I guess a lawyer is a handy thing to have in the family when you spend so much time breaking the law."

She stood. "I think it's time for you to go now."

"I'll be over later tonight," he said.

"No!"

"I'll park my car a couple blocks away—near that mechanic, with all the cars in the yard. And I'll leave early, before anyone is up."

"I won't let you in."

She turned away, but he grabbed her wrist and leaned closer, his voice low but insistent. "I can't leave you alone, not with some man neither of us knows asking about you. At least let me protect you until your handler from the Marshals office shows up."

Her eyes told him she hated being in this position— hated having to depend on anyone, but especially him. But she'd always been more intelligent than most people he knew; she could be reckless, but she was never foolish. "All right," she said, and pulled out of his grasp. "But only until the marshal gets here. And you'll sleep on the sofa."

By the time Anne reached her house, she was jittery with nerves and fear and anger. Jake—she couldn't think of him by any name but Jake—had no right to come here like this. After all he'd done, he owed her peace and an illusion of safety.

But of course her safety was an illusion. It always had been. No matter how many promises the Marshals made to her, she'd never really believed they could protect her from her father.

The phone was ringing when she unlocked the door. She fastened the locks behind her and went to answer it. "How was coffee?" Maggie spoke with a musical lilt, her joy at having the scoop on Anne's love life—or so she thought—barely contained.

"Coffee was...tense." The Marshals had drilled into her that sticking as close to the truth as possible was the best way to keep from getting caught in a lie.

"I take it the two of you didn't part as friends."

"You could say that." She and Jake had grown so close in the weeks they'd spent together, but their final night had been all chaos and confusion. One moment they'd been dancing, her head cradled on his chest, wondering how soon they could make their excuses and head upstairs to bed. Nights in Jake's arms were heaven to her then. The next moment her world exploded in a hail of bullets and blood. Jake lay shattered on the dance floor, the front of her dress red with his blood. Her screams echoed over the music as two men she didn't recognize dragged her backward out of the room.

Later, still wearing the bloodied dress, huddled over a cup of bitter, cooling coffee in some gray-walled interrogation room, the agents had told her their version of the truth—that Jake West was really Jacob Westmoreland, accountant turned undercover FBI agent, assigned to infiltrate her family and bring down her father.

She hadn't hated him immediately. Hatred had come later, when the weight of his lies had settled on her. He'd told her he loved her. He'd said he wanted to protect her. He wanted them to get married, to live happily ever after. And all that time she hadn't even known his real name. How could anything else he'd said be true if his very identity had been a falsehood? He'd used her to betray her family. As much as she'd come to despise her father, she'd despised Jake almost as much.

"Are you going to tell me what happened?" Maggie asked. "'Cause if I want to talk to myself, I can do that without holding a phone to my ear."

Maggie must have been talking while Anne took her trip down memory lane. "Nothing happened," she said. "He said he was sorry. I said I was sorry, too. End of story."

"Uh-huh." Maggie sounded skeptical. "How long is he staying in town?"

"I don't know. Another day or two. We don't have plans." As soon as she got off the phone with Maggie, she'd need to call the number her WitSec handlers had given her. Denver was only five hours away—they could have someone here tomorrow, surely.

"He was really good-looking," Maggie said. "And I think he still has a thing for you. You have to admit, coming so far to say he was sorry took guts. Maybe you'll get together again while he's here."

"Maggie." Anne said her name as a warning.

Maggie laughed. "I know. I'm an incurable romantic. All right, I'll shut up about it. What are you doing tonight?"

"The usual. Schoolwork. Maybe some TV."

"Have a good night. See you tomorrow."

"Goodbye." Anne replaced the phone in the cradle and started to the kitchen to make tea. She was only halfway across the room when a knock on the door made her jump. She glanced out the window; the sky was a gray smudge against the black-and-white shadows of mountains, the day rendered in charcoal by the disappearing sun. Jake had said he would come by after dark—maybe a city boy used to all those lights thought this was dark enough.

She strode to the door and took a deep breath, bracing herself, then checked the peephole. She registered a man, about Jake's height, huddled in the shadows. Apparently, the bulb in her porch light had burned out. As long as Jake was here, she'd ask him to replace it. She threw back the chain, turned the dead bolt and jerked open the door.

A burly, dark-haired man shoved her back into the room and slammed the door behind him. He looked her up and down, his face expressionless. "Long time, no see, Elizabeth."

Chapter Five

Jake parked the rental car amid the jumble of vehicles at the auto-repair shop and began walking the few blocks toward Anne's house. The old joke about small towns rolling up the sidewalk when the sun set must be true; no one else was out and the only traffic was the occasional car on the central thoroughfare that connected with the state highway. Here on the side streets, it was as silent as a tomb. A quarter moon and the occasional glow from a porch light illuminated his path. The crunch of his footsteps on the unpaved shoulder of the road sounded too loud in the profound stillness.

For a man who'd spent all his life in the city, the silence felt vaguely threatening. He studied the shadows the trees and buildings cast, anticipating an ambush, but nothing moved.

He kept one hand wrapped around the gun in his coat pocket as he walked. Maybe he was being overly cautious and he and Anne had nothing to fear in this sleepy little town. But who was the man who'd been asking for her at the gym? Jake wouldn't leave her alone until he found out. He'd failed at protecting her from her father and his thugs before; he wouldn't let them near her again.

He approached the house from the back, though he doubted any of her neighbors were watching. He kept to the shadows along the side of the house, moving quickly toward the back steps. Maybe they should have agreed on some kind of signal, so she'd be sure it was him when he arrived. As he turned the corner toward the back of the house he froze, heart pounding.

The back door to Anne's house was open—not wide open, but cracked a few inches, sending a shaft of bright light onto a patch of trampled snow at the bottom of the steps. Jake drew the gun and sidestepped toward the door, keeping to the deepest shadows against the wall of the house. When he was sure the coast was clear, he took the steps two at a time, moving silently, and paused on the small landing at the top, holding his breath, listening.

"You don't remember me, do you?" The man's voice was nasal, the words clipped and staccato.

Anne's answer was unintelligible, but the terror in her voice made the hair on the back of Jake's neck stand on end. He nudged the door open a little wider with the toe of one shoe and leaned in.

"I worked for your father, but you never noticed me. You were too high and mighty to pay attention to the help."

Jake heard a scraping sound, as if someone had shoved a chair out of the way. He decided they were in the living room, just beyond the kitchen. Was it just Anne and this man, or had the intruder brought along help?

Jake slipped silently into the kitchen, keeping close to the wall, out of sight of the doorway between the kitchen and living room. "You deserve to die for what you did to your father," the man said.

"No!" Anne cried out and Jake rushed forward. He burst into the room and saw Anne struggling with a burly, dark-haired man. He aimed his pistol, but there was no way he could get off a clean shot without risking hitting Anne instead.

Anne's attacker wrapped one arm across her chest and pulled her against him, crushing her rib cage, lifting her off the ground. She writhed in his arms, kicking out. The man still didn't know Jake was in the room. That gave him a slim advantage, but he didn't yet see how to use it.

Anne kicked out, knocking over a table, on which sat a lamp. The glass base of the lamp shattered, and then the lightbulb exploded with a shower of sparks. Anne wailed—whether in pain or frustration, Jake didn't know, but the sound enraged him. He aimed the gun again, determined to get off a good shot.

Anne beat her fists against her assailant, who held her with one hand now while he groped in his jacket pocket, probably for a weapon. If he drew a gun, Jake would have to fire, and pray Anne was not in the way.

But just then, Anne leaned over and bit her attacker on the hand, hard enough to draw blood.

The man howled and released her, and Anne whirled and landed a solid punch on his chin. Her attacker reeled back, but in the same moment he drew a gun from his coat. It was the last move he ever made, as Jake shot him, twice, the impact of the bullets sending him sprawling across the back of the sofa.

Anne screamed, then stood frozen, her hands to her

mouth, her face the same bleached ivory color as the wall behind her. "Is there anyone else?" Jake asked.

She shook her head, still staring at the dead man draped across her sofa. Jake pocketed his gun and dragged the man onto the floor and laid him out on his back. He was a burly man in his forties, dressed in jeans and a flannel shirt and wearing a new-looking ski jacket, hiking boots and a knit cap. Anyone seeing him on the streets would have taken him for a local, or a visiting tourist.

Except most tourists didn't carry a Glock. Jake checked the weapon; it hadn't been fired. He slipped it into his other coat pocket and took out the man's wallet. "Robert Smith," he read the name on the driver's license.

"That's not his real name." Anne's voice was shaky, but surprisingly calm, considering she had a dead man laid out on her living room rug. "His name's DiCello. Some of my father's men called him Jell-O. He hated that."

"What's this on his jacket?" He tugged at a laminated tag hanging from the zipper pull of the jacket. "It's a lift ticket, from Telluride Ski Resort. Dated for yesterday." Had Mr. DiCello decided to take in a day on the slopes before driving over to Rogers to do a little business with his boss's estranged daughter?

The loud jangling of the phone surprised a cry from Anne, who immediately put a hand to her mouth, as if to hold back further cries. Jake stared at the ringing instrument. Had someone heard the shots? "You'd better answer it."

She nodded and picked up the phone. "Hello?"

She listened a moment, then forced a smile. "How

sweet of you, Mrs. Cramer, but everything's fine....
Yes, I heard it, too. It must have been a car backfiring."

She hung up the phone and looked at him. "The
neighbor lady, checking on me."

"You did great." Better than great. She'd sounded
perfectly calm and reasonable. As if thugs got shot up
in her living room every night. "That was quite a punch
you landed," he said.

She massaged the back of her hand—she'd likely
have a bruise there tomorrow. "I've been taking boxing lessons. So I'd know how to defend myself. But it
wouldn't have saved me. Not if you hadn't come along."

He moved toward her, intending to comfort her,
but she stepped away from him, and hugged her arms
tightly around her waist. He swallowed his disappointment. It didn't matter if she hadn't forgiven him; she
still needed his help. "Your father's found you. You
have to leave."

"Maybe my father didn't send him. Maybe he came
on his own."

"Anne, look at me."

She met his gaze, and the anguish in her eyes cut
him. He wanted to hold her close, to tell her again that
he would protect her. But now wasn't the time. "You
don't really believe this man, who you know works for
your father, came here without your father's knowledge,
do you?" he asked.

She shook her head. "No."

"Is there some place near here we can go that might
be safe—just until we can make a plan?"

She straightened, visibly pulling herself together.
"There are some cabins in the mountains about fifteen
miles from here. The area is remote, on National Forest

land. In the summer, a few people live there, but in the winter they're closed up. There's a gate over the road, but I know the combination to the lock."

She hadn't hesitated with her answer; she had all the details laid out. "You've been planning for something like this."

"I always knew I might have to leave. I didn't want to, but…" Her voice died, and her gaze dropped to the man at their feet.

"Pack a few things you'll need and we'll go. Now."

"What about him?"

"I'll drag him out back and hide the body under a pile of firewood. As cold as it is, it could be a long time before anyone finds him. If the police come looking for you, they might inadvertently lead your father to us."

"You think he'll send someone else after me?"

"You know he will."

She nodded. "Yes. What about the blood?"

"I'll clean it up. Now go."

Without another word, or a glance in his direction, she went into her bedroom and shut the door.

Jake stared at that shut door; it wasn't half as solid a barrier as the one she'd put around her heart. Fine. She could hate him all she wanted. Maybe he even deserved her hate. But that wouldn't stop him from protecting her. And it wouldn't stop him from finding the man who'd caused her so much pain, and making sure he could never hurt her again.

ANNE SHOVED UNDERWEAR, a change of clothes and a few cosmetics into an overnight bag. She added a phone charger and a box of ammunition. The thought of needing those bullets made her shake, but if forced, she would defend herself. She wouldn't hide behind Jake; she wouldn't trust her life to him alone.

Her own father wanted her dead. She'd accepted the truth of this intellectually, but in her heart she'd nurtured a kernel of hope that he would never follow through on his threats.

Tonight had destroyed that hope. If she let herself think too much about what had just happened, she might fall apart. So she clung to anger and nurtured that instead. A man had invaded her home—her sanctuary—and tried to destroy her. She wouldn't let that happen again.

Even if that meant depending on Jake in the short term. She needed him—and his gun—for protection right now. But as soon as she had a plan that would keep her safe, she'd say goodbye to him. She didn't need—or want—him in her life again. In his own way, Jake was as tied to violence as her father had been. The fact that he wanted revenge, even though he wasn't in law enforcement anymore, proved he was still a part of the violence. She was done with living that way, with danger and bloodshed as commonplace as Friday-night pizza or Sunday drives for other families.

When she emerged from the bedroom with the overnight bag and her coat, DiCello's body was gone. Jake had cleaned the floor and thrown a quilt over the back of the sofa to hide the bloodstains. "I've done the best I can," he said. "Are you ready?"

"Yes."

"We'll take my rental car. It's parked just down the street."

"What kind of car is it?" she asked.

"A Pontiac Vibe. What difference does that make?"

She shook her head. "It isn't four-wheel drive. We'll take my Subaru."

She could tell he wanted to argue. Jake liked to take charge, to have every situation under control. But this was her plan and she'd thought it out very carefully. "We'll need the four-wheel drive on the Forest Service roads," she said.

"Then give me your keys. I'll drive." He held out his hand.

She wrapped her hand more securely around the keys. "I know the way to the cabins and I'm a better driver in mountain snow than you are." And focusing on driving would keep her from brooding over the man who had attacked her, and the images of him dying right before her eyes. Though her father had been responsible for many deaths, the only other one she'd seen close up had been Jake. She moved past him, out the door.

She expected him to argue more, but he didn't, he merely slid into the passenger seat as she started the car. "You should call your friend Maggie, and tell her you're going out of town for a few days. Tell her your mom is sick or something."

"All right. I need to stop for gas. I'll call her then. And I'll call the U.S. marshal assigned to my case and let him know what's going on."

"Don't tell him you're with me."

"Why not?"

"I'm supposed to be retired. They'll see my presence as interfering."

"You *are* interfering." She gripped the steering wheel so tightly her fingers ached. "I was fine until you showed up."

"It was a coincidence that your father's goon showed up right after I did."

"A pretty big coincidence, if you ask me." She turned onto the main highway out of town. A few cars filled the parking spaces in front of the town's only bar, but there was no one outside to see her car glide past, or to wonder what the teacher was doing out so late.

"Where is this gas station?" He changed the subject.

"About five miles, by the lake. It's closed this time of night, but the electric pumps will take a credit card."

"I suppose we'll have to risk it. I'll stay out of sight of the security cameras, so it will look like you're alone."

"Why do I need to look like I'm alone?"

"If you're really on your way to visit your sick mother, why do you have a strange man with you?"

Right. She'd already forgotten the cover story he'd concocted. Not that she expected anyone to believe it. But maybe it would buy them a little time, and if anyone came around questioning Maggie, she'd have something to tell them.

Jake hid in the backseat while she fueled the car; then she parked around the side of the building, out of sight of the security cameras, and dialed Maggie's number. A sleepy voice answered on the fifth ring. "Hello?"

"Hello, Ty? I'm so sorry to bother you this late. This is Anne. May I speak to Maggie?"

"Sure, Anne. Everything all right?"

"It's fine. I just need to talk to Maggie a minute."

After a few seconds of fumbling with the phone, Maggie came on the line. "Anne, what's wrong?"

"I just learned my father is in the hospital in New York. I need to go up there and see him." She was surprised how smoothly the lie rolled off her tongue. She felt like an actress, delivering a line in a play.

"Oh, honey, I'm so sorry. What's wrong?"

"His heart. It...it doesn't look so good, I guess." Her father didn't have a heart where she was concerned, but as far as Anne knew, his health was fine.

"You never talked much about your parents before."

"My mother died when I was little." True. "My father and I aren't particularly close." Also true.

"I understand. You want to try to patch things up before it's too late. Don't worry about a thing. I'll call Mr. Strand first thing in the morning and explain."

Anne had been hoping to avoid a phone call to the principal. Lying to her best friend was bad enough; the more people she spoke with, the greater the chance of getting her story mixed up. "Thanks. I'll call you again when I know when I'll be home."

"Don't worry. Have you told Jake?"

"Jake?" She glanced at the man in the passenger seat and he sent her a questioning look. "Why would I tell Jake?"

"He's from New York, isn't he? He could fly back with you. Then you wouldn't have to be alone."

Maggie made it sound so romantic—the old flame comforting her in her time of need. In some ways, having Jake with her *was* comforting; at least he knew the truth about her. But she shouldn't trust him, and being with him complicated the situation even more. "I haven't seen Jake. He never knew my father, anyway." More lies. She hoped her friend would forgive her one day for her deception. Not that Anne would be around to accept that forgiveness. Now that her father had learned her identity, the Marshals office would give her a new one. If she kept this up, she wouldn't even remember who she was.

"I have to go now," she said. "I'll talk to you soon." She hung up before Maggie could ask more questions.

"Do you think you convinced her?" Jake asked.

"I think so." She scrolled through her phone directory until she found the number for U.S. Marshal Patrick Thompson.

He answered on the third ring, his voice as crisp and alert as if he'd been expecting her call. "Anne. Is something wrong?"

The concern in his voice brought a knot of tears to her throat. Marshal Thompson had always been kind, gentle even, treating her the way a caring big brother would look after his little sister. He'd done his best to make a horrible situation better, and the memory of that came rushing back at the sound of his voice. She struggled to rein in her emotions. Now was no time to break down. "One of my father's men, a man named DiCello, broke into my house tonight," she said. "He's dead and I'm leaving. I thought you'd want to know."

"Did he say how he found you? Did he say where your father is now?"

"No. We...we didn't talk much."

"You shot him?"

She hesitated, and looked again at Jake. "Yes." When they found the body, they'd probably figure out she'd lied; DiCello had been shot from behind, with a different gun from the one she owned—the gun Thompson himself had most likely given her. But none of that mattered now. "I'm headed to a place where I think I'll be safe, at least temporarily."

"Stay in touch and we'll send someone to get you. We'll set you up with a new identity."

"I'll call you tomorrow."

"I was going to contact you soon, anyway," he said. "To warn you that Jacob Westmoreland might try to get in touch."

"I...why would Jake...Jacob...be in touch? I mean, he's dead, isn't he?" She hoped he'd take her surprise at his mention of Jake as confusion.

"He was badly injured the night of the raid, but he didn't die. Apparently, he's been asking a lot of questions about you. He's been in contact with some friends at the Bureau."

"Why would he be asking questions about me?" She didn't look at Jake, but she could feel his eyes on her.

"You're sure the man who came after you tonight was from your father?"

"Yes. I knew him. He worked for my father." Why was Patrick changing the subject?

"Word is, Westmoreland is pretty upset about what happened. He's probably blames you for what happened to him and he may come after you, seeking revenge."

Chapter Six

Anne caught her breath, and almost dropped the phone.
Patrick sounded so certain, and his words made sense:
Jake had lost everything the night of the raid—his career, his bright future, and almost his life. If he thought
she'd betrayed him to her father…

"I'll be careful," she said. "And I'll be in touch."

She disconnected the call, then switched off the
phone and dropped it into her purse.

"Why did he ask you about me?" Jake asked.

She started the car and backed out of their parking
spot. She had to remain calm and not let on that Patrick
had warned her about him. "He heard you were looking
for me. I told him I hadn't heard from you."

"Good girl."

The fact that he was so pleased by her deception
made her even more nervous. What if Patrick had been
telling the truth? So far, Jake had played the role of the
wounded lover, but he'd been a good actor before, hadn't
he? He'd fooled her father into trusting him. His love
for her had felt real, but what did she know about love?

She didn't really know anything about Jake. When
they'd been together before she'd only known the man
he was pretending to be. Only later had she learned

he worked for the FBI. She didn't know his real background, or what had happened to him during the months of his recovery.

She glanced at him as she turned the car onto the highway once more. He had his back to her, scanning the road for traffic. He was definitely different from the man she'd known before: he was less brash and more intense. Driven—by revenge? But revenge on her father, or on her?

"What have you been doing with yourself since you got out of rehab?" she asked, trying to keep the conversation light. If she kept Jake talking, maybe she could figure out his real motives for being here.

"I've spent most of my time looking for you."

That wasn't exactly reassuring. "Did you work, or... date?"

"I wasn't interested in dating, and looking for you was my work. I lived off my savings, and I was on disability pay for a while."

"You didn't think about maybe, I don't know, getting on with your life?"

"Not while I had unfinished business." She could feel his eyes on her in the dark.

She tightened her fingers around the steering wheel. She didn't like being afraid of Jake; it felt so wrong, since she'd once trusted him with her life.

"What do you think went wrong that day?" he asked.

"Wh-what do you mean?"

"I didn't have a clue your father suspected me. He never said anything, and he never tried to hide anything about the business from me."

"He never said anything to me, either," she said.

"If you'd known he planned to attack me, would you have warned me?"

"Yes!" She'd loved Jake more than she'd known it was possible to love a man. "I would have done anything for you. I thought you knew that."

"And now you just think I'm scum for lying to you."

"I don't know what to think, Jake. I gave everything to a man who didn't even exist. Can you understand how that might make me suspicious of your motives now?"

"I can understand. And I'm not asking you to pick up where we left off. But believe me when I say I want to help you and protect you."

"And you want revenge on my father."

"Only so he can't hurt you—and others—again."

She wanted to believe him. She wanted to believe that his feelings for her hadn't been lies. But a lot had happened to change both of them in the last year. Maybe in running away from her father's thugs, she was running into even worse danger with Jake.

AN HOUR LATER, Anne hunched over the wheel of the Subaru wagon, easing it over frozen ruts in the Forest Service road, watching the thick wall of spruce and pine on either side of the narrow path for the gap that would indicate her turn onto an even narrower, less-used route. Clouds obscured the moon and the night was as black as a crow's wing. They hadn't passed another car since they'd turned off the main highway half an hour ago.

She'd decided she'd be cautious around Jake, but she wouldn't let fear get the better of her. She was armed, and McGarrity had taught her how to defend herself with her fists. She didn't have to be helpless, and that knowledge alone gave her power.

"Where are we, exactly?" Jake frowned at the darkness around them.

"We're in the Gunnison National Forest. In the summer it's a popular hiking and camping area."

"And in the winter?"

"In the winter the campgrounds are closed, the trails are usually covered in snow and the roads don't get much use." She pressed down on the gas and the car plowed through a snowdrift. It slid and fishtailed a little, but she steered it back onto firmer ground.

"When my handler from the Marshals office, Patrick Thompson, first showed me this car, I was horrified," she said. The green Subaru Outback was five years old and had clearly seen better days. Worse, it was a wagon, a vehicle for suburban moms and grandpas, not a fashionable young woman. In New York she'd had a BMW convertible, a silver Roadster she'd driven with the top down on all but the coldest, wettest days.

"This definitely isn't a car Elizabeth would have driven." Jake patted the dash. "But it suits Anne."

She sighed. "It does. Half the women in town, including most of the teachers, drive similar cars."

"It must have been very strange for you, starting over as someone else."

"It's still strange, but it got easier. When I first moved here, I put a coffee mug with my new name, Anne, on the table beside my bed, where I'd see it first thing every morning, to remind me I wasn't Elizabeth anymore. My name was Anne." She glanced at his profile in the darkness. His head was turned slightly and she knew he was watching her, but she couldn't make out his features, only the curve of his skull and the jut of his nose and chin, like one of those silhouette portraits that had been popular in Victorian parlors. "I spent my whole life until coming here trying to stand out, wanting to be noticed. I had to learn to do the opposite, to become invisible."

"I don't think you have to be invisible," he said. "You just have to blend in with your surroundings, to fit in context. You've done a good job of that. I might not have recognized you if I hadn't known what I was looking for."

"DiCello obviously didn't have any trouble, either." She spotted the break in the trees and slowed the car further. "There's our turn. We're almost there."

The steep, narrow drive was choked with snow. Anne gunned the car up the pitch, relaxing only when it leveled out in front of a gate formed by a single length of heavy pipe suspended across the road between two fat lodgepole pines. She set the brake and took a small flashlight from the console between the seats, then climbed out of the car. Jake followed.

"How do you know the combination?" he asked as he watched her dial the numbers into the lock on the chain that fastened one end of the pipe to a tree trunk.

"I came here with my camera to take pictures of the fall colors. You can't see it now, but there's a lovely little aspen next to this pine. Back in September it was covered in golden leaves. I took picture after picture of that tree, while the summer visitors packed up and left their cabins. I had a zoom lens focused in on this keypad, though no one ever suspected." The lock popped open and she unwound the chain. "My father had employees who used the same trick to steal people's ATM pin numbers. Wait here until I drive through, then replace the lock."

She drove past the gate, then waited while he swung the pipe over the road once more and refastened the lock. "Are you shocked, that I knew so much about my father's dirty dealings?" she asked as she drove on once more.

"You mean, would I rather think of you as an unsullied innocent who had no idea her father was a thief and drug dealer and pimp and murderer? I don't think anyone can live for years in a world of crime and not be touched by it, and that includes me."

She hadn't been unsullied or innocent, but she'd perfected the art of looking the other way, and of telling herself the things her father did were none of her business, that they didn't matter to her. Jake had made her see things differently. She couldn't be grateful to him for that, not when it had destroyed the only life she'd known, and taken away the only family she had.

The cabins sat in a rough semicircle amid the trees, separated from each other by several hundred yards and piles of boulders that rose almost to the roofs. There were five; she chose the smallest, the farthest from the road. Even in summer it had been closed up tight. Unused.

She parked the car behind a screening stack of boulders and they climbed out. It was after midnight, and the cold was like a slap, hard and stinging. Anne led the way to the door and felt for the key above the lintel. Jake took it from her and unlocked the door and pushed it open.

The cabin smelled of stale ashes and dust. Jake fumbled along the wall by the door and she laughed. "There's no light switch," she said. "No electricity." She scanned the area with her flashlight beam until she spotted a kerosene lantern sitting on a table next to a box of kitchen matches. She lit the lantern and turned down the wick. Its golden glow illuminated the small main room, which consisted of a kitchen area, a table and two chairs and a worn love seat and armchair.

Jake opened the door on the far side of the room and looked in. "Bedroom," he announced, then checked the second door on an adjacent wall. "Bathroom—or at least a toilet and sink."

"The water's probably shut off for the winter so the pipes don't freeze," she said. She turned her attention to the empty woodstove that squatted between the front room's two windows. "There should be some firewood out back," she said.

He left, and returned with an armload of wood. She laid a fire, building a bed of small sticks and crumpled paper, then adding split pieces of wood. When she touched a match to the paper, it caught, and smoke curled up the chimney. After she was sure the fire was blazing, she closed the stove door. "It will be warmer in a little bit."

"I'm impressed," he said. "Were you a Girl Scout?"

"I've learned a lot of things since coming here." The instinct to survive was a powerful teacher. She made sure the curtains were pulled shut over the windows, then checked the contents of the two cupboards in the kitchen. "There's coffee and hot chocolate, and some canned soup and stews. We won't starve."

"Do you know who owns this cabin?" Jake asked. He slid onto a stool at the small breakfast bar.

She filled a kettle from a ten-gallon bottle of water on a stand beside the old-fashioned round-top refrigerator. The refrigerator was propped open by sticks held in place with bungee cords. "According to the county land records, it belongs to a man in Minneapolis. He inherited it from his parents. I don't think he comes down here very often—the cabin was empty every time I checked this last year."

"And the other cabins?"

"They belong to summer people. That's what everyone around here calls them. They live somewhere else and they come here every summer for a few weeks to hang out in nature."

"But we're on Forest Service land?"

"That's right." She lit a burner on the gas stove. "The cabins were here before the land was taken as National Forest, so the families were allowed to keep them and use them, but they're not allowed to make any changes without government approval—so no insulation, no electricity, no modernization, except ten years or so ago they made everyone fill in their outhouses and install flush toilets. Water comes from cisterns or a pump dropped in the creek down there."

"A creek that is frozen this time of year."

"Right. So we won't be using the indoor toilet. The cabins weren't designed for winter use, only as summer retreats."

"How did you ever find this place?" he asked.

"I came hiking with Maggie and her husband, Ty, not too long after I moved here. She told me all about the cabins. A few weeks later I came back on my own to check them out."

"And you brought your camera."

"I thought it would be a good idea to have a plan— someplace to go if I needed to hide. Even in the summer many of the cabins are empty, but if someone had asked,

I could have posed as a friend of the guy who owns the cabin, using it for the weekend, or something like that."

"That was good thinking. But then, I'm not surprised. You were always one of the smartest people I knew."

She busied herself finding cups and spooning cocoa into them, afraid if she looked at him he would see how pleased she was by the compliment, and how uncomfortable that made her now. It reminded her too much of one of the things she had loved about him, before: he didn't think that because she was beautiful, she was dumb. The other men in her life—her father and brother and her father's friends—dismissed women as empty-headed dolls.

"What's the rest of the plan now that we've made it here?" he asked.

She poured boiling water over the cocoa and slid a cup toward him. "I suppose I wait for Patrick—Marshal Thompson—to take me someplace new where I can start over again."

"Does that bother you?" He looked thoughtful as he stirred the cocoa. "I mean, how many times will you have to start over before you forget who you are? Or before your father stops looking for you?"

"My father will never stop looking." He could make all the speeches he wanted about her being dead to him, but until she was actually dead, and he had proof of it, her betrayal would eat at him like a cancer. "I've heard that hate is another side of love. As much as my father loved me, I think he hates me that much now." She would be his obsession, as other enemies had been. He had destroyed the others, every one. He wouldn't let her be his one failure. "The Marshals tell me they can protect me, that they've protected thousands of other people."

"They haven't done a very good job keeping you hidden so far," he said.

"No. You found me."

"I'm not the one you have to worry about."

Patrick hadn't been so sure about that. He thought Jake was out for revenge; maybe so, but he seemed willing to keep her safe as long as he thought she might help him find her father. "The problem with the Marshals is that too many people know who I am and where I am. They can talk about how secure their system is, but there are always leaks."

"True. But what other choice do you have?"

"I could head out on my own, go to Denver or Los Angeles or some other big city. I can buy a passport with another name and leave the country."

"You know how to get a fake passport?" He sounded skeptical. "But then, I guess you are your father's daughter."

"Don't judge me. I know how to do what I need to do to stay alive."

"I wasn't judging you." His tone softened. "You have another choice."

"What's that?"

"Work with me to find your father. See him arrested again and locked up for good. With him out of the picture, you'll be safe. You won't have to hide."

She stirred the chocolate, the spoon hitting the side of the cup with a tinkling melody. "He escaped before. He can escape again."

"There's something you ought to know about his

escape," he said. "Something I uncovered in my research that was hushed up at the time. Maybe knowing the whole story will help you make up your mind."

Chapter Seven

Anne glared at him, anger growing. "Jake, I'm tired and I'm stressed and I don't like playing games," she said. "If you have something to say, come straight out with it."

"First, tell me what you were told about your father's escape."

"Patrick met with me in person, before it was even in the news." She'd only been in Rogers a month then, so he'd arranged to meet her in a mall in Grand Junction, where they'd purchased tickets to an afternoon matinee, then ducked into an empty auditorium. "He told me my father's lawyers petitioned for a transfer to a different prison unit. No one in law enforcement expected the request to be granted—my father was too much of a risk. But the transfer was granted. The officers transporting him to the new facility were ambushed and overwhelmed and my father got away. By the time authorities discovered what had happened, hours had passed and there was no trace of my father."

"It all sounds very convenient, doesn't it?" Jake asked. "At the very least, it sounds as if someone paid off the judge to grant the transfer, and then pulled other strings to delay the reporting of the escape."

"Patrick said it took place in a remote area. They thought my father got away via helicopter."

"Did he also tell you the FBI suspected your father had help from higher up?"

"Higher up? What do you mean?"

"I don't have any proof, but my friends in the Bureau tell me they think a prominent politician pulled strings and paid off some guards to look the other way."

"Because my father paid him?" Sam had said once that he could make anyone do what he wanted if he waved enough money under their nose.

"Either that or he was connected to Sam in some way that he didn't want to come out."

"Maybe so," she said. "But how is knowing this going to help me decide whether to go back into Wit-Sec or stay and help you?"

"Because my friends in the Bureau say they're closing in on the people who helped Sam escape. They're going to make an arrest soon. Your father won't have so many friends to rely on next time."

She shook her head. "You make it sound so simple. But I don't have any idea where my father is."

"I think he's near here. I don't think DiCello had to travel all that far to find you in Rogers." He reached into his pocket and took out a piece of paper. She recognized the lift ticket that had been on DiCello's coat. "This is from Telluride. Dated yesterday," Jake said.

"Maybe DiCello stole the coat."

"Or maybe he went skiing. Does your father ski?"

She hesitated. She didn't want Jake to be right; she didn't want her father to be so close. "Yes. Every winter when I was a kid we took a family ski vacation." For one week every winter they'd been like any other family, renting a condo, riding up the lifts together, racing down the mountains. They drank cocoa and went for sleigh rides and gathered around bonfires. Just like ordinary people, as long as you ignored the beefy bodyguards who accompanied her father everywhere. When they were very young, her mother had taught Anne and her brother to call the men "uncle." Uncle Ramon and Uncle Frankie and Uncle Tiva. Four-year-old Sammy had asked once why there were so many uncles but no aunts, and her father had repeated the joke over and over for weeks, always to uproarious laughter.

"Did you ever come to Telluride?" Jake asked.

She shook her head. "Mostly we went to Europe or Canada. Once to California, but never Colorado."

"Getting out of the country might be tough for your father right now. He's at the top of the FBI's Ten Most Wanted list. Does he know anyone in Telluride? Any friends?"

"I don't know. He had connections all over the country. All over the world."

"Search your memory. Maybe he's combining a little vacation with business."

The business of hunting down his own daughter. She shuddered.

"Do you have any idea how DiCello knew where you were?" he asked.

"I've been thinking about that." She pushed aside the cooling cocoa. "Maggie told me my picture was on the front page of the Telluride paper yesterday. I was helping with a fundraising booth at the Winter Carnival and a reporter took a picture without my knowledge. Someone who knew me before might have recognized me."

"I think that's a pretty strong indication that your

father is in Telluride. It's not that far from here, right? I saw a brochure at my hotel in Rogers."

"It's about an hour away. But all that lift ticket tells us was that DiCello was in Telluride. Maybe he was on vacation."

"We could go there tomorrow and find out."

"I'm supposed to call Patrick tomorrow. We're going to arrange to meet somewhere."

"You can meet him in Telluride."

She opened her mouth to say no—to tell him she didn't care if her father was in Telluride or Timbuktu. But as much as she could lie about other things, she couldn't lie to herself. Not about this. She wanted to know if her father was nearby; she needed to know.

"Maybe I could arrange to meet Patrick in Telluride."

"We can go in the morning. When are you supposed to check in with Thompson again?"

"We didn't set a time."

"Then leave your phone off and call him when we reach Telluride. After we've had a chance to look around."

He didn't press or plea, just waited for the answer he probably already knew she would give. "All right," she said. "I can do that."

He looked around the cabin. "We should be safe enough alone here tonight."

His words were innocent enough, but they struck a chord deep inside her. The last time she'd spent the night alone with Jake they'd been lovers. They'd slipped away to his apartment and celebrated like honeymooners, oblivious to the rest of the world and its problems.

Only two days later that world had come crashing down around them. They weren't the same people they'd been in that apartment so long ago—how could they be? But the memory of all she'd felt for him rose up in her. She didn't love Jake anymore—she couldn't, after the way he'd lied to her, and all he'd put her through. But that didn't stop her from wanting that kind of love again. She just needed to remember the difference between the fantasy and the reality and not make the mistake of confusing the two.

"You take the bed," he said. "I can bunk on the sofa."

"All right." The sofa was really a love seat, too short for him. He'd be pretty uncomfortable, but it wouldn't kill him for one night. In the morning they'd drive to Telluride and find nothing to alarm them. She'd call Patrick and arrange to meet him somewhere nearby. She'd say goodbye to Jake and probably never see him again. The thought brought a lump to her throat and she had to turn away.

JAKE HAD GIVEN ANNE a lot to mull over and she was obviously upset—not to mention dealing with the shock that someone had really tried to kill her, which was probably just now beginning to hit her. "Give me the keys and I'll get your overnight bag from the car," he said. She'd probably appreciate a few moments alone to pull herself together.

Stepping outside was like stepping into a cave—dark and bitingly cold. Trees blocked the stars, and there probably wasn't another occupied house for miles in any direction. He stood on the steps of the cabin, allowing his eyes to adjust to the darkness and listening to his own breathing. He had never been anywhere so dark and silent and remote.

Click. The sound, like metal striking against a stone,

rang loud in the stillness. Jake froze, one hand on the switch of the flashlight he'd brought from the cabin, the other on the gun in his pocket. Nothing.

He waited, until his feet grew numb and he could no longer feel his nose, but he heard nothing. Maybe an animal had made the noise, or the wind rubbing tree branches together. Moving slowly, placing each foot silently in the snow, he made his way to the car. He switched on the flashlight and aimed the beam low, shielding it with his body. The beam illuminated a confusion of footprints in the snow—his and Anne's steps, when they'd arrived at the cabin.

When he opened the car door the dome light came on. He crouched down behind the door, trying to stay out of sight of anyone who might be watching. Of course, no one was out there, but he couldn't shake the sensation that he wasn't alone.

He retrieved Anne's bag from the backseat, then opened the glove box and pulled out a map of Colorado. He wanted to study it, to figure out where they were now, and to determine the best route to Telluride tomorrow.

He switched off the flashlight and slammed the car door, plunging himself into darkness once more. Retracing his steps to the front door by memory, he opened and shut the door, but remained outside. Then he stood very still, waiting in the deepest shadows beside the steps.

He counted off a full three minutes before he heard the faint crunch of footsteps in the snow, the creak of a car door opening and the quiet *thunk* of it closing again. Then an engine roared to life. None of the sounds were close—the car was probably a quarter of a mile away or more. Sound carried farther out here in this profound silence.

"Jake?" A strip of light fell across the snow as the door to the cabin opened a few inches and Anne peered out. "Jake, are you all right?"

"I'm fine." He stepped out to where she could see him.

"What have you been doing out here so long?" she asked.

He debated whether to tell her; he could worry enough for both of them. But maybe she'd have a simple explanation for the sounds—a neighbor he didn't know about or something like that.

"Let me come inside and I'll tell you," he said. "I'm frozen."

She opened the door to let him in. He dropped her bag on the table, then stripped off his coat and stood in front of the fire, warming his hands. "I thought I heard something," he said.

"What, exactly?"

"Someone walking around out there—not too far away, maybe up by the road. I pretended to go inside, then I stood in the dark and waited. After a few minutes, I heard footsteps again, then a car door opening and someone driving away."

She frowned. "What time is it now?"

He slipped his phone from his pocket and checked the display. "Twelve minutes after one."

"Kids come out here to party sometimes, but not in the winter, and not on a weeknight," she said. "And when we drove in, I didn't see any sign that anyone else had been here, not since the last snow at least."

"Maybe I should walk up to the road and check."

He didn't relish the idea of venturing out into that cold blackness again, but he would if he had to.

"And then what?" She began to pace, arms folded across her chest. "So someone drove in here, then turned around and drove out. It might not mean anything."

"Or it might mean you were followed."

"I wasn't followed. I was watching and I'm sure of it. And if someone had followed and they wanted to harm us, why leave, having done nothing?"

"I'll feel better checking."

"Fine. Go check."

"I don't like the idea of leaving you here alone." Maybe whoever it was wanted to lure him away, so they could get to Anne when she was more vulnerable.

She stopped in front of him. "Well, I'm not going out there with you," she said. "It doesn't make sense to me to go stumbling around in the dark in the freezing cold instead of staying in this nice warm cabin behind locked doors. We're bound to be more vulnerable outside than in."

He nodded. Leaving shelter didn't make sense, especially with no obvious assailant. "You're right. It was probably just someone who was lost or something. I can check in the morning."

"Good. I found some sheets and blankets in the bedroom closet, and a pillow you can use."

He took the items, though he doubted he'd sleep. He'd sit up and keep watch. "Try to get some rest," he said.

"You, too." She started to turn away, then turned back and added, "I'm glad you were with me tonight. Not only because you saved my life, but because I'm glad I don't have to do this alone. That was always the worst part, when I was making my plan—knowing I'd be running away alone, with no one to tell me I was doing the right thing, that I wasn't crazy or paranoid."

"You're not crazy or paranoid. And I'm glad I'm with you, too." As horrible as the events of this day had been, the one good thing was that he'd been able to help her. He'd begun to make up for the way he'd let her down before.

ANNE WAS TOO EXHAUSTED, emotionally and physically, to change into a nightgown, so she crawled into bed in her clothes. She expected to lie awake, worrying about whoever had been in that car up near the road, and about where Patrick planned to send her next, and where sticking with Jake might lead. But weariness won out over worry, and she fell into a fitful sleep.

She awoke to pitch darkness, and the disorienting feeling of not knowing where she was. She stared into the darkness, awareness slowly returning, and the memory of the man who had attacked her at her home in Rogers. She didn't like to think what would have happened if Jake hadn't shown up when he did.

Something tickled her nose, and she sneezed. Then she sat bolt upright, fear making her heart pound. The smell of smoke filled the room, and she heard the unmistakable crackle of flames. "Jake!" she shouted as she threw back the covers and shoved her feet into her boots. "Jake, wake up! The cabin's on fire!"

Chapter Eight

Anne groped her way to the bedroom door and pressed both palms against the wood. The door was warm—too warm. Local firefighters had given a fire safety talk at the school earlier this year. She remembered their warning to never open a warm door in a fire, that doing so could send the flames rushing into the room. If the door was warm, you were supposed to find a window and escape that way.

But Jake was on the other side of that door. The love seat where he slept was near the woodstove, where the fire had likely started. Had he awakened in time and fled out the front door—or was he already dead, overcome by smoke? She pushed the thought away and hurried to the window. She'd go around to the front of the cabin and try to reach Jake that way. Or maybe she'd find him outside, safe and trying to reach her.

She tugged hard at the window, until it opened with a screeching protest. Bitterly cold air rushed in—air that might feed the fire and engulf the bedroom. She started to climb out, then reached back and yanked the heavy wool blanket off the bed. Maybe she could use it to beat out flames, or as an extra layer of protection if she had to go in after Jake.

Dragging the blanket behind her, she jumped out the window and made her way through the snow to the front of the cabin. The brilliant glow of the blaze momentarily blinded her as she rounded the corner of the house. She shaded her eyes with one hand, and stumbled on, but when she reached the front of the house, she drew back, gasping. The entire front wall of the cabin was ablaze, flames licking at the windows and door, and swiftly devouring the wooden shingles of the roof. "Jake!" she screamed above the roar of the inferno.

No answer came to her cries, and she saw no sign of him in the area illuminated by the fire. He must still be inside. Reaching him through the front door would be impossible. But the side walls remained intact. There was a chance she might get to him through the window. Still dragging the blanket, she ran back the way she'd come, and stopped at the window that opened into the cabin's main room. The sash refused to yield to her tugging, so she raced to the wood pile, grabbed a length of stove wood and ran back and swung it at the window, shattering the glass. Then she draped the blanket across the sash and boosted herself inside.

The flames that engulfed the front of the cabin illuminated a cavern of swirling smoke and shadows. "Jake!" she shouted.

Harsh coughing answered her. "Over here!" said a hoarse voice.

She wrapped herself in the blanket and shuffled toward the voice, trying to hold her breath, but unable to avoid the choking smoke. "Jake!" she called again, and began to cough.

"Here!"

She stumbled forward once more and almost fell over

him. He pulled her down beside her. "Stay low. The air is better down here."

Not much better that she could tell, but now wasn't the time to argue. She handed him a corner of the blanket. "Use this to shield your face. We've got to get to the window."

"I was trying to get to you in the bedroom, but I couldn't find the door in the smoke and darkness."

"Don't talk. Just move."

Together, they crawled across the floor, toward where she hoped the window was situated. A current of colder air told her they were getting close, so she stood, and helped Jake to stand also. They rushed to the window and half jumped, half fell onto the snow outside.

They lay side by side, wrapped in the singed blanket and gasping for breath. She felt Jake's hand, heavy on her back. "Are you...all right?" he gasped.

"I'm fine. The smell of smoke must have woken me and I climbed out the bedroom window."

"I planned to sit up all night, keeping watch, but I must have drifted off. I didn't wake up until the front wall was on fire. By then the smoke was so thick, and I was disoriented." He raised himself up on his elbows and looked at her. "I don't think I'd have made it if you hadn't come after me."

"I couldn't leave you." She blinked, trying to hold back a sudden flood of stinging tears. She'd been alone so long. Jake was the first person in a year who really knew her story, who had some inkling of what she was going through. For that reason alone, she couldn't turn her back on him, not yet.

He sat and helped her to sit, too. "Should we call 9-1-1?" she asked.

"With what? My cell phone is in the cabin."

"Mine, too. And my purse and, oh no—the car keys."

"I have the keys." He pulled them from his pocket. "I must have automatically stuck them in my pants when I came back from getting your bag."

A section of the cabin roof collapsed in a shower of sparks and she flinched. Even from a distance of ten yards, she could feel the intense heat of the blaze. "I hope it doesn't spread to the other cabins," she said.

"I don't think it will." He stood and offered her his hand. She grasped it and pulled herself up. "This cabin is set away from the others, and there's no wind. I think when the fuel—the cabin—is gone, the fire will burn itself out."

"I don't understand what happened," she said. "I checked the woodstove before we went to bed and everything seemed fine. But I guess all it takes is one spark—"

"The fire didn't start from the woodstove," he said.

She stared at him. "Then how?"

"Come on." He grabbed her hand and urged her toward the front of the cabin. "The fire started in the front."

She nodded. "The whole front wall was burning—that's why I had to come through the window on the side."

"For a whole wall to burn like that, so quickly, blocking the main exit, I'd think it would take some kind of accelerant."

"You mean—someone deliberately set the fire? But who? How?" She looked around, fighting rising panic. She'd chosen this place because it was safe. Now he was telling her danger had followed her even here?

"Look." He pointed to twin lines of tire tracks in the snow. "They weren't here earlier, I'm sure."

"But you heard a car earlier, and footsteps."

"Maybe the same people, checking to make sure we were here. They waited until we fell asleep and came back. Or maybe there was no connection at all."

She stared at the tracks, anger quickly overtaking panic. "You think someone planned the fire, knowing we were the ones in the cabin?"

"Yes, but they probably haven't gone far. They'll be back soon, to make sure the fire did its job."

"They must have followed us here."

"If they did, they're much better at tailing someone than anyone I've ever seen. I was watching and I never saw anyone, and you didn't either. On these deserted roads, any other vehicle would stand out."

"They couldn't have known I'd be here. I never told anyone—not even Maggie."

"We can't worry about how they found you right now. The point is, they did. And we have to leave before they come back."

"You're right." She headed toward the car. He put his hands on her shoulders and steered her toward the passenger side. "I'll drive."

She didn't argue. She was too shaken to face negotiating the narrow, snow-choked Forest Service road. She hoped Jake was up to the task; she had no idea what kind of driver he was. In New York, they'd taken taxis or the subway, or her father had sent one of his drivers to take them wherever they needed to go. She kept her convertible for weekend trips upstate or to the coast.

"Is there another way out of here?" he asked as

he started the car. "I meant to check the map, but I never did."

"You have to take this road up to the gate, but there you can turn right instead of left and take another series of forest roads that come out near a little town called New Richmond. It's a lot farther back to the highway than the way we came in."

"We'll take it. I don't want to risk running head-on into the arsonist on these narrow pig trails."

At the gate, he stopped and waited for her to dial in the combination, but she'd only taken a few steps from the car when she saw there was no need. The chain hung loose, the lock lying in the snow. She forced herself to move forward and swing open the gate, then closed it and climbed in the car again. "Someone cut the lock off," she said.

"Whoever followed us didn't have the combination."

She hugged her arms across her chest and shivered. "We'll buy coats in Telluride," he said. "Meanwhile, turn the heater up."

"It's not the weather making me cold," she said. "I just can't believe someone followed us—and tried to burn us to death."

"I'm guessing they think two accidental deaths would be easier to deal with than two obvious murders."

"They weren't very smart," she said. "An arson investigator would have spotted the accelerant."

"Maybe. Maybe not. We don't know what they used."

"And we don't know who they are."

"Except they probably work for your father."

"Maybe. Maybe not."

"Do you have other enemies?"

"No. Do you? Maybe we're looking at this wrong.

Maybe they're not after me at all. If my father knew you were still alive, he'd be very happy to see you dead." The idea that Jake might be the target of her father's wrath—that Sam Giardino might not even know anything about her—flooded her with relief. Not that she wanted Jake to be in danger, but she dreaded starting life over with yet another new name and profession.

"I don't think you're right," Jake said.

"You don't know that I'm wrong."

"All right. I'll concede it's a possibility that whoever set the fire was after me, and you were only a secondary target—a bonus. That still leaves us with the same problem. Until your father is behind bars again, neither one of us is safe."

"He was behind bars before—I testified to put him there. But he didn't stay there for long." Despair had engulfed her when Patrick had told her of her father's escape from prison. She'd given up everything in order to see him convicted; his escape made her sacrifice worth nothing.

"He'll stay there this time. The authorities won't risk being made to look like fools twice."

"People will do a lot of foolish things when confronted with the kind of money and power my father can offer."

He fell silent, negotiating a particularly bad section of road. Anne clenched her teeth, and prayed they wouldn't end up stuck in a snowdrift here in the middle of nowhere, with an unknown assailant out to silence them.

She let out a sigh of relief as Jake turned onto a slightly wider, smoother section of road.

"You're right," he said. "I can't guarantee your father

won't get out of prison again. But if we do nothing, he definitely won't be arrested, and he'll continue to do everything in his power to see that both of us are dead. You can go back into witness protection and hope he doesn't find you again, but he's already beat the system once."

Denying his words wouldn't make them any less true. And if she ran away again, without even trying to change things, she'd have one more thing to regret. "All right," she said. "I'll do what I can to help. But only for a few days. I can't give you any more time than that."

"And I won't ask for any more."

His words should have made her feel relieved; instead, they filled her with sadness. That's what she got for thinking about regrets. Surely she would regret the love she and Jake had had, and could never regain, for the rest of her life.

"Patrick told me I should be careful of you," she said.

"Oh? When did he tell you that?"

"When I talked to him last night. He said you'd been asking about me and he thought you were looking for revenge."

"I am looking for revenge, but on your father, not you."

"I know that now."

"How do you know that?"

"Setting a fire that you almost died in would be a pretty stupid way to try to do away with me."

"Thanks for agreeing that I'm not stupid."

"You're stubborn and reckless—but not stupid." And the same might have been said of her, once upon a time, back when she was daring Elizabeth, not quiet and cautious Anne.

"*Nil opus captivis.* Do you still believe that?" he asked.

The idea of doing whatever she had to in order to get what she wanted had appealed to her when she was a young, spoiled socialite, to whom very little had ever been denied. From the perspective of a woman who had paid the price for that kind of ruthlessness, the words she'd once had tattooed on the base of her spine struck her as a sick joke. "I'm ashamed I thought those words were important," she said.

"We're both a little older and I hope a lot wiser now," he said. "Suffering and loss make you understand what's really important in life."

But what if the really important things—love and home and family—were all the things you had lost? "What's important to you?" she asked.

"Right now, what's important is seeing that your father is back behind bars, where he can never hurt anyone else again."

So revenge was most important to Jake—not home or family or love. For all he'd suffered after her father's attack, he didn't value the things that were most precious to her. She shouldn't have been surprised, really. How could a man who had made a living out of lying and pretending to be someone he was not ever be happy with simple truths?

She had to remember that, for all her strong feelings for Jake, she hadn't really loved him. She'd only loved a mirage he'd created to fool her. The man she loved didn't exist, and he never would.

AN HOUR BEFORE DAWN, Jake stopped the car at the intersection of the Forest Service road and the highway. True darkness had receded, and the trees along the side of the road looked like black smudges against a gray sky. They hadn't seen another car since leaving the burning cabin; maybe they'd lost whoever had been tracking them. "Which way do I turn?" he asked.

Anne pointed right. "Telluride is that way."

"How are you holding up?" he asked. Her hair was disheveled and she wore the same clothes she'd had on last night, reeking of smoke. She had to be tired and hungry, yet she hadn't made one complaint. He couldn't imagine Elizabeth enduring such discomfort gracefully. She'd been used to living like a princess and taken for granted she should be treated like one.

With all that finery and privilege stripped away, Jake could see that Anne was made of stronger stuff.

"I'm fine." She offered a weary smile. "Before we reach Telluride, we'll go through New Richmond."

"What's in New Richmond?"

"Not much. But there's a convenience store where we can stop for gas and coffee, and to clean up a little." She leaned forward and touched his cheek. "You've got a smudge of soot."

The gesture was innocent; she'd leaned back and was looking out the car window again almost before he'd realized what was happening. But the sensation of her cool fingers against his cheek lingered, calling forth all the other times she'd touched him, sometimes not so innocently.

Enough, he cautioned himself, and he turned the car right onto the highway. He needed Anne's help to find her father, and he wanted to protect her, but he shouldn't waste time trying to recreate something that had been built on lies and fantasy. They both lived in a harsher, if more honest, world now.

Half an hour later, he pulled the car alongside the gas pumps at the Gas and Ready in New Richmond. She went inside while he filled the car, and then he made his way to the men's room, where he did his best with soap and paper towels to make himself look presentable. He needed a shave and a change of clothes, but this would have to do.

When he emerged from the restroom, she was waiting. She handed him a cup of coffee. "Do you still drink it black?" she asked.

He nodded. She'd washed the last of the makeup from her face and pulled her hair back into a sleek ponytail. She looked very young and vulnerable. The thought that someone out there was trying to kill her made him shaky with anger.

"They have breakfast sandwiches, too," she said. "And we should get these." She handed him a dark blue bundle of cloth.

He set his cup on the counter and unfolded a thick sweatshirt, and read the slogan printed on the front. *Telluride—Higher, Steeper, Deeper.*

"I got this one for me." She held up a pink shirt, printed with the words *Official Ski Bunny.*

"I guess this will help us look like tourists," he said.

"At least we'll be warmer, and have one thing that doesn't smell like smoke."

He paid for their purchases, thankful he'd still had his wallet and credit cards when he'd crawled from the burning cabin. "We'll get a room in Telluride and shower." He rubbed his sandpapery chin. "And I need to shave."

"I hope you have a big expense account for this little expedition." She settled into the passenger seat and fastened her seat belt. "Hotel rooms in Telluride don't come cheap."

"I think I can manage." He'd remained at full pay all the months he'd been recuperating, the money piling up in the bank with no way for him to spend it. And he had savings; he didn't care if he had to spend every penny to make sure Sam Giardino ended up back behind bars.

"We'll need some more clothes, too. Those won't be cheap, either." They turned onto the highway once more, the view of snowcapped mountains against the pink clouds of sunrise worthy of any tourist postcard. "Telluride used to be a sleepy little hippie hangout," she said. "But now it's home to the rich and famous."

And the infamous, he hoped. "We have to have new clothes," he agreed. "It's pretty hard to sneak up on someone when you reek like a campfire."

"Good point. I know a chichi thrift store on the main drag that won't break your bank."

He laughed.

"What's so funny?"

"Elizabeth would have never shopped at a thrift store," he said.

"Elizabeth's dead. You need to remember that." The finality of her words sent a chill through him. Of course Elizabeth was dead. And he was after the man who had destroyed her. The loss had been a tragic one, though he couldn't help thinking now that maybe the woman beside him was stronger and wiser than the pretty, naive socialite he'd once loved.

They drove on in silence. Maybe she was as mired in thoughts of the past and what might have been as he was. But after a few miles he became aware that they weren't alone on the highway anymore. He checked the rearview mirror and saw a black SUV, windows heavily tinted to prevent any view of driver or passengers, approaching at a fast clip. "We might be in for trouble," he said.

"What is it?"

"I think we're being followed, and this time they're not even trying to hide it."

Chapter Nine

Anne stared at the black vehicle barreling toward their car. It was driving much too fast for the narrow, winding highway, but the driver expertly negotiated the sharp curves, and the powerful engine appeared to manage the steep grades without strain. "Are you sure they're after us?" she asked.

"No, I'm not sure." Jake pulled his gun from beneath his shirt and laid it on the console between them. "But there's no one else out this time of morning, and I don't like the looks of them. If they pass us by, no harm done, but I want to be ready."

"Of course." There was something sinister about the vehicle, with its blacked-out windows and swift approach. She glanced to the side of the road, where the world fell away into a steep, rocky canyon. On Jake's side of the car, sheer rock walls rose beside the road. They were stuck on the side of a mountain, with a swiftly approaching enemy who would probably like nothing better than to knock them off into the abyss below.

"They won't shoot us," she said. "They'll try to make it look like an accident. They'll try to run us over the side."

"I think so." He gripped the steering wheel with both hands, and constantly shifted his gaze from the road to the rearview mirror and back. "I'm going to do my best to keep that from happening."

"What do you need me to do?" she asked.

"Tighten your seat belt, and if they start shooting, duck."

"I could try to shoot at them."

"Don't waste ammunition unless they get really close."

She picked up the pistol and checked that there was a bullet in the chamber. "Have you shot much before?" he asked.

"After I came to Rogers, someone sent me a gun in the mail. I think it was probably Patrick, though he wouldn't admit to it."

"Your father didn't teach you to shoot?"

"Absolutely not. Women weren't supposed to concern themselves with that sort of thing. That's what the muscle was for."

"What did you do with the gun Thompson sent you?"

"I took it to the local shooting range and practiced, but firing at a moving vehicle is a lot different from hitting a target on the range."

"It is. But if they succeed in running us off the road and then come after us, you might be able to hit one of them."

"If they run us off this road, I don't think either one of us will be shooting anyone." She took in the steep drop-off to her right and shuddered.

"Good point." The Subaru sped up and the passing scenery became a blur of gray rock, blue sky and white snow. Anne clutched the armrest and bit her lip to keep from crying out as they careened around one hairpin turn after the next, all the while steadily climbing the mountain. The screech of protesting brakes tore into the early morning silence as the SUV followed, skidding around the turns. "He's got a higher center of gravity," Jake said. "He can't corner as well as we can."

His logical analysis of such an emotionally charged situation made her feel calmer. But then, she reminded herself, Jake was trained as an accountant to measure evidence and sift facts. Focusing on the things he knew, rather than the things he felt, allowed him to remain in control of an impossible situation.

She took a deep breath, and tried to follow Jake's example. But the first fact that came to her mind offered little comfort. "They've got a more powerful engine than we do," she said. "They're gaining on us." One glance over her shoulder proved the SUV was quickly closing the gap. Sunlight glinted off the windshield, making it impossible to see who was behind the wheel. Somehow, that made the situation more menacing, even though she doubted she'd recognize one of her father's many "associates." When she was growing up, they had been a series of faceless, muscular men who accompanied her father everywhere; they'd meant nothing to her.

The Subaru lurched as the back wheels skidded on the gravel shoulder. Anne shrieked, and clutched the dashboard with one hand, the fingers of her other hand digging into the armrest. "Slow down!" she pleaded. "We're going to run off the road."

He eased off on the gas pedal a little—enough that she felt she could breathe again. "We can't outrun them," he said. "So I'm going to slow down and see what they do."

"You're going to let them catch up with us?"

"They won't expect us to stop trying to outrun them. I'm hoping to catch them off guard."

"All right." She had to trust his judgment on this; she had no one else to turn to.

He eased off the gas and the Subaru slowed to forty, then thirty miles an hour. Anne watched in the side mirror as the SUV raced toward them, closing the gap between the two cars in an alarmingly short time. "They're going to ram us!" she screamed.

"No, they're not." He wrenched the steering wheel to the left, sending the Subaru shooting into the next lane, which was thankfully empty of oncoming traffic. The SUV flew past, a blur of black paint and red taillights.

Jake turned the wheel hard right, ramming the front end of the Subaru into the left rear quarter panel of the SUV. The SUV slid onto the gravel shoulder, sending up a rooster tail of mud and rock. The Subaru fishtailed wildly; Jake leaned forward, struggling to maintain control. "Hang on!" he shouted.

The car veered wildly to the left, narrowly avoiding a collision with the rock wall. The SUV slid along the right shoulder, only one wheel still in contact with the pavement. Anne watched in horror as the bulky black vehicle swayed, then began to topple, momentum taking it over the side. Time seemed to slow as the SUV plummeted, sending up sparks as it struck rock, bounced up, then tumbled out of sight.

Jake pulled the Subaru to the shoulder of the road and set the parking brake, but left the engine running. "Stay in the car," he ordered, and opened the driver's door.

She ignored the command, and followed him out of the car. On shaking legs, she walked along the shoulder of the road to the place where the SUV had gone over. Black skid marks cut into the gravel; a mirror torn from the side of the car rested on the rocks a few feet below. Trees blocked their view of the wrecked vehicle, but a plume of smoke marked the site of the crash. "Should we call for help?" she asked. "Do you think anyone is alive?"

"We'll call at the first place we come to with a phone," he said. "Meanwhile, we'd better get out of here."

She hugged her arms tightly across her stomach, fighting a chill that had nothing to do with the air temperature. "We can't just leave, can we?"

His eyes met hers, his gaze hard. "Do you want to answer a bunch of questions for the police?"

Questions that had no right answer, starting with "Who are you?" and "What are you doing with this man?"

She shook her head. "No, I don't want to get involved with the police."

"Come on, then." He took her elbow and led her back to the Subaru.

He didn't say anything for several minutes after they drove away, and she could find no words. Finally, as they neared a scenic overlook outside of Telluride, he pulled in and shut off the engine. "Are you okay?" he asked.

She laced her fingers together in her lap, as if she might squeeze all her turbulent emotions into a ball in the palms of her hands and keep them confined there, with no danger of them rocketing out of control or overwhelming her. "I think it's all just beginning to hit me," she said. "The man you killed at my house in Rogers—

DiCello—I remember him at my sixteenth birthday party. He wished me happy birthday. I'd forgotten all about that, and it came back to me this morning. And now he's dead."

"Because he tried to kill you."

"Yes, but…" She swallowed hard. "I don't think anyone is ever prepared for the idea that someone else—especially a parent—wants you to die. It's too bizarre."

"So is starting life over with a new name and a new story, trying to pretend the person you were never existed."

"I thought I was getting used to that." She stared out the window at the view of snow-capped mountains against a cobalt sky. So different from the jutting spires of city skyscrapers that had formed the backdrop of her old life. "When you go into witness protection, they give you a little training," she continued. "The counselors tell you to think of your new life as just that—a rebirth, a new beginning. They want you to focus on the positives and all the new possibilities, and not what you left behind. I thought I was handling it pretty well, until you came along."

"Because I brought all the memories of your old life back?"

"Because you brought back the memories of what happened at the end—why I had to hide in the first place." She studied his face, and curled her hands into fists to keep from reaching out and touching him, to reassure herself that he was indeed flesh and blood, and not a hallucination of her fevered imagination.

"I thought about you every day while I was in the hospital, and during rehab." He spoke low, the roughness in his voice catching at something in her chest and pulling. "I tried to get my friends at the Bureau to tell me where you were, but all I could get out of them was that you were safe. When I was well enough to be on my own, I started looking. I found the obituary for Elizabeth and figured out you must be in WitSec. It took a few more months of digging to find you after that—and only because I knew exactly what to look for."

"Was it awful—after the shooting? You haven't talked much about your injuries."

"It's not the most fascinating subject. I had some liver damage, shattered bones in my legs, pneumonia from a bullet in my lung. It took a lot longer to get back on my feet than I'd have liked, but I was motivated. And I was lucky. I trained for triathlons before I went undercover, so I was in good physical shape."

"I thought you were dead. Knowing my father had killed you was the final straw—the thing that turned me against him."

"I did die, in a way. Jake West died. Agent Westmoreland died. I had to learn to walk again, but I also had to learn to live a different kind of life. A life without you."

She tried to look away, but he reached up to brush her cheek, and gently turned her to face him once more. She raised her eyes to meet his; he was the same man she'd once loved so passionately, and yet he was not the same. In his eyes she saw a pain that touched her, and a new hardness that made her tremble.

He kissed her, his lips silencing her gasp. She closed her eyes and he deepened the kiss, his hand cradling her cheek, the tenderness of that touch, even more than the caress of his lips, breaking down some barrier within her. She sighed and leaned toward him, craving the closeness that had been denied her so long. Eyes closed, lips pressed to his, she gave herself up to memories of the intimacy they'd shared, and love she'd been sure would last forever.

The wail of a siren ripped apart the early morning silence. She shuddered, and pushed him away. "This is wrong," she said.

"Because I lied to you about my real identity?" His face was still very close to hers, so close she could see the individual bristles of the stubble along his jaw, and the fine lines of tension that radiated from the corners of his eyes. "I don't see how I could have done anything differently."

"It's wrong because neither one of us is the person we used to be. We don't even know each other."

"I know you're still as brave and beautiful as you ever were. And you understand loss and sacrifice. Those are hard lessons to learn, but in the end they make you a stronger, and hopefully a more compassionate, person."

He made her sound so noble and virtuous, like a saint, not a woman. "We don't want the same things," she said. "You want revenge. I just want to be left alone."

"You'll never be left alone until your father is behind bars again."

"You can't know that."

"I can't know anything, except that someone— probably your father—wants us dead and I have to do what I can to stop it."

He leaned back against the driver's seat and she breathed a little easier, relieved to shift the subject away from impossible emotions. "I can't understand how they keep finding us," she said. "I thought DiCello recognized my picture from the Telluride paper. But how did someone follow us to the cabin—and then find us again on the road? It's as if they have someone telling them our every move."

His expression hardened. "Not someone. Some*thing*." He shoved open the car door and climbed out.

"What are you doing?" she asked, but he ignored her. She exited the car in time to see him lie on the grimy snow and slide under the car.

"I don't know why I didn't think of this before." He emerged from beneath the car and stood, holding up a black plastic box about the size of a deck of cards. A green light glowed at one end of the device.

"What is that?" she asked.

"It's a GPS tracking device. It allows the person who planted it to track your movements—or the movements of the car. DiCello must have planted it before he entered your house."

"But he was there to kill me."

"Yes, but he probably had orders to plant the tracking device as insurance—in case you managed to get away."

She stared at the small black object, feeling sick. "What do we do now? Destroy it?"

"If we destroy it, they'll know we're on to them. We need to think of something else."

"What?"

A second emergency vehicle raced by, siren blaring. "Someone must have seen the smoke from the accident and reported it," he said.

She drew hands into the sleeves of her sweatshirt and hugged her arms across her stomach. "We have to get rid of that thing."

"Yes. And I think I know the perfect place. Get back in the car."

She returned to the passenger seat and had scarcely fastened her seat belt before he turned the car around and headed back the way they'd come. "What are you doing?" she asked.

"You'll see."

As they neared the place where their pursuers had run off the road, they saw the flashing lights of emergency vehicles. Jake parked on the side of the road behind a Colorado Highway Patrol SUV. "Wait here," he said.

He got out and walked alongside the patrol vehicle. An officer approached. "Sir, you need to leave," he said.

"I just wondered if there was anything I could do to help." He craned his neck to see down into the canyon, a nosy tourist drawn to the excitement.

"No sir, we have everything under control."

"What happened?" Jake asked.

"A car went over the side. It happens. People drive too fast, or maybe he fell asleep. We don't know yet."

"That's too bad. I'll have to be more careful out there."

"You do that. Now if you'll please leave."

"Of course." He turned, and stumbled, bracing himself against the side of the patrol car. "Sorry," he said. "Must have tripped on a rock." He straightened, nodded to the officer and returned to the car, walking briskly. "Someone went over the side," he said to Anne. "Shows you how dangerous these roads can be."

She waited until he'd turned the car and headed back toward Telluride before she asked, "What did you do?"

"When I stumbled, I stuck the tracking device on the side of the patrol vehicle."

"Why did you do that?"

"Instead of tracking us, whoever is after us can track the cops for a while."

"You don't think we're putting the police in danger?"

"If your father sends someone else to follow you, that person will recognize a cop car from a long way off. But chances are the cops will discover the tracking device long before your dad's thugs show up. Until they do, it buys us time to get settled in Telluride."

"If my father is there, what then?"

"We make sure he's there, and contact the authorities."

So he didn't intend to go after her father himself. The knowledge flooded her with relief. "There's a reward for finding him, isn't there? Patrick mentioned it."

"Yes. But that's not why I'm doing this."

"I know. But I like thinking you'd have the money from the reward to live on after I'm gone."

"Right." He looked grim. "While you're teaching school or working as a secretary in your new life."

"Teaching was the best part about starting over. I loved my students—I loved making my own way, based on my own merits. That's something I never had to do as Elizabeth Giardino."

"Then I hope you get the chance to do that again."

"What will you do when this is over?" she asked.

"I don't know. I suppose it depends on how things turn out. Come on. We've got to find a place to stay and do some shopping. We'll play tourists for a few hours, anyway, and worry about your father later."

"What about Patrick? I promised to contact him today."

"You can call him from the hotel later. But you'll need to try to put him off for another day or two, to give us time to look for your father."

"Patrick isn't the easiest person to put off."

"Then wait to call him. Tonight, let's just try to relax, and worry about the rest tomorrow."

She nodded. She'd grown used to not thinking much about tomorrow. Knowing, as she did, how things could change in an instant, she'd spent the last year focusing on right now, today. Tomorrow was a luxury she almost felt she couldn't afford, but for a little while, maybe, she could pretend things were different. Maybe, with Jake by her side, she could even be Elizabeth, a woman without a worry in the world, with the man who loved her more than anyone ever could.

Chapter Ten

The kiss had been a mistake. Jake had known that the moment his lips touched Anne's. If he was going to pull this off—if he was going to find Sam Giardino and see him locked away for good—he couldn't afford to make mistakes. He couldn't let emotion or nostalgia or plain old lust interfere with the job he had to do.

He glanced at the woman walking beside him. Showered and freshly made up, dressed in a fake-fur-trimmed parka, designer jeans and knee-high boots they'd purchased at a thrift store on Telluride's main drag, Anne looked more like Elizabeth when he'd first met her—polished and fashionable and way out of his league.

"What are you staring at?" she asked.

"I'm not staring." He turned his attention back to the crowded street in front of them. Men and women filled the sidewalks and spilled out of shops and restaurants, talking and laughing, carrying shopping bags or schlepping skis and snowboards toward the gondola that would take them up to the ski resort above town. Conversations in four languages drifted to him, and he heard accents that identified the speakers as hailing from New York and Texas and half a dozen foreign countries. February was the height of the tourist

season in Telluride, and somewhere in all this human-
ity was one man who'd managed to evade the law for
the past year. Jake had to admire Giardino's cunning;
a crowded tourist town with people from all over the
world was the perfect place for a fugitive to hide, lost
in a crowd of people who didn't know one another and
would likely never see each other again.

Jake and Anne had arrived in town a little after ten
in the morning and found lodging at a new hotel that
had been built to blend in with the town's Victorian
architecture. He'd booked them into adjoining rooms
and they'd agreed to meet later for lunch and shopping.
The afternoon should have been a pleasant break from
the tension, but the events of the past two days, and
the real reason they were here, prevented them from
completely relaxing and enjoying their roles as tourists. "I've been thinking about how we're going to find
your father," he said.

"Yes. How are we going to do that?"

"If he's here to ski, we need to hit the slopes."

"Do you ski?" she asked.

"Not in a long time. What about you? Do you make
it to Telluride much from Rogers?"

"I've been a few times. Enough to be fairly familiar
with the runs."

"Good. Then you can take us to the places your father's likely to hang out."

"It's a big mountain, with a lot of people. I don't
think our chances are very good that we'll see him."

"You say that because you don't really want to see
him."

She stiffened, and started to protest; then she clamped

her mouth shut and shook her head. "No, I don't want to see him. Why should I?"

"Help me find him and you'll never have to see him again."

She took hold of his arm, stopping him. "Why is this so important to you? You're retired. You don't have to do this anymore."

"I told you—neither one of us will be safe as long as he's walking around free."

"This isn't about safety—it's about revenge. You want to make him pay because he hurt you."

"I want to make him pay because he hurt *you*."

She released his arm as if she'd been burned. "Don't make this about me. I was happy with my life the way it was."

This was all about her. If Jake hadn't fallen in love with her, if he hadn't let his emotions get the better of his training and common sense, he might not have been so careless and let himself be found out. He wouldn't have almost died in a hail of bullets and she wouldn't have been dragged away and persuaded to testify against her father. She wouldn't have had to hide out in WitSec and she wouldn't be running from her father's thugs right now. If he did nothing else with his life, he had to fix this mistake. He couldn't give her back the life she'd had, or even repair the damage to their own relationship. But he could see that she was safe. Then, even if he had to leave her—and he did have to leave her, she'd made that clear enough—he'd have done what he could to make up for the mistakes of the past.

"Fine. It's not about you," he said. "It's about me. I screwed up and I have to make this right. Your father belongs behind bars. It was my job to put him there and I want to finish the job."

"You don't work for the Bureau anymore."

"No, I don't. Which makes this both easier and more difficult."

She looked at him, head tilted slightly to one side, one eyebrow raised. He remembered that look from before, imperious and demanding answers. He almost smiled, seeing her so easily slip back into the role of the pampered princess who was used to getting her way. "Easier, because I don't have to wait and go through channels, or play by their rules," he explained. "Harder, because I have no authority, and I don't have the Bureau's resources at my fingertips, or a team backing me up."

"Only me." She looked away before he could judge the expression in her eyes. "Do you think finding my father will prove they were wrong to dismiss you?" she asked. "Do you think it will get your job back?"

"This isn't about getting my job back." He wasn't a good fit for the Bureau; he was always stepping outside the boundaries of his job description and questioning dictates from higher up the chain of command. Going to Sam Giardino's warehouse hadn't been part of his job. He was an accountant, and he was supposed to stay chained to his desk in front of a computer. But his bosses had badly wanted the dirt on the Giardino family, and when they'd learned Jacob had an in, they had been willing to overlook him breaking the rules. Only when his rule-breaking had resulted in a disaster had they been more than happy to let him go. "Though I would have preferred to leave on my own terms, not theirs," he said. And yes, it would feel good to prove to them they had been wrong to dismiss him so easily.

"You said something before about my father escaping prison with the help of a politician. Do you mean the governor?"

"I don't know who. I couldn't find anyone who would admit to being part of the investigation, only that there is an investigation. Someone with power pulled strings so that your father got what he needed to get out of prison. Two guards died during the escape, did you know that?"

"Yes. I know my father is a murderer." Her expression grew bleak. "I've known it for a very long time, but I either ignored the killings or tried to tell myself they were justified. You opened my eyes to the truth of what he'd done, and when he tried to kill you…"

He put his arm around her. "I read the trial transcripts. Your testimony was the key to convicting your father. I know speaking out against him wasn't an easy thing to do."

"It wasn't as hard as you might think. I was so angry. I wanted to hurt him."

"And now?"

"Now I'm more sad than angry. And tired." She stifled a yawn.

He patted her shoulder and released her. "You must be dead on your feet. We've both hardly slept."

"I'm too keyed up to sleep." She shrugged away from him. "Maybe we could get something to eat."

At the mention of food, his stomach growled. He couldn't remember his last real meal. "There are plenty of places to choose from. See anything you like?"

"There was a little bistro a few blocks back. Let's try that."

They retraced their steps. The sun was sinking fast behind the mountains; with dusk came a deeper cold, and more crowds, as vacationers and locals alike returned from a day on the slopes. Jake kept one hand on Anne's back to prevent them from being separated, but also because he felt the need to hold on to her. Today he'd glimpsed the vulnerability beneath her strength. He wanted her to know she wasn't alone in this, that he'd do anything to protect her.

They'd almost reached the restaurant when Anne froze. Tension radiated from her body, like a hunting dog on point—or a rabbit that knew it had been spotted by a dog. Jake moved in close behind her. "What is it?" he asked softly.

"I thought I saw Sammy."

"Your brother?"

"Yes." She continued to stare in the direction of the brewpub across the street. "He just went into that restaurant. I'm sure it was Sammy. He's here in Telluride."

ANNE HADN'T SEEN her brother since the trial, but it wasn't as if he would have changed that much in a year. "Are you sure it was him?" Jake asked.

"Yes." She'd scarcely glimpsed the dark-haired man who'd entered the restaurant with two burly companions, but something in the set of his shoulders and the back of his head had sparked instant recognition. Her heart had leapt in her chest, blood calling to blood.

"Did he see you?" Jake asked.

"No."

"Then we'd better not give him the chance." He took

her arm and led her away. She went reluctantly, finding it difficult to move, when all she wanted to do was run toward her brother. She wanted to feel his arms around her and hear him tell her he was glad to see her—that everything would be all right.

She shook her head, as if she could shake out that fantasy. It had been a while since she and Sammy had been really close; he was four years younger and involved in his own life. As the only son he'd been groomed to follow in her father's footsteps. While she'd been spoiled and pampered and indulged, Sammy had endured lectures and ordeals designed to toughen him up and teach him the ins and outs of the various family "businesses."

They turned onto the next block. Jake stopped in the shelter of an overhang in front of a boutique and let the crowd flow around them. "I don't think we were followed," he said.

"I'm sure he didn't see me."

"If your brother is here, that means your father is probably here, too," Jake said.

"Maybe. Or he could have come here on vacation with his family." His family and a few spare goons to act as bodyguards and lookouts. The thought made her stomach churn.

"I didn't see too much of Sammy while I was with your family. He was away a lot."

"My father had sent him to Atlantic City to learn about the Giardino operation there."

"Were you close?"

"We were when we were younger. I always looked out for him." She smiled, remembering the nights she'd sneaked into Sammy's room with a peanut butter sandwich when he'd been sent to bed without his supper, or the times she'd finished his homework assignments for him. "We were the only kids around most of the time," she said. "So the two of us would band together to spy on the adults. But as we got older, we kind of grew apart." Her smile faded. "It's hard to be close in a family where there are so many secrets and lies."

He put his hand on her shoulder, a comforting gesture. She fought the urge to lean into him. She was physically and emotionally exhausted, not just from the events of the last few days, but from months of bearing everything alone. WitSec had helped her start over with a new life, but it couldn't erase the memories of everything that had happened. Figuring out what to do with those memories, how to process and deal with them while not letting them destroy her, was wearing.

"I'm going to ask you a question you may not like, but I want you to answer honestly," he said. "Your brother is next in line to assume power. Do you think he'd order a hit on you?"

"If you mean is he the one behind everything that's been happening lately, I don't know." She met his gaze and saw her own exhaustion and frustration reflected in her eyes. "Since Sammy is the only son, he was always more involved in the business side of things than I was. I saw more of his wife those last few years than I did him, so I have no idea what he thinks of me these days. I never would have believed my father wanted me dead, and he actually threatened me. I can't wrap my mind around my brother feeling that way about me."

"I don't recall that you and his wife were that close. Stacy—that was her name, right?"

"Yes. I liked her well enough, but she never really fit

in well with the rest of the family." Stacy was neither brash and outspoken, nor meek and compliant, the two models for Giardino women. She held herself aloof, and maintained a slightly disapproving air. "I didn't understand her at the time, but now that I'm on the outside, I have more sympathy." Barely nineteen when she'd married Sammy Giardino, Stacy Franklin had been thrust into a world where she didn't fit. She must have felt trapped in her contentious marriage; divorce was not an option in the Giardino family, since ex-spouses had the potential to reveal family secrets.

"I got the impression she wasn't very happy in her marriage," Jake said.

"Probably not. It was more a political move on my father's part than a love match."

"You mean your father arranged the marriage? And Sammy went along?"

"Sammy will do anything to please my father." Even though Sam Senior was almost impossible to please.

"Maybe he resents the control your father has over his life."

"Maybe."

"Then maybe we can use that. Maybe he'll help us get to your father."

"I doubt that. I mean, he might want to get back at my father, but doing so would mean destroying everything Sammy is supposed to inherit—everything he's spent his life working toward. I can't see him giving up all that."

"If I could arrange for you to talk to him, would you?"

"I don't know. Yes. But because I want to see him, not because I think it will be of any help." To spend even a few minutes with someone who knew her—knew her childhood and her relatives, with whom she had shared so many memories and experiences—would be such a gift. Of all the things she'd experienced since going into witness protection, the loneliness of having no family at all had been the most unexpected pain.

She became aware of Jake studying her intently, as if trying to read her mind. "Are you all right?" he asked.

"I don't feel like braving a restaurant right now," she said. "Let's go back to the hotel and order room service."

"All right."

They didn't speak as they walked back to their hotel, though Jake radiated tension. He scanned the crowd, watching for her brother or father, she supposed. She couldn't help watching, too, but saw no one familiar in the sea of strangers' faces.

At the hotel, he followed her into her room and checked the bathroom and closet. "Do you really think someone is hiding out here, waiting to pounce?" she asked when he returned from the bathroom.

"Probably not. But better to be safe." He picked a room service menu from the dresser. "What do you want to eat?"

"Some soup. I don't care what kind."

He called in the order, then settled into the room's one chair, while she sat on the side of the bed. "All right if I eat in here with you?" he asked.

She shrugged. She didn't want to be alone, but she didn't want him hovering, either. "I should call Patrick," she said.

"And tell him what?"

"Whatever I want," she snapped. She picked up the

receiver from the phone by the bed. "If I don't call, he'll think something's wrong." But of course, a lot of things were wrong. Someone—probably her father—was trying to kill her. A man she thought was dead had come back to life. She'd seen her brother for the first time in a year, and part of her had been afraid to let him see her. Nothing in her life was as it ought to be.

She dialed his number. One of her first assignments as an enrollee in Witness Security had been to memorize the number.

He answered on the second ring. "Hello?"

"Hi. It's Anne. I wanted to let you know I'm all right."

"Where are you? What have you been doing? Why haven't you been answering your phone?" The rapid-fire questions betrayed his agitation, though his voice remained calm.

"I don't have my phone anymore. I, uh, I lost it." She doubted he would believe the lie, but she felt compelled to try it. She didn't want to alarm him, to make him want to rush her back into WitSec. She wasn't ready yet to change her name and her job and her life all over again. Not when she had a chance to stop her father—and to make things right with Jake.

"Where are you now?"

She hesitated. Lying to this man who'd been her only real friend this past year was impossible. "I'm in Telluride. At a hotel."

"Are you alone?"

She glanced toward Jake and found him watching her, eyes burning. "Jake is with me," she said.

"Are you all right? Has he tried to hurt you?"

"No! I mean, I'm fine. Jake has asked me to help

him find my father." Jake was shaking his head, but she turned away from him.

"He has no business contacting you." Patrick sounded angry. "And he has no business with your father. He's not a federal agent and he could be charged with interfering with an ongoing investigation. He's putting you in danger."

She had put herself in danger by agreeing to come with him. "Patrick, listen," she said. "I think my father might be here—in Telluride."

"What makes you think that? Have you see him?"

"No. But today I thought I saw my brother, Sammy. And the man who attacked me at my house in Rogers had a Telluride lift ticket on his jacket."

"Then you shouldn't be there. I want you to leave town immediately. Go back to the cabin where you were staying. You said that was safe, right?"

"Someone set fire to the cabin last night," she said. "Or rather, very early this morning, while we were asleep. We got away, but then they tried to run us off the road. Jake found a tracking device on my car. He thinks the man who came to my house in Rogers planted it."

Jake stood and made a move as if to grab the phone, but she leaned out of his way. "I really think we're close," she told Patrick. "As soon as we've located my father, I'll call and tell you. You can send federal agents in to make the arrest."

"I should come now, and get you away from there," Patrick said. "We can take it from here."

"If you send a bunch of feds into town, my father is going to find out," she said. "Let Jake and me see what we can find out first. We'll be careful."

"This isn't your fight anymore."

"I'm sorry, Patrick, but it is. He's my father and he's trying to kill me. I have to see for myself that he can't harm me anymore. That's the only way I can get on with my life."

"Letting you stay goes against everything I've pledged to do."

"If you come to town now and interfere with this, I'll leave and you'll never hear from me again."

"Don't do that."

"Then don't force my hand."

Silence. She could almost hear him thinking. Jake stood beside her, hands on his hips, glaring down at her. "I'll compromise," Patrick said. "I'll station a team near there, and when you give the word we'll move in. If you need anything in the meantime, call me. And don't do anything foolish. And don't let Jake do anything foolish."

"I won't."

"Be careful around him, Anne. He's not the man you knew before. Word is he's been obsessed with this case. Obsessive people don't act rationally."

What was rational about any of this? But she didn't bother pointing that out to Patrick. "I'll be careful," she said. "And I'll stay in touch."

"I'll only give you a few days. Then I will find you."

"A few days is all I'm asking. My father is either here or he isn't. We should know soon."

She hung up the phone. "What did he say?" Jake asked.

"He's going to station a team nearby, but he won't make any move until I tell him."

"Do you believe him?"

"I do. They want to find my father as badly as you do."

"Did you mean that—about leaving if they interfered?"

"Yes." She met his gaze, resolve strengthening in her. "I've run away from my father long enough. I need to end this once and for all."

Chapter Eleven

The next morning Anne and Jake dressed in the ski clothes they'd also purchased at the thrift shop, and rode the gondola up the mountain to the ski resort, where they rented equipment and purchased lift tickets. "What now?" Anne asked, when she'd followed Jake up the stairs to the base of the first ski lift.

"Now we wait. We hang out here, watch people coming off the gondola and boarding the lift, see if you spot anyone familiar."

She looked around at the skiers and snowboarders who stood in groups on the cobblestones of the ski village or queued up to board the lift. Dressed in helmets or knitted caps and brightly colored jackets and pants, they looked like circus performers, or aliens. "How am I going to recognize anyone when they're dressed like this?" she asked.

"You'll recognize your father or your brother."

"Will I?" Maybe she'd been wrong about seeing Sammy yesterday. After all, she'd only glimpsed him for a second. Maybe her imagination had played tricks on her.

"You will." Jake patted her shoulder. "Your subconscious will, even if your conscious self doubts."

"Is that the kind of thing they teach you at the Bureau?"

"No. I read it in a book somewhere."

"Don't believe everything you read."

She started to move toward the lift, but he stopped her. "We can see more hanging out down here than we can actually skiing."

"I think we can see a lot from the lift."

"No. This is where the action is."

Reluctantly, she slotted her skis alongside his in a rack and found a chair outside the bar and restaurant at the base of the lift that transported skiers up the mountain. "If this is all we were going to do, we could have worn our street clothes," she grumbled. "We could have told anyone who asked that we were waiting for our children to get out of ski school."

"Really? How many children? Boy or girl? Or maybe one of each."

She glared at him.

"If things had worked out differently we might have a child by now," he mused. "Though he—or she—would be too young to learn to ski."

Pain squeezed her heart as she thought of the baby she and Jake might have had. First, there would have been a huge society wedding, maybe at St. Patrick's Cathedral. Her father would have spared no expense for his only daughter. She'd have had a designer gown and a diamond tiara and a reception that people would have talked about for months afterward.

She and her new husband would have settled into a condo her father owned, and her husband would work in the family business, while she stayed home and raised children. On Sundays, they'd dine with her parents and her brother and his family, and there'd be no such thing as a holiday alone.

It was an old-fashioned lifestyle, one in which the women didn't work or have any independence of their own, so the reality would have been much less comfortable than the fantasy, but it had been her dream, until Jake had showed her the cruelty and ugliness beneath that pretty picture of family devotion. Once he'd opened her eyes, the dream hadn't seemed so lovely.

"Pay attention." Jake tapped the back of her hand. "Do you see anyone in the lift line or skiing down the mountain that you recognize?"

She scanned the crowd. "No."

"I think I'd recognize your father," Jake said. "I didn't see Sammy enough to be sure of recognizing him. But I'm guessing anyone who's skiing with a couple of burly bodyguards will stand out."

"You might be surprised," she said. "A lot of celebrities ski here. Some of them probably have bodyguards."

"I don't think even I would confuse your dad and some pop star."

Would a year on the run have aged her father? Or would time spent apart make her see him differently? "I don't think sitting here waiting is going to do us much good," she said. "From the lift we can see more."

"Fine. You go ski. I'm staying here."

She stood. "You can't ski, can you? You lied to me."

"I can ski. Or I could, before last year."

The image of him lying in a pool of blood on the floor of that hotel ballroom flashed into her mind and she felt sick. "I'm sorry. Your legs were injured. I didn't think—"

He waved away her apology. "I could probably still do it if I had to, but I'll be more mobile here. You go on and if you see anything, call me."

"All right." She should be safe enough by herself with people all around, and she had her phone to summon help. She put on her skis and moved into the line for the lift. This wasn't her first visit to Telluride; she'd come last year with a group of teachers and spent the day exploring the slopes. It had been one of her best days since coming to Rogers—one of the days when she hadn't felt so alone.

She rode up the lift with a mother, father and daughter from Texas. The ski runs spread out below the lift like a white carpet, skiers and snowboarders zipping along like toys on a track.

Her father would have moved away from the main ski area as quickly as possible. He didn't like crowds or waiting in line. The lifts farther from the base area would be less crowded, the terrain more challenging. She thought back to her previous visit to the resort, and other ski vacations she'd taken with her family. What runs would most appeal to her father?

At the top of the lift, she skied to a map of the area and studied it. Her father liked to show off. He liked to prove to himself, and to the men around him that, though he was getting older, he was still a man to be feared. He didn't, as he'd said on one of those long-ago vacations, want to ski with a bunch of women and children.

Anne decided he'd head for a group of double black diamond runs that hurtled down narrow, tree-lined slopes into territory that had been backcountry skiing until only a few years before. She'd make her way over to Revolution Bowl. There would be fewer skiers there; if her father was among them, she'd be sure to spot him.

As she skied to the next lift, she began to relax a little. The snow was smooth and perfect, the sun bright and the temperature not too cold. She was a strong skier, and she was safe here. No one was likely to recognize her in her secondhand ski clothes, her hair stuffed under a rented helmet. She was an anonymous tourist, free to move around as she chose.

She rode a second lift farther up the mountain and made her way to yet another lift that took her to the top of Revolution Bowl. From the top, she had a view of the entire resort and the town below. Half a dozen other skiers joined her at the start of the group of runs, none of them her father. Only one other woman was there— she smiled and nodded to Anne, who returned the nod.

Maybe she'd been wrong. Maybe now that her father was older, he no longer attempted such challenging terrain.

She pointed her skis down the slope and started down the run, her heart in her throat. It was steeper than she'd anticipated. The group she'd been with last year hadn't ventured into this terrain, labeled *expert only* on the map. Trees formed a dark green wall on either side of the narrow chute, forcing her to make tight turns. So much for her brilliant ideas. It was going to take all she had in her to get down from here onto more manageable terrain.

She stopped to rest at the side of the run and looked back up at the section she'd just skied. Probably a mistake, since it was steeper than anything she remembered skiing before. But she told herself if she'd come this far, she'd be fine....

Something about the stance of the skier coming down the mountain toward her made her breath catch. She shrank farther into the shelter of the trees and stared as the man moved nearer, trailed by a burlier man. The first skier wore black pants and a dark blue jacket, while his companion was dressed all in black. He descended the run in a series of sharp, aggressive turns, attacking the snow as if determined to subdue it.

Her first thought was that she was watching her father, but as the man skied closer, she thought it must be Sammy. He was broader across the shoulders than her father, younger and more athletic. She prayed he wouldn't notice her, hiding here in the trees.

In horror, she watched as he skied to a stop directly in front of her. "Hello," he said. "We don't see many women over on this side of the mountain."

She angled herself away, and pulled her fleece neck gaiter over her nose and mouth. *"Excusez-moi, je ne parle pas anglais,"* she said, in a high, breathy voice that was partly an act and partly due to the fact that she was having trouble breathing.

"I might have known, a European," he said to his bodyguard, who'd stopped slightly behind him. He turned back to Anne, and in perfect French, said. "I usually ski in Europe myself, but decided to try here this year. Are you enjoying the runs?"

Idiot. She'd forgotten Sammy had studied with the same French tutor she had. Her father had seen knowing French as a sign of sophistication, and useful when the family traveled to Europe. "I really must join my husband now," she said, still in French, and started to move away.

Sammy's grip on her arm was firm, but not too rough. "Don't run off so soon," he said. "Did your husband leave you up here alone? That wasn't very gentlemanly. You should stick with me and we'll make him jealous."

She stifled a groan. She'd forgotten that her brother was an incorrigible flirt. He was convinced no woman could resist him—and many of them didn't. Though he wasn't the handsomest of men, money and power were an amazing aphrodisiac.

"That really would not be a good idea, monsieur," she said, and shot past him.

"Well, if you want to play it that way," he called, and took off after her.

On the edge of panic, Anne hurtled down the narrow, steep chute, skiing faster and more recklessly than she ever had. Why had she ever come up here? She should have listened to Jake, and stayed safely at the bottom of the mountain. No telling what Sammy would do if he found out his flirt was instead his sister—that is, if she even survived this perilous descent.

She shot out of the trees, into the open bowl. If she hadn't been so frightened, she might have enjoyed the treeless, more moderate terrain. But her only thought now was to get away from Sammy and lose herself in the crowd.

She glanced over her shoulder and saw that he was still close behind her. "Wait!" he shouted. "I only want to talk to you."

She took off, sure she would get away now. He was red-faced and out of breath, heavier and more out of shape than she was. She was skiing well, gaining confidence, and she began to relax, energized by her narrow escape. Wait until she told Jake about this…

Suddenly, she was falling. Her ski caught an edge and she faltered and was thrown to the ground, landing in a heap in soft snow, unhurt, but stopped.

As she struggled to her feet, Sammy skied up beside her. "Are you all right?" he asked, sticking to French.

She nodded, careful to keep her head down, her eyes focused on finding one ski that had detached in the fall and clicking back into it.

"You don't have to be afraid of me, you know," Sammy said. "I'm a good guy. Isn't that right, Carl?"

Carl, a looming hulk on Sammy's right, nodded. "Of course."

Anne said nothing, having decided that silence was the best option. Maybe he'd mistake her terror for shyness, or even a European disdain for the pushy American.

"You look so familiar," Sammy continued. "I'm sure we've met before. Where are you from? Paris? Or maybe Nice?"

She shook her head, and skied away. There was nothing he could do here on the slopes, she'd decided. He could follow her and he could talk to her, but he wouldn't grab her or force her to reveal her face. He still saw her as a possible romantic interest. With any luck, he'd give up before they reached the bottom of the mountain.

"Seriously, I'm sure I know you," he called, and raced after her.

He skied so close she was afraid he was going to cause a collision. Maybe that was what he wanted—

another fall he could help her up from, maybe while pulling the gaiter from her face and seeing her more clearly.

She pushed on, skiing faster. Recklessly. Her legs were shaky with fatigue, and her pounding heart wasn't helping matters any. If only there was some way to get rid of him.

She managed to put a little distance between them, but Sammy was determined and she had no doubt he'd catch up to her soon. She looked around for some escape—a run she could dart onto, or other people who might intervene.

Her rescue came from the most unlikely quarter. Hurtling toward them in an awkward half-crouch came a figure dressed in bright orange pants and a blue jacket—the clothing Jake had chosen at the thrift store yesterday.

Chapter Twelve

As Jake neared Sammy and Carl, he straightened and began windmilling his arms—the picture of an out-of-control skier. He slammed into the two men with a sickening thud. Anne winced, but couldn't look away. Sammy and Carl went sprawling into the snow, while Jake slid off to the side, skis still on his feet as he crouched over them.

She watched in amazement as he straightened, then skied past her without a word. She took off after him. By the time Sammy and Carl recovered, she and Jake would be long gone.

She followed him onto a series of blue and green runs that crisscrossed through the trees. He left the run and skied into the trees, stopping at the base of a large pine. He was breathing heavily, his face flushed when he pulled the bandana he wore from over his nose. "I think…we lost them," he gasped, doubled over, his hands on his knees.

She looked back up the run they'd just descended. No sign of her brother or his bodyguard. "What were you doing up there?" she asked. "I thought you were going to wait at the base."

"After you got on the lift I decided it was a bad idea

to leave you alone. If your father or one of his men recognized you, it would be too easy for them to kidnap you—or worse—without me to watch your back. So I followed."

"And I'm glad you did. But I thought you couldn't ski with your injuries."

"After that run I don't have much more left in me. I thought I was going to have to take off my skis and come down on my butt. Then I saw you with those two and adrenaline kicked in. Was that your brother?"

She nodded. "He didn't recognize me. I pretended to be a French tourist."

"And he believed you?"

"Oh, yes. My brother fancies himself a real Casanova, a man no woman can resist."

"You mean, he was *hitting* on you?" Jake's outrage was almost comical.

"Yes. It's funny now, but at the time, I was terrified." She looked him up and down. "Are you sure you're all right? That was quite a crash."

"I was a lot more stable than I looked, and I wasn't going that fast when I hit. Mainly, I surprised them and caught them off balance."

"I don't think they were hurt, either, but it bought us the time we needed to get away." She looked again up the empty run. "Do you speak French?"

He shook his head. "Why?"

"I was thinking that if we run into them again before we get off this mountain—if they see us together—you need to pretend to be my husband. I told them I was trying to get back to you."

"Tell them I have laryngitis."

She laughed, as much from relief as from any real

mirth. "I'm so glad you came along when you did," she said. "I was sure any moment he'd recognize me. He'd be embarrassed and angry, and there's no telling what he would have done. Or rather, what he would have had Carl do."

"At least now we know for sure he's here. I don't suppose he said anything about your father?"

"No. And I certainly wasn't going to ask."

"We'd better go. We'll head back through the beginner area. Something tells me your brother and his bodyguard aren't likely to venture onto the bunny hill."

"I think the bunny hill is all I care to tackle right now," she said. "My legs are jelly."

"Mine, too. Just hang in there. We'll return to the hotel and decide on our next move."

"I vote for the hot tub," she said.

He grinned. "Sounds like a great idea."

He led the way out of the woods and she followed. Later, when the impact of her encounter with her brother really hit her, she'd probably be even more shaky. For now, she pushed those emotions away and focused on keeping her weight even over her skis and making nice, easy turns. She was safe, and Jake was watching her back. Amazing how good it felt to know that.

"ARE YOU SURE you're all right?" Jake asked for the third time since he and Anne had clicked out of their skis and headed back toward the hotel.

"I'm fine." She strode along beside him, skis on her shoulder, goggles shading her eyes—and hiding her expression, so he couldn't decide if she was telling the truth or putting up a brave front.

"Are you sure? You look pale."

"You're the one who's limping, not me."

He made an effort to lessen the limp, though his legs felt like they were made of broken glass, jagged edges sending jolts of pain through him with every step. "The physical therapist said exercise was good for me." Exercise, but probably not a kamikaze plunge down a double-black ski slope.

"I'm sure I could have gotten away from Sammy and his sidekick on my own," she said. "I hate to think you hurt yourself coming after me when it wasn't really necessary."

"A while ago you were grateful to me for saving you."

"Yes, but now I've had time to think about it and I realize I didn't really need saving. I could have kept up the pretense of being French and eventually gotten away from him. Once we'd been around more people, he wouldn't have wanted to make a scene."

Maybe Jake had risked himself for nothing; even when he'd known Anne before, she'd been very good at looking after herself. "If nothing else, you could have shown off your boxing skills and punched him," he said.

She laughed. "There is that."

"So what now?" he asked. "Back to the hotel and that hot tub?"

"First, I have to buy a swimsuit."

"Can you buy a swimsuit in a ski town?"

She smiled. "Of course."

She led the way down a side street to a boutique that, as it turned out, had a large section devoted to both men's and women's swimwear. They left their skis in a rack just outside the door and pushed their way inside. Shoppers, mostly women, milled around the racks and displays, while several men congregated on benches in what was clearly a waiting area for patient spouses.

Anne selected several suits and headed for the dressing room. "Need any help?" Jake asked.

"You need to get your own suit," she said, and ducked into a changing room.

He wandered over to a rack of Hawaiian-print swim trunks and began flipping through them. "You're taking a risk coming here, Senator," a voice behind him said.

"Even politicians are allowed to take vacations."

"The issue isn't your vacation. It's who you're vacationing with."

Jake maneuvered around the rack of suits until he had a view of the speakers—two middle-aged men seated on a bench near the door, apparently waiting for their wives or girlfriends to finish shopping.

"I'm vacationing with my wife and with you and your wife, Al," a portly, white-haired man with a florid face said. "Do you have a problem with that?"

"I'm not the one you should be worried about," the other man, shorter with iron-gray hair, said.

"This really isn't a discussion I want to have in public," the senator said.

"Should I get the red or the blue?" Jake turned to see Anne holding up two swimsuits for his inspection.

"No bikini?" he asked, surveying what looked to him like relatively demure one-pieces.

"I guess you'll have to use your imagination," she said.

"I have a very good imagination." And a good memory.

"Have you picked out a suit?" she asked.

"How about this one?" He grabbed a pair of trunks from the rack.

"You don't think they're a little big?"

He checked the tag. Extra large. He found the same pair in a medium. "Okay, how about these?"

"Great. What have you been doing while I've been in the dressing room? Ogling other women?"

"Not exactly." He pulled out his credit card to pay for their purchases, then steered her outside. When they were a block away from the shop, he asked, "Does your father know Senator Greg Nordley? He's a senator from New York state."

"I know who he is, but I have no idea if Pop knew him. Maybe. Probably. He made it a point to know people like that."

"People like what?"

"People in power. Politicians. Why?"

"I just saw a man I think is Nordley in that shop. He was talking to another man who apparently thought Nordley was taking a risk by vacationing in Telluride with someone the other guy didn't approve of."

"You think Nordley is here to see my father?"

"It makes sense if Nordley is the man who helped your father get out of prison. Maybe Nordley is here to collect a favor."

She said nothing as they negotiated a crowded corner. "Did your FBI contacts say the man who helped my father was a senator? Or that it was a politician from New York?"

"They didn't say. But it makes me wonder."

She looked doubtful. "It's not much to go on."

"Let's file the information away for future reference. It could come in handy."

"I don't see how, but all right." She shifted her skis to her other shoulder. "Right now all I want is a shower and a soak in that hot tub."

"Sounds good." He was looking forward to seeing her in her swimsuit, but he'd keep that comment to himself—for now.

AN HOUR LATER, Jake, wrapped in a hotel robe and carrying a towel, rode the elevator to the rooftop hot tub, where Anne had agreed to meet him after her shower.

The elevator opened and he stepped onto the deck, which offered an extravagant view of snowcapped peaks and azure sky. At this time of day, just after noon, the deck was empty, the large, bubbling hot tub awaiting the après-ski crowd later in the day.

He made his way to the spa, grateful Anne wasn't around to see him limping. That mad dash down the mountain had taken more out of him than he would admit to her. Only sheer will and obstinacy had gotten him through. Then again, that was what had been driving him ever since he opened his eyes in the hospital after the shooting—a will to survive and a determination to finish the job he'd started and see Sam Giardino behind bars permanently.

He carefully lowered himself into the steaming water and positioned himself to watch the elevator doors. He didn't want to miss a moment of Anne in her swimsuit. The modest one-piece she'd purchased was not the daring bikini Elizabeth would have chosen, but he had no doubt she'd be more beautiful than ever in it.

And he was going to do his best to not show his reaction to her. They had a business arrangement and a tentative friendship; he wouldn't do anything to jeopardize either.

The elevator doors opened and he sat up straighter, heart pounding in anticipation. But instead of Anne, a man stepped onto the deck. He was tall, with light brown hair showing beneath a red knit cap. He wore hiking boots, dark jeans and a fisherman's sweater. To most people, he probably looked like a tourist, but something in his alert attitude—a sense of coiled energy and vigilance—told Jake this guy was either law enforcement or a paid hit man.

Chapter Thirteen

Jake froze, and tried to keep his breathing steady and even. Had Sam Giardino discovered that Jake was alive and in Telluride, and sent someone to take him out? After killing Jake, would the assassin wait on the roof for Anne?

He glanced at his robe hanging on the back of a chair, just out of arm's reach. There was a gun in the pocket, but he'd likely be dead before he could reach it. Gripping the edge of the hot tub, he looked around for something else he could use as a weapon. In the meantime, he needed to remain calm and avoid overreacting.

The newcomer walked straight to the hot tub. "Jacob Westmoreland," he said in a smooth, deep voice that belonged on the evening news. "I'm Patrick Thompson. I thought the two of us should talk."

Thompson. Jake released his grip on the side of the tub and sat up straighter. He might have known the marshal would show up sooner rather than later. "Does Anne know you're here?" he asked.

"No. I wanted to talk to you first." The marshal's gaze swept over him, assessing, though his expression betrayed nothing about his opinion of Jake.

"You wanted to check me out."

"That's my job." He looked around the empty rooftop. "I'll wait for you over by those tables."

Jake debated refusing, or making Thompson wait until he'd finished his soak. But that would allow more time for Anne to arrive, and he'd just as soon get this over with before she showed up.

Thompson walked over to the tables and took a chair facing Jake. Conscious of the other man's eyes on him, Jake took his time climbing out of the spa, toweling off and shrugging into his robe. Then he joined the federal marshal at the table. A propane heater shaped like an oversize copper lamp bathed the table in warmth, and provided a low, dull roar to further mask their conversation from passersby—if there had been anyone to overhear.

"Can I see some ID?" Jake asked, choosing a chair with a view of the elevator.

Thompson produced a leather case and opened it. Jake studied the U.S. marshal's credentials and nodded. "What do you want to talk about?" As if the two of them had any shared interests other than Anne.

"You were out of line, getting in touch with Anne. And you're stepping way over the line, bringing her here."

"She's in WitSec. She's not your prisoner. She can see whoever she wants, and go where she wants."

"You're not a federal agent anymore. This is not your case, and by getting involved you're jeopardizing a federal investigation."

"No, I'm a private citizen. I can visit a friend if I want to."

Thompson's jaw tightened, the first sign that the guy could show emotion. "You had no right to compromise

Anne's identity. If someone who knew her before sees the two of you together, you could be putting her in danger."

"You let her think I was dead." All the time he'd been worrying and wondering and dreaming about her, she hadn't even known he was alive.

"We thought it was best," Thompson said. "She needed to start over, with no ties to the past."

"I'm doing my best to give her a future. One where she doesn't have to be looking over her shoulder every minute."

He expected Thompson to object to that. Fine. Jake was ready to have it out with the man who thought he had the right to dictate the life Anne would lead. Instead, the marshal leaned back in his chair and studied Jake, relaxed and thoughtful. "What makes you think you can find Sam Giardino when no one else has?" he asked.

"Maybe because I want him more than the rest of you do."

Thompson stiffened and Jake bit back a smile. He didn't like criticism, did he? "What do you mean?" Thompson asked.

"I mean that it's in some people's interests to keep Sam Giardino free—people in power who owe him favors."

"Who are you talking about?"

He glanced toward the elevator—no sign of Anne. "I don't know yet," he said. "But you must have heard the same rumors I did."

"That depends on what you've heard."

"All I heard was that an elected official who knew how to pull strings worked it so that Sam Giardino got away, and provided the means for Giardino to stay free. Someone in power made it his business to see that Giardino didn't spend much time behind bars."

"But you can't give me a name?"

"No." He sat back, debating whether to share the next bit of news—or non-news—with Thompson. He decided to let the man decide for himself if the information was valuable or not. "I saw Senator Greg Nordley in town today. He was arguing with another man who thought the senator was taking a risk in coming to Telluride."

"Who was this man?"

"I don't know. But I'd recognize him again if I saw him."

"Maybe he was worried the senator would hurt himself skiing."

"This other man objected to whoever the senator was vacationing with."

"Anything else?"

"No. The senator said this wasn't something they should be discussing in public."

Thompson took a notebook from his pocket and wrote something—maybe Nordley's name. Or his assessment that Jake was nuts. "A U.S. senator could be doing any number of things—ethical or unethical, legal or illegal—but that doesn't mean any of them have a connection to Sam Giardino."

"Yeah. Maybe it's just a coincidence. But if I've heard this rumor about Sam's powerful friend, I know you have, too. And if we find Sam, he could lead us to that person."

"We?"

"Do I look like a one-man SWAT team? When I

find him, I'll let you and whatever posse you want to bring do the rest."

Thompson fell silent. His gaze dropped to Jake's legs, visible beneath the hem of the hotel robe. The scars from the surgery that had put him back together were clearly visible, white, waxy lines against his skin. "You're something of a legend, did you know?" Thompson asked. "They say you died twice on the operating table, and almost bought it again when you had pneumonia."

Was Thompson trying to flatter him? Jake had heard the legend line before—when the Bureau showed him the door and handed him a pension.

"All the more reason for me to want Giardino, to make him pay for the hell he put me through."

"They also say you're too obsessed with Giardino—that you've made this fight personal."

"Who is they? And I just told you this fight *is* personal."

"You lose your objectivity, you lose all sense of caution."

"Did they teach you that in Marshal school?"

To his surprise, Thompson laughed. "You don't sound like any Bureau man I ever met."

"I never was a typical FBI guy. I was an accountant who thought it would be fun to play secret agent. I found out otherwise."

Thompson leaned forward, elbows on his knees. "You and I are on the same side," he said. "We both want to protect Anne."

"Are you in love with her?" Jake looked Thompson in the eye, trying to gauge the marshal's reaction to the question.

The other man never flinched. "I like Anne and I have a lot of respect for her, but no, I'm not in love with her."

Jake believed him. "Of course not. Because that would be unprofessional and possibly unethical, and all the things that are probably in a file with my name on it somewhere at the Bureau."

"I haven't seen that file, but I heard you were in love with her once. Are you still?"

Jake looked away. "The point is, she's not in love with me, so let's leave it at that."

Neither man said anything for a long moment, the hiss of the propane heater and the bubbling hot-tub jets filling the silence between them. Jake went back to watching the elevator, wondering what was taking Anne so long, yet, at the same time, hoping she'd put off her arrival a few moments longer.

Thompson blew out a breath and sat up straight once more. "If you find Sam—and I still think that's a big if—what will you do after we arrest him?"

"I don't know."

"You mean you didn't plan for the future?"

"All those times on death's door taught me not to think too far ahead."

"Why do you think Sam Giardino is in Telluride?"

Jake was tired of Thompson's questions, but he figured the guy wouldn't leave unless he thought he had all the answers. He turned to face the marshal once more. "He's probably not right in town, but he's somewhere near here. Anne tells me he has lots of friends with money. One of them probably has a house around here they're letting him use as a secure hideout."

"That doesn't mean he's here."

"His son, Sammy, is here."

"When we spoke on the phone, Anne mentioned she thought she saw him, but it wasn't a positive ID."

"She saw him again this morning."

"Is she sure it was him?"

"Yes. She talked to him. He didn't know it was her. She pretended to be a French tourist and he decided to flirt with her. She was having trouble shaking him."

This news clearly alarmed Thompson. "She needs to leave here right away. This isn't worth endangering her life."

"It's my life, Patrick. I appreciate your concern, but I'm not going to run away again."

Both men looked up and found Anne walking toward them. She wore one of the white hotel bathrobes cinched tightly around her waist, and brown Ugg boots, the combination seeming somehow chic on her.

Thompson stood. Jake was slower to rise to his feet, but if Thompson was going to be such a gentleman, he wouldn't be outdone, even if his stiffening limbs protested.

All her attention was focused on Thompson, however. "Patrick, what are you doing here? I thought we agreed you were going to wait for my call."

"My job is to look after you. That includes keeping track of where you are."

"How did you find me?" she asked.

"Telluride isn't that big of a town. I only had to contact a few hotels with your description before I found the right one. And if it's that simple for me to locate you, your enemies wouldn't have any difficulty locating you, either."

Jake wanted to punch the man for trying to scare

her, but he should have known Anne wouldn't frighten easily. "I'm fine. You didn't have to follow me here."

"I had to make sure Jake wasn't putting you in danger."

She looked at Jake, a half smile playing at the corners of her mouth. "And what did you decide?"

"He told me you saw your brother today. That you talked to him. That's getting much too close."

"Sammy didn't recognize me."

"You were lucky this time. What if next time your luck has run out?" He fixed his dark gaze on her. "I know it's difficult to see family—people you love—as a danger to you. But you know your father is ruthless. He would kill you, if given the chance, even if you don't want to believe it."

"I don't want to believe it," she admitted. "But I know you're right. Which is why it's so important to lock him up again, where he can't get to me."

Jake realized she was repeating his words. Did she believe them now, or was she using them as a convenient way to put off Thompson?

"Now that we suspect he's in the area, you can leave," Thompson said. "We'll take it from here."

"How are you going to find him? My father hasn't avoided jail time all these years by not being able to spot law enforcement a mile away."

"He didn't spot Jake."

She flushed. "Jake isn't a typical agent, I don't think."

The frown lines on Thompson's forehead deepened. "I don't like it."

"But it's my decision to make," she said. "And I want to stay here and see if we can find my father. When we do, I promise I'll let you handle it."

Thompson looked at Jake. "Do you really trust him?"

"He hasn't given me any reason not to so far," she said.

"That isn't an answer."

"Then, yes. Yes, I trust him."

Jake moved to Anne's side. "Give us another couple of days to see if we can locate the Giardino hideout," he said. "We'll keep you informed, but give us room to work."

Thompson looked grim. "All right. I'll give you two days." He turned to Anne. "But at the first sign of trouble, call me. We're already working on a new plan for you, someplace where you'll be safe."

She nodded, though her eyes looked bleak. Jake wouldn't blame her if she balked at starting over yet again, with another new name, new job and new identity. How often could a person do that before she didn't know who she was anymore?

Thompson left them. When the elevator doors closed behind him, Jake said, "Let's get in the hot tub. We can talk there."

He lowered himself into the water quickly, submerging his legs before she got a good look at the scars. He wasn't a vain man, but he didn't want her feeling sorry for him, or thinking he was a freak. She took her time pulling off her boots, then slipped out of the robe and folded it neatly across the bench beside the hot tub.

His heart stopped beating for a few breaths, or at least it felt that way as he stared at her, at the blue Lycra swimsuit hugging the swell of her breasts, at the indentation of her waist and the flare of her hips. Her long, bare legs seemed perfect, and looking at them made him feel even more glad to be alive. As long as he lived, she would always be the standard by which he'd judge other women; time and the differences between them hadn't changed that. The beauty he saw in her wasn't merely a matter of physical appearance, though she'd always been a woman who turned heads wherever she went. He knew the loveliness of the woman she was inside—the intelligence and compassion and bravery that made her, to him, the most gorgeous person in the world.

"You can put your eyes back in your head now," she said as she slipped into the water across from him.

"Can't blame a guy for looking," he said. Too bad looking was all he'd do. Once she had welcomed his touch, but that seemed a long time ago. Despite the way she'd warmed to him over the last twenty-four hours, and her response to the one kiss they'd shared in the car, she'd made it clear that she didn't think the man she loved existed anymore—and the real man who'd showed up to take his place didn't measure up.

"Mmmmm." She sank lower in the water and closed her eyes. "So now that we've convinced Patrick that we can track down my father, how are we going to do it?"

"You could talk to Sammy. Arrange to meet him in some neutral location and see if you can persuade him it's to his benefit to turn the old man in."

"I don't think it would work."

"Because Sammy is more loyal to his father than you were?"

"He married Stacy to please my father."

"One more reason to resent the old man." Jake drummed his fingers on the side of the tub. "I wasn't a part of your household long, but from what I saw, your father rode Sammy pretty hard. He wasn't spoiled like you."

She opened her eyes. "That's because I was a woman—my father didn't expect anything from me. He was hard on Sammy because he thought that was the way to make him hard, to prepare him to be the boss one day."

"Maybe so. But that kind of treatment gets old, especially now that Sammy is a grown man. He'd probably jump at the chance to run the organization without your dad to interfere."

"Sammy wouldn't refuse to work with us out of loyalty to my father so much as he'd refuse in order to protect himself. If anyone thought he was on the side of the cops, he wouldn't have any power, even with my father out of the way. And he could think that this would be letting the police get a wedge in. First, they take out his father, then they start in on him. He wouldn't risk it."

"Then what else can we do? Sammy is all we've got."

"I've been thinking about that." She sat up straighter, water streaming off her shoulders and the tops of her breasts, distracting him. "There's somebody else we can lean on to try to find out where my father is staying," she said.

He forced his attention back to her face. "Who's that?"

"His driver. He always has one. He's not going to ride a shuttle like a common tourist, and he doesn't drive himself. Instead, he has a car take him from wherever he's staying, and drop him off at the base of the lifts. If we find the driver, we can either follow him back to the hideout, or we can try to persuade him to tell us the location of the house."

"Talking is probably better than following. He's

liable to spot a tail and get suspicious. Outside of town, there isn't much traffic."

"Tomorrow morning, we should go to the drop-off area near the gondola and look for the driver. We might even see my father, which would confirm he's here."

"Have I told you lately that you're brilliant?"

"Not brilliant enough to think of it before now."

"That's still brilliant." He checked the elevator again; no one had come up. They were still alone. "Patrick Thompson is worried about you," he said.

"He takes his job seriously."

"Because he's in love with you?" Thompson had denied any romantic feelings for Anne, but maybe she felt more deeply for the man who had rescued her from possible death.

She regarded him coolly. "Why? Are you jealous?"

"Yes."

"Jake, don't." She put up a hand as if to physically push him away.

"I know things can't be the way they were between us before," he said. "But I want you to know, it meant a lot to me when you told Thompson you trusted me."

"I do trust you, Jake. I'm just—we're both different now."

"I know. Just trust that I'm here if you need me—for whatever."

She nodded and looked away. He wanted to reach across the foaming water and pull her to him, but he held back. He cared about her, but maybe some of what he felt for her was merely nostalgia for what they'd had once before. She had been right when she'd said they were different now. He didn't know if he had it in him anymore to trust anyone the way he'd once trusted her.

The elevator opened, and a trio of young women emerged, giggling and talking, robes open over bright bikinis. They headed straight for the hot tub. Jake stifled a groan. So much for quiet relaxation. He turned to suggest they leave, and found Anne moving toward him. Before he could say a word, she covered his mouth with hers, and wrapped her arms around him. All coherent thought fled as he responded. For whatever reason, Anne was suddenly kissing him as if her life depended on it.

Chapter Fourteen

Jake's lips against Anne's felt both wonderfully familiar and excitingly new, she thought as she moved in closer. He wrapped strong arms around her and pulled her onto his lap, where the evidence of his desire pressed against her thigh, sending an almost-forgotten thrill through her. He slid one hand down her back to cup her bottom, and the thrill coalesced into full-on desire. She squirmed closer, and deepened the kiss, tasting him, unable to get enough of him.

"Ewww. Get a room!" a high-pitched voice said, followed by a chorus of giggles. Then the voices moved away.

Jake pulled back, just enough to slide his mouth to her ear. "Not that I'm sorry in the least, but what brought this on?" he asked.

"I didn't want those girls disturbing us."

"Mmmm." He nibbled her ear, and pure, erotic pleasure shivered through her. "Now you're the one who has me disturbed." He moved his mouth back to hers and kissed her again, a deep, shuddering kiss that left her breathless and clinging to him, as if he'd turned her bones to butter.

"I...I was just trying to get them to go away." She tried to move out of his arms, but he held her fast.

"So you were just acting. You didn't really want to kiss me." He traced the hollow of her neck with his tongue.

"Maybe I did." Maybe she'd wanted to kiss him since that first night in Rogers, when he'd held her in his arms. "I just don't know if this is a good idea." Why start something they couldn't finish?

"I think it's a very good idea." He cupped her bottom more tightly, and slid one finger into the leg opening of her swimsuit.

She gasped. "I..." But words failed her as he slipped one finger into her. He moved his other hand up to cup her breast, rubbing his palm over the sensitive nub of her nipple.

"Do you remember that night after your father's birthday party?" he asked. "When we sneaked out to the pool after everyone was asleep?"

She had a sudden vision of moonlight on water, the cityscape behind them. Moonlight on the hard planes and honed muscles of Jake's lithe body, naked as he dove into the water. She'd been naked, too, bold as she swam after him, then with him. They'd teased and tantalized each other, unashamed, then made love on a chaise longue by the edge of the water, no doubt providing entertainment for the guards who remained unseen, but whom she knew were on duty. Guards were always on duty in her father's house.

"Th-that was Elizabeth," she stammered, as he moved his finger to stroke her. "I'm Anne now."

"And Anne doesn't do things like this?" He bent his

head and covered her breast with his mouth, kissing her through the thin, wet fabric of the suit.

"Jake, we can't." She put both hands on his shoulders and pushed him away. She retreated across the hot tub and wrapped her arms across her chest. "I shouldn't have done that," she said. "I'm sorry."

"I'm not." His eyes burned into her. "We can go up to the room and finish this."

She swallowed hard, fighting the images his invitation suggested, of naked bodies writhing in the sheets, of Jake doing things to her he did so well. "I don't think that would be a good idea."

"Is that your brain or your heart talking?"

"Jake, I don't love you anymore. I can't."

"Can't—or won't?"

"It's too dangerous." She'd seen him die on that ballroom floor, bleeding to death in front of her, and for a while she hadn't wanted to live, either. She couldn't go through something like that again.

"Don't tell me you don't still want me," he said.

"Yes, I want you. But…" Heat suffused her cheeks and she almost laughed. After all they'd done, to think she could still be embarrassed. "I haven't been with anyone in over a year."

"No one since me, you mean?" His voice grew husky. "I haven't been with anyone, either."

It would be so easy to move back into his arms, to give in to the longing that thrummed in every fiber of her being. To forget, for a blissful hour or so, about the danger that surrounded them and the uncertain future that loomed before them.

But the events of the past year had proved the folly of ever taking the easy route, or of letting emotion get the upper hand over sense. "I can't start something with you that we can't finish," she said. "I'm not that reckless anymore."

"Then I'll be reckless enough for both of us," he said.

"You know that's not wise."

"Since when was I ever a wise man? Especially where you're concerned."

"You're one of the smartest men I know. Right now we need to concentrate on staying alive and finding my father."

His expression grew pained. "You're right, but it doesn't make me happy to admit it."

She'd once believed her job was to make herself happy, that everything would fall into place if she just focused on that. Her self-indulgence had almost gotten Jake killed, and had destroyed the life she'd known.

"I'd better go in," she said.

Not waiting for his answer, she climbed out of the tub and slipped back into her robe and boots. As she crossed to the elevator, the three bikini-clad girls descended on him. She fought back a stab of jealousy. Maybe those girls were just what he needed to take his mind off her. She was determined not to complicate matters by getting involved with Jake again, but she wasn't so strong she wouldn't spend time mourning what might have been.

THE NEXT MORNING, Jake and Anne were at the drop-off area at the base of the gondola at eight-thirty. The lifts opened at nine, and Anne said her father liked to get an early start, to beat the crowds and get the best lines in the freshly groomed snow and unpacked powder.

Neither of them had said a word about their exchange

in the hot tub, though Jake couldn't stop thinking about it. His skin still felt feverish from her touch, and he'd spent a restless night fantasizing about making love to her, hearing her scream his name in delight the way she used to.

For the hundredth time, he shoved the fantasy away. He had work to do. And she was right—he couldn't afford to let himself get distracted.

From a table on the balcony of a coffee shop that overlooked the drop-off area, they watched a procession of SUVs, shuttle buses and sedans drop off skiers and snowboarders. A figure in red pants and a red jacket, his short-cropped white hair shining in the sun, crossed the courtyard on his way to the lift. "That's Senator Nordley," Jake said.

Anne studied the stocky man, who'd paused to speak with a trio of women near the lift. "He doesn't look familiar," she said. "I don't think he was ever at the house while I was there."

"It would be interesting to follow him and see what he does while he's here."

"He probably skis, and hits the bars and the shops, like everyone else who comes here on vacation," she said. "And you're supposed to be looking for my father, not politicians."

"Right." Just then, a black four-door sedan pulled into the line. He and Anne both leaned forward. "Is that him?" Jake asked.

"I don't know yet," she whispered, though there was no chance the occupants of the vehicle would hear her from up here.

The car eased into position at the head of the line and the back door opened. A man dressed in black ski pants and a black and white jacket slid out, followed by a second man, who went around to the trunk and took out two pairs of skis.

The first man looked up at the gondola, and for a moment the sun caught him full on the face. Anne gave a small cry, and Jake put his hand on her arm to steady her. "That looks like him, doesn't it?" he asked.

She nodded. "Yes."

Jake studied the man more closely. He was trim, and tanned, silver hair showing beneath a black watch cap. Sunglasses shaded his eyes, but Jake remembered Sam Giardino's intense blue gaze. Even from this distance, dressed in ski clothes, Sam radiated command. He strode toward the gondola, the man with him shouldering both pairs of skis. The car pulled away from the drop-off area, into the line of vehicles waiting to exit.

"Come on, we'd better get down there." Jake stood and Anne followed him down the stairs and across the cobblestoned courtyard.

They'd discussed the plan last night and decided Anne would approach first—a tourist asking directions. While she had the driver distracted, Jake would make his move.

She hurried to the driver's door. Jake wiped the sweat from his palms and gripped the pistol inside his coat pocket. The last thing he wanted was a shootout here, with all these people around, but if the driver tried anything with Anne…

She knocked on the driver's window. Waited. Knocked again. Jake's chest hurt from holding his breath. Maybe this wasn't going to work.

Finally, the driver's window lowered. Anne was supposed to play the role of the pretty, flirtatious tourist, buying time for Jake to slip in and surprise the driver. But the smile on her face vanished when she saw the driver. She covered her mouth with one hand, and used the other to brace herself against the car. Then she opened the passenger door behind the driver and climbed in.

The car inched forward in the line of departing vehicles. Anne was being driven away by a killer—or at least by a killer's employee. This definitely wasn't part of their plan. Gripping the gun in his pocket, Jake sprinted toward the car. Anne leaned forward and said something to the driver and the door locks clicked. When Jake tried the door, it was open, so Anne must have told the driver to let him in.

"Mr. Westmoreland. I'm surprised to see you here." The driver looked at Jake in the rearview mirror, his expression hidden by dark glasses.

Jake leaned forward and pressed the muzzle of the gun against the back of the driver's neck. "Drive us to the overlook just outside of town. Pull in there."

Anne stared at him, eyes wide. "Jake! This is Doug. He used to drive me to school when I was a little girl. He would never hurt me. Put that gun away."

"Your father wants you dead, and he works for your father."

"I'm a driver, not a killer." Doug put the car into gear and turned onto the street that led away from the ski resort. "I'm glad to see Miss Elizabeth looking so well, but I can't say the same about you."

"Jake isn't with the feds anymore," Anne said. "He's just trying to protect me."

"No offense, Miss Elizabeth, but I always thought

you could do a lot better than the likes of him. I thought so the first day you brought him home."

"I didn't ask for your opinion." Jake shoved the gun harder against the chauffeur's neck. He recognized the man now, a weathered, reedy sixtysomething, who chewed spearmint gum nonstop and did Sudoku puzzles while he waited for Sam to summon him.

"Jake, please." Anne put a hand on Jake's arm, but he shrugged her off. She wanted him to be gentle with the old chauffeur, but these people didn't deserve gentleness. They only understood violence.

Doug removed his sunglasses and his eyes met Jake's in the rearview mirror. Clearly, he thought Jake was the equivalent of something he'd wipe off the bottom of his shoe, but he had apparently decided to humor him, for Elizabeth's sake. He put the car in gear and drove toward the overlook. No one said anything, though Jake could feel Anne beside him, disapproval radiating from her like strong perfume.

The paved pullout overlooking the town was empty. Doug nosed the car up to the rock wall that separated visitors from the canyon below and shut off the engine. "We're here," he announced.

"Anne, get out of the car and leave us," Jake said.

"No." She glared at him. "I won't let you hurt him." She turned to Doug. "I want to see my father," she said. "Please tell us where he's staying."

"You know I can't do that, Miss Elizabeth. I'd do almost anything for you, but I can't do that."

"Tell us where Giardino is staying, or I'll blow your head off." Jake cocked the gun. Anne gasped, but he ignored her. Anger made his pulse pound and formed a painful knot in his chest. After so many months of suffering and planning, he was finally close to the people who had caused him so much pain—people who had hurt Anne and destroyed her life. He was a professional; he would control himself. But that didn't mean he didn't long for a little revenge.

Sweat dotted the driver's forehead, but he remained calm, eyes fixed on Anne. "I can't tell you where Mr. Giardino is staying," he said. "But I can give him a message from you, if you'd like."

"No!" Jake barked, before Anne could answer. The tears that shimmered in her eyes made him feel about two inches tall. He gentled his voice. "If he knows you're here, he'll send someone to kill you."

"He must know I'm in the area," she said. "He sent those other men after us."

"If you care anything about her at all, you won't betray her to her father," Jake told the driver.

Doug nodded, the barrel of the weapon scraping the soft flesh of his neck, making a red mark.

"Tell Sammy I'm here and I want to see him," Anne said.

Jake sent her a questioning look, but she avoided his gaze.

"Where will he find you?" Doug asked.

"Tell him she'll meet him at the bar at the base of the gondola in town tonight at seven," Jake said. The bar was public enough Sammy probably wouldn't try anything, yet they'd be able to have a private conversation.

Doug nodded. Anne looked sick, but she nodded, too.

The sound of an old-fashioned telephone ringing made Jake flinch, though he kept the gun steady. "That's my cell," Doug said.

The ringing sounded again, out of place in the morning stillness. "Answer it," Jake said.

Doug picked up the phone. "Hello… Yes, Mr. Giardino. I'll be right there."

He clicked off the phone and looked at Anne. "That was your father. He forgot his neck gaiter and wants me to bring it to him. Do you want to come with me and see him now?"

She hesitated. Jake wanted to tell her no, but he held his tongue. She knew what was at stake here.

She shook her head. "No. I won't see him now. Just… just give Sammy my message." She sagged back in the seat. "Please drop us off before you get to the gondola."

Ignoring Jake, despite the gun that was still pressed to the back of his neck, Doug started the car again, and pulled onto the highway.

"Drop us at the grocery store on the edge of town," Jake said.

"Miss Elizabeth?"

"Yes. The grocery store is fine." Anne hugged her arms across her chest and stared out the window, her expression distant, her face pale. No doubt she'd have plenty to say to Jake later. Fine. Let her be angry with him; anger wouldn't stop him doing whatever he had to in order to keep her safe.

Doug pulled the car into a space at the edge of the grocery store parking lot. "It was good to see you, Miss Elizabeth," he said.

"It was good to see you, too, Doug."

"Take care of yourself."

"I will."

"I'll give Mr. Sammy your message."

"Thank you."

Jake stowed the gun in his coat and followed Anne out of the car. As soon as he shut the door behind them, Doug pulled away. Anne wrapped her coat more tightly around her and angled her body away from Jake. "I thought you didn't think Sammy would help us," he said.

"But he's all we've got, isn't he?" She whirled to face him, anger restoring some of the color to her face. "If you hadn't pulled that gun and started making threats, I could have talked Doug into telling me what we need to know."

"Or, he'd have pulled his own gun and marched you straight to your father."

"I couldn't let you hurt Doug. I thought if I did what you wanted in the first place—agree to talk to Sammy—you'd let the old man alone."

He leaned close, almost, but not quite touching, his voice low, his gaze locked to hers. "I know this is hard for you. These people are your family. But you know they're also killers. And I will do anything—including risking your anger—to protect you from them."

The resentment was gone now, replaced by grief and resignation. "I know." She stared at the icy pavement beneath their feet. "Maybe Sammy will help us. You were right when you said there's no love lost between him and my father. Things may have gotten worse since I left."

"Are you okay?" He studied her face, trying to read her emotions, but she refused to meet his gaze. So much for thinking he'd fully gained her trust.

"I'm scared," she said after a moment. "Scared this trip is a waste of time and I'm going to have to run away again. Scared we've somehow made things worse."

"I won't give up until I find your father," he said. "I won't leave this alone until you're safe."

He started to pull her into his arms, but stopped as a black SUV braked to a stop in front of them, so close it almost brushed against them. The front passenger window lowered and Sammy Giardino looked out at them. "Doug told me you wanted to see me," he said. "No reason to wait until tonight when I'm right here."

Chapter Fifteen

Anne stared at Sammy, feeling as if she'd been thrust into a dream—one of those she'd had often in the early days of her exile, in which she ran into a member of her family on the street. The dreams had various outcomes—sometimes the other person embraced her, sometimes they turned away. In the worst dreams, they came at her with knives or guns. But Sammy did none of those; he merely regarded her calmly. Without his ski helmet and goggles, he looked more like the young man she remembered—a twenty-five-year-old version of their father, dark-haired and black-eyed, with the same hooked nose and square jaw that made Sam Giardino look so intimidating.

"Hello, Sammy," she said, trying to keep the shakiness from her voice. "You're looking well."

"And you look like a schoolteacher." He wrinkled his nose. "Where did you get those clothes—a thrift store?"

Was he goading her because he knew the answer to that question? Had he been aware of her the whole time she'd been in town? No, it was just a logical guess. The fact that it was all true was just a coincidence. "How have you been?" she asked.

"Well enough." Behind them, a car honked. Sammy

glanced around the crowded parking lot. "This isn't exactly the right place for a private conversation. You must have a hotel room or something we can go to."

"You don't need to know where she's staying." Jake spoke up. Tension radiated from him, and he regarded Sammy with obvious suspicion. Anne knew the hand he kept in his coat pocket rested on his gun; she hoped Sammy wouldn't be foolish enough to try anything here in this public place.

"It's all right." She turned back to Sammy. "I'm staying at the Columbia. Meet us there in the lobby and we'll go up to my room together."

"I'll give you a ride." He hit the button to unlock the car doors.

"We'll walk." Jake took her arm. "And come alone." Not waiting for an answer, he pulled Anne away.

As soon as they were out of the grocery store parking lot, she jerked out of his grasp. "I don't appreciate being bullied," she said.

"Then I'm not the man you need to worry about right now. What are you doing, letting him know where you're staying?"

"We need somewhere private to talk. And we need to get Sammy to trust us. We can't do that if we don't at least pretend we trust him. If you don't think it's safe, we can change hotels after he leaves."

She expected him to argue with her, but he merely took a deep breath and nodded. "All right. But we need to be careful. We don't know if he's on our side yet. If we can't persuade him to help us, we'll have to leave town in a hurry. And I hope you have Thompson's number on speed dial."

"It will be all right. You'll see." She couldn't believe

her brother would hurt her—but then, she never would have believed her father would want her dead. The events of the past year had made her wary of her own instincts.

"I won't leave you alone with him," Jake said.

The words made her feel stronger. "And I won't leave you alone with him, either." She smiled, trying to lighten the mood, but his expression remained grim.

"I'm not the one he's liable to hurt," Jake said.

"Don't be too sure of that. In case you haven't noticed, my family doesn't have a lot of fond feelings for you."

"Was it like that before, and I didn't know it? Or did finding out I worked for the FBI taint their opinion of me?"

"What do you think? If I'd known you were with the Bureau, I wouldn't have come within ten feet of you." She smiled to soften the sharpness of her words.

"But now my irresistible charm and sex appeal have overcome those reservations."

His tone was teasing, but the heat of his gaze made her heart pound and her breath catch, especially as she remembered how close she'd come yesterday to giving herself to him once more. If only life were less complicated, and love was simply a matter of acting on feelings, without worrying about the consequences of those actions.

Sammy was already waiting when they reached the hotel, standing under the portico, hands in his jacket pockets, his expression somber and unreadable as he watched them approach. Did he see the big sister he'd once adored, or the traitor who had destroyed the family? "I sent my driver away," he said. "So it's just me. And no one else knows I'm here."

"Thank you. It's better for all of us if we're careful."

She led the way to the elevator, Jake bringing up the rear. He and Sammy hadn't exactly been friends when they'd known each other before; she suspected Sammy had been jealous of this other young man who had claimed her father's attention.

When she started toward her room, Jake moved up beside her and took the card key from her hand, then moved past her door to his. His gallantry touched her, though she thought it was unnecessary. If Sammy really wanted to know where she was staying, she had no doubt he could find out. But she said nothing and let Jake lead the way.

She waited until they were in the room with the door shut before she spoke. "How have you been, Sammy? And how are Stacy and Carlo?"

"Carlo is getting big, talking up a storm. Stacy still hates my guts, but nothing new about that."

"I'm sorry to hear that," Anne said. She knew her brother's marriage had been more a business arrangement than a love match, but she'd hoped with time the couple would be happier.

"What about you? Please tell me you haven't gone and married this scum." He scowled at Jake.

"Don't hold back, Sammy," Jake said. "Let us know how you really feel."

"I never liked you from the moment I laid eyes on you," Sammy said. "You were too cocky by half. It was bad enough you fooled Elizabeth, but then you had the old man believing your lies. I thought the one good thing to come out of that night was that we were rid of you."

"Sammy, stop it." Anne stepped between the two men. "I didn't invite you here to listen to you two bicker with each other."

"Then why did you want to see me?" He sat in the room's only chair and crossed his arms over his chest. He was a big, powerful man, and the posture only emphasized this. Anne had a hard time seeing the little boy he'd once been in the muscular, scowling figure before her. She'd counted on his fond feelings for her swaying him to her position, but now she wondered if that was even possible, especially given his antagonism toward Jake.

"I was hoping you'd tell me where Sam and the others are staying," she said.

"Why? So your boyfriend can swoop in and finish what he started a year ago?"

That was why they were here, but she didn't think stating it so boldly would help their case. The key to dealing with Sammy, ever since he was a toddler who wanted to stay up past his bedtime, was to persuade him to see how doing what you wanted would benefit him. First, she had to get past his animosity for Jake. "Jake isn't my boyfriend. Until recently I thought he was dead. And he doesn't work for the FBI anymore."

"Then what are you doing with him? And why are you here in Telluride?"

Jake was here for revenge—but why was she here? Not to rekindle her romance with Jake. They'd already agreed that wasn't possible. But being with him had reminded her of all she was missing by hiding from life.

"I'm tired of running away," she said. "Tired of

living a lie. I want to be able to go places and meet people without always looking over my shoulder. You can help me."

He looked wary. "How can I do that?"

"Tell us where Sam is. Help us put him in prison again."

"He'll just get out. He has powerful friends in high places."

"Is Senator Nordley one of those friends?" Jake asked.

"What's it to you, Mr. Not-a-Fed?"

"I still have contacts in the Bureau."

"It doesn't matter who my father's friends are, just know that he's got them."

"They're closing in on your father's benefactor, whether it's Nordley or someone else," Jake said. "He won't be able to help the Giardinos much longer."

"I didn't ask Sammy here to talk about all that," Anne said. She put her hand on her brother's shoulder. "Did you know Sam is trying to kill me? He's sent people after me three times now."

"Three times and you're still alive?" Sammy uncrossed his arms and looked her up and down. "You're either very good or very lucky. I'm thinking lucky."

"You think it's all right that your father is trying to murder your sister?" Jake's voice rose; Anne feared he was in danger of losing his temper.

"You make it sound like a Greek tragedy." Sammy shrugged. "But in a way, I guess it is. She betrayed the family honor, so now she has to die."

His words sent a chill through her. "Is that really how you think?" she asked. The idea that even Sammy could regard her with such coldness filled her with immense sadness.

He shook his head. "My opinion doesn't count. Ask Pop—he'll tell you that."

"If your father is back in prison, where he belongs, you'll be head of the family," Jake said.

"And then you can come after me."

"I don't have a beef with you."

"Yet." He turned his attention back to Anne. "Are you sure Pop is behind these attempts to off you?"

"I recognized one of the men as having worked for him. And you heard him in court. He said I was dead to him, and he'd make sure that was the case."

"He said that in court because he was furious at being taken in. Since then, he's calmed down a lot."

"What do you mean, calmed down?" Sam had always had a volatile temper, and he was not a man prone to forgiveness. Anne could think of more than one person who'd met with an "unfortunate accident" after incurring her father's wrath; no doubt there were many more she didn't know about.

"Now you're the prodigal daughter," Sammy sneered. "You're his darling Elizabeth who could do no wrong. You were led astray by that FBI scum. And you never meant for things to turn out the way they did."

"He said those things about me?" she asked. "Really?"

"Only a hundred times. And in the next breath he's telling me how worthless I am. Why couldn't I be the one who went away, and not his darling Elizabeth?"

"So you're saying he doesn't want me dead?" She fought back the surge of hope that threatened to overtake her.

"I'm saying he doesn't talk like he wants you dead."

He turned to Jake. "He'd gladly see you in hell, though. If he finds out you survived the attack last year, you'd better watch your back."

"So he doesn't know I'm alive?" Jake asked.

"He never mentioned it. And I think he would have." He grinned at Jake, a horrible smile that made Anne shudder. "Maybe I should take you out—earn some points with Pop."

Jake never flinched. "Why mess up your clean record? The feds don't have anything on you. They don't have any reason to come after you once your father's out of the way."

"Except I'm a Giardino and they've got it in for us."

"No one has it in for you, Sammy." Anne began to pace back and forth in front of her brother. "I'm the one people are trying to kill."

"And I told you, I really don't think Pop is the one who's out to get you."

She stopped. He sounded so certain. And part of her wanted more than anything to believe that her father did not want her dead. "Then who is after me?"

"I can't answer that. But maybe the feds think you're a risk and they've decided it would be an easy out to kill you and make your death look like a mob hit."

"Sammy, that's crazy! The government has gone to a lot of trouble to put me in the Witness Security Program and keep me safe. Why kill me now?"

"Since when do the things the government does make sense?" He turned to Jake. "But don't you think it's suspicious how *he* showed up in your life again just about the time all these attacks started happening?"

Anne wrapped her arms around herself to ward off

a sudden chill. What Sammy was saying was preposterous. Jake had no reason to want to harm her. The timing of his arrival and the attacks on her was just coincidence. But Patrick had tried to warn her about him, too.... Her eyes met his, and she saw the challenge there. Would she believe her brother, or her former lover?

"How do you know the attacks on your sister started when I arrived?" Jake asked.

"I'm sure she mentioned it," he said.

"But I didn't," Anne said.

"You did," Sammy said. "How else would I have known?"

How else, indeed? "What else do you know about the attempts on my life?" she asked.

"Nothing. Pop only tells me things he thinks I need to know, which is almost nothing."

"But you said your father wasn't behind these attempts to kill your sister," Jake said.

Sammy squirmed, and Anne was reminded of a time when he was nine, and had been caught stealing change from their father's desk. "I'm punishing you because you took the money," her father had said, as he removed his belt and prepared to give Sammy a whipping. "But I'm throwing in a few extra licks because you need to learn to be a better liar." Family values, Giardino style.

"I don't think Pop wants Elizabeth dead," Sammy said. "That's all I know."

"We're not getting anywhere with this." Jake turned to Anne. "Tell your brother to leave. We never should have bothered him."

"I didn't say I wouldn't help." Sammy stood. "But I

think before you go in with guns blazing, you should come and talk to Pop. Make your peace with him. When you see he's no threat to you, you'll have no reason to turn him in."

Except for the fact that he was a killer who'd broken the law, she thought, but she didn't dare say the words out loud.

"That's the worst idea I've heard all year," Jake said. "Once she goes to her father, he'll have her. It's like asking her to volunteer to show up at her execution."

"I told you he won't hurt her. Are you calling me a liar?"

The two men glared at each other, two bulldogs arguing over a bone. But ultimately, this was her decision to make, wasn't it? "If I did go and talk to Sam— Pop—could you guarantee my safety...and Jake's?"

"You'll be safe. I'd be a fool to make any promises where Jake's concerned."

"Fine. Then I'll go by myself."

"No, you won't," Jake said.

"I have to do this, don't you see? I have to find out how my father really feels about me."

"He could kill you."

"I believe Sammy. He has no reason to lie to me."

"I can think of half a dozen reasons," Jake said.

"Watch it." Sammy moved toward them.

"Stop it! Both of you." She turned to Sammy. "Can you set up a meeting? Soon?"

He nodded. "I can send a car for you tomorrow."

"Give us the address and we'll come in our own car," Jake said.

Sammy shook his head. "And risk you tipping off the feds? No way. I'll send a car. And Elizabeth comes alone—without you or anybody else. And if we catch anyone tailing our car, there'll be hell to pay."

"All right," Anne answered before Jake could object again. "But Jake will be waiting for me, and if I don't check in with him every thirty minutes, he'll contact the U.S. Marshals office."

"I don't like it," Jake said.

"It's not your decision to make." To soften her words, she went to him and put one hand on his chest. "This is the only family I have. If I can find a way to make peace with them, I have to risk it."

He studied her face, as if something there might help him understand. Finally, he nodded. "If you're going to do this, then I'm going to do what I can to protect you."

"If you lovebirds are done with your little tête-à-tête, I'll go now." Sammy moved toward the door. "I'll call you here at the hotel and let you know what time."

"Are you going to tell Pop ahead of time that I'm coming?" she asked.

"Are you kidding? I wouldn't pass up the chance to have him thank me for bringing back his favorite child."

She followed him to the door, Jake close behind them. "I still can't believe you'd trust a fed," Sammy said as he stepped into the hall. "Or that he'd trust you."

"Why wouldn't I trust her?" Jake asked.

"After the way she betrayed you? If a woman did that to me, I know I wouldn't be so forgiving."

"Betrayed me?" Jake sent Anne a puzzled look.

"Sammy, I don't think—" she began.

He grinned—that horrible, gloating smile that didn't quite reach his eyes. "You mean he doesn't know?" He nudged Jake. "Your girlfriend here is the one who gave you up to Pop. She's the reason you almost died that night."

Chapter Sixteen

Anne waited until her brother had stepped into the elevator down the hall before she shut and locked the door of the hotel room. She could feel Jake's gaze on her, burning into her back. Her stomach churned and she had trouble taking a deep breath. Sammy was a fine one to talk of betrayal; the obvious delight he took in revealing her secret to Jake wounded her almost as much as her father's turning his back on her that day in court.

She forced herself to face Jake once more. His expression was grim, lines of strain deepening around his eyes. "Is it true?" he asked. "Did you betray me to your father?"

"Not deliberately. Though, in the end, the result was the same."

He crossed his arms over his chest, his posture rigid. "Tell me," he said.

How many times over the last year had she revisited that fateful day? How often had she played the depressing game of "what if?" What if she'd never spent that night at Jake's apartment? What if she'd never said what she had to her father? What if she'd been smarter, or shown more discretion, or at least hadn't been so trusting…

"Do you remember when I spent the night at your place, two days before the party where you were shot?" she asked.

"Yes." His voice were clipped, his expression wary.

"Then you remember how you went downstairs to get takeout from the deli on your building's ground floor." She forced herself to continue. "I stayed behind to wait."

"You didn't want to get up and get dressed," he said. "So you waited for me in bed. Naked."

She shivered, as if chill air had just crossed her bare skin, though the room was warm, and the look he gave her heated, despite the anger she sensed that lay just beneath the surface. "I decided to fix us a drink, so I got up and went into the kitchen. I found a bottle of wine that looked good, so I started looking through drawers for the corkscrew."

"And you found something besides the corkscrew," he said.

"Yes." She met his gaze, silently pleading for understanding. "I found a mini digital recorder. I didn't play the recording or anything—I really didn't even think anything of it. I put it back in the drawer and kept searching until I located the corkscrew and opened the wine."

"And then I came back with dinner and we continued our evening together."

"Yes." They'd drunk the wine and eaten salad and calzones and made love until they were both sore and sated. She closed her eyes against the images her mind insisted on replaying—of Jake, naked and reaching for her, a look of such tenderness and passion in his eyes it still left her trembling.

"I don't understand what this has to do with your supposed betrayal," he said.

She opened her eyes again. "The next day, I was in my father's office at our apartment. I was looking for a stamp to mail a thank-you note and he was complaining that the tape system he used to record all his phone calls was malfunctioning again. I told him he ought to get one of those mini digital recorders. It would take up so much less space and he wouldn't have to mess with tapes. He wasn't very tech savvy, and he didn't know what I was talking about, so I told him you had one— that you'd probably be glad to show him. It was small enough to put in your pocket and no one would ever even know it was there."

"And that made him wonder why I had a recorder that could be hidden so easily."

"Later, he came to me and started asking more questions—about what you did when you weren't with me, who your friends were, what else I'd seen at your apartment. I was confused, but I thought he was just being the typical overprotective father. I told him what I knew, but I truly didn't think anything of it. When I asked him why he was so interested, he told me not to worry, that he would take care of everything."

"Meaning, he would take care of me."

"If I'd had any idea what he was planning, I would have warned you, I swear. I never thought—" Her voice broke and she covered her face with her hands, reliving the horror of Jake bleeding to death in her arms. "I'm so sorry. When I think if all you suffered because of my foolishness…"

He closed the distance between them and put his arm

around her shoulders. "I believe you," he said softly. "You never meant for me to be hurt. For both of us to be hurt."

She curled into him, her face pressed into the hollow of his shoulder. Closing her eyes, she breathed in his scent—cotton and fabric softener, and the aroma of clean male skin that was uniquely him. It was the scent she associated with strength and safety and long nights of lovemaking.

"The worst days in the hospital, I would distract myself from the pain by trying to remember every detail of that evening—how you looked, what you said, the way you felt." He took her hand in his and trailed his thumb across her knuckles, tracing the ridges and valleys, his touch light but sending a jolt of awareness through every nerve.

A fierce desire stabbed her, a need to feel him around her and in her, affirming life in the most elemental way she knew. She raised her head and found his gaze fixed on her, his eyes reflecting the same wanting she felt. "Make love to me," she whispered.

He caressed the side of her neck, then trailed one finger along her jaw until it rested lightly against her bottom lip. "I've wanted to make love to you since the first night I saw you again," he said. "But are you sure?"

"I'm sure." She wrapped her hand around his, and kissed his fingertips. "I have no idea what's going to happen tomorrow, or the next day, or the day after that. All we can count on is now. And right now, I want to be with you."

"Then I'll stay. And I won't leave you until you tell me to go."

JAKE HELPED ANNE pull her sweater over her head, then steadied her as she stripped off boots and pants. He was glad of something to do to hide the trembling in his hands as he acted out the fantasy that had played in his dreams too long. When she stood before him, naked, he smiled, remembering how bold she'd always been with him before. For all the ways she'd been forced to change in the last year, she hadn't left that boldness behind.

She took hold of the waistband of his ski pants. "You're still dressed," she chided. "We must do something about that."

He unsnapped the pants, then hesitated. "I have a lot of scars from the shooting and the surgeries afterward," he said. "It's not a pretty sight."

"I saw a little yesterday and I didn't think you were too horrifying."

His face must have betrayed his dismay at her choice of words. She laughed and reached for him. "I'm not afraid of scars," she said. She grasped the tab of his zipper and slowly lowered it. His erection strained against the fabric, eager for her touch. As if answering the unspoken summons, she slipped her hand into his underwear and wrapped her fingers around his length. He pulled her close and lowered his mouth to hers in a fierce, claiming kiss.

Cupping her bottom, he pulled her tight against him, his erection pressed to her stomach, the soft fullness of her breasts flattened against the hard plain of his chest. Desire pulsed between them in time with their pounding hearts. After so long a time apart he forced himself to draw out the waiting a little longer, to savor the anticipation.

Her mouth still locked to his, she tugged at his pants

and underwear. He broke the kiss and quickly stripped out of the garments, and pulled his wool sweater and thermal top over his head. While his face was still buried in the tangle of clothing, she placed her hands over his ribs and began kissing her way around the puckered, white scar on his chest that marked a bullet's path. The touch of her lips was light, little more than a flutter, but he felt the kisses deep within, touching wounds he'd shied away from examining too closely, wounds of doubt and fear and loss, soothed by her tender caresses.

He grasped her by the shoulders and urged her to stand straight. "Let me look at you," he said.

She stood without shame, letting his gaze take in the full, firm breasts, indented waist and gently curved hips. She was thinner than she'd been before, her ribs standing out more, but she could have gained thirty pounds or lost twenty more and he wouldn't have cared. To him, she would always be beautiful, the one woman whose body fit him perfectly.

She traced her finger along a network of scars across his chest. "Are all of these from when you were shot?" she asked.

"Some of them are from surgery to remove the bullets, and a port for IV antibiotics to fight an infection."

Her gaze fell lower, to the scars on his legs. "I suppose you could always tell people you played football or something."

He laughed, as much from sheer happiness as anything else. "There's only one athletic pursuit I'm interested in at the moment," he said, pulling her close once more.

They moved to the bed, slipping between the crisp sheets to lie facing one another. She smoothed her hands down his side, fluttering her fingers along his ribs and coming to rest on his hips. "Every time with you is new," she said. "And yet so familiar."

"So right." He began kissing her again, tracing the line of her jaw, running his tongue along the tender flesh of her throat, relishing the swell of her breasts, and the way her breath caught as he drew the sensitive tip into his mouth. He nipped and licked and teased until she was breathless and writhing beneath him, her body arching upward in a silent plea that made his own desire quicken and intensify.

He moved lower still, to kiss her stomach, and the tender flesh of her inner thighs, and the softly furred mound between her thighs, stroking and coaxing while she moaned her delight. He ached for her, but refused to give in to that aching until he had shown her every pleasure.

She put her hands on his shoulders, urging him upward. "I want you in me," she pleaded.

"Your wish is my command." He moved his body alongside hers, then leaned over to open the drawer beside the bed.

"What are you doing?" she asked.

"I thought we needed this." He opened his palm to reveal the condom he'd taken from the drawer.

She smiled. "You think of everything."

"I try to be prepared."

"Were you so sure you'd get me into your bed?"

"I wasn't sure, but I wasn't going to let anything spoil the moment if I had the chance."

She held out her hand. "Allow me."

He handed her the packet and she tore it open and removed the condom, then knelt before him and rolled it on. He held his breath and tried to think of something mundane—multiplication tables or tax codes or anything else to keep him from flying apart as her hands closed around him.

Condom in place, he pushed her gently back against the pillows and knelt between her legs. She flashed a coy smile and reached down to guide him in, and then together they began to move in a dance whose moves they had not forgotten in a year apart. She smiled up at him, face suffused with joy as they increased their tempo, anticipation and tension building.

He slipped his hand between them to fondle her, and was rewarded with a breathy "Yes!" Her eyelids fluttered and her head fell back as passion overtook her. "Jake," she cried, then louder, "Jake!" A sound of triumph and completion as she tightened around him.

He held on for a few more thrusts, then surrendered to his own need, months of fear and worry and denial vanquished in the letting go.

They lay crushed together for a long moment, coming back to themselves, waiting for breath and heart to slow. At last, he rolled off of her, but she clung to him, pressing her face against his chest.

"What are we going to do, Jake?" she asked after a while, after he'd pulled the covers over them and was drifting toward sleep.

"What are we going to do about what?" He forced himself out of slumber, and smoothed his hand down her back, reassuring himself that yes, she was real, and this was no dream.

"About tomorrow, to start with. I know you don't think I should go with Sammy to see my father."

So reality would insist on intruding on this moment.

Well, that was what had brought them here, after all. "I don't trust Sammy," he said. "He was too smug. Too sure of himself."

"He was like that before—don't you remember? He's my father's son, and all the men in my family have that cocky attitude. It's all about power and control. Never let anyone see you sweat."

"He's jealous of you and of your relationship with your father." As much as he disliked Sammy, he didn't blame him for the jealousy. Even in Jake's brief time with the family, he'd seen the difference in the way Sam Giardino treated his children, spoiling his daughter and denying his son. "Maybe he thinks he can raise himself up in your father's eyes by delivering you to the old man on a platter."

"Maybe you're right. But my father loved me more than anything else in the world," she said.

"You said before that kind of love might turn to hate."

"Did your love for me turn to hate?" she asked.

"No." He kissed her forehead. "Never."

"I thought I could convince myself to hate you, but it turned out to be impossible." She settled her head against his chest once more. "Once I knew you were alive again, all my old feelings for you started growing again. I don't think you can ever turn off or put aside love like that."

"No, you can't," he agreed. Love like that could keep you going through hell. It could make life worth living—and make you miserable, sometimes at the same time. "And you still love him."

"Yes. In spite of everything, I do. If there's a chance to patch things up with him, I have to take it."

"And then what? You let him go on his way, back

to his life of crime? He welcomes you back into the family fold and you go back to being the pampered mafia princess?"

She rose up on one elbow, so she could look him in the eyes. "I could never go back to that life," she said. "I'd have to leave again, but at least I could do so knowing I still had a family. I still had a father who loved me, no matter how flawed he is."

"And after you leave, I'll have to bring in Thompson and his men to arrest your father. And your brother, too, if he tries to interfere." One thing he wouldn't do was lie to her—not ever again.

She nodded. "I know. And I'll admit part of me would feel guilty, but I've learned to live with guilt."

"Have you considered that your father might not let you leave?"

Her expression clouded. Clearly, she hadn't thought about this possibility. "He couldn't keep me prisoner," she said.

"I think he has the manpower and the resources to do whatever he wants," Jake said. "Including keeping his beloved daughter by his side forever—whether she wants to stay there or not."

She shook her head. "I wouldn't stay. I could never live like that again. He'd have to see—"

"I think your father has made a life out of seeing what he wants to see."

Her eyes met his, filled with sadness, but also determination. "You're probably right. If he tries to keep me with him, you should contact Patrick."

"I'd do that. But I wouldn't leave rescuing you up to the Marshals. I'd have to do what I could to save you."

"I'd be counting on it." She lay back down, nestled

against him once more, and he held her closely, wishing that was enough to protect her, to truly keep her safe.

He never heard her crying, but he felt the tears, hot and damp on his chest. He lifted her chin and his anxiety rose at the sight of wet tracks down her cheeks. "Why are you crying?"

She shook her head, smiling through the tears. "It's just… Why does the world have to be so screwed up?"

Why, indeed? He lay back, and cradled her head in the hollow of his shoulder. "Don't think about that now," he said. Soon enough, they'd have to face the future, a future that didn't hold any promise that they could be together. But worrying wouldn't change anything that was to come. Better to hold on to the present for a little bit longer.

Chapter Seventeen

Sammy called as Anne and Jake were finishing breakfast. She'd spent the night in his room, doing her best to savor the moments and not worry about the future. She could admit now—if only to herself—that she still loved Jake. But how could she ask him to give up everything to join her in hiding in witness protection? And if she left WitSec she doubted she'd fit into his life. Though he hadn't said, she suspected he had hopes of returning to a career in law enforcement; being linked to the daughter of a mafia don would make that ambition impossible to realize.

So it was with a heavy heart that she answered the phone and heard her brother's voice on the other end. "I'll pick you up in front of your hotel at ten-thirty," he said, then hung up before she could ask any questions.

"That was Sammy," she said as she replaced the phone in the cradle. "He says he'll be here at ten-thirty."

"Did he give you any idea of what your father thinks of this reunion?"

"No. He didn't say anything else." She studied the silent phone. "Maybe we should call Patrick."

"Maybe we should. He'll tell you the same thing I did—don't go. Will you listen to him?"

"If I don't go, I'll spend the rest of my life wondering what would have happened if I had." She took a deep breath and straightened her spine. *Courage.* "Besides, this is our best chance to pin down Sam's location. This is the closest anyone has come to him in a year." She forced a smile. "Once I've left the house, you'll be able to get him." They'd already discussed the possibility that her father might not allow her to leave. No sense bringing that up again. She'd deal with that problem if it presented itself.

"I know I said that's what I wanted," Jake said. "But it's not worth risking your life over."

"If I don't confront him I could lose my life anyway. He's either responsible for sending those men to kill me, or he knows who is."

Worry made Jake look ten years older. "I wish you'd let me come with you."

"You'd never even get into the car. I don't trust Sammy not to shoot you on sight."

She expected him to argue more, but he only nodded. "I'll be waiting for your calls. Every half hour or I'll send in the cavalry."

"Don't worry, I'll call." Just hearing his voice would give her the courage she'd need to get through this. She and Jake had both purchased new phones yesterday—cheap pay-as-you-go models that would allow them to keep in touch today. She stood. "I'd better get ready."

She took her time with her hair and makeup. Her father appreciated glamour in a woman, and though she didn't like to admit it, Sammy's comment yesterday about her looking like a schoolteacher had stung.

When she emerged from the bathroom shortly after

ten, Jake let out a low whistle. "You look gorgeous," he said, and pulled her to him.

"Don't smudge the makeup," she said, and offered her cheek for a kiss.

He squeezed her waist, and brushed his lips against one cheek. "You'd better go down," he said. "I'm going to watch from the lobby, just in case."

Promptly at ten-thirty, the black SUV pulled under the portico. Anne was surprised to see Sammy driving. People in her family seldom ventured out without a bodyguard. She opened the door and slid into the passenger seat.

"I see you didn't chicken out," he said as she fastened her seat belt.

"Did you think I would?"

"You never would have before, but it's been a year. No telling what kind of brainwashing the feds have been doing."

There was no right answer to an accusation like that, so she chose to ignore it.

"So what have you been up to for the past year?" Sammy asked. "The old man spent a fortune trying to track you down and came up with zilch."

"I thought you said he wasn't after me." Renewed fear that she was, in fact, on the way to her execution, rose up to paralyze her.

"He didn't want to kill you—he wanted to bring you home. Where he thought you belonged."

"Oh." She forced herself to look more relaxed, though her heart still pounded.

"So where have you been?" he asked. "Did they really give you a new name and everything?"

"Yes, they gave me a new name. And a new job and a house and car. It's a very well-organized program."

"I'll bet. But you're not going to share any details."

"I really don't think I should." She looked out the window, at the crowds moving toward the ski gondola or filling the shops along the town's main street. "How far is it to the house where you all are staying?"

"Not far." He hunched over the steering wheel, tapping out a jerky rhythm with his fingers as they inched through morning traffic. When a car somewhere behind them backfired, he jumped and swore.

"Is everything okay?" she asked.

"Why wouldn't everything be okay?"

"I don't know. You seem nervous."

"You're the one who should be nervous. Pop isn't going to be happy when he finds out you're still with Jake."

"I'm surprised you haven't already told him."

"I haven't told him anything. I told him I was bringing to see him this morning who he needed to talk to."

"So he doesn't know it's me."

Sammy grimaced. "I wanted it to be a surprise. One he'd remember me for."

A shiver went through her. Was Sammy intent on making a good memory, or a bad one?

"He won't like knowing about Jake, though," Sammy continued. "He'll probably send someone to take him out."

"I'm not 'with' Jake," she said. "I didn't even really want to come here with him, but he didn't give me much choice. I'll probably never see him again after this."

The lies rolled off her tongue, but she couldn't tell if Sammy believed her.

"Pop will be glad to hear it," he said. "Maybe with you back in the fold, he'll get off my back—though I doubt it. He always had a double standard where the two of us were concerned."

"You know I always took your side against him."

"You did. And he'd listen to you, when he wouldn't listen to me." He looked thoughtful, less agitated. Though she struggled to remain outwardly calm, her insides were roiling, heart pounding with fear—fear for her physical safety, yes. But also fear of being disappointed, of seeing her father look at her once more with hatred instead of love.

They left behind the last buildings of Telluride and turned onto a gravel county road that climbed into the mountains, past clusters of small houses and abandoned mine machinery. After a few more miles they turned onto a paved road that wound through acres of carefully positioned trees and miles of five-rail wooden fencing. She might have been looking at a painting entitled "A Colorado Estate in Winter."

In the distance, Anne spotted what appeared to be a gray stone castle set on a rise overlooking a broad valley. Twin turrets flanked a facade of glass and stone blocks that rose three stories, with two-story wings sprawling on either side of the main house. A separate three-car garage and various other outbuildings in matching stone dotted the grounds around the house. "Who owns this place?" she asked. "It's gorgeous."

"It belongs to a friend of Pop's. Somebody who wants him to partner in some business ventures."

Business ventures. It sounded so prosperous and

legitimate. Just another American capitalist doing his part to build a vital economy. Except that the Giardino family "businesses" always had the taint of the shady and illegal. Everything was shiny and respectable on the outside, but underneath was a layer of filth, too often tainted by blood.

They stopped at a stone guardhouse. A man dressed in black and openly cradling a semiautomatic rifle stooped to peer into the vehicle, then pressed a keypad to open the iron gate and waved them through.

A second armed man met them in front of the house and opened Anne's door. "Mr. Giardino is waiting for you," he said.

She smoothed the front of her coat, wishing she could as easily smooth down the butterflies in her stomach, and studied the entrance to the house, buying time. Stone columns rose three stories, supporting an arching portico in front of a fortune in stone and plate glass. She'd seen hotels that were less lavish. A massive chandelier made of hundreds of antlers strung with lights glowed from the top of the portico. A ten-foot oak-and-iron door stood open, providing a glimpse into a stone-floored foyer and more antler lighting.

Sammy moved up beside her and took her arm. "Come on," he said. "We don't want to keep Pop waiting."

"Of course not." In some ways, they'd both been waiting for this moment for the past year. There was no going back now, only forward. "Take no prisoners," she whispered to herself as she let her brother lead her into the house, and into her future.

"THEY'VE JUST TURNED onto a paved drive. The number on a post says five-twenty-four." Jake spoke softly into his phone, as if someone might overhear, though he was sitting in the battered Subaru alone, parked between a rusting ore cart and a leaning spruce, a quarter mile before the estate where Sammy had turned in.

"I've found it on our map." Patrick's voice was a low growl in Jake's ear. "Property belongs to a developer out of Denver, Jason Castle. Our friends at the ATF have had him on their radar for a while now, though they've never been able to make anything stick."

"I don't care about him," Jake said. "Can you get up there to look after Anne?"

"The place is guarded like a fortress. No way can we come in from the front."

"What about the back?"

"It's rugged country. You'd have to come in over the top of a mountain."

"What about a helicopter?"

"You obviously think I have a bigger budget than I do."

"Don't tell me the government wouldn't pull out all the stops to nail Sam Giardino."

"We still don't know for sure that he's there," Patrick pointed out.

"We know Anne's there. And she could be in danger."

"Then why did you let her go?"

"I had no right to stop her. Besides, what was I going to do—tie her up? Lock her in her room?"

"You could have tried harder to talk her out of going. You could have called me."

"I did call you. I'm talking to you now."

"Now that she's gone, there's not a lot I can do. You should have called me before."

"And you really think you could have talked Anne out of doing something she'd made up her mind to do?"

Thompson didn't answer. "What do you want me to do now?" he asked.

"I thought that was obvious. I want you to get a team in there to protect her."

"I'll see what I can do. It's going to take a little time to pull things together. Meanwhile, you stay put. I'll be in touch." He broke the connection.

Jake set his phone on vibrate, then took an extra ammunition magazine from the glove box and shoved it into the pocket of his ski jacket. He stowed his gun in the other pocket, pulled on a stocking cap and gloves, and climbed out of the car. He could just make out the snow-covered ridge of rock that rose up behind the massive stone house. Giardino and his men would never expect someone to come at them from that direction. Nothing but a mountain goat was likely to traverse that approach and live to tell about it.

He leaned back into the car and retrieved a county map he'd purchased from a local outdoor adventure supplier. In addition to roads, it showed all the Jeep trails, cross-country ski routes and hiking paths in the area. Jake traced the broken line of a path that led to the top of the peak behind the house. There was no corresponding trail down the other side, so he'd have to make his own. He glanced toward the house again. Anne's first call was due any minute now; he'd wait for it, then head for the mountains. One man against all of Giardino's thugs wasn't the best odds, but he'd have surprise on his side. And he'd promised Anne he'd protect her. It wasn't a promise he could afford to break.

SAMMY LED ANNE into the house, past more guards, who stood like armed statues on either side of the door leading into a great room with a twenty-foot ceiling and three stories of glass that looked out onto soaring mountain peaks. Two more guards waited inside the room, and regarded Anne and Sammy with blank expressions.

Patrick and his men would never get in here, she thought. Even if they found this place, they'd never get past her father's troops—not without an army of their own. She pushed aside her nervousness. She had to stay calm and keep thinking clearly. "Where's Pop?" she asked, looking around the room.

"He'll be here in a minute," Sammy said.

The alarm on her phone chimed. "I need to call Jake," she said. "If I don't check in, he'll be worried."

"Go ahead." Sammy nodded to her phone.

She hit the speed dial for Jake's new cell. He picked up on the first ring. "I'm here and I'm fine," she said. "This place is amazing." That was the code phrase they'd settled on to reassure him that everything was, in fact, okay.

"Have you see your father?" he asked.

"Not yet."

"Say goodbye now." Sammy moved over to her— close enough to snatch the phone away.

She fought the urge to stick her tongue out and turn her back on her brother, the way she would have when they were both teenagers. But she and Sammy weren't teenagers anymore, and as a grown man, second in command in the Giardino family, he had the power to do her real harm. "I'd better go now," she told Jake. "I'll call you again in half an hour."

She slid the phone back into her pocket. Sammy sank into an oversize leather chair and motioned for her to sit also. "Make yourself comfortable," he said. "Isn't this a fantastic place?"

"Very nice." She perched on the edge of a sofa that matched the chair. The room was full of overstuffed, oversize pieces, as if a race of giants lived here.

"Sammy! Do you have the lift tickets? I put them on the dresser and they're not there." An elfin woman with a cap of white-blond hair hurried into the room. She was dressed in a Nordic sweater, black leggings and short leather boots and was pulling on a pair of gloves as she spoke.

"Don't worry about the lift tickets," Sammy said. "You're not going skiing today."

"What do you mean I'm not—" She looked up, her voice trailing away in midsentence as she focused on Anne.

"What are you staring at?" Sammy asked. "Don't you recognize your own sister-in-law? Elizabeth is back with us."

All color fled from the face of the woman—Sammy's wife, Stacy. "What are you doing here?" she asked, her voice scarcely above a whisper.

"What kind of a question is that?" Sammy barked. "We're her family. Why shouldn't she be here?"

Stacy turned cold eyes on him. "I thought once she was lucky enough to get away, she'd be smart and never come back." She turned and left the room, her boot heels hitting hard on the plank floors as she hurried toward the stairs.

Sammy mumbled an obscenity under his breath as he watched his wife leave the room. "You should be nicer to her," Anne said—not for the first time.

"Why should I? She isn't nice to me."

"She'd probably respond better to kindness than cursing. And she's your wife. She's the mother of your son."

He grunted, his usual response to an argument he couldn't win.

The guards by the door snapped to attention, and Sammy rose to his feet. "What is it?" Anne asked, straining to see.

"Pop is here," he said. "I hope you're ready."

Her heart pounded, and she wanted to shout that she wasn't ready. But it was already too late. She stood also, and prepared to meet her father.

Chapter Eighteen

The trailhead that climbed the peak behind the estate where the Giardinos were hiding was a fifteen-minute drive from the road where Jake had been parked. He found the start of the trail without too much trouble, despite the snow. Fresh boot prints marked the route, and he wondered if they belonged to casual hikers or people who, like him, had come to check out the Giardino compound.

The trail was steep, but he powered up it, running until his lungs threatened to burst, then resting only long enough for his breathing to return to normal before he started up again. His legs, held together with pins in places, screamed in protest, but he ignored the pain. He had to get to Anne. No matter what Sammy said about her father being glad to see her, he didn't trust the Giardinos. They were a family of killers, and he didn't think they'd hesitate to kill one of their own.

After forty-five minutes of hard climbing, he came to the end of the trail at the top of the ridge, in a leveled-off area about five feet square, stamped clear of ice and snow. Someone had definitely spent time up here recently. Had Giardino sent some of his men up here to check out the approach? That would have been a smart move.

Or maybe the feds knew about this place and were keeping an eye on it. Thompson obviously knew more than he let on; Jake hoped the marshal would use his knowledge to save Anne.

He scanned the area below with binoculars. He counted four guards patrolling the perimeter, though they paid little attention to the back of the house, which was separated from a sheer natural rock wall by less than ten feet. The wall itself rose about twenty feet, and above that the mountain sloped back at what he judged to be a sixty-degree angle.

No doubt any scouts that had been sent up here to assess the situation had determined that approaching the house from this direction was impossible. Such an assault would require technical climbing equipment, not to mention nerves of steel.

Jake had been accused of having more nerve than sense, and he hadn't come this far to give up. He turned his back to the house and carefully lowered himself over the edge, gripping what rock he could with his hands, and feeling with his feet for the next best hold. Loose rock, icy slush and chunks of snow rained down, and it was impossible to determine stable footing from useless debris in the mix of snow, mud and ice that covered this aspect of the mountain. But he managed to advance a few feet.

At this rate, it would take him hours to reach Anne—hours she might not have. He should have purchased technical climbing equipment from that shop in town. But then, he'd have needed lessons in how to use it. This wasn't a skill the Bureau had bothered teaching in the classes he'd taken at Quantico.

It didn't matter. He couldn't see any other way to help Anne, so he kept on climbing, ignoring the pain and the fear and the voice inside his head that argued that no woman was worth risking his life this way.

But he didn't listen to the voice. He had promised Anne he'd do whatever it took to keep her safe, and it was a promise he intended to keep.

SAM GIARDINO STRODE into the room, looking more like Sammy's older brother than his father. Anne had imagined that the ordeal of a trial, prison time and escape, plus months evading recapture, would have aged her father, who was almost sixty. Instead, he looked younger than ever, his dark hair showing only a touch of gray at the temples, his tanned skin smooth and unlined. Hair dye and plastic surgery probably accounted for his youthful appearance, but whatever was behind the transformation, it sent a clear message that Sam Giardino was a long way from being counted out. He had the vigor and intelligence—and the power—of a much younger man.

Standing next to their father, Sammy looked soft and tired. His hair was thinning, his skin sallow, and he had the beginnings of a paunch, despite the powerful musculature of his chest and arms. Worse, Sammy lacked his father's attitude of command. He kept his gaze fixed on his father, alert for clues as to Sam's mood, and doing so gave him the attitude of a faithful dog who was trying to avoid being kicked.

Sam stopped halfway across the room, and studied his daughter with the burning blue gaze she remembered too well—a look that said if it was possible to read another person's thoughts, he would do so. "Elizabeth, is that really you?"

"Don't you recognize me?" she asked. She'd meant her tone to be defiant, but it came out in the voice of a lost little girl.

Then he opened his arms, the same gesture he'd used when she was a toddler heading toward him on unsteady legs, or a weeping preteen who'd been hurt by her first middle-school boyfriend. Those arms had been her refuge, a place of certain safety, and she could no more turn away from them now than she could then.

While Anne embraced her father, Sammy paced around them. "I tracked her down," he said. "I knew you'd want to see her."

Sam drew away, his expression solemn, but his eyes misty. "That was a good thing for you to do," he said. "Go tell Angie we will have an extra person for lunch. And she should fix something special. We have a lot to celebrate."

Sam's back was to his son, so he didn't see the scowl on Sammy's face when his father addressed him like an errand boy. But after a hard look at the older man, Sammy left the room, presumably to talk to the cook.

With his arm still around Anne, Sam led her to a sofa. "Come here and tell me why you stayed away a year."

The question was so preposterous she almost laughed out loud. "Dad, you swore you'd have me killed," she said. "I didn't think it was safe for me to come anywhere near you."

"And you were probably right, those first few months." His eyes met hers, the look chilling. "You did a very bad thing. An unforgivable thing. But a man gets weaker as he ages, and I wasn't strong enough to hold on to a hatred of you. Not having you in my life was worse than being in prison."

"Oh, Dad." She hugged him close and kissed his cheek. She wanted to believe his words, but doubt still nagged at her. She drew back.

"What is it?" he asked. "What's wrong?"

"A man came to my house last week—a man who used to work for you, DiCello. He tried to kill me."

"Frank DiCello left my employment six months ago," he said. "He went to work for an outfit in St. Louis, closer to his mother and sister."

"Then you didn't send DiCello after me?"

He looked genuinely puzzled. "No."

"He was wearing a lift ticket from Telluride on his jacket, so I thought he was here with you."

"I haven't seen DiCello since August."

"After the attack by DiCello, I hid out in a cabin in the National Forest," she said. "Someone set the cabin on fire while I was inside, sleeping. Later, on our way here, someone tried to run my car off the road."

"None of this has anything to do with me," Sam said. "I swear on my mother's grave."

This was the ultimate oath in the Giardino family, so Anne had no choice but to believe her father. "Then who is trying to kill me?" she asked.

Sammy returned. "Angie says lunch is in ten minutes," he said.

Sam's only reply was a nod. Tension stretched between father and son, worse than Anne remembered from before. She'd hoped, now that Sammy was older, her father would show him more respect, and give him more responsibility. But he still seemed to treat his only son like some low-level flunky.

The alarm on her phone beeped. "What was that?" Sam asked.

"I promised a friend I'd check in," she said.

"She needs to call Jake West," Sammy said. "You remember him, don't you, Pop? Though I take it these days he goes by his real name, Jacob Westmoreland."

"Jake West is dead," Sam said.

"We believed so, but turned out he's tougher than we thought." Sammy gripped Anne's shoulder, hard enough to make her flinch. "And it looks like he and Elizabeth here are still an item."

"Is this true?" Sam asked.

"It's true that Jake survived your attack on him. And that he came with me to Telluride." She chose her words carefully, wary of sending her father into a rage.

"Elizabeth still thinks she's in love with the guy," Sammy goaded.

"Is this true?" he asked again, her father's sharp gaze sending a shiver through her.

She opened her mouth to deny the words, but could not. Part of her did love Jake, even though she knew a relationship with him was impossible. "Jake is a good friend of mine," she said, and hoped she wasn't damning him with this faint praise.

"I meant it when I said I could never kill you," Sam said. "But Jake West is someone I would gladly kill— and I will, if I see him."

"Even if killing him hurts me?" she asked. Would she be able to live with herself if her father murdered Jake? Thinking about the possibility made it difficult to breathe.

"You'd be better off without a lying fed in your life," her father said with a sneer.

She swallowed hard. "I still need to call him, to let him know I'm okay."

Her father frowned, but said nothing, so she took out her phone and punched in Jake's number. After five rings, the call went to voice mail. "Leave a message," came the clipped recording in Jake's voice.

"This is Anne. I'm just checking in."

"You go by Anne now?" Her father gave her a curious look.

"Just...sometimes," she hedged. In the back of her mind, she could hear parts of Patrick's lecture on compromising her identity. But after today she'd have to start over again anyway, wouldn't she? Even if her father wasn't behind the recent attacks, someone was, and her luck against that unknown assailant wouldn't hold out forever. She'd have to question her father more later about who he thought might be after her.

A gong rang somewhere toward the back of the house. Her father took her hand. "It's time to eat," he said.

He led her to the dining room, another sunny space that looked out over the valley and the side of the estate. A long table, set with crystal and china, filled the center of the room. Sam took his seat at the head of the table. Anne sat on her father's right, across from an attractive, thirtysomething woman with long dark hair worn in a chignon, and the lithe body of a model or dancer. "This is Veronica. Veronica, this is my daughter, Elizabeth," her father said.

Anne nodded at what was probably her father's latest mistress. He'd had half a dozen such women in his life since her mother's death years before. They were all cast from the same mold—beautiful, classy and quiet. They voiced no opinions of their own and seldom joined in family conversations. When one left, to be replaced by a similar model, the rest of the family scarcely noticed.

Sammy occupied the other end of the table, with Stacy on his right and their son, Carlo, in a booster chair at her side. The boy, who had blond, curly hair and a winning smile that showed twin dimples, smiled shyly at his aunt. "I can't get over how big he is now," Anne said, as she made faces at the boy, who giggled in response.

"He just turned three," Stacy said. "He already recognizes some of the words in the books I read him."

"To hear Stacy tell it, the kid's some kind of genius," Sammy said.

"There's nothing wrong with being proud of him," Stacy said. "He *is* very smart."

"He's a three-year-old, not Einstein."

The diners at the other end of the table ignored the bickering. Anne suspected they were used to it.

"Levi, open a bottle of champagne," Sam directed one of the guards by the door. "We should celebrate."

Levi did as asked, and passed full glasses of the bubbly. Sam stood at the head of the table and held his glass aloft. "To Elizabeth."

"To Elizabeth," the company echoed.

Anne cautiously sipped the bubbly. After so many months abstaining, she didn't want to end up light-headed.

Lunch was grilled steak and roast potatoes, salad and asparagus and a lemon cake for dessert. "You're not eating much," her father observed after a while. "What's wrong?"

"It's all delicious," she said. "But I'm watching my weight." The truth was, her stomach was in knots. Why hadn't Jake answered his phone before? Had her father or brother sent someone after him as soon as she was out of the way? Or was he in some other kind of trouble? And was her father really going to let her walk away from here today, back to Jake and her life separate from the Giardino family?

She decided as soon as she could steal a moment alone, she'd call Patrick. She shouldn't have come here without telling him first, even though Jake had agreed to contact the Marshal when it was time to make the arrest. Patrick wouldn't have liked their plan and would have tried to stop her, but he had the manpower to protect her—and to protect Jake.

She turned to ask her father if he'd enjoyed skiing in Telluride, but his attention was focused on a car making its way up the drive to the house. "Who is that?" Anne asked.

"No one you need to be concerned about." Sam turned to the guard behind his chair. "Show our guest into my office," he said.

Anne pretended to focus on the food, but she watched the entrance to the dining room out of the corner of her eye. She could just see the front door from here. After a few moments, the door opened, and a white-haired man was ushered in. Was this the same man she'd seen at the gondola yesterday? The one Jake had identified as Senator Nordley? Had Jake been right that he was the one who'd engineered her father's escape? And was he here now to collect his payment?

PARTWAY DOWN the rock face, Jake realized he was probably clearly visible to anyone looking up from the back of the house. A bright blue jacket was not very good camouflage. He'd originally thought he could climb down quickly enough that being spotted wasn't much of a concern, but the rough terrain made the descent agonizingly slow. He spent most of his time clinging to the side of the mountain, plastered against the snow, freezing, his fingers aching as he clung to the barest projection of rock, praying he wouldn't slip and fall to his death. A lot of help he'd be to Anne then.

He'd missed her second check-in call. The one opportunity he'd had to pull out his phone, it had reported *No Service*. They'd discussed what he'd do if she failed to contact him, but had made no plans in the event that he didn't respond.

She was a smart woman, and not prone to hysterics. She'd be all right. He thought he would have heard gunfire, even at this height, if there'd been any trouble below. Of course, a small-caliber weapon with a silencer was another story.... He pushed the thought away and focused on inching farther down the slope. This next section of the climb was covered in deep snow, making it difficult to plan stable footing.

He stopped to rest, and to review his plans once he reached the house. He'd find cover, preferably with a view into the house, and try to locate Anne. If she was all right, he'd simply observe until she left safely, and he'd somehow make his way around to the road and back to the car. That was the most optimistic scenario, but not the most likely.

The most likely scenario was that there'd be trouble, probably when Anne tried to leave. Though her brother had promised a happy reunion and safe passage, Jake couldn't believe Sam Giardino would give anyone who had betrayed him once—even his daughter—the opportunity to do so again. He might not kill Anne, but he'd make her his prisoner, and Jake would be the only one who could save her.

His determination renewed by this thought, he resumed his descent, pushing himself to move faster, to be bolder. He had no time to waste. If the Giardinos decided to move Anne to another location, he might lose her again, a chance he didn't want to take.

Clinging to a rock handhold, he lowered himself onto a narrow ledge and checked his progress. He'd made it almost halfway. The house, a sprawling assemblage of glass and gray rock, looked much larger from this angle. If Jake moved faster, he could be to the wall directly behind the structure in another half hour or so. Encouraged, he positioned himself for his next step down.

The ledge gave way beneath him and he began to slide. He scrambled for a handhold in the rock, but found only loose dirt and ice. Snow filled his mouth and nose, and jagged rock tore at his clothes as he gained momentum, sliding and bouncing down the steep slope, unable to stop his fall.

Chapter Nineteen

The meal finally ended with coffee and brandy. Sammy had switched to scotch, despite the fact that it was only twelve-thirty. "I have to go the ladies' room," Anne said as they stood to leave the table. It was true, but she also hoped to use the opportunity to try Jake's phone again, and to call Patrick.

"Show her where it is, Stacy," Sam said.

Stacy, who was cleaning Carlo's hands and face, looked annoyed, but she handed the boy to Veronica and motioned for Anne to follow. Sammy grabbed his sister's arm as she passed. "Give me your phone," he said.

"No!" She tried to pull away from him.

"We can't have you sneaking off to call someone you shouldn't. Now, hand it over."

"Let go of me." She kicked him hard in the shin. He grunted and lashed out, catching her on the side of the face.

Levi moved to intervene, pulling Sammy away. Anne glared at him, and straightened her clothes. Her father came up behind her and put his hand on her shoulder. "You know I don't hold with manhandling women," he said. "But Elizabeth, I do need you to hand over your phone."

"If I don't check in with Jake, he'll send someone after me," she said.

"I'm sure we can deal with anyone who tries to get too close," Sam said. "You may have noticed when you drove in that this place is well-positioned for defense."

She'd counted six guards on the way in; there were probably twice that many out of sight, patrolling the grounds. They'd be well armed and well-trained, a private army sworn to defend her father from anyone he perceived as an enemy. Why had she and Jake ever assumed that Patrick had the forces at his disposal to take this place? Even if he could assemble a large enough force, he couldn't move in without risking the lives of innocent—or mostly innocent—women and children.

"Your phone." Sam held out his hand.

She surrendered the phone, then followed Stacy to the ladies' room. To her surprise, the other woman followed her inside. "Are you supposed to guard me?" Anne asked.

"I wanted to talk to you." Stacy glanced over her shoulder. "Alone."

"About what?"

"Why did you come back here?" Stacy asked, keeping her voice low.

"I wanted to see my father. And I wanted to find out who has been trying to kill me. Sammy says it isn't my father, and I think I believe him."

"I don't know anything about that, but you've stepped into the middle of a war zone. Your father and Sammy are at each other's throats all the time. I'm sure they're going to kill each other."

"Sammy's always had a temper, but he isn't stupid," Anne said.

"I used to think that, too, but now I'm not so sure. If I could get out of here with my son, I would. You were a fool to come back."

On that note, she turned and left, slamming the door behind her.

Anne used the bathroom, washed her hands and stepped out into the hall once more. Levi was waiting for her. "I'll take you back to your father, Miss Elizabeth," he said. He spoke in the tone of some staid family retainer. If she closed her eyes, she might imagine he was a butler or footman from a fine home at the turn of the last century.

But when she opened her eyes, his muscular build and the shoulder holster he wore in plain view would give away his true role. And to think she'd grown up accepting this as a perfectly normal way to live.

He led her, not to the great room where they'd been before lunch, but to a smaller side room that served as a study or library. Her father sat in a leather chair before a fireplace lit by a gas log, and motioned for her to sit across from him. "Is this your office?" she asked, remembering he'd instructed the guards to have his guest wait there.

"No."

"Don't you need to deal with your visitor?" she said. "I can wait."

"Don't worry about things that don't concern you."

How many times growing up had she heard those exact words? Strangers coming to the house, phone calls in the middle of the night, the need to suddenly relocate for a few weeks or months—these were all deemed matters that were none of her business. The women in the family, including Elizabeth, were supposed to keep quiet, obey and never ask too many questions. She couldn't believe she'd accepted this role for so long, though, as her father's clear favorite, she'd been allowed more leeway than anyone else. Would he accept the same degree of rebellion from her now?

"Elizabeth, tell me what you've been up to," he said.

She smoothed her hands across her thighs, and chose her words carefully. "I've been fine," she said. "Staying busy." She wouldn't tell him she'd been living in a small town and teaching school; he'd think such things beneath her. All her life she'd heard how she wasn't like "working people." He might even become angry if she told him she'd become one of that despised lot.

"I've been thinking about what you said before," he said. "About someone trying to kill you. I wonder if one of my enemies sent this DiCello fellow after you as a way of getting to me. Perhaps he wanted to frame me."

"Can you think of someone who would do that?" she asked.

A ghost of a smile played about his lips. "I have many enemies, but I can't think of one in particular who would take that convoluted approach to revenge. Or maybe DiCello knew about my outburst in court and thought he could impress me and work his way back into my good graces by doing me this 'favor.'"

"I thought you said he left to be closer to his mother and sister."

Sam waved his hand in dismissal. "We had a bit of

a disagreement before he went. I thought his loyalties were too divided."

"Between you and who?" Who else would one of her father's men be loyal to?

"He and your brother had become good friends. Sammy thought he had the right to give orders to one of my people. I had to set him straight."

She winced inwardly. She was sure Sammy wouldn't have enjoyed that particular "lesson," which probably involved humiliating him in front of the men.

"Did you say this attack in your home wasn't the only one?" Sam prompted.

"After DiCello died there were two more attempts on my life," she said. "The fire in the cabin, and the car that tried to run us off the road."

"Two of my men disappeared last week, along with one of our cars," her father said. "I've been too busy with other matters to trace them, but I wonder if there's a connection." He leaned forward and patted her hand. "Let me check into it and see what I can find out."

Silence stretched between them while her father stared into the fire and Anne wondered how she was going to get away from here. "Would you please return my phone?" she asked.

"I'll get you a new one," he said. "One of ours." Meaning a phone on which he could monitor the calls, she knew.

"It's been wonderful seeing you again," she said, making her voice as gentle as possible.

"It's wonderful to have you back." He took her hand between both of his.

"I hope I'll see you again soon," she said. "But I can't stay."

"I'll send someone to your hotel for the rest of your things," he said. "Until then, I'm sure Stacy has clothes you can borrow if you need anything."

"Dad, I have to go." She pulled her hand from his and stood.

"You don't have to go anywhere," he father said. "Not now that you're back where you belong."

She backed toward the door, knowing there were guards there to stop her, but determined to try. She wouldn't quietly surrender to being made a prisoner. She would fight, and she wouldn't stop fighting.

A heavy hand on her shoulder stopped her. "You always thought you could get your way, didn't you?"

She smelled the scotch on her brother's breath before she turned to look at him. "Perfect Elizabeth," he sneered. "The child who could do no wrong. But you've done nothing but wrong lately. Starting with bringing a federal agent home and into your bed. You sold out your family for the sake of lust. Does that make you proud?"

"I won't have you talking to your sister that way," Sam said. "She's made some mistakes, but now she realizes she was wrong—"

"She doesn't realize anything. You didn't see them, Pop, I did. Her and that fed, two cozy lovebirds, plotting to hand you over to the authorities. As soon as she walks out of here, the agents will swoop in and lock you in handcuffs." He moved to stand between her and his father. "Don't you see, she's just here to betray you again. She's not your perfect little girl. She's a viper who wants to destroy you."

Sam stared at her. "Is that true?" he asked. "Did you really come here to betray me?"

"No! I wanted to see you. And to find out who was

trying to kill me and…" And to help Jake and Patrick arrest him again. To him, that was betrayal. To her, it was justice, but in this case they meant the same things.

"I already told you, I had nothing to do with those attempts on your life," he said. "You're my daughter, and you always will be."

"It would be better for all of us if you were dead," Sammy said. "I should have gone after Jake from the beginning. With him out of the way, you never would have survived the fire, or the drive to Telluride."

Anne stared at him, stunned and sick to her stomach. How could her brother, whom she'd loved, speak such hate-filled words? "Are you saying you were the one who was after me?" she asked.

"Samuel, what is the meaning of this?" her father demanded.

"I was doing it for you, Pop," Sammy said. "She didn't deserve to live after what she did to you. And with her finally out of the way, we could move on. You'd stop worrying about her and focus on me."

Her father's face was ashen. "You had no right," he said.

"I had every right. I'm the one who stayed home. The one who remained loyal. But it didn't mean anything to you." His voice shook, and his eyes were dilated, wild.

"Sammy, calm down," Anne said.

"No! I'm tired of waiting around for what is rightfully mine." He reached into his coat and pulled out a pistol.

"Sammy, no!" she screamed.

But it was too late. Sammy fired the pistol, the report deafening in the small room. Sam clutched at his chest, blood spurting between his fingers while Anne looked on, horrified.

While Sam was still falling, Sammy turned the gun on Anne. "You won't get away from me this time," he said.

She screamed, but the scream was drowned out by another gunshot. Sammy jerked back from the force of the blow, then sank to his knees. Anne stared at the window behind her father's chair, the glass shattered in a thousand pieces. Jake stepped through the opening, his gun fixed on Sammy. "Are you all right?" he asked Anne.

She nodded, too shocked to speak, then knelt beside her father just as her brother collapsed beside her.

THE DEEP SNOW had saved Jake's life, and delivered him to the house in record time. He'd ended up tobogganing down the slope on his belly and landing in an avalanche of thick powder at the base of the rock wall behind the house. He was banged up, with a rip in his pants and a gash in his leg that oozed a thin line of blood, but he was alive and whole—and apparently no one had noticed his spectacular descent.

He stood and brushed off as much snow as he could, then drew his gun, removed the safety and checked the load. All around him was quiet, and he saw no one. Keeping low and out of sight of the windows, he reached the back of the house, then crept around the side toward the sound of raised voices. Before he could identify the speakers, a gunshot shattered the silence.

Jake rushed forward, in time to see Sammy turn his gun on Anne. He fired, shattering the window and striking the younger man in the middle of the back. He didn't even remember stepping through the broken glass and moving to Anne's side. "Are you all right?" he asked.

She nodded, and knelt beside her father, but he was beyond help, his face forever frozen in an expression of surprise.

Jake turned to Sammy, who lay gasping on the rug, blood seeping from a hole in his chest. "We should call an ambulance," Anne said.

Jake thought it was too late for that, but who was he to say, considering how he himself had defied the odds? He looked for someone to make the call and found himself face-to-face with three men with guns, all of them pointed at him.

"Call 9-1-1," he ordered, ignoring the weapons.

No one moved. "Put those guns away and call for help!" Anne shouted.

The men looked at each other. "All right, Miss Elizabeth," one said, and the rest followed him out of the room.

Anne moved to her brother's side. He stared up at her, vacant-eyed. "Sammy, hang on," she pleaded, gripping his hand.

"I just…wanted him…to be proud…of me," Sammy gasped.

"He was," she said. "I know he was."

Sammy's eyes closed and Anne choked back a sob. Jake pulled her into his arms. "I'm sorry," he said. Not sorry he'd protected her, but sorry she had to go through this, to lose her family, no matter how bad they were.

Shouting and the sounds of running feet came from the front of the house. Jake stood, and pulled Anne to her feet behind him. "What's going on?" she asked.

"Jake! Anne!" a man bellowed.

"Patrick!" Anne called. "We're in here."

The U.S. marshal, dressed in black fatigues and carrying an assault rifle, appeared in the doorway of the room, flanked by two similarly clad officers. He took in the two men on the floor. "Sam Giardino and his son?" he asked.

"We need an ambulance," Anne said. "Sammy—"

Thompson was already kneeling beside the younger Giardino. "It's too late for an ambulance," he said. He moved to Anne. "Come with me. I've got a team ready to relocate you right away, before anyone here even realizes you're gone."

"I..." She looked around the room, confused. "Sammy's dead?"

Thompson nodded. "Come on," he said, one hand on her shoulder. "We have to go."

"Wait!" She wrenched away from him. "Senator Nordley. You've got to stop Senator Nordley."

"What about Nordley?" Thompson asked Jake.

Jake shook his head. "Is the senator here?" he asked Anne.

"He arrived while we were eating lunch and my father told one of his men to put him in his office to wait."

"And you're sure it was Greg Nordley?" Thompson asked.

"I think so. I only caught a glimpse, but he had white hair, and he looked like the man Jake pointed out to me in Telluride this morning."

"I have my men searching the house," Thompson said. "If he's here, we'll find him." He took Anne's arm again. "Now you need to come with me."

Anne stared at her fallen brother and father. "I can't just leave them," she said.

Thompson started to argue, but Jake stepped in. "Can't you see she's in shock? Don't ask her to make that kind of decision right now."

"Stay out of this," Patrick said. "We have to get all the women out of here. We don't know who else might move in to take over, and we need to take down their testimony before someone else gets to them. This is our chance to dismantle the Giardino operations while the family's in disarray."

"You can give her a little more time," Jake said.

"I tell you, we don't have time." Thompson turned her toward the door. "I promise she'll be safe."

Jake watched as the marshal led Anne away. Her head was bowed, and she moved blindly, letting Thompson guide her around the carnage in the room. Jake turned away, cursing under his breath. He shouldn't have let them take her—not like this.

"Sir? I need you to come with me."

He turned and faced another black-clad marshal. "We'll need you give a statement about what happened."

He looked over the man's shoulder, at Anne's retreating figure. "What will happen to her?" he asked.

"She'll be taken care of. You don't have to worry."

But of course, he would worry. And he'd start over, looking for her again. And this time, he wouldn't let her go.

ANNE SAT IN THE SMALL interrogation room, in an office whose location she couldn't have named, and stared into a foam cup of long-cold coffee. Patrick had taken her statement, then left her here to wait for the typed transcript, while he made the final arrangements for her to travel out of state. Tomorrow she'd start over—a new life, with a new name, a new occupation and a new past.

Before, she'd been grateful for the chance to make a fresh start. She'd longed to distance herself from her family, and from the pain of losing Jake. Now, all she felt was numb. Her father, a man she'd spent a lifetime both loving and hating, was gone. Her brother, who had been both ally and enemy, was dead, too.

And Jake. He was the one man who'd stood by her, and she'd realized his value too late. He'd saved her life, but more than that, he'd saved her from thinking she was only good enough to be her father's daughter, a pretty, spoiled socialite who turned her back on the suffering of others. Jake had shown her she had the courage to do the right thing—not once, but over and over again.

A knock on the door startled her out of her musings. "Come in," she called, and sat up straighter, trying not to look as exhausted as she felt.

Patrick leaned into the room. "There's someone out here who's asking to see you," he said.

"Who is it?" Patrick wouldn't let a reporter in to see her. But maybe Stacy wanted to speak with her. Or even Veronica…

Patrick held the door open wider and Jake came into the room. He stopped halfway to her. "I wasn't sure you'd want to see me," he said. "Now that you've had time to think about everything."

"Jake!" she cried, and ran to him.

He crushed her in his arms, and kissed the top of her head, over and over. "I'm sorry," he said. "I'm sorry about your brother and your father…and everything."

"Don't apologize for saving my life." She drew back,

just enough to look him in the eyes. "I'm glad I got to see you again. Thank you for coming."

"I couldn't let you go. I called Thompson and I made him tell me where you were."

"You must have been pretty persuasive. He thinks I'm still in danger from others in my father's business."

He cradled her face in his hand. "I told him I loved you and I didn't want to live without you."

Her breath caught, and tears stung her eyes. "I love you, too," she said. "And I don't want to live without you, either."

"Sounds like we're stuck." He kissed her, a sweet, gentle brushing of his lips against hers that said more to her heart than all a poet's words of love.

"I told Thompson I'd come with you into WitSec," he said.

"What about your career?" she asked. "Don't you want to get back into law enforcement?"

"You said yourself, I was never a typical agent." He smoothed his hands down her arms. "I'll find something to do. Don't worry about me."

"There's only one problem." Patrick moved into the room and shut the door behind him.

"What's that?" Anne asked.

"Jake's not in my budget. I can't enroll random people into Witness Security just because I feel like it."

"That's not a problem," Anne said.

"It isn't?" Jake sent her a questioning look.

"No." She took a deep breath. "I don't want to start over with a new life. I like the life I have. As Anne."

"Anne Gardener?" Jake asked.

She met his steady gaze. "Or Anne Westmoreland."

His grin erased all the weariness and pain of the past hours. "I like the sound of that," he said.

They kissed, and Anne marveled that so much sadness and happiness could be mixed up together.

Patrick cleared his throat, and reluctantly the lovers moved apart. "I can't guarantee your safety if you don't stay in the program," he said.

"I don't think I have anything to worry about now that my father and my brother are both gone," she said. "My father's business partners or his rivals will take over his operations, but there's no one left in the family to take over. And certainly no one who cares about me."

"We'll be offering protective custody to your sister-in-law and to your father's mistress," Patrick said. "You won't see them again."

"I understand." Jake would be her family now. The only family she needed.

"What about Senator Nordley?" Jake asked. "Was he at the house?"

Patrick shook his head. "No sign of him. He must have left before we arrived."

"I was in the bathroom for a few minutes right after lunch," Anne said. "My father might have sent him away then."

"We may ask you to confirm that he was at the house, but right now the investigation is ongoing." He put a hand on Anne's shoulder. "Are you sure you'll be all right?"

"I can look after her," Jake said.

Patrick studied them a long moment, then nodded. "All right. I'll take care of the paperwork. You're free to go."

She hurried to collect her coat, and to leave the office before Patrick changed his mind. Outside, it was snowing, soft flakes drifting down to dust her hair and the shoulders of her coat. Jake gathered her close. "It's going to be all right," he said.

"I know it will be." She kissed his cheek. In Jake's arms, she felt safe and warm, and more at home than she had ever been anywhere else.

* * * * *

*Be sure to pick up Cindi Myers's
ROCKY MOUNTAIN RESCUE,
coming out next month.*

MILLS & BOON®
Book Club

Join the Mills & Boon Book Club

Want to read more **Intrigue** books?
We're offering you **2 more** absolutely **FREE!**

We'll also treat you to these fabulous extras:

- Exclusive offers and much more!

- FREE home delivery

- FREE books and gifts with our special rewards scheme

Get your free books now!

visit **www.millsandboon.co.uk/bookclub**
or call Customer Relations on **020 8288 2888**

FREE BOOK OFFER TERMS & CONDITIONS